Neil Bartlett was born in 1958. His books include *Who Was That Man?*, a study of Oscar Wilde, and the novels *Ready To Catch Him Should He Fall* and *Mr Clive and Mr Page*, which was shortlisted for the Whitbread Novel Award and has since been translated into five European languages. In 2000 he was awarded the OBE for his work in the theatre, which includes productions for the Royal Shakespeare Company as well as controversial performance pieces. From 1994 to 2004 he was Artistic Director of the Lyric Hammersmith in London.

www.neil-bartlett.com

Also by Neil Bartlett and published by Serpent's Tail

Ready to Catch Him Should He Fall

"If he can do this with his first novel, what heights will his fourth or fifth reach?" Ruth Rendell, *Sunday Times*

"Stands head-and-shoulders above any British or American gay novel to have appeared in several years" *Gay Times*

"A writer who can really change the way people think" *Literary Review*

Mr Clive and Mr Page

"A strange, yet perfectly poised tale of male sexual longing and violent fantasy, with a chilling whodunnit at its core" *Mail on Sunday*

"Neil Bartlett's second novel establishes him among English fiction's fiercest historians of gay male suffering" *Independent*

"A curious and original novel that is compulsively readable" *Observer*

Skin Lane

Neil Bartlett

A complete catalogue record for this book can
be obtained from the British Library on request

The right of Neil Bartlett to be identified as the author
of this work has been asserted by him in accordance with
the Copyright, Designs and Patents Act 1988

Copyright © 2007 Neil Bartlett

First published in 2007 by Serpent's Tail,
an imprint of Profile Books Ltd
3A Exmouth House
Pine Street
Exmouth Market
London EC1R 0JH
www.serpentstail.com

Designed and typeset by Sue Lamble
Printed in Italy by Legoprint S.p.A., Lavis, Trento

ISBN: 978-1-85242-919-5

10 9 8 7 6 5 4 3 2 1

James, without whom

1

"Under certain very particular circumstances, there may be some dispute as to who has jurisdiction over the body itself."

The Coroner's Office: An Introduction
Corporation of City of London Publications, 1967

The stories we are told as children do, undoubtedly, mark us for life. They are often stories of dark and terrible things, and we are usually told them just before the lights are turned out and we are left alone; but we love them. We love them when we first hear them, and even when we are grown, and think we have forgotten them entirely, they never lose their power over us.

The man who is the subject of this story had, when he was a little boy, one particular bedtime favourite. This was despite the fact that the old-fashioned book of fairy tales which contained it had only one picture, and that a small steel engraving printed in black and white. He would ask to be read this particular story again and again – every night, in fact. The voice that read him the story was, on some nights, calm, reassuring – as warm as lamplight; on other nights his father (for it was to his widowed father, and not to either of his older brothers, that the duty of the bedtime story fell) would be tired, and eager to get downstairs to his dinner, and could not conceal his irritation at being asked to rehearse the words of the story for the fourth time that week. The boy never especially paid attention to his father's mood, or tone of voice; he was rapt whether the sentences of the story were repeated clumsily or well. The first few pages never particularly interested him, but he never asked for them to be skipped; he would lie quite still, and wait patiently for the two moments in the telling of the story that he loved the most. The first was when the Beast, having lured the famished Beauty to his table with the promise of fine wine, and finer food – chickens with meat as white as milk, jellies as red as rubies – suddenly says out of nowhere "Beauty, will you be my wife?" and she, weak with hunger and terror, faints dead away; and the second was the story's very end. It wasn't the odd music of the final words about living in happiness "for years and years and many years to come" that he always looked forward to (he was of course too young to understand why his father sometimes read that sentence too quickly, as if eager to get to the full stop and back downstairs); nor was it the fireworks, or the strange sound of the invisible orchestra that played when the Beast's place at the dining table was suddenly taken (disappointingly, he always thought) by "the loveliest prince that ever eye beheld" – no; it was the quiet noise that the paper of the last page of the little book always made as his father turned it – a whisper meant for his ears only – because that meant that there, at the bottom of the last page of the story, there, at last, was the picture. He would always ask to see it. "Show me, show me—" he'd say, "I'm not frightened; show me."

According to the picture (– yes, I have the book here in front of me), the Beast is a small and oddly wounded-looking creature; small, dark and indeterminate. It snuffles, half in wonderment, half in ignorance – half bear, half boar – at the exposed neck and breast of a swooning, Empire-dressed Beauty, who has fallen backwards across a bed. Whether she is really asleep, or has fainted, or is merely playing dead, the little boy is never quite sure; but he can see that her eyes are firmly closed.

The story over, and the picture inspected, the boy lets himself be told to go to sleep; he enjoys lying back on the clean white pillowcase and feeling his father's big hands tucking the weight and warmth of his very own paisley-printed eiderdown firmly down around him. Then he lies straight and still, with his feet together and his arms down by his sides, like he's been told (like a good boy), and listens for the three last sounds that he hears his house make each evening; the soft, satisfying click of the bedroom light switch; the gentle shutting of the bedroom door; and then, finally, his father's footsteps making their way across the landing and down the stairs. He lies there in the dark, and counts the steps *(seven, eight) – watching the strip of light under the bedroom door (thirteen, fourteen); waiting for the moment when his father will reach the bottom of the stairs and turn the landing light out. Then, and only then, when both the darkness and the silence are complete, will he prepare to close his eyes.*

Before he closes them, there is something that he has to do. First, he pulls down the eiderdown; then he unbuttons the top two buttons of his pyjama jacket, uncovering his chest to the air. Next, he twists his whole body slightly to one side, rearranging his legs and arms under the covers so that he is now lying just as Beauty is lying in the picture – eyes closed, breast exposed, head thrown back to one side, luxuriant black ringlets spread across the pillow. And then he waits, just as he knows she must have waited all those nights. Waits, for the first sound of snuffling in the dark. For the first touch of bristle or guard-hair on his cheek. For the first hot, stinking breath to brush against his neck.

Here it comes.

one

Since this story is to be so much about bodies, I should probably start by describing Mr F's as well as I can.

At the age of forty-six (three months short of forty-seven, in fact) it is well preserved, but largely unused – by which I mean that there is nothing very conspicuously athletic about it. Not that he was thin, or worn-out-looking; in fact he was rather a large man, nearly six foot, with broad shoulders and the sort of build that most people would describe as *sturdy*. He had the usual pale skin of a city-dweller, and the conventionally cut short dark hair of his period, with only the expected shading of grey. His blue eyes, on the rare occasions when he looked directly at anybody, could give the impression of being rather strikingly pale. He had rather fine, strong arms, lightly dusted with black hair on the forearms, and a still almost hairless back; this he always carried consciously upright when he walked, perhaps because he spent so much of his working day standing stooped over a bench. A slightly military edge to his stride – but only when he hurried, which was rarely. A perfectly reasonable waistline for a man of his age – in fact, rather trim. Rather large feet. Though he looked as though he would still be well capable of, say, rowing a boat, you wouldn't have said that it was a body well suited to dancing. His physical demeanour was, well – self-effacing, I suppose, describes it best. Contained.

If there was anything unusual or distinctive about him, it was his hands. Always framed by an impeccably clean pair of cuffs (fastened with his one pair of plain gold-plated cuff-links) they were also large, but not at all rough or conventionally masculine. They were not at all the sort of hands you would have expected to find on a man who had been using them to earn his living for over thirty years. The long, tapering fingers were white, except for the nicotine staining on the index and forefingers of his right hand, and well manicured; there were no calluses. He wore a wristwatch, but no wedding ring. The fine, slightly perfumed and almost uncreased skin of the palms would have told anyone who inspected them closely – anyone who might have kissed them, for instance- that these hands were not only scrubbed, but also cared for, every night.

Not that anyone ever did, of course. Inspect them closely. Or kiss them.

Every morning of the working week, at twenty minutes past six, Mr F got promptly out of bed, knotted a plaid dressing gown over his pyjamas, used the bathroom, returned to his bedroom, took off the robe and his pyjamas, hung up the former and folded the latter, and then proceeded to conceal this middle-aged body of his beneath a well-ironed white cotton shirt and a three-piece medium-weight brown worsted suit. He wore this same suit all year; if it was cold, he only needed to put on a cotton vest under his shirt to be warm enough – and if it was one of South London's rare days of high summer sunshine, and already a touch too warm for comfort at a quarter past seven in the morning, the fabric was still lightweight enough to allow him to make the brisk ten minute walk to the station without sweating. Even with the waistcoat and all four suit-buttons done up, and his tie tightly knotted.

This was important to him.

With its double-breasted jacket and two-inch turn-ups, this brown worsted ensemble of his could have been tailored at almost any time in the middle thirty years of the last century. On a younger man, it would have seemed markedly out of date by the time this story takes place – but this Mr F was of a generation and a class for whom the idea of fashion in men's clothes didn't really exist. In fact, he was still in effect wearing the same suit to walk to work in in 1967 as he had been in 1938. When that first suit, the one he'd bought for himself to mark his eighteenth birthday, had finally given way (unsurprisingly, after spending the whole five-and-a-half years of the war tightly folded in a damp tin trunk) he'd seen no reason to change his mind about either cut or fabric when replacing it. This meant that it was in a more or less exact copy of what he'd worn at eighteen that he stood bareheaded at first his father's funeral and then to watch the cold, rain-drenched funeral procession of King George VI. When that second suit in turn had finally given up the ghost, and he'd gone out shopping for its third and current incarnation, he had been briefly tempted by something in a chalk-stripe and what he was assured, by an eager young sales assistant on Oxford Street, was a much more modern cut – but then he had found a gentleman's outfitters on Camberwell High Street who still stocked brown worsted, and in his usual style, and once again, he had seen no reason to change.

Mr F was a man who didn't often change his mind about things.

*

Having put on the suit, tightly tied his laces, checked his wristwatch against the kitchen clock and collected his trilby from the hallstand (together with an overcoat or umbrella if the day threatened rain), Mr F always left his flat at more or less exactly five minutes past seven. He took some pride in the fact that he was never late for work, and would often make a point of completing his whole journey into town without once needing to look at his watch; like most people who make a daily journey to work in London, he always made it by the same route, and so knew exactly how many minutes each part of it took. From his front door to Peckham Rye Station, for instance, took either nine or eleven minutes, depending on whether or not he stopped to buy a morning paper. To save time at the station itself, he liked to always carry the exact change required for the purchase of his ticket in his right-hand pocket, together with that day's clean linen handkerchief. He always travelled in the second, least crowded carriage of the train, if he possibly could, since that minimised delay on arrival at London Bridge. Once there, he always looked to see if the stopped clock on the bomb-damaged façade of the station forecourt still said the time was ten minutes to twelve; it always did. When he crossed the bridge itself, it was always on the western, upriver side; this way, he avoided becoming part of the almost impossibly thick bowler-hatted crowd of office-workers that walked north in silent unison towards the City on the eastern pavement. Once across the river (he seemed not to notice the sudden upward swirl of the breeze, the faintly metallic stink of the water) he again avoided the main flow of the crowd as it surged across King William Street and left towards Cannon Street, choosing to reach his destination by a much less direct, but much less crowded, route. Turning left down Arthur Street, and then cutting down the steps of Miles Lane, he would head down Fishmonger's Hall Street until he emerged out onto the open wharf at its southern end. Before the war, his route from here on had been via a network of narrow riverside lanes and enclosed alleyways, but now at least half his journey was past partly cleared bombsites still awaiting redevelopment. The concrete monolith of the City's first multi-storey car-park was just nearing completion by the river at Swan Lane, and he had to walk right under its scaffolding; the east side of All Hallows Lane, up which he turned right to join Upper Thames Street just as it disappeared into its dark, roaring cavern under Cannon Street Station, was still a bare-branched scrubland of buddleia bushes. Further on, the ruined churchyard of St Michael's Paternoster was being replaced with a "modern" garden that seemed to consist mostly of concrete paving slabs dotted with wilting, thin-trunked saplings – but Mr F ignored all these signs of redevelopment and disruption. As far as he was concerned, the important thing was that this was the way he had always walked to work.

At the end of the working day, some nine and a half hours later, he would retrace his steps exactly. The only time he would use a different pavement from the one he had used in the morning was if he crossed the street to avoid some noisy crowd of men gathered outside the one of the two pubs he had to pass (they are still always almost all men, those early evening crowds outside the City pubs, even now, nearly forty years later; have you noticed that?). As he turned left at the bottom of All Hallows Lane, he would ignore the anonymous threat tolled out by the river barges moored for the night under Cannon Street rail bridge; the slow, funeral clanging-together of their empty metal hulls, weirdly amplified by the bridge, was too familiar to disturb him. If it was summer he would, as he emerged back up out onto the sudden open space of London Bridge, give a quick backward glance across at the sunset as it flared over the whole of the western city; but the view, no matter how bloody or sulphurous, never detained him. He always knew exactly how many minutes he had before the five-forty nine train departed from platform eleven, or the six-o-two from platform eight – and would have already calculated exactly how much time he would need to stop and buy his nightly copy of the *Evening Standard* at the station kiosk.

The old London Bridge, which was to be demolished just a few months after our story takes place, was famous for the narrowness of its York stone pavements. They constricted the rush-hour crowds into almost intolerable crushes. But even when the black river of commuters was at its densest – that twice-daily human tide, rolling north at eight, receding south at five, as relentless in its way and thickening and gathering pace just as swiftly as the waters which slapped and surged and came to a rolling boil twice daily against the four great granite piers which supported the bridge – it is extraordinary how rarely any one of them ever bumped into anyone else. Mr F certainly never did. Even when he was forced to queue to go through the ticket barrier – even if he was obliged (on a rainy day) to cram into an overcrowded compartment on his train – he was expert at avoiding contact. If he did find himself having to stand, and the train lurched unexpectedly, he would brace himself with his knees, never reach to share an improvised hand-hold on a luggage rack; he never dropped his umbrella and had to stoop and grope to retrieve it; never accidentally grazed the back of an adjacent hand when attempting to open his evening paper. Since he was tall, there was rarely any danger that anyone's wet hair would brush inadvertently against his face. If the crowding was so bad that contact became inevitable, the combined thicknesses of his suit and his overcoat meant that he would feel at most only a general pressure, never the exact shape or temperature of a specific limb or joint as it was pressed gently against his leg or into the small of his back. And even if his face was only inches from that of his neighbour, he would never look at them. Certainly not in the eye.

Of course, as you will know if you have ever made such a daily train journey yourself, none of this made him in any way particularly unusual.

Once he reached Peckham Rye Station, he would retrace his morning journey exactly, stopping only to buy some milk if he needed it, and would arrive back at the mansion block which contained his one-bedroomed, third-floor flat at twenty past six at the very latest. Earlier, of course, if it was a Friday night in winter.

two

Mr F lived, you will not be surprised to hear, on his own.

Although the street as a whole was now fairly down-at-heel, the hundred-year-old building in which he lived retained, under the shabbiness of its flaking paint and the grime of its blackened brickwork, enough gentility to announce that this had, when everything was new, at least aspired to being a respectable address. The block, which held twelve flats, had kept all of its original ironwork; an unkempt privet hedge was kept hemmed in against the ground floor windows by a set of heavy cast-iron railings, and an elaborate fire escape (the latest thing at the time of construction) reached right to the third floor at the back. The handle of the panelled front door was still large and brass, the letterbox an incongruous neo-gothic maw more suited to a vicarage than a mansion block. The tessellated hallway had the usual nineteenth-century geometric design in red, black and white; the curving banister was mahogany, and the second-floor landing of the stairs boasted a small, dim window of stained glass. These features were of course still years away from being valued as "period" by the inhabitants; the wood of the stained glass window's frame, for instance, was being allowed to rot under its chipped white gloss paint. It rattled in any kind of wind, and one or two of the small diamond-shaped panes of glass that made up the central panel (*fleurs de lys* on alternating lozenges of grey and yellow) were missing. This central panel was framed by bevelled strips of a plain but violently red glass, and because the window faced west, at sunset, these threw a lurid carmine frame, a bloody, disembodied trap-door, right across the shabbily carpeted turn of the landing. This meant that on summer evenings Mr F had to walk straight through this strange and intensely coloured rectangle of light on his way up the stairs; there was no way round it. He would have avoided it if he could, but having no choice except to walk straight through it, he would always (and I'm sure he didn't know he was doing this) hold his breath while he did so. For some reason, he intensely disliked the way the strips of pure red, running across his right arm, looked strong enough to soak into the cloth of his suit; the way the white skin of his wrist, as he held his front door key in readiness, was stained scarlet. On warm summer evenings it was with some relief, that he finally reached his front door, slipped the key into the lock, and turned it.

Mr F was a man who valued his privacy. He still remembered each and every one of the grimy bedsits he had been forced to occupy in the two years it had taken him to find the relative comfort of this flat. Relative; the kitchen and so-called living/dining-room were tiny, the bedroom only just big enough to hold, besides his single bed, an over-sized stained-oak wardrobe and a tiny bedside table. The white-tiled bathroom, however, was of a reasonable size, and after two years of padding along shared hallways to see if there was any hot water left, Mr F particularly valued being able to lie down in his very own, full and full-sized bath more than once a week if he felt so minded. The moment he entered the quiet darkness of the flat, he felt reassured. After returning his overcoat to the hallstand, hanging up his key on the hook by the front door and his suit jacket on its hanger in the wardrobe, he would always repair first to the bathroom. There, he would remove his links and wristwatch, roll his sleeves up to well above the elbow, and proceed to conscientiously first wash and then scrub his hands, using a big wooden-backed nail-brush and a cracked brick of the pink carbolic soap that he favoured. He did this for several minutes, with the water running as hot as he could get it.

Once this ritual was complete, his evenings in the flat were simple, quiet – and predictable. Whatever the night of the week, his supper, the washing up, the finishing of his evening newspaper with one roll-up and then an hour or so of sitting with the radio and smoking several more – "Golden Virginia" was his preferred brand – always came and went in the same order. Every Friday night, as often as not on a Sunday and occasionally on a mid-week evening as well, he took a hot bath before going to bed. This was as much for the pleasure of it as because he felt he ought to, and it was after this bath, standing in front of the misted washbasin mirror in his dressing-gown, that he carefully rubbed his hands with the lanolin lotion that gave them their distinctively soft skin and faint night-time perfume. He worked the lotion in by wringing his hands firmly together, until every trace of it was absorbed; he never would have dreamed of going to bed with them still greasy. Had anyone been there to witness it, this gesture – repeated, like the scrubbing, for several minutes – would surely have perplexed them; after all, isn't it women, not men, who wring their hands, and then only to express some hidden grief? But of course, there was no one there in his bathroom, and Mr F himself never looked up to see the image framed in the washbasin mirror, never wondered from whom he had inherited or by whom he had been taught this strangely intent and melancholy gesture. Once back in the bedroom, he took off the dressing-gown and buttoned himself into his pyjamas. Standing at the foot of the bed, he could hardly avoid catching sight of himself in the half-length mirror with the bevelled edges which was set into the wardrobe door – but once again, he never stopped to stare at or scrutinise himself. When you live with someone for years, you barely notice how the slow, incremental changes in their body accumulate; and Mr F. had lived with himself always. He saw nothing worth staring at.

Mr F was one of those fortunate men who never have much trouble getting off to sleep. As a child he had shared a bedroom with his two brothers, both of whom were much older than him – nine and eleven years, respectively – and he had developed the younger sibling's characteristic trick of not letting anything wake him, not even the sound of two occasionally drunk young men undressing in the dark at midnight. As an adult, since he had kept to the same job all his working life, he had (with the exception of the war years) been in the enviable position of never having to go to sleep at night worrying about what the next morning would bring, or whether he would wake up in time. His body could be relied upon for that; his eyes opened promptly at twenty minutes past six, Monday to Friday, regular as clockwork – with an extra half hour at weekends – regardless of whether it was cold dark winter, or whether the sounds and colours of summer had already been probing and testing the faded red lining of his bedroom curtains for nearly two hours. It was the same in the evenings; once the ten o'clock pips had sounded on the radio, his body would go through the routine of turning off the gas, cleaning his teeth and getting undressed almost by itself. This meant that it was invariably ten-fifteen – almost exactly – when he folded back the counterpane.

Once he was in bed, Mr F would close his eyes and be straight off to sleep in minutes. Or that was what he usually did, anyway. But

But on this particular evening, which is a Thursday evening, early in the freezing January of 1967, as our story now more or less officially commences, he does not go straight to sleep. He places his wristwatch on the bedside table, folds back the bed-cover, turns the bedroom light out, gets into bed, lays his head carefully in the centre of the pillow – and then lies there and stares at the ceiling for a good twenty minutes. This is because now, at the age of nearly forty-seven, after nearly thirty-three years of working at the same address – after nearly thirty-three years of the same domestic routine, of his own company almost every solitary evening – something new has started to happen to this man.

He has started to dream.

More specifically, in the space of the last ten days, he has had the same dream three times in a row.

Come to think of it – and ever since the last time it came, the third time, he has found himself thinking about it often, because the dream, as you will see, is of a peculiarly troubling nature – he may even have dreamed it more than three times; for all he knows, he may have dreamed it every single night, and simply not remembered it. After all, he thinks, which of us remembers all their dreams? The last two mornings, when he's sat down with his cup of tea and made a conscious effort to see what he can remember, there's been nothing, nothing at all; but the morning before that –

The morning before that, he could remember *everything*.

And the thing was, the *everything* he could remember was exactly the same – exactly the same the third time as it had been the first two times. He was sure of it – the dream hadn't been just more or less the same, but *exactly* the same – as if he'd stayed in his seat at the end of the programme at the Odeon and watched the film all over again. As if he'd got up three mornings in a row and found exactly the same unaddressed brown envelope lying on the mat, waiting for him.

This worries him, as well it might. In fact, he's starting to think that this way that the dream repeats itself so exactly is perhaps the most disturbing aspect of the whole business.

And so perhaps it is no wonder that tonight, even though it is a Thursday night, and he is tired, Mr F lies there in his narrow bed with his eyes wide open and stares up at the ceiling first for twenty minutes, and then thirty. Eventually, it is nearly an hour before his eyes begin to slowly, reluctantly – because it does wear him out, this job of his, and the journey there and back again on the train, and all the walking, some days, really it does – before his eyes begin to reluctantly, finally close. And as he lies there, waiting for the dark, he tries to guess whether the dream will come again tonight or not, and if it does, whether it will be the same.

It does. And when it comes, this is what he sees.

★

Mr F is coming slowly up the stairs (this shot is a close-up, of his feet; well-polished oxfords, and two inches of turn-up). The stair-carpet is so worn and thin that every other tread creaks – except that in the dream his footsteps, like everything else, are silent. Muffled. He passes the bloody window. The bars of scarlet light slide across his shoulder, down his arm and across the white skin on the wrist of his outstretched right hand; however, he makes it to the door unstained. Now his right hand is inserting the key into the lock. The key turns; the door opens; now the door is closing behind him again. The lock clicks shut. Then there is a long sequence in which, as on most of Mr F's evenings, nothing much happens. There is the washing of the hands, the preparation and clearing away of his supper, the cleaning of his shoes ready for the next morning over a spread out sheet of newspaper – and all of this Mr F watches (over his own shoulder, as it were, and as if the film had the sound turned off) with some dread, because he knows by now what is going to happen when this is all over. He knows what is going to happen once the dishes are all done and the paper folded and the polish and brushes put back in the cupboard. Despite himself, he goes into the bedroom – and this is where the dream begins to diverge from what *ought* to happen next, from what actually happens when he gets himself ready for bed every night – and instead of hanging up his suit-trousers and putting on his dressing-gown to go and have his bath, he finds himself standing at the foot of the bed and staring at himself in the wardrobe mirror. He stands there for a long time – for what feels like several minutes. What the camera is looking for when it scrutinises his face and body like this, Mr F really doesn't know. Is it looking to see whether the suit still fits him properly? Whether the hems of his trousers are too worn? Whether that smudge of dirt on his collar (which he doesn't for the life of him know how he acquired) will come out, whether his tie is the right colour with this jacket, whether it's tight enough – he has no idea (of course, he knows that it is him doing the staring really, not some camera; he knows that. That this is all a dream, not some peculiar modern film). He frowns, and notices that his eyebrows are slightly bushier than they used to be. Slightly bushier than they used to be back when he was... when he was... when he was what? When he was twenty? When he was *younger*? Is that it? And now, when he holds up both his hands like that, as if offering them for inspection, palms towards the mirror, why does he do that? To check if he's got all the ink from his *Evening Standard* off? To make sure they're white and clean and soft, soft enough to kiss – not that anyone ever does bend down and kiss the palms of another man's hands. Why on earth would they do a thing like that?

All the while, there is still no sound.

When this staring in the mirror eventually stops (just as

he never knows what he is looking for, so Mr F never knows quite how long the looking is going to go on for) he frowns at himself again, turns on his heel and walks down the hall to the bathroom. There is no sound of the taps running, so he knows he isn't going in there to have a bath. It's dark now, of course, so as he pushes open the bathroom door he reaches in and pulls the cord, automatically, without thinking, and the light comes on.

The white ceramic tiles on the walls have never been so white and cold, or the light so bright; for some reason, the single high-wattage lightbulb is bare. The door swings open, and he walks in, and walks to the washbasin to get himself a drink of water, and then he looks up, squinting in the brightness of the light and sees, O God, he sees

Mr F sees, reflected there in the mirror over the washbasin, right there behind him, with its feet tied, its ankles lashed with a thick rope to the cast-iron brackets which hold up the lavatory cistern, a body.

A man's body.

Naked.

A man's body, hanging upside down, with the torso twisted across the seat of the lavatory, twisted sideways so that the head is tipped back over the rim of the bath and the hair and both arms are hanging down into the bathtub and the hands are lying palm up, lifeless and defenceless, right there on the chilly, medical-looking white enamel: the hanging, lifeless, naked body of a white-skinned, black-haired, athletically well-built young man.

Yes, that's right; there are now two men – two men's bodies – in the confined space of Mr. F's bathroom, one standing (his eyes opening wide with shock as he stares in the mirror – he would if he could, but he can't seem to take his eyes off it –), and one hanging; one in a brown worsted suit, the other as naked as a beast on a butcher's hook. And now Mr F suddenly can't bear to look in the mirror a minute longer, he needs to know if it's really there or not, this body; he spins round – and of course it's there, it really is – and the weight of all that hanging flesh in such close proximity sends him stumbling back against the washbasin, so hard that he hurts himself, and then backwards, back towards the door, which is just as well really because he badly needs to get out of this room now, to just get out of there (he can hear himself beginning to whimper) – except that of course fear is making him clumsy (it does that), and his back slams against the bathroom door, slamming it shut, and he starts to slide down it, starts to go sliding down it as his feeble white hands scrabble uselessly for the door-handle behind his back, as he tries to close his eyes to shut out what he's seeing, but can't believe he's seeing, but for some reason he can't, he can't shut them, they just won't close, and

Don't men sound funny when they scream?

three

The first time it happened, after the terrible initial panic of waking up in the dark had subsided and he'd lain there for a bit and got his breath back, Mr F's first really conscious thought about this dream of his was to wonder if any of his neighbours had heard him making that peculiar noise. He couldn't quite be sure if he'd actually screamed out loud, or if that was only the effect of the sound coming back on in his dream. Either way, real or not, he was sure he'd never made a noise like that before in his life. It wasn't like him. He wouldn't want anyone to think he had been –

He collected himself, sat up, put the bedside light on and looked at his wristwatch on the bedside table. Ten to four – just time enough to go back to sleep and get some proper rest before going to work, he thought. Two and half hours, in fact.

In other words, despite the screaming, the dream disturbed him less on its first visit than you might imagine it should have done. Three hours later, once he'd used the toilet, washed his face and cleaned his teeth, he was able to tell himself that the memory of how dreadful he'd felt in the middle of the night was nothing that a strong cup of tea and the first cigarette of the day couldn't put right. It was probably just something he'd eaten – that was it. On the way into work on the train, he read his morning paper a little more thoroughly than usual, and by dinnertime Mr F really had forgotten all about it.

This shouldn't really surprise you. As you probably

know from your own experience, the ease with which the daylight mind explains away or erases its own nocturnal wanderings is extraordinary, but commonplace.

The second time the dream came, two days later, perhaps because his sleeping mind recognised the sequence of events as soon as he saw the key going into the door, and therefore knew what was coming next, it didn't seem quite so terrifying. His memory of it in the morning was hazy enough to suggest that perhaps its images were already beginning to fade. Perhaps because of this, he even felt a little reassured, rather than threatened, by this first return – he told himself it was just his body flushing something out of his system. He was sure that was normal. Healthy, even. It was only after the third time, when he suddenly looked up at his face in the washbasin mirror in the middle of shaving himself the next morning and found that he could remember everything, could remember exactly and in vivid detail what he had seen reflected right behind him there in the mirror last night, that he actually started to wonder what was happening to him. The razor paused in mid-air; he

He had to physically stop himself from turning round to check there was nothing there.

★

As you have probably (and rightly) assumed from the way I have talked about him, Mr F was not the sort of man who was given to thinking about himself a great deal. Mostly, he just got on with things. And he would certainly never have thought of discussing such a personal matter as this with anybody else; even if he had had somebody else with whom he could have talked about his dream, nothing in his upbringing would have equipped him to begin a conversation which would inevitably have had to include a description of exactly what it was that he saw in it. In the absence of talking, all he could do was think; but reflect as he might, he could come up with no possible reason why this strange dream should have come to him three times in a row at this particular point in his life. Nothing about that life had recently changed, dramatically or otherwise; there had been no discoveries, no strange meetings. No one he knew had died. He did briefly wonder whether it was only coincidence that the dream had first appeared on New Year's Day – but then he told himself that from where he was standing, there was nothing very different about the first days of 1967 as compared to the last days of 1966; the pavements were still icy, the mornings were still dark and the trains were still crowded. Everything was as it had been; routine.

Even the dream itself, for all its outlandishness, had, when he thought about it, an aspect of routine. As it became familiar – on the Thursday night I've just described, for instance, the fourth time the dream had come, he was sure he felt the peculiarly alarming sensation, just before he opened the bathroom door, that he was going to make a fool of himself in there *again* – he began to feel exasperated by it. He felt – what was the word – *mocked*. What right had it to wake him up night after night? Didn't it know he had to work the next day? He particularly resented the fact that the dream was beginning to take away from how comfortable he normally felt in his bathroom – first thing in the morning for instance, or when he turned the hot tap on full for his bath. Tomorrow, he decided, he'd try scrubbing the bath out with bleach before he went to bed. He was not used to being disturbed like this, and he didn't like it. He was not used to finding himself mysterious.

He had no idea what the dream "meant", or why it was plaguing him. The only thing that he was sure of was that he wanted it to stop. Consciously or not, he had started to defend himself against it; the way he arranges himself when he first gets into the bed now, for instance, at the end of the second week of his strange new affliction – lying on his back with his feet together and his arms straight down by his sides – he never used to do that.

Not since he was a child.

★

On the Friday morning after the dream had come for the fourth time, after he had lifted the screaming kettle off the stove with a teacloth, poured the boiling water over the leaves, stirred the pot three times exactly, put the lid back on and stood it to brew on the kitchen worktop, Mr F decided to try and tackle this dream of his by asking it a simple, straightforward question. He often did this – put his thoughts into actual sentences. Walking to the corner shop on the way back home from the station, for instance, the sentence would be *Now, do I need milk?*; as he went into the kitchen, it would be *Now, shall I put those chops on?* One of his favourites, which he invariably used when he had finished clearing away at the end of his evening meal, and was wiping down the kitchen table, was *There, that's better.* Sometimes he even found himself saying it out loud.

He couldn't exactly see at first how to put his thoughts about the dream into a single sentence – he had two ideas he was juggling with, and he couldn't quite get them to fit together. One idea was that perhaps the body in the bathroom was best explained away as being like finding a stranger on your doorstep; some sort of unexpected guest. Perhaps a stranger who you'd met somehow on the street the day before and who you could see needed help. Someone who you'd offered shelter for the night, perhaps – and then when you came home from work the next day, he was still there, and helping himself to all the hot water... The problem with this idea was that Mr F couldn't really see how any of this could ever actually happen. Who was this hypothetical stranger he was supposed to have met, for instance; what did he look like? What did his voice sound like – and at what point on the walk home from Peckham Rye station was Mr F supposed to have met him exactly? And what sort of a desperate story would a filthy stranger like that have had to tell in order to talk his way into Mr F's private bathroom? It was ridiculous.

The second idea, which was more of a memory really, seemed more vivid – more precise – but was just as hard to put into words as a single question. It was a memory of something he'd seen once on his dinner-break, down by the river. A great baulk of timber, a great sodden log as thick as a telegraph pole and six feet long, had suddenly broken the surface of the water trapped in the dock at Queenhithe. For a moment, because of its size and shape, he had thought it was something truly dreadful bobbing and rolling there in the oily water, something rotten and stinking that the rivermen would have to come and drag out with their boathooks. Even when he had realised it was just a piece of wood, it still seemed terrible; dangerous, somehow, as if it had lurched up out of the stinking Thames looking for something to smash into. Why had it stayed hidden for so long? What had dislodged it from its filthy bed? Where had it come from?

Mr F was pouring his tea at this point. As he looked down at the steady stream of undrinkable black liquid (it was bound to be stewed by now, and practically cold) he realised that he'd just found the exactly right sentence for his question. He stopped pouring just as the tea threatened to overflow the rim of the tea-cup; he'd got it. He'd found his sentence.

Where have you come from?

Yes; that was it.

Putting down the teapot, and looking up at his kitchen clock to check his watch, Mr F was horrified to discover that he must have been standing there staring into space and thinking about filthy strangers for a good ten minutes now, and that if he didn't get a move on, he might well be late for work. Leaving the breakfast tea-things unwashed on the draining-board (something he never did), he collected his rolling papers and tobacco, quickly buttoned a scarf under his overcoat, slipped on his gloves (it was a raw morning, barely getting light; he'd need them) and walked briskly to the station, striding out (but still taking due care with that ice) and repeating his question over and over in his head all the time to make sure he didn't forget it. Once he'd got his ticket and was on the train, the rhythm of the repeated sentence began to soothe him; he wasn't going to be late at all. And now that he'd found the right question, he was sure that finding the right answer was only a matter of time.

Where have you come from?

The words started to jiggle comfortably against the rhythm of the train, and he checked his watch again; everything was fine.

Where have you come from
Where have you come from

The January of 1967 was a cruelly cold one, and the warmth of the crowded carriage was welcome. Queen's Road and Bermondsey stations slid past behind the misted windows. He decided he'd have plenty of time for a proper hot cup of tea when he got to London Bridge.

Where have you come from

Where have you been…

As his body relaxed in the warmth, the sound of the question began to fade to the back of his mind, and as he sat there, he congratulated himself on the fact that nothing about him made him look any different to anyone else on the train. In particular, nothing of the previous night's adventures showed on his face. Not even the people sitting directly opposite him could possibly have known that this was a man who had woken up screaming just three and a half hours ago. You see, people say that what happens to you in bed at night shows in your face, that people can always tell: but it doesn't, and they can't.

four

Mr F may well be busy asking himself questions about this bizarre night-time visitor of his, but I'm sure he's not the only one; I'm sure that by now you also have a few questions you'd like to ask about our Mr F. Why does this man have such a strange, abbreviated name, for instance? Where is he actually going, when he sets out on this circuitous journey of his each morning? What sort of a job does he have that he always gets home early on Fridays – but only in the winter – and why this curious business of scrubbing and anointing his hands for so long each night?

The answers are all connected. Let me start with the scrubbing of the hands. There is nothing untoward about this. As it happens, Mr F is a fastidious man – for instance, he always leaves the sash window in the bathroom open after he has used the toilet in the morning, despite the fact that the window is easily big enough for someone to climb in through, and the cast-iron fire escape is right outside. No; the reason why he washes his hands so thoroughly when he gets home in the evenings is simple. At the end of the working day, and before he starts to prepare his evening meal, he wants to get rid of the faint but distinctive smell that clings to them. It isn't a particularly unpleasant smell, but it is unusual; dusty, pervasive, oddly animal – hard to place until you realise what it is.

The destination of Mr F's morning journey should provide the necessary clue. The last of the network of narrow lanes on the north bank of the Thames into which we have watched him disappear rejoices in the slightly sinister name of Skin Lane; it is so-called because, together with the other five streets leading off Garlick Hill – Great St Thomas Apostle, Upper Thames Street, College Hill, Trinity Lane and Miniver Court – Skin Lane is the heart of the London fur trade. Mr F's business is the slicing and stitching of skin; he is a furrier.

★

According to the British Fur Trade Directory for that year, there were still over three hundred businesses handling fur – mostly commissioners and importers, but also some dressers, furriers and finishers – on these seven adjacent streets in 1967. Together, they made up an entire and self-contained world; because every single step of the business was still represented – from the first unpacking of the stinking pelts to the final immaculate hand-stitching of the silk linings – a skin could complete its complex journey from broker to dresser to dyer to furrier to finisher – from beast to beauty – without ever leaving the confines of the parish. Commissioners worked next door to pattern-cutters, importers were crowded onto the same staircases as workshops. The neighbourhood had its own distinctive smell (Mr F's stained hands were only one pair amongst hundreds) and even its own arcane vocabulary; urgent telephone conversations were punctuated by trade names and terms that no customer would ever have recognised, and in the workshops themselves you would have overheard strange talk of things being *dropped, drummed,* and *pointed*; of something (a skin; a person – a cheque?) being *fleshed*, and *faced*, and *stayed*. The streets themselves had their own peculiar and local names: Garlick Hill, to its inhabitants, was always just The Hill, while Skin Lane, to Mr F and his colleagues, was only ever The Lane.

This world was, in effect, a secret one; as is often the

way, few outsiders had any idea of the outlandish transac-
tions and transformations that made up its daily business,
despite the fact that the Lane, for instance, was (and is) only
three minutes away from the busy and familiar tube-map
destinations of Cannon Street and Mansion House. This
shouldn't really surprise you, though – in London, it's all a
question of whether you turn right, or left, isn't it? You live
in this city for years, and then one day you turn an
unfamiliar corner to keep an appointment with a stranger –
and suddenly you sense that behind the doorways and
blacked-out shop-fronts of the particular street on which
you've found yourself are the workings of a business that
you know nothing about; one, indeed, that you may not
even have known existed. And they are never fixed, these
secret back-street or High Street worlds – the infamous
"Hidden Worlds of London" which tourist guidebooks like
to dismiss on behalf of their readers in one short, pictur-
esque paragraph (the worlds that the guidebook writers
have heard of, that is; believe me, there are others); they
appear, flourish, and then mysteriously remove, only to
reappear elsewhere. The Hill is a case in point; the most
remarkable thing about the streets that Mr F was heading
for each morning is not that they once held such a unique
concentration of one trade, but that having once been
synonymous with it, they have now been so completely
abandoned. Not a single one of those three hundred
businesses now remains, and the first word of the old black-
and-white cast iron street-sign for Skin Lane affixed to the
corner of College Hill is perhaps the only physical reminder
of the commodity these streets once dealt in.

Even though the businesses have gone, I still think you
will (especially if you arrive from the west down the wide
modern canyon of Cannon Street) get a strong sense of
stepping down into an older, darker – a *separate* – part of the
world, should you choose to interrupt your journey to

wherever it was that you were meant to be going, and ask the driver to turn right down Garlick Hill. This is one of the rare parts of the City that the Blitz left almost untouched, and you'll find that most of the lanes here are too narrow for your taxi. Perhaps it is the cobbles that you'll suddenly find under your feet that make these streets feel different; perhaps the memory of the strange life that once teemed in them still lingers.

★

The Hill is a steep, dark street, hemmed in by nineteenth-century office-buildings and warehouses, and it seems to lead nowhere. At the bottom of the hill, the tower of Wren's church of St James Garlickhythe closes off the view to Upper Thames Street, and here, at the bottom of hill, on the left, is where you'll find Skin Lane. It too is dark; now as then, the south side of the Lane is dominated by the great bare wall of the church, and the bottom two storeys of the business premises which still make up its north side are kept in almost permanent shadow. The first of these, on the corner, is the building where Mr F worked – at least, the address is the same, if not the actual building. The block which now occupies the site dates from a couple of years after the events of this story, but it is the same size and shape – indeed, the outer walls at least are more or less a reconstruction of the building of a hundred years earlier which Mr F would have known. To judge from a photograph of the earlier building taken on the Lane in 1962, showing the nineteen staff of the firm which he worked for assembled outside their workplace, he would still recognise the front door. Just as it was then, it is still painted black, and still set back from the Lane at the top of a steep flight of eight stone steps. The bottom four of these seem to be of a much older and darker stone; I assume they must be survivors from the original building. The people in the photograph are assembled in two distinct groups – the men at the top, all in their white cutters' coats (most of their faces are in shadow; I have no idea which of them might be Mr F himself), and the women on the bottom steps in their pinnies. The black-painted front door appears to be unnumbered, and there is no brass name plate to announce either the name or nature of the business. This doesn't entirely surprise me; on these streets, everyone must have known more or less everyone else's business. Looking at that door, at the top of its flight of dark steps, I get the distinct impression that, as with certain other highly specialised businesses that the City still considers are best conducted well out of sight, it was expected that anyone who needed to seek out the services on offer on the Lane would already be in the trade; in the know. If they were a customer, they would certainly have been given directions – if not a personal recommendation.

I'm sure you know the sort of thing.

The building Mr F entered when he pushed open that door was a warren, cobbled together out of several even older premises. According to the Corporation of London Survey produced as part of the plans for the redevelopment of the north bank of the Thames in 1966, this corner block was Number Four, Skin Lane; and according to the Fur Trade Directory, Number Four housed three separate businesses; The Astoria Fur Company, A&D Eshkeri Ltd (both of these are listed as importers, who presumably only used the building as their City office address; their store- and workrooms are listed as being in Wembley and Plaistow respectively), and M. Scheiner Ltd, which is listed as a manufacturing furriers. This last was Mr F's employer. The firm was unusual, in that it was an actual manufacturers – the relatively high rents in the City meant that most of the actual workrooms were to be found further out – and in its scale of operations. With nineteen workers (most of the firms on the Lane were much smaller), the building must always have felt crowded – and it was far from being purpose-built.The machine-room, for instance, was in a half-basement at the bottom of the building, while the cutting-room was right at the top – a highly inconvenient arrangement that necessitated endless journeys up and down the building's narrow staircases. Offices, lavatories and stockrooms were hidden on each of the landings, and most of the rooms were small, and dark. There was one exception; if you stood out on the corner of the Lane and looked up, you'd have seen that the top storey of the building at least was paradoxically open to inspection. A strip of south-facing windows ran the entire length of the cutting-room, overlooking the roof of St James's church, and these windows were kept permanently uncurtained. This was were the cutting-benches were; the intricacy of the work required constant and direct illumination, and so you might have said that this was the one part of the trade which was conducted in broad daylight – except that up there on the top floor, the windows were too high for anybody to have looked in through them anyway.

The rest of the building was as secretive as its front door. The glass of the lower half of the ground floor windows, for instance, was kept whitewashed, to prevent any passer-by from watching the proceedings inside. The windows were also barred – the trade is, after all, a luxury one, and its raw materials are sometimes of considerable value. In the retail branch of the business, of course, up on Bond Street and Wigmore Street, things were done differently; the West End showrooms of this period were all plate glass windows and acres of polished parquet floor – but even there, discretion was exercised; tact. The finished coats and stoles were displayed on decorous, sexless stands, or at best stiffly draped on extremely ladylike dummies. Nothing hinted at what was, by common consent, best kept hidden. The stench of the pelts when they arrived, stiff and greasy, skin out; their raw sensuality as they hung in glistening rows at auction; their unnerving softness as they submitted to the knives and needles – all that was kept out of sight, down on the Lane.

There was one further twist to the odd air of secrecy about Scheiner's old premises, and it is clearly shown in the photograph I mentioned. The barred basement window to the left of the front door looks as if it is glazed in plain frosted glass, but the one to the right has somehow managed to retain its old plate glass from before the war – they must have kept it sandbagged. In black letters, on white paint, it still bears, for no apparent reason, the cryptic legend "And Sons".

*

So far as I can see, the employees ranged on Scheiner's front steps in the photograph are all smiling. The women in particular – with the exception of one short, fierce-looking lady standing in the middle of them with her arms crossed – look cheerful. There is nothing secretive about *them*. However, if ever he was asked what he did for a living, or where he worked, Mr. F would usually evasively answer that he worked "over in the City". For reasons that he himself didn't quite understand, he still worried, even after all these years, that to describe too accurately what he actually did every day would seem grotesque. There was too much skin and hair involved, too many knives – and there was the smell, of course. He worried that it might still be there, clinging to him; worried that despite the nightly scrubbing, the carbolic and the lanolin, he would never quite have got it out of his skin. On occasion, he resorted to telling people he was actually a bank-teller. Once, bizarrely, when filling in a form to join a library, he had even put down *Zookeeper*.

Mr F had joined Scheiner's in 1934. He'd started in the downstairs workroom, as a sweeper – which was the first time in his life he'd been surrounded by women. They didn't make it easy for him, it must be said. Something about this big, quiet boy fresh out of school made the half dozen female machinists delight in competing to see who could make him blush the deepest. They would surreptitiously kick at the scraps of fur caught under their treadles, sending up an invisible cloud of floating hairs to catch in his nostrils and mouth, forcing him to spit to get them out. The boy would always try and do this when he thought no one could see him – he'd bend over his broom and try and do it in a corner, because he thought it was disgusting, the sensation of hair between your teeth, and he hated spitting anyway – but their eyes were sharper than his, and someone would always spot him and sing out *Are you alright there, darling?* which was everyone's cue to stare, and for the blood to rush to his face. He hated that, too, but the women were merciless – *Aaah; bit of someone's fur stuck between your teeth – anyone we know, darling?* If he could have understood all of the accompanying ribald comments about the promising size of his feet and hands – at fourteen, he had still to grow into his extremities – he would have blushed even harder, but the young Mr F was one of only two or three non-Jews in the twenty-strong workforce at Scheiner's, and since the ladies' filthiest comments were always screeched above the din – the constantly blaring radio, the staccato, guttural whirring of their fur-sewing machines – in Yiddish, he was spared the explicit details of his humiliation. (That explains why Mr F got home when he did on a winter Friday, by the way; like most of the rest of the London garment trade, the workforce at Scheiner's had to be home before sundown on a Friday night, and so the workshops always closed early.)

At sixteen, Mr F had been offered an apprenticeship as

a cutter, and, swapping his brown apron for a four-buttoned white coat, had moved up the narrow, twisting staircase to the all-male workroom at the top of the building. This was where the knives were kept; where the furs were sorted, cut and nailed to their patterns, ready for seaming at the machines downstairs. The segregation of the workforce into male and female workrooms was not peculiar to Scheiner's; tradition dictated that in the fur trade there was no such thing as a female cutter or a male machinist. Everything in the trade was sexed; even the skins themselves were sorted into male and female before going to auction, and priced accordingly (the boy never forgot being taken to the great high-ceilinged Beaver House auction room for the first time, and hearing the words themselves – *male!, female!* – shouted out across the echoing floor). Once the skins arrived on the Lane, both men and women handled them, of course – but their hands moved in very different ways while they did it. Men sliced; women stitched. Men owned the businesses (in this case, Mr Maurice Scheiner, a fifty-year-old second generation Londoner), men ran the auction houses, men ran the showrooms, it was always men who paid for the finished furs – but it was only ever women who wore them. Somehow, the unspoken rules and principles of sexual division clung to the garments as insidiously as their faint but unmistakeable smell; they were worked into them with every delicate stitch, with every painstaking incision. Even though it is hard to describe in figures, and rarely features in anyone's accounts, there is an economy of desire, and of beauty, just as there is of everything else – and that economy was the Lane's business. Men brought their women to be dressed in fur because they thought it was right and proper; they thought it bestowed on a woman all the qualities she should have – elegance; obviousness; animal heat. It put all her secrets right where they needed them to be – on the outside. It could (and, of course, can) make a wife as desirable as a secretary, or a shop-girl as grateful as a wife; even more importantly, it can confer on even the most ordinary of men, as he writes out his cheque for a wrap or coat, a long list of all those things that people who don't have it mistakenly think money just can't buy. Generosity. Princeliness. Dominion.

No wonder they pay. No wonder the trade still flourishes.

Of course, the women on the machines at Scheiner's used rather blunter words than I have to talk about the men who visited the Lane. *"New Styles This Season my arse"*, as one of the younger girls put it, extinguishing her fag before starting work on seaming up a big new order. No one in the machine-room ever spoke to the young boy directly about any of these things – no one ever does – but surely, at the tender age of fourteen, he must have sensed them. Sensed them, hanging there behind the jokes in that hot, dense air – thick with fur, and loud with raucous laughter.

Whatever the reason, he was glad to get upstairs.

*

Nearly thirty-three years later, he was still there, up on the top floor of Number Four, and *Mr F of Scheiner's*, as he was universally known, had become one of the fixtures of the Lane. Despite his seniority (it was the Head Cutter's place he now occupied, in the centre of the long workbench, and even Mr Scheiner himself occasionally deferred to his judgement), no one ever called him anything else. The nickname had originally been given him when he first moved upstairs; this particular junior's arrival had meant that the cutters' benches were then staffed by a Mr Davison, a Mr Eisenberg, a Mr Freeman (which is our Mr F's proper name), a Mr Greenberg (who preferred to be called Mr Green) and a Mr Hoffmann. Naturally the clerk in charge of wages had saved himself time by entering them in the company's wage-ledger as Mr D, E, F, G and H – and the names on the wage-packets had stuck. After the war, out of the five, only Mr F had returned to his job, and indeed by 1967 out of all his colleagues probably only Mrs Kesselman, the head machinist and supervisor, could still remember how he had acquired his name. She is the rather forbidding woman (still wearing both her dyed hair and her thick make-up in the extreme fashion of the late nineteen-forties) who is standing in the middle of her colleagues in the photograph – and she, paradoxically, was the only one of them who would sometimes insist on calling Mr F by his full surname. Mrs Kesselman had been with the firm longer than even he had, and her *Mr Freeman* was the only person in the firm she considered – and treated as – her equal. She wouldn't hear a word against him.

Mr F took this use of his nickname as a mark of respect, which it probably – mostly – was. He knew it implied neither familiarity nor affection. Despite the fact that he had worked there all his adult life, he didn't have anyone at Scheiner's who he would have described as a friend; *acquaintance* and *colleague* were the words he preferred. Their formality suited him. No one who worked with him feared or disliked him, exactly, but they all left him alone. His solid build and his always immaculate appearance combined to suggest a temper being contained; his reprimands were certainly never vulgar, but they were always prompt, and meant. The cutters under him knew enough about the seriousness with which he took his work to never be late in the morning, and never to spoil a skin – not when he was watching, at least.

The world of which Skin Lane was part was a small and crowded one, and almost everyone working in that dense network of streets knew or claimed to know the habits and faults of their rivals. Sometimes a cutter from another firm would remark *That Mr F from Scheiner's, he's not the cheeriest soul on the Lane* – and it was true that even after all these years neither Mr F's body nor his voice had acquired the characteristic Yiddisher inflections of his trade. His hands never gesticulated; he rarely joked. His manner was at all times sober and, to a degree, withdrawn; this was a man who definitely kept, you would have said, himself to himself. Though no one ever said anything to his face, some of the younger girls downstairs did occasionally (not in front of Mrs Kesselman, mind) raise their eyebrows at this apparent stand-offishness of his. As was only natural, there was some speculation about him.

About his single-ness, I mean.

When a man is solitary, people always want an explana-tion, don't they – have you noticed that? Especially if he ends up doing something notable, committing a crime for instance, or even just surviving to a very old age. At some point in the conversation, someone always says, *I wonder what made him that way?*

★

As it happens, Mr F's air of solitariness was something that he had always had. When he was a child, it had had the most obvious of explanations, the one that the female neighbours always liked to dwell on when commenting on the fact that he wasn't as boisterous as his brothers; *of course, you know the boy never knew his mother.* That's why, in the few memories he has of childhood outings to the circus or the pictures or the zoo, it is always his father's hand that he is holding. The faces of the succession of ladies "down the street" – some kind, some less so – who looked after him while his father was at work are lost to him now; he remembers the house he grew up in as only ever having men in it, and as being small, and dark, and quiet. He remembers how cramped the kitchen was, and how the meals were eaten without conversation; he can still vividly picture his father standing, silent, at the kitchen sink, his shirtsleeves rolled up and his face turned away. He can remember being short enough to have to struggle to reach the kitchen table on a Sunday night, when it was always his task to polish his brothers' giant shoes over a sheet of spread newspaper – and he can remember a lot of listening. In particular, he can remember sitting at the top of the stairs with the lights turned out and his forehead pressed against the banisters, straining to catch the strange, half-heard sound of men's voices booming and drifting up the stairs. There were several noises in the house that fascinated him like this. There was the small *chink* of his father's wedding ring as he put it in the china saucer on the windowsill when they started on the dishes; the muffled laughter downstairs when his brothers came home after he'd been sent up to bed; and strangest – and perhaps best – of all, the occasional sudden shout or woman's shriek from beneath his bedroom window late on a Saturday night, followed always by the mysterious sound of someone running (from what? he wondered), by the receding clack and clatter of a pair of high heels.

He sometimes thought of asking what these noises meant; but he was not a child who ever asked his questions out loud. They stayed inside his head.

At school, he was what they called "quiet". At the dinner-break, he often stood apart from the others in the playground, but luckily, he was saved from the bullying usually meted out to any boy less than eager to join in by the reputation of his brothers. In the classroom, he rarely, if ever, volunteered an answer, which gave his teachers licence to ignore him; this reticence infuriated his father, but only sometimes, and not enough for his annoyance to develop into either worry or any great care. Later on, when he started on the Lane, the boy's inability or disinclination to contribute to the workroom banter was certainly remarked on; but when his apprenticeship proper began upstairs, his quietness was for the very first time appreciated, and even, on a couple of occasions that he still remembered, commended. In a workplace that crowded, his colleagues were probably grateful that for once the junior had little to say for himself. Certainly, no one ever learnt faster or mastered the intricacies of the craft with more studied concentration than Mr F did; at sixteen, he may have showed no desire to learn to swear in Yiddish, and he may never have wanted to go to a dance-hall or yet have struck up a conversation with a stranger on a bus, but the methodical, brow-furrowing dexterity required to handle a furrier's knife seemed to come naturally. It was as if this was what he'd been waiting for. Even Mr Scheiner, who'd been in the trade long enough to have forgotten more about it than most people had ever known, was impressed. So, the boy was cold fish. By whom was that a problem?

*

Where else in this man's life should we look for explanations of this impression that it was always lived more or less to one side of everybody else's? His experiences in the war? People often think that men of Mr F's particular age must be hiding some invisible wound, some secret damage that means they could never be quite the same man again after 1945 – but actually the clean and orderly life, the regular pay and food, and above all the anonymity of the army had all suited him; the foul things, the hours of panic and squalor, had if anything only made him more self-reliant.

Those years left him with two harsh lines drawn under his eyes, which for some reason never faded, but apart from that he came back to his life determined to resume it exactly where he'd left off; he put his self-contained habits back on with his brown worsted suit.

No; scrutinise him as they occasionally may, as he approaches his forty-seventh birthday there is nothing obvious to explain to his colleagues (or to you) why this man should seem so separate. Nothing in his history marked him out as different from any other single man of his age; his clothes and manners were no more or less old-fashioned than those of most of his generation. If you had been walking two paces behind him in the morning rush hour you would have noticed nothing unusual – no twist in the spine or built-up shoe, no tell-tale disfigurement or limp. If you'd found yourself sitting opposite him on the 5.49 train home to Peckham Rye, you would have had no reason to either stare or avert your eyes; there was no scar or bloody blotch of birthmark on his face that I've failed to mention. He was nearly six foot tall, had large hands, pale blue eyes, a short-back-and-sides and a brown worsted suit that had perhaps seen better days – but that was all. The pallor of the eyes was perhaps a bit unusual, and the skin on the hands unusually soft, but not by any stretch of the imagination could this man be said to have any of the physical peculiarities or deformities that are usually held to explain why some men are left well alone by their fellows; the reasons why, in stories like this one, men turn violent or strange – why they become, or are deemed to be, unlovable. But

But there is something, of course.

Something nobody can *see*, but which I can tell you about.

There is something about Mr F that sets him apart from his fellow commuters on the 5.49 train, something which most of us – certainly now, and, I think, even then – would, if we were being honest, think of as a deformity. In all of the nineteen years since the first night when he sat there testing the springs of the mattress and smoking a thin celebratory roll-up (he knew how lucky he was; one-bedroomed flats for single men were in short supply in the hungry, still-shabby London of 1948) from the age of twenty-eight to the age of almost forty-seven, he has never invited anyone to join him in that single bed of his.

How do some people miss it, sex? How has this man missed it? Shall we say *by accident*? After all, a very few words can do it; a few tiny hints. If his older brothers had still been living at home by the time the little boy's body had started to sprout its own mysterious patches of dark hair, he would probably have been taken into their confidence – when he was watching them get dressed on a Saturday night, he would have heard who that dirty wink in the mirror was being practised for, whose eye the clean white shirt was meant to catch; what the half-whispered words of that song could lead to after the last dance of the evening. But both of his brothers had already left home by the time his tenth birthday came around – and his father's bedroom was forbidden territory for advice as much as for affection. When he was taken to the older of his two brothers' wedding (a grim, hurried affair, with a white-faced bride and the two families barely speaking to each other) he was surely old enough to have been told why the marriage had been arranged so quickly – but there too, nothing was explained to the boy. By the time he was what we would now call a teenager, his father, never quite sure what a widower was meant to do with children anyway, had taken to spending every evening alone in the front room with the evening paper; this meant that although by the age of sixteen Mr F knew how to contribute a week's wages to the household budget, how to scrub and bleach and to cook, no one had ever taught him how to feel. Indeed, the only real lesson his father had ever taught him was that feelings should never be spoken of; his dead mother, for instance, was never mentioned, and there were no pictures of her in the house. When the younger of his brothers was killed, it was Mr F who went to the door to get the telegram, and when he had given it to his father to read, the old man (men were old at fifty in those days) had done nothing but sit stony-faced in his usual armchair, never saying a word, waiting until night had fallen and the house was dark before walking slowly upstairs, closing his bedroom door behind him, and shouting out his lonely, foul-mouthed, broken-hearted grief to the empty bed on which his children had been conceived. That night, Mr F again found himself sitting on the stairs, with his head on one side, wondering what the noises meant. Wondering why the door had to be closed before they could be spoken.

It is the words that do it, I think. The words that men use to each other. Those muffled howls of his father were not the first obscenities the boy had ever heard, not by any means; but they were the ones he never forgot. There were other phrases, too, that he heard later, in an army bunk, when the other men were smoking and talking about the women they'd left behind, about what they were going to do to them when they got home. And of course there were the very earliest ones, the words from way back, from so far back he's forgotten them now, as we all do: *Don't look. Don't be silly. Hands straight down by your sides now, like a good boy. Lights out.* These are the words that none of us can quite remember being used on any particular occasion, but which we know – and knew, somehow, even then – all add up to a warning, a prohibition. Stone by stone, they place all the things we wish we could see and touch on the other side of a high, forbidding wall.

And perhaps even more than the words, it is the silences. They aren't necessarily sinister or malicious in intention; no one means them to maim or deny. When he was little, for instance, eight or perhaps nine, how Mr F used to stare all the time at his older brothers – O, how that little boy used to love being allowed to stay up and watch them getting dressed on a Saturday night! He'd stand in the bathroom doorway in his pyjamas, keeping quiet like he'd been told to, and stare, fascinated, while they took it in turns to strip down to their vests and shave. He loved everything about it; the unwrapping of the brand-new razor blade from its mysterious little paper envelope; the careful whipping up of the soap with the little badger-bristle brush; the silent concentration. The way the white suds were mysteriously flecked with black when the razor got wiped on the little squares of newspaper. The way they smiled at him and said *You wait. You just wait, our kid. You'll find out... one day.* Sometimes he thought they looked so splendid, when they were all done and dressed up, that he wanted to clap. They'd sweep him up, kiss him goodnight (cologne and soap on a smooth chin; the smooth dazzle of a white collar), call him *our kid* again and tuck him in and leave him alone in the dark, whistling and singing their way down the stairs and out of the front door. Then, on Sunday mornings, he'd try his very hardest to wake up while it was still almost dark, so that he could sit up in his bed in his pyjamas and stare at them while they lay side by side in the early morning half-light, sleeping off their big night out. He always wondered how they'd managed to creep back into his bedroom and get undressed without waking him up – they were princes, he decided, princes who'd been out dancing all night like in one of his stories, and now they'd come back again and cast off their magic robes and changed back into ordinary, exhausted mortals. He'd sit there for a whole hour, holding his breath lest they wake up and catch him, trying to read in their blurred faces and dishevelled hair the details of their nocturnal adventures. He loved the quiet, and the half-light made by the still-drawn curtains, and the sound of their breathing – even the faint stink of cigarette smoke from their clothes on the back of the chair was a mystery. He wondered if their slack, half-open mouths were about to tell him something.

Yes; maybe it's in the silences, the silences in which we imagine the answers to the questions that we never dared ask, that the damage is first done. Who knows.

★

Of course, all around this man, because of the year in which this story takes place, the city he lives in is far from silent. In fact, it's getting noisier by the week.

Because it's still early in January, the copies of the *Evening Standard* which he buys at London Bridge station on the way home still have all their usual "New Year" articles, articles headlined *The Year Ahead Of Us*, or *So What Can We Expect In 1967?* This year, they all seem to agree that great changes are imminent. They are cheerfully strident about overcrowded roads, and the preposterous cut of youthful suits and skirts and hair; they are littered with the phrase *these days*. Mr F is kept informed about *young people who live in the shadowy half-light of an illicit world*, and he wonders what exactly it means when the article says that *an estimated 800,000 young women are now believed to be regularly taking the contraceptive pill*. He looks at the adverts for all the new films, but rarely recognises any of the faces.

When people look back – people like us, I mean – they're going to point to this hubbub and chatter and to all the music and the films and they're going to agree that everyone in London must have known that this was one of those years when nothing was ever going to be the same again. But Mr F, carrying his copy of the *Standard* home on the 5.49 train, doesn't know that; he doesn't know that any more than he knows it is going to be an exceptionally hot summer this year. He reads his newspaper every day, as most people do, but, like most people, he thinks the things described there are happening in somebody else's world, not his; that they are happening to other people, but not to him. Sometimes he will look at the page which lists the television programmes for that evening and wonder if perhaps he should buy himself a set and try it; but in the end he always decides that he's happy with just the radio. He notices, amidst the regular items on strikes, deaths, robberies and actresses, the news that a ranch mink coat has been reduced in the Harrods Sale to £895. He reads the whole of a half page advertisement with an odd little photograph of a grinning couple in swimsuits pretending to be on a beach, informing him that this summer he can choose between spending *Two weeks in Sorrento for forty-one guineas*, or *One in Switzerland for only twenty-nine and a half!* – but he never thinks for a moment that he might ever be the sort of man to put his arm around someone's naked shoulder like that, or to smile like that, or indeed that he might ever go to Italy. He reads his horoscope (he's an Aries), which on Thursday the thirteenth of January 1967 tells him that *Though you may have good cause for feeling mad about something or someone, it would be best to disguise your feelings for the time being. You will only make matters worse if you speak out.* He looks forward to getting home.

But it would be a mistake for you to think of Mr F as unhappy. If anyone had ever asked him if he felt old-fashioned or lonely or hidden away, he would have never have dreamt of answering *yes*. Far from it. He believed in keeping himself active. Every weekend, for instance, he would always be sure to make at least one trip out. He had tried the cinema – had even gone as far as the Odeon Leicester Square one evening, to see a new film which had been in all the papers and which he'd thought from the sound of it that he might, unusually, like. He'd chosen Leicester Square because he could remember being taken there once as a child, but the whole experience was very different to how he'd remembered it, and he'd found the whole thing too noisy, too crowded and not at all – well, not at all *improving*. His preferred treats were the galleries and museums; they were just more him, really. The quiet, and the fact that it was considered perfectly normal to stand and stare at things you didn't really understand, and to be alone while you tried to work them out, all suited him. If he felt like a bus journey, the National Gallery was always a reliable favourite; if he wanted a walk, then the Dulwich College pictures were only a determined uphill half-hour away. It wasn't that he loved pictures, especially; if he was walking, he was just as likely to choose the Horniman Museum in Forest Hill as his Sunday afternoon destination. It was the atmosphere, really; the quiet. There was something about all those neatly labelled cabinets of curiosities, the long, gloomy galleries of birds and beasts, each one perched or prowling under a thin coating of dust, that both fascinated and calmed him. He often stayed until almost closing time, waiting until the galleries got dark and empty and mysterious. Perhaps it was the odd life in all those pairs of staring, artificial eyes that he liked. Perhaps it was the way each specimen was alone in its cage of glass.

The peacock, forever displaying to an absent mate: the shambling, stupid rhino. The black panther, forever screaming on its dusty forest branch.

All of them, so quiet.

five

Two whole weeks of dark January nights later, Mr F still had no answer to his question – this, despite the fact that his dream was now returning more or less every other night. Every time it came, he still found himself starting awake with his throat jerked back in a scream; but as the second week turned into the third, and then into the fourth, his attitude towards his uninvited guest began – inevitably, perhaps – to change.

As he got into bed each night, he would still find himself straightening his limbs under the sheets in preparation – but now it was not so much to defend himself against what he knew or feared was coming as to brace himself for it. The moment when he finally let himself close his eyes became not unlike that strange moment when the car reaches the top of the roller-coaster, and pauses; the moment when you find your legs involuntarily stiffening and your hands holding on tight because your body, despite itself, knows the thrill that is coming. Of course, in the moment of waking, there was no pleasure for Mr F, only fear – the truly horrible fear that comes with a thumping heart and twisted sheets – but when the dream began, as the pictures which heralded his nocturnal visitor's arrival began to repeat themselves in predictable, stately succession – the blood, the key, the door; the mirror – there was no getting round it: the fear was definitely starting to be mixed with anticipation.

I suppose you could say that Mr F was simply getting used to living with his dreams. Men do, of course. No matter what you see them actually doing by daylight, it is nothing compared to the ferocity and oddity of what they imagine when their eyes are closed.

Another thing that began to change was that instead of trying to shake the details of his dream out of his mind – to not dwell on it, for instance, on the train into work – he now found himself making much more deliberate efforts to recall them. Especially in the few minutes just after he had woken up. Before, he had always turned the bedroom light on straightaway, to reassure himself that he was still lying safely in his bed, with his bedroom walls all reassuringly close, and his watch still lying just where he'd left it on the bedside table; but now, he doesn't do that. He sits there, panting, in the dark, eyes screwed shut, trying to replay what he has just seen stretched across the blank, black screen of his eyelids.

Of course, Mr F didn't – I suppose I should be kind, and say *couldn't* – Mr F couldn't admit to himself the obvious reason for these changes. He told himself that he *had* to dwell on the details of his dream like this, because that was the only way he was ever going to find an answer to his question: the only way he was ever going to work out where this naked man had come from, and who he was. How else was he ever going to make him go away?

There was a problem with this plan, however. To know who someone is, obviously, you have to be able to see his face.

And Mr F can't.

No matter how many times the dream comes, and no matter how many times he screws his eyes back shut and replays it in his mind, he can't ever seem to see the young man's face.

Perhaps it's because he turns round too quickly, he tells himself. Perhaps he ought to try and look in the bathroom mirror longer. Or perhaps it's just that he screams too soon – he really should try and hold out longer. After all, it's not as if he doesn't know what's coming. But what with his heart racing like that, and that terrible, animal need to get out of the room, that awful useless scrabbling behind his back for the door handle (the way his fingernails slide over the smooth surface of the paint makes his stomach lurch) – it's no use; he just can't help himself. And then, by the time he's got his breath back, it's no good. It's too late. The young man's face just isn't there. It's gone. Even with the light kept off and his eyes screwed shut to preserve the darkness, Mr F just can't see it.

That is why, late on the last Sunday of the month, instead of putting the radio on after he has finished his supper, he makes himself a cup of tea, collects his Golden Virginia and his rolling papers, goes into his living-room, turns on his gas fire and the living-room lamp, sits down in his armchair and prepares himself to really concentrate. Even though he knows this is going to take quite some time, he leaves the lights on in the kitchen, and in the hall – which is odd, because he is normally very careful about not leaving any lights on in an unoccupied room. I don't think he is aware of doing this; perhaps it reassures him. He lays out his tobacco and his papers next to the cup and saucer on the arm of his chair and then, starting at the beginning, he tries to make the whole dream come back as clearly and slowly and completely as he can.

He tells himself that he knows how to do this; it's just like staring at something in a gallery or the museum. And since they're all closed, it being a Sunday evening, he'll just have to do his staring here at home. And since he's at home, he'll be able to have a smoke while he does it – three cigarettes, he's going to allow himself. He doesn't want to get morbid about it. Doesn't want to find himself staying up all night with it, for instance; that wouldn't be right. Tomorrow is Monday, after all.

*

The first bits come back easily; the bloody light from the
landing window as he comes up the stairs; the key sliding
into the lock of the door; his frown in the wardrobe mirror.
It's only when he gets to the bathroom door that he has to
start to really concentrate. He tries to slow everything down.
Opening the door. Reaching in for the light-switch. Looking
up and seeing the body reflected in the washbasin mirror –

He pauses here, and has a drag on his cigarette. Then he
closes his eyes.

That's better.

The tiles are very white – too white. And the bulb's too
bright – it makes the flesh hanging there behind him look
like there isn't a single drop of blood in it. He can feel his
stomach starting to clench in panic, but

but he tries to turn round slowly – *properly*. Not
spinning round and bruising his hip against the washbasin
like he normally does. But it isn't easy, staying calm. He
tries telling himself that this is what it must be like in a
mortuary, when they call you in to identify the body. The
bright overhead light. The white tiles. The being allowed to
take your time and stare.

That's right. Being *allowed* to stare.

(It's very cold, for some reason. Must be that bathroom
window being left open. Good job he's got the gas on.)

He wonders if they really do leave you alone in the
room with the body like this – surely, there must be an
assistant or somebody, in case you get upset. That's it, he
decides; there's bound to be somebody else in there with

you. Somebody in a white coat. Somebody whose job it is to stand right close beside you, saying very gently *It's alright, sir, you can go closer than that if you want to.*

He does – but then he decides that before he gets to the face, he ought to make a conscious effort to search the body all over for any clues as to how it got there. He tells himself not to be embarrassed – after all, looking at skin, in a way it's what he does for a living. If he doesn't know what he's doing after thirty-three years, what's the point.

He starts at the top, with the feet.

What with the weight of the body, there is some slight bruising where the ropes are cutting into the skin just below the ankles. The feet are half-crossed – and very pale. White, really; no blood in them, I suppose –

Wait a minute. He's seen them before, those feet…

Mr F gets up out of his chair, and goes and stares out of his living-room window, pulling the curtain aside. Of course, it's dark outside, and there's nothing to see but blackness. He lets the curtain fall back. Aren't Jesus's feet always crossed like that – though obviously not pointed up at the ceiling like these are. *That's it.* (He sits back down again.) But where? Where has he seen them like that before? He isn't a Catholic, and they didn't have anything like that in their church at home that he can remember (not that they went very often) but he is sure he can remember seeing a pair of white feet like that. Yes; being a little boy, and staring up at a pair of white feet – at how very big they were, bigger even than his brothers'. It must have been outside that big red-brick church on the High Street he was always hurried past on the way to school. That's it – yes. He can see them now. Pinned up on the end wall. White; white-gloss-painted carved wood, they were. And big, bigger than life-size, with a big metal nail through them. Bright splashes of red paint for the blood. Big, and shiny, and dead – and then when you looked up there was the whole body looming up over you, with that awful downward-sagging face with its closed eyes. Right out there on the street for you to stare at – except that you weren't supposed to – he remembers that, too. He remembers being dragged past in a hurry even if he wasn't late for school. He remembers the man's hand, tight around his, dragging him away.

He sits back down (without realising it, he has stood up and started pacing up and down in front of the gas fire) and rolls himself another cigarette – and then forgets to light it.

This skin he's staring at now is white, too – but it doesn't have that hard, painted look at all. It's soft. It soaks up the light. And it's unbroken – there are none of the carefully painted holes that Jesus has. Mr F checks every inch of it, just as he would check every one of a bundle of skins at work. There are no wounds, splits, snare-cuts or shot-holes anywhere. Starting at the feet again, he moves his eyes slowly down over the whole body.

He notices that the fine black hairs on the crests of the shins are so sparse that he could, if he wanted to, count them. Normally he would touch them, part the hairs with his thumb to check the quality – but he's sure that's not allowed. He can't imagine the voice in his ear ever telling him he's allowed to do that; *Go on, sir, it's quite alright. Do touch him if you want to.* He notices how the insides of the two upside-down thighs – just – touch, and then, lower down, are pressed together. When he looks at the soft folds in the skin of the genitals (they look so peculiar, hanging upside-down like that) he thinks that the hair around them is like... like Persian lamb, he decides. The individual hairs glitter slightly in the light. Like black wires.

He's never stared at anyone like this; not even at himself in the bath. He's surprised he's being so calm about it. He lights his cigarette, and carries on.

He notes the three creases across the stomach where

the body is slumped and twisted over the toilet seat; the way the muscles are stretched across the upper ribs by the dead weight of the arms. The exposed fan of flattened hairs in each open armpit. The long muscle of the inner arm; the veins on the inside of each forearm, and then the wrists, and then, finally, the hands. The soft palms; the backs of the upward-curving fingers, resting on the cold white enamel (why do they unnerve him so, the hands? Is it their helplessness? The way they seem more dead than any other part?). Then, making sure he does it slowly – *properly*, because this is the point of the whole exercise – he runs his eyes back up the arms. Up the forearms: across the faint veined shadow on the inside of the elbow. Up across the open armpit: up the cording of the tipped-back neck-muscles to the line of the jaw, and then –

He can't see it.

He can't see the man's face. It doesn't matter how long he sits here in his armchair with the third cigarette burning unheeded between his fingers – he can't see it. Which is ridiculous. He can't even say for sure what colour his eyes are. Can't even remember if they are open or closed. Except he knows when he thinks about it that of course they must be closed. They must be. He tells himself that somehow next time he should get down on his knees at the side of the bath and stare at it, really *study* it, make a deliberate effort to memorise it, but for now – what's the sentence? – oh yes; *I just can't put a face to him.* He's heard Mrs Kesselman use that phrase to one of her girls when discussing some actor or other in a film they'd both seen; *I just can't… I just can't seem to…* (He reaches down and turns out the gas – it's not helping him, that hissing sound.) He has one last go. He screws his eyes shut – so tight, that the blood in his eyelids sends strange patterns of smoke and shifting clouds across the screen.

There is one thing, actually. Yes; he may not be able to see his face, but he can see his hair. It's dark; yes, dark, definitely, and long enough to flop over his forehead and spread out on the enamel. Which is too long, Mr F thinks. Too long for a man. He can't understand these young men's haircuts, the way they let it grow down almost over their collars; he wouldn't feel comfortable with that at all – he has to change his shirt every day as it is. Still, that's the fashion these days, so they tell him; long – and dark. Definitely dark. He had thought at first it was black, but now that he looks closely, he can tell that it isn't – he will say that for his bathroom, you get a good working light from that naked bulb, especially with all that white tiling round the bath. It's almost as good as his workbench at Number Four. After closer inspection, he thinks the colour of the young man's hair is much more like this so-called "black" fox which Scheiner's is using a lot of for collars and cuffs at the moment, which isn't a true black at all when you get it in the light, but still has a dark mahogany under-fur where the dye hasn't taken. Or sable, of course. Yes, Mr F decides, that's it; sable. Wild dark Russian sable, the kind you hardly ever see these days. Male skins, of course. With that beautiful shine to it, which not even the best of the dyers can ever convincingly fake. That beautiful *lustre*. Something special, that is. And the way it feels, under your hand…

He opens his eyes, blinks, takes a sip of his cold tea and starts to roll a fourth cigarette. *Sod it. Never mind the colour of his hair, what about the face,* he tells himself. *That's what they'll want to know about. You can't just say "The man who did this to me had curly black hair, officer. Well not black exactly, but certainly very dark." They'll need a full description. Otherwise how are they ever going to identify him for you?*

★

If it had been real, of course, the body – if it had been a real, actual corpse in his bathroom – then his life would probably have been a lot easier, he knew that. There'd have been the unpleasantness of actually discovering it to get over of course, but once he'd done that, and scrubbed out the bathroom, and they'd taken the body away or whatever they do, then a couple of mornings later he'd be in the newsagents on the way to the station – or buying his *Evening Standard* from the kiosk at London Bridge on the way home – and there the young man's face would be all over the front pages. They'd use one of those artist's reconstruction drawings, probably, to make the appeal – and he wouldn't be surprised if it was in all the papers, not just the *Standard* – shelves of them, all stacked up one on top of the other, whole rows of front pages, and all with the same caption: *Do You Know This Man?* And then somebody would come forward with the necessary information – some relative, probably – and then he'd finally have the answer to his question. He'd *know*.

He wondered if the police would be able to tell him not just where the young man had come from, but how he'd got in there – how he'd ended up in his bathroom. Up the fire escape and in through the window, probably – and definitely at night. It was a wonder they'd managed to creep in and do all that without waking him up – because there must have been more than one of them, mustn't there. More than one person involved. Yes; it would have taken more than one person to hoist the body up and tie it to the brackets with the ropes like that. And they must have had a reason, mustn't they, though heaven knows what it could possibly have been. I mean they could have just put him face down on the bed, but no, hanging him up like that, like a beast or a piece of meat, they must have been making a point – they must have been trying to tell someone something, mustn't they. Mustn't they, *officer?*

＊

As the living-room grew colder, Mr F elaborated this story of himself talking to a policeman. He tried to work it all out, all the details – but he wasn't very good at it, it must be said. He didn't have a television, remember, and rarely went to the cinema, so his ideas about how to express bewilderment or to lie convincingly were necessarily sketchy. He did his best, however. He imagined for some reason that this interview with the police would take place in the downstairs office at Scheiner's, not at his flat, and that they'd call him down from upstairs in the middle of the morning, so that he'd be standing there explaining himself still wearing his white coat, with his knife in his hand – and his hands all unwashed. That last detail bothered him – it seemed impolite to be bringing his smell into the room like that. He decided (he even went to the lengths of imagining himself pausing on the stairs outside the office and working all of this out) that he'd better tell them he'd been working late that night, and so hadn't left Skin Lane until gone seven. Allowing time for the walk and the train, it would have been nearly eight o'clock before he'd slid the key into the lock of his front door – he thought he'd leave out the detail of the light from the bloody window staining his sleeve, because he didn't see how that was relevant – which would mean that he'd discovered the body shortly after eight o'clock, officer. Then (he'd explain, carefully) he'd had to go into his living-room and roll himself a cigarette, just to calm his nerves – and then go into the kitchen and make himself a cup of tea with three sugars in it. To get over the shock, officer. In fact it must have been nearly a quarter to nine before he'd been able to summon up the nerve to walk back down the hallway past that bathroom door and go downstairs and ask in Number Two could he please use the phone as it was an emergency.

That was it; he'd tell them how he'd had to have a little

cough just before he spoke, just gently, seeing as how his throat was still slightly bruised from the screaming – just to open it up a little, so that he could speak clearly and in a relatively normal manner to that kind officer who'd answered the telephone at the station, but –

But then his story betrayed him. His voice faltered, and he knew

Mr F knew, as he sat there in the chill of his now-cold living-room, that he was only making up all of these details about having worked late and the cigarette and the cup of tea with three sugars in it so that he would never have to tell anybody – certainly not some young police officer who he'd never even met before – the real reason why it took him so long to go downstairs and make that fictitious telephone call. Which was that the sooner he made it, the sooner they would come and take the body away. He was afraid that when they did that – and he had to stand there in his front doorway and watch them carrying it down round the bend of the stairs, with the red light from the window catching the sheet or blanket draped over it – that the expression on his face would reveal his secret.

Which is that he wants it to stay.

Which is that far from wanting to be rid of it, he thinks the sight of this young man slumped in his bath, the dark target of his pubic hair set against the white marble of his unmarked flesh, is probably the most

Well (Mr F gets up and starts pacing the room again), he knows that he doesn't want anyone to come and take him away, that's all.

He has no idea at all what to do with this feeling.

six

Each year, as January turned into February, visitors to Skin Lane who weren't in the trade themselves would often find themselves stopped in their tracks by one of the strangest sights that London's backstreets had to offer. Great swaying, disembodied cloaks of fur, slung over porters' shoulders, appeared to stagger from doorway to doorway of their own accord; the buried porter's breath, rising in the winter air, completed the illusion that some hitherto-unrecorded species of beast was blundering, hunch-backed and wounded, through the narrow city streets.

The annual appearance of these strange hybrid creatures is simply explained. These were the weeks when the previous year's Russian and North American winter skins had to change hands as quickly as possible, so that the manufacturers could meet the retail orders of the new season. At Number Four, as on the rest of the Lane, the whole pace of the building would pick up. The ceiling of the cutting-room would be festooned with bundles of freshly bought-in pelts, while all along the length of the south-facing window the cutters in their white coats would be bent over their benches like hard-pressed, conscientious doctors. Downstairs in the machine-room, the women's voices rose in volume as the needles raced to meet the weekly deadlines; the radio was kept turned up so loud, sometimes you could hear the lyrics of the songs they chose to shout along to even right out in the street.

For Mr F, who was in charge upstairs, and Mrs Kesselman, who ran the machine-room, the new month had its own particular pressures. They usually met on the stairs first thing in the morning – they both made a point of always being at work in good time to monitor the prompt arrival of the rest of the workforce. One bitter February morning, towards the end of the second week, having bid him her usual *good morning,* she replied to his daily enquiry as to her health, *And how are we, Mrs Kesselman,* in a more than usually aggrieved tone.

"Well, nothing gets easier, Mr Freeman."

Although he would just as soon have gone upstairs and made sure everything was ready, because he knew it was going to be a particularly busy day, Mr F was always polite.

"And why is that, Mrs Kesselman?"

As she briskly unbuttoned her coat, she explained that in order to meet the extra workload, Mr Scheiner had asked her to take on two new girls who were, as she put it, *not from the trade.*

"So now I have to say everything twice – and no offence, Mr Freeman, but these girls they are slow – slow. Not willing, I might say. Still, since the war, young people – yiddisher, not yiddisher – do they want the job or not, I sometimes wonder."

She hung her coat up, beating at the dyed marten collar with her hand to get the last of the morning damp off it.

"And today of course we have Mr Scheiner's nephew starting his six months if you don't mind."

Mr F hadn't heard about this, and said so, and so Mrs Kesselman explained. Apparently the boss's sixteen-year-old nephew was being given a try-out with the family firm, starting as a sweeper downstairs. She reminded him that that was where he had started.

"Who knows, Mr Freeman, if he's keen this boy, maybe one day he'll be in your shoes."

Mr F thought, but didn't say, *Well, let's give him thirty-three years, shall we, and then we'll see*; he headed upstairs with just the reply

"I think there's a few more years still to go before I need replacing, Mrs Kesselman."

Mrs Kesselman, who had the sharpest eyes and ears in the building, didn't think anything at all of the rather sharp way Mr F ended the conversation – it was a Monday morning in February, and an unpleasantly cold one. She knotted on her overall, patted her raven's-wing hair into place, and started to get ready for the girls.

★

Later that same morning, when Mr Scheiner insisted on taking his nephew all round the building and introducing him to everyone, it must be said that the young man in question looked far from keen. He could hardly be blamed; at sixteen, machine-room sweeper was not the most glamorous of jobs. He clearly found being paraded round by his uncle in front of everybody as The New Boy hideously embarrassing. In the upstairs workroom, Mr Scheiner insisted on everyone stopping work while the introductions were made, and this made it worse. Mr F looked at the boy's sharp suit, and at his dark, clever face, and thought *We'll be lucky to get six weeks out of you.*

After the boy had been sent back downstairs again, Mr Scheiner stayed on to see what sort of progress Mr F was making on the cutting of his current piece, a mid-length jacket in ocelot. Although the firm's bread and butter was retail orders of the commoner furs – ranch mink, musquash, lamb – they did occasionally make one-offs for personal clients, usually family or business associates of Mr Scheiner's. Ocelot is difficult fur to work, and if the client can afford the best-quality skins, it can be expensive. These particular skins were Brazilian, the best, and the ten of them required for a decently cut jacket represented a considerable investment – which was why Mr F, as Head Cutter, had been entrusted with the job – and why Mr Scheiner was keeping a close eye on it.

Like most small-scale manufacturers, his habitual language was that of complaint, and while he watched Mr F work on cutting the skins for the collar (always the trickiest seam on a jacket) he launched into a running commentary on how difficult it was to turn a proper profit on the individual pieces these days, crowning his argument with one of his most frequently heard catch-phrases: *But the hidden costs, do they consider? The* **hidden** *costs. That's my point, Mr F.* He wasn't expecting any response to his monologue – the man was taciturn at the best of times, and the job was a delicate one – and so was surprised when the knife stopped moving, and hovered.

"I'm sure the lady concerned will be happy," said Mr F, not looking up from his bench, "and that's the main thing – "

Mr Scheiner couldn't resist a chuckle:

"I should think she should be, when he tells her what this is costing him."

The knife was still poised above the fur:

" – because I should hate to be going to all this trouble for no reason."

Clearly Mr F wanted to be left alone to get on with the job. His boss was happy to leave him to it and go back downstairs; he could see that the piece would be a knock-out. And he didn't mind the somewhat surly tone – he was used to it. The man was concentrating.

"Just checking to see my investment is in good hands, Mr F," he said, lowering his voice conspiratorially, "And would I let just anybody touch skins of this quality?"

As he made his way back down to the office, Mr Scheiner considered his long-term plan, which was that at some point quite soon in the six months he should ask Mr F to take the boy on in the workroom, give him a try with the knives. He was a firm believer in management knowing the skin side of the business – after all, he'd been a cutter himself in the early days. And then, after the boy had found his way around the workroom, he'd start to show him the office and invoice side of the trade, introduce him to some people ... after all, a boy from the family to head the firm, he had to come from somewhere (Mr Scheiner himself, despite the constant admonition of that *And Sons* painted on the window by the front door, had none). He had thought that now might have been a suitable moment to mention the idea to Mr F, but later would do. Let the boy get settled downstairs in the machine-room first. And besides, the man was clearly preoccupied. And no wonder; ocelot – tricky. Tricky on the seams.

★

He was right, of course; Mr F was preoccupied that morning. But not with the task in hand – this wasn't the first time he'd had to match two spotted skins across an exposed collar-seam, after all. That was what they paid him for. No; he was having trouble concentrating. Not on the knife – that more or less knew its own job. It was his mind that kept on wanting to wander. To slip. He found himself having to keep on collecting himself.

As I'm sure you know, this is what happens once you admit to yourself that you have a secret. You find yourself carrying it around all the time – especially if it's a secret which you know you can never, under any imaginable circumstances, share. You can never be quite sure where exactly might be a safe place to put it down for a moment, and this worry does begin to eat up your hours. You have to actively stop yourself thinking about it – and thinking about his secret is exactly what Mr F finds himself doing these days, far more often than he intends. Both in the evenings, when he sits with his tea, and in the mornings when he's getting ready for work. Quite often over the past few days he's found himself staring at himself in the washbasin mirror when he's shaving, or scrubbing his hands, and thinking about it. Or stirring the teapot and thinking about it. Pausing, just as he closes the front door – standing there, at the top of the stairs, slipping the key back in his pocket and imagining what it would feel like to watch them carrying the body away down round the turn in the stairs and past the window, so that the light

And that's the problem, you see. That's all very well at home, in the living-room or in his bedroom, but he doesn't want to start all that nonsense here at work as well.

Mr F adjusted his grip on the brass knife-handle, and returned to his task. The beautiful rosette-strewn skin opened under the blade like a flower.

seven

The next weekend, he just felt like a visit to the National Gallery. The fact that the great dark rooms on Trafalgar Square remained hushed even when they got crowded always reassured him. The sombre dark reds and greens of the damasked walls, the weight of the heavy gold frames on their chains, the high double doors that swung silently closed behind you – it all suited him. He especially liked the fact that you knew no one was ever going to speak to you – that you could be quite sure there'd be no one there who knew you. It made him feel well and truly left in peace.

He finished his dinner punctually at one o'clock, stacked the dishes on the draining-board, put on his weekend tie and, carrying his raincoat just in case, set out to walk to Camberwell Green. From there, he caught the number 36A to Kennington, where he had to change. As it happened, the first bus to come along was a number 59, and he could have stayed on it all the way to Trafalgar Square; but he preferred to get off early and take the short bracing walk along the river up past County Hall, then across Hungerford Bridge and up Villiers Street. He liked to walk; it was good for you.

Seated up on the top deck of the bus as it made its way up the Kennington Road and into Lambeth, Mr F could see just how much of London was being torn down and rebuilt. It always struck him, when he saw it all in one sweep like this, just how many new buildings were going up these days. Ugly great things, most of them, he thought. Incomprehensible. *Still, the streets; they can't move them*, he told himself. *At least they're still all in the same place.*

As he strode across Hungerford Bridge (he always found the way the walkway was so close to the trains slightly alarming; the way the metal shook, and rumbled) it started to squall with rain, and he was glad of his raincoat. He picked up his pace, and decided that when he got to the gallery he would start with the English paintings, as he usually did – the big green room with all the landscapes – then break his visit with a cup of tea, and then perhaps take a walk through some of the more far-flung galleries until he found one which he didn't know so well. Just for a change.

He'd see what caught his eye.

As always, he walked straight through the first three rooms, the French pictures, without looking, because he didn't really care for them – too many hot, bright colours, to his way of thinking. Then, when he got to the English room, he slowed down, and began to work his way dutifully round the walls. Like most people when they visit a gallery, Mr F was always conscious of how many more pictures he still had to get through, and so never quite exactly came to a stop in front of each one; unless it was a favourite, his eyes would just slide over it, and then on to the next. There were two paintings he did pause for, the big brown and green painting of Salisbury Cathedral with the rainbow, which he always admired, and next to that the one of the lady with her little grey dog, pretending to be out for a walk in front of some rather flat-looking grey-green trees. Then there was rather a dull stretch of portraits (he was never quite sure about staring at the faces of people he didn't know), and he half-wondered if now would be too soon for that cup of tea he'd promised himself – but then, half-way round the room, there was a picture that stopped him; genuinely stopped him. It must have been there before, but for some reason he couldn't remember ever having seen it. It was a smaller picture than the rest, and oddly shaped, with the corners cut off to make it almost an octagon, and for some reason, in this room full of pictures of placid English countryside and well-fed people, this one showed something frightening: a small, ferocious and bright yellow lion, clinging to the back of a terrified white horse. Hemmed in by the thick gold frame, the horse rolled its eyes, tossed its mane and helplessly lifted one of its front hooves – as if it wanted to rear and bolt, but was too frightened or in too much pain to move. The lion sank its teeth into the muscles on the back of its neck, all the time staring straight out of the picture with its two blank tawny eyes – straight at you, as if to say; *Yes?* – digging its claws so deeply into the horse's neck and rump that you could see how the individual talons were raking at the hide, gathering it slightly, the way your fingers pluck and clutch at the sheets when you – Mr F moved on to the next painting. He didn't want to look at that one any more. Anyway he'd got too close to it – other people were waiting to take a look, he could feel their disapproval behind him. He stepped back and turned away, telling himself that perhaps he should stop dawdling now and go and find that new room to look at. It wasn't really yet time for his cup of tea, that would be cheating. In the end he decided that the next thing he ought to go and do was leave his raincoat in the downstairs cloakroom; he was getting rather too warm in here with it still on.

Having left his raincoat, and washed his hands, Mr F set out, as planned, in search of something he had never seen before. He moved away from the busier part of the gallery and found himself walking through a sequence of nearly empty rooms where the walls were covered in a damask patterned in various shades of a dusty old gold colour, and the paintings were first of all all Spanish, and then Italian. The weather outside was obviously worsening; the dull drumming sound of heavy rain started to drift down from the gloomy skylights. As he kept walking, the sequence of rooms gradually darkened. Then, suddenly, just when he was standing in the middle of the last one, trying to see what there was there, all the lights in the gallery came on at once. Someone, somewhere, must have pressed an unseen switch. The dull gold of the walls blazed; the picture frames glittered.

With all the lights on, Mr F could see that there was something about this last room (it was a dead end, with only one door) which, if there had been anyone else in there with him, would have embarrassed him. Luckily, however, there seemed to be no other visitors in this part of the gallery at all; the polished parquet floor was empty, and the guard (Mr F checked), was asleep in his chair. The problem with this room was that every single painting on the walls (again, he checked), every single one of the paintings on the walls seemed for some reason or another to feature naked white arms and legs. Or even whole bodies, naked. And mostly men's. Which meant that whichever way Mr F turned and looked, he found himself doing in public the thing which up until now he'd only ever done at home in private, sitting in his chair with his eyes closed and the cup of tea going cold at his elbow. And right out in public, too – right in the middle of the room. Staring at a body.

The sound of the rain on the skylights thickened; looking up, he could see that it was starting to get properly dark outside. All around him on the walls, the limbs of the various saints and warriors stretched, sweated and gleamed as they were variously martyred, massacred or entombed; skin and armour and marble and silk were pressed together as their bodies soared or were bound to pillars or hurled together in confusion. The paintings were so big that almost all of this white-limbed flesh was shown life-size – and under these lights, it seemed to be shining. Looming out of

its great gloomy canvas, one despairingly out-flung arm in
particular seemed to be straining straight towards him. He
checked that the guard by the door really was asleep; he was.
Then he looked right round the room again, and decided
that he ought to pick one painting, and really look at it
properly. He told himself quietly that it was alright, he was
supposed to stand and stare. It was what this place was for.
*Go on, sir, it's quite alright. You can go closer than that if you
want to.* He began to give his undivided attention to the
painting which hung in pride of place in the middle of the
end wall of the gallery.

It showed two men, on their own, in a darkened upstairs
room. According to the label, it was called *The Incredulity of
St Thomas*. He couldn't quite remember which of the Bible
stories it was that involved St Thomas, but he was sure from
his face that the man on the left, the younger one, had to be
Jesus, even though there wasn't any halo. In fact, when you
looked at the way he had been painted, he looked nothing
like the Jesus he remembered from the church – big and
dead and frightening – but actually quite ordinary-looking.
Quite human. Slightly – well not fat exactly, but certainly
fleshy. The painter had dressed him in just a twist of dirty
white bed-linen, and he was pulling it to one side to show St
Thomas the wound cut into his flank.

Mr F started to stare at the wound.

It must be an old one, he thought. *There's no blood.*

*

In this painting, St Thomas, who is an older man, with a
beard, bends down to peer at the wound, right up close, as if
he's short-sighted – and now Jesus does a very odd thing.

He takes hold of St Thomas's right hand by the wrist, quite firmly, and guides his hand so that the older man's index finger is sticking right inside him, right deep inside the wound.

Mr F tries to see what the expression on Jesus's face is as he does this, but even with all the lights on there's too much shadow; the paint's too dark. He can't tell. He wonders if Jesus has just said something to St Thomas – if he's just said, for instance, very gently, *It's alright, you can touch me if you want to*. He could have done; the picture seems very quiet.

Just as he is about to step forward and get really close to the picture, to try and really see what's going on, Mr F is interrupted by the sound of an actual voice – a man's voice. Somebody says, in a rather high and very well-educated voice (one of those men's voices that really carry, though this man must be actually standing right beside him, because the voice is very close, almost in his ear) –

"He does do hands better than anyone, don't you think?"

Mr F looks round, of course, and there is indeed a man standing right beside him. Standing much too close, in fact. The man is slightly older than Mr F – silver-haired – and tall, and very distinguished-looking. He is holding a pair of yellow gloves in one hand, and in the other a pair of gold-wire-rimmed spectacles, which he has evidently taken off to inspect the painting. He isn't looking at Mr F, despite the fact that he is standing right next to him, but staring straight at the painting. Right at the wound, in fact. Mr F has no idea how he got there, right out into the middle of the room – he certainly didn't hear him come in – nor of how to reply to what he's just said. Because the man isn't looking at him, but still at the men in the painting, he's not even sure if the comment was really addressed to him in the first place. But he knows it would be rude not to say anything at all, so after a while he says the only thing he can think of, which is

"If you say so."

"Such a marvellous sense of how tangible things are. I mean you can really see that finger sliding in, can't you?"

The man gestured towards the painting, waving at it with the hand holding the pair of spectacles.

"And the way He's guiding his hand like that. The contact. Marvellous. Quite marvellous."

Mr F was going to say that yes it was, marvellous, very cleverly done indeed – because it was, when you looked closely, especially the way you could tell he was insisting that the other man push his finger right inside, so far in that the skin around the edge of the wound was just beginning to pucker – but by the time he had turned to speak to the stranger at his shoulder, he wasn't there any longer. He had already moved away, as suddenly and as noiselessly as he had materialised. He was now standing on the other side of the room, apparently rapt in front of a big brightly coloured painting which showed some sort of a sky-blue curtain being drawn aside to reveal a tangle of pink and white bodies and bright gold jewellery. He did look back, just once, over his shoulder, giving Mr F an odd, thin-lipped smile; but then, after a few moments more with his new picture, he left the gallery without another word, walking slowly and deliberately, letting the high doors swing silently closed behind him.

Perhaps in the days before he had started having his dream Mr F, who normally hated any sort of forwardness, would have responded to this stranger's rather rude behaviour by simply giving a small snort of derision to himself and then carrying on with his inspection of the rest of the room before heading off to the cafeteria for his cup of tea. As it was, he watched the man go (oddly, the heels of his highly polished shoes sounded a very definite set of ringing footsteps on the parquet floor as he made his exit), and then turned back to the painting.

He didn't want to stop looking at it, you see. Not just yet.

The man had been right, you see; it was marvellous. The way the flesh was done. The finger going into the wound, all the way in like that, gentle but firm. Inside.

Mr F stayed looking at this picture for several minutes. He even tried taking hold of his own right hand by the wrist, and stretching out his index finger just like the man in the painting was doing, and wondered how it would feel to do that; wondered if, when you touched somebody like that, he would feel cold or warm. Thinking about the young man in his dream, he wondered if he would still be warm. Inside.

Even if he was, he thought, even if he was still warm inside, surely that white skin of his would be stone cold to the touch by now. Hidden away in the dark like that. Lying stretched out on the cold enamel like that, all day long and half the night, waiting for Mr F to come and turn on the light and find him.

*

This experience in the National Gallery had an odd effect on Mr F. It was the picture that did it, probably – the way that it seemed to be waiting for him there in that dark final room, as if it knew he was coming. As if it was expecting him. Or perhaps it was the way that that elderly stranger had stared at it so blatantly, as if he had a perfect right to. Whatever the reason, Mr F now began to keep a close but discrete eye on all the parts of men's bodies that their clothes left visible on his way to and from work every day. To put it bluntly, he too began to *stare*.

We all do it; we pretend not to, of course, but we do.

In order to keep it in its proper place (he wouldn't have wanted anyone to think he was doing anything *untoward*), Mr F told himself there was a perfectly good reason for this new habit of his. If he could only find some detail from his mysterious dream on an actual body – the right shape of hands, for instance, or the right colour hair – then that might give him just the clue he needed as to the features, the face – to the person, if you like. He knew of course that he was never going to find an *exact* match; that he was never going to suddenly discover that the missing face in his dream belonged to some complete stranger who he'd look up and see walking towards him across the forecourt of London Bridge Station – that would be ridiculous; but nonetheless, he felt compelled to search. I suppose he must have thought that if he could only find something to jog his memory, then perhaps the part of his dream that was so mysteriously missing would somehow come back to him.

He was still after an answer to that question of his, would be another way of putting it.

*

It was a particular kind of colouring that most often caught his eye. A patch of especially white skin exposed to the morning cold above the black velvet collar of a Crombie overcoat, just where the dark hair was razored high on the nape of the neck; a bare right wrist, just flecked with one or two dark hairs, famed between a pristine white shirt-cuff and the handle of a black leather briefcase – *Probably left his gloves on the train*, thought Mr F, when he saw that; *his fingers must be getting cold in this raw air.* To make his search more thorough, he took to using the more crowded eastern pavement to cross London Bridge in the morning, and even tried to walk where the stream of dark-suited and over-coated men was at its thickest. He still had to take care not to bump into anyone, of course, which meant that he couldn't spend his entire time scanning the people around him – he had to *watch his step*, you might say – but nonetheless his searching was at least partially rewarded. Between his visit to the gallery and the end of March, he reckoned there were at least seventeen occasions when he caught a glimpse of something which reminded him of his dream.

Out of these, the closest he came to finding what he was looking for was probably on a Friday night towards the end of the month. The cutting-room having closed early for the Sabbath, it wasn't yet rush hour proper when he got to London Bridge Station, and he had no difficulty getting a seat in his preferred second carriage. Once he'd settled, he took a quick glance round at his neighbours, tucked his *Evening Standard* down by the side of him on his seat, and then started to have a good proper stare at the hands of all the men sitting near him.

He always started with the hands. He'd noticed in the course of his searching that people – men, especially – don't guard their hands like they do their faces, and especially not when they fall asleep. I'm sure you've seen it happen yourself; when a man starts to fall asleep on a train (and Mr F had recently started to notice just how often this does happen, even on a relatively short journey like that from London Bridge to Peckham Rye), first his head lolls forward, but then, as he starts to fight it, jerks back up again as he frowns and tries to pull his features together as if to prove to whoever might be watching him that nothing at all untoward is happening – but all the time, he leaves his hands lying unsupervised in his lap. On this occasion, Mr F found himself sitting directly opposite a young workman who'd already lost the battle; he must have closed his eyes almost as soon as he'd got on the train. As Tower Bridge slid unnoticed past the windows, the young man's neck relaxed vertebra by vertebra, and his chin sagged right down onto his chest. He began to snore, very quietly – and all this time, his hands lay undefended in his lap. Quite *open*.

Palm up, with the right hand held gently over the left.

Cupped by it.

Mr F looked away, disconcerted – when he saw that, for just a moment he thought he could feel the hairs going up on the back of his neck. But then he had to look back; he had to check. It was the fingers, you see. The fingers of this sleeping workman were curving softly up and away from the palm of his right hand in exactly the same way as the fingers Mr F saw spread on the white enamel of his bathroom every other night did. Exactly.

Since the man was so deeply asleep – and since everyone on a homeward-bound Friday afternoon train is always too tired to take much notice of their fellow passengers anyway – Mr F knew he was quite free to stare. The copy of the *Standard* remained folded and unread down his side. He let his eyes travel from the palm of the young man's right hand up across the veins on the inside of his wrist, to the spot where they were cut off by the worn cuff of his paint-stained overalls. Since he knew so much about clothes, and how they can either disguise or fit the body – how the cut of a jacket across the shoulders can straighten a man's back for instance, or the set of a collar lengthen his neck – Mr F found it quite easy to imagine how the young man's arms must look under the dark blue cloth. His forearms; the crooked elbows; and then the long thin muscle of the upper arm. Then the shoulder. The set of the collar-bone, and above that, just where the corded muscles of the neck met the line of his unshaven chin –

Suddenly the train lurched to a halt at Queen's Road station, and the young man woke up with a confused start, looking wildly around to see if he'd missed his stop. Mr F immediately snatched his eyes away, because obviously he didn't want to be caught staring, not at someone's face – but even so, he couldn't help but see what the young man looked like. And at once, he could see that he looked nothing like what the man in his dream should look like at all. Nothing like him. He was too

He was too what, exactly?

Mr F was bewildered. How could he be so sure, just from that one quick glimpse, that this young man's face was the wrong one – so sure that he couldn't be *him*? After all, it wasn't as if he had ever seen the face he was trying to compare it to. It wasn't that this workman was too old – in fact he was just the right age, he must have been nineteen at most; so what was it? Mr F risked another look. As the young man peered out through the steamed-up window to try and see which station they had stopped at, he could see that his eyes were wild with tiredness, and his blue-stubbled cheeks hollow and grey-skinned. It was Friday night, after all, and whatever it was he did for a living, his week had clearly worn him out. The tenderness with which his sleeping face had sunk down onto his chest was deceptive; in that odd moment which we all know, the moment after we've started awake but before we've remembered to compose our features, he looked completely brutalised. Exhausted. His lips were drawn back over discoloured teeth, and there were broken veins under the plaster dust smearing his cheeks. That was it, thought Mr F; he looked *finished*.

It wasn't that the man he was looking for necessarily had to be young, Mr F decided in that moment; it was just that he had to be somebody who was beginning, not ending. Somebody who wasn't used up.

He had to be *unmarked*; that was it.

Just before he got off the train at Peckham Rye, Mr F looked again at the young man's hands (he was safely asleep again by now), and he noticed for the first time that the fingernails were all split and blunt, the fingers calloused and paint-stained. Which wasn't right. Not right at all.

He'd just have to keep looking.

★

I said we all do it; but there was of course a very particular quality to Mr F's staring. A particular *hunger*, I should say. After all, he had a much more specific template he was trying to find a match for than the ones that most of us carry in our heads; his morning journey often came only three or four hours after he had been woken up by a vision of a body of almost hallucinatory clarity. Indeed, we might compare these seventeen "sightings" of Mr F's to the seventeen visions of poor deluded Bernadette Soubiroux, the girl who claimed she saw the Blessed Virgin – that elusive creature whose face no one else but her could ever quite, somehow, see; or perhaps to the row of paintings with which the Beast, in one version of the story I've read, lines the Long Gallery of his fabulous palace, each one commissioned from a different painter and each one, supposedly, granting him a glimpse of the features of his long-dreamt-of bride. In both of these cases, however, the hapless dreamer was eventually rewarded with the absolute certainty that the face they'd once only imagined did finally look down on them and smile – the miracle happened – whereas all Mr F felt he'd ended up with, by the time he'd got to the end of the last week in March, was a collection of a few tiny dislocated pieces of skin. As the spring began to thaw, the crowds on London Bridge began to discard their gloves and scarves –

but still all he got was a quick glimpse of a wrist or nape, or at best the suggestion of the line of a shoulder under a heavy overcoat. It wasn't much to work on. Of course, he did his best – tried to stitch all these fragments together in his mind – but it was no good. Most of them had to be discarded as unsuitable; even with the workable ones, he knew he was never going to end up with a whole body, with something *recognisable*. He felt the same sort of frustration as when the machinists at work were set to stitching together all the scraps and off-cuts into what the trade called *plates* – panels of mismatched fur-scraps which the cutters then had to work up into the cheapest possible capes or coat-backs. To his way of thinking, a garment made up from scraps like that was never going to hang properly, not even on the shop-rail. All you ended up with was a big piece of dead skin, not something that was ever going to move properly. There was no suggestion of a living person there at all.

No *life* to it.

All through these five weeks, despite this strange and growing preoccupation of his, once he got to Skin Lane each morning and went upstairs and got his white coat on, Mr F did by and large manage to keep his promise to himself not to let his mind wander at work. He'd finished the special order in ocelot, all to Mr Scheiner's satisfaction, and had now moved on with the rest of the cutting benches to a big retail order of plain dark ranch mink jackets, all with the new season's wide lapels. He was glad of the routine, frankly, and only once did he find himself thinking anything untoward. Late one afternoon, as he was finishing cutting a batch of skins destined for shoulder pieces, he found himself trying to imagine what kind of woman would end up wearing the jacket he was working on. What she might look like. He wondered what she'd be wearing underneath when her husband gave her the big box to open and she tried her present on for the first time. Probably something a bit special – one of those dresses with the thin straps, he thought. Jewel-coloured. As he imagined this woman feeling the growing sensation of heat across her bare shoulders (people are often surprised by just how hot a mink can get next to the skin; you wonder what they think the animals have fur for) he had a very odd thought, one that didn't quite make sense to him. Thinking about the expression on the woman's face, about her parted lips and the flush spreading slowly across her shoulders, he found himself wondering for the very first time in his life *why am I doing all this for someone else? Why am I making this for someone I don't even know?*

eight

Even though none of his colleagues noticed any changes in his face or manner, it is important to remember how very tired Mr F must have been during these first three months of our story. Carrying a secret is tiring; having to keep an eye on every other man you pass in the street is exhausting. And on top of this, remember that his dream was still visiting him – not quite so often, perhaps, but still every third or fourth night of the week. Just as his gratefully unconscious body was beginning to drift out over the shallows of the early hours, beginning its descent into the deep, dark salt-water of true, deep sleep, the dream would seize hold of him and shake him awake. Every time it came, the pictures were still the same; and every time, he'd wake to find himself suddenly in the dark, twisted in his sheets, shouting at the top of his voice. He was sleepless in the same way that a pregnant woman is sleepless – kicked awake, thumped in the stomach.

I told you that Mr F was nearly forty-seven; well, on the twenty-seventh of March, 1967, which was a Wednesday, he was. This was just two days before the incident with the young workman on the train. He had never made a fuss of any kind over his birthday, and his colleagues at Scheiner's didn't even know when it was, much less help him celebrate it. His horoscope in the paper that evening – there was always a special entry for people whose birthday it was – was so ludicrously optimistic, it made him wince: *A spectacularly fulfilling year lies ahead of you,* it said, *especially if you have reached, or passed, the age of forty. It seems you cannot go wrong.*

This would be a good time to form alliances and try out experiments, starting this evening. Oh yes? Pull the other one, he thought.

The only event that usually marked the day was the arrival of a card from his older brother, who was now living in Canada. For many years the envelope had used to include a brief note, with phrases like *Maybe we'll come over some day, who knows?* – or, *It would be great to see you and the old town again, brother,* but latterly, there had just been the card, signed, he assumed, by his sister-in-law, his brother's second wife, a woman he had never actually met. This year, even that failed to turn up; when he pushed open his front door, thinking perhaps it might have come by the second post, the mat was still as empty as it had been when he'd left for work that morning. *Not that that's unusual,* he told himself, hanging up his jacket, and rolling up his sleeves.

When the card did finally arrive, two days late, there was no note; just the two names, both in the usual handwriting, and, underneath them, in blue biro, the scribbled phrase *Hope this finds you well as always.* Recognising what it contained from the stamp, Mr F hadn't bothered to open the envelope before going to work, and so it had still been lying on the kitchen table when he got home. It being a Friday, Mr F felt so tired that night that he even considered not cooking himself any supper, but just going straight to bed instead. For want of anything better to do, he sat down at the table, opened the envelope, and read the card. Nothing particular happened when he read the scribbled message, but a few moments afterwards, the silence in his kitchen seemed to suddenly thicken; the ticking of the kitchen clock became almost deafening. The thought that it was still not even five o'clock became somehow intolerable to him. He stood up, scraping the back legs of the chair against the lino, but then the thought of going and getting undressed at that hour, of climbing between the sheets and lying there and watching the light fade through the curtains and waiting for it to get dark, seemed impossible. He sat down again.

Talking to yourself is something that few people will admit to doing, but most people who live on their own do it often – nobody likes to live in silence, after all. Mr F did it rarely; usually the things he said to himself stayed inside his head. But this one came out – it had to – and it came out good and loud. As if there was some other noise in the room that he had to raise his voice over, as if for instance the kitchen clock really had started to tick inexplicably loudly, or as if he was calling an instruction to Mrs Kesselman over the sound of the machines and the radio in the downstairs workroom, Mr F said, very firmly and definitely, *If I'm going to be by myself, then I want to be on my own, thank you very much.* And then again, after a short pause, and this time even more firmly, he pronounced the sentence *This has got to stop.*

*

Later that night, as he lay in bed, he tried talking to himself again, repeating the same few phrases over and over. But now, even though he knew it was his mouth shaping the words, it somehow wasn't his own voice that he heard speaking them. It was somebody else's; whose, he had no idea. The voice was quiet – gentle, even – and it seemed to have something to do with another bedroom, and with the way things had been years ago – yes; that was it. Something to do with lamplight, and the feeling of the sheets being drawn tight around you; and the sound of a man's voice saying gently in your ear *That's better. There we go. All done. All over now: all done.*

Whoever's this voice was, it worked its magic. As if at

this man's command, the dream left Mr F in peace that
night.

*

He slept late that Saturday morning, until gone eight – he
must have been more tired than he'd known. He did it again
on Sunday, and even on the Monday morning, didn't open
his eyes until nearly twenty-five to seven.

He knew it wasn't over though. As he hurriedly drank
his tea and worried about catching the train, he had to
suppress the obvious thought that his nocturnal visitor had
probably just gone elsewhere for the weekend, and was just
as probably already planning his return. Walking to the
station, he decided that since he just had time to stop at the
newsagents, he should – a newspaper might take his mind
off things. The placard with the Sunday paper's headline
had for some reason been left up outside the shop in its
wire-fronted case, and was still announcing *Missing Body
Finally Found* – this was the spring of a famous murder case,
and the reports of any development always made the front
pages. As he stood in the short queue, ready as always with
the exact change for his paper in his right hand and trying
not to worry about the train, Mr F found that the first word
on that poster was snagging at his thoughts. *Missing.* Surely,
he thought, there can't ever really be a person who *nobody*
misses – somebody must always know who they are. Know
where they're *from.* Obviously the police hadn't been asking
the right people. Or hadn't been asking the right questions.
By the time he got to the front of the queue, he was
worrying that he'd done the wrong thing in stopping for his
paper, and really was anxious now that he was going to miss
his train – but for some reason, instead of just handing over
the newspaper, the newsagent, who normally never said
anything beyond "Thank you" or "Good morning", felt

moved to conversation. As he took the offered change, he said to Mr F

"Well, at least they're at peace now, eh?"

Mr F didn't say anything, because it was now gone quarter past, and he didn't have time; he simply snatched his paper from the pile on the counter, turned, and went, not caring if the man thought he was being rude or not – but he wanted to. For just a moment, as his hand reached for the paper, he wanted to look the newsagent right in his stupid eye and snap right back at him *Peace? What's that then? Is that what you call what I've never had?* Out on the pavement, he took a deep breath, folded the paper and tucked it neatly under his arm. He walked the fifty yards to the station as briskly as he could without actually breaking into a run, and as he walked, he started talking to himself under his breath again. The morning air was just cold enough to fog his breath as he muttered *What on earth are you talking about? That's not true, is it? Not true at all. You've had a good life. A good life. A good life.*

Fortunately, I don't think anyone heard him. Like I said, he must have been tired.

nine

The walk to work that morning did nothing to improve his temper. As he made his usual detour along the river, the wind that came slicing across the water was a cold one, and he couldn't for the life of him remember why he didn't take the sheltered route west down Cannon Street like everybody else; the uphill cobbles of All Hallows Lane seemed steeper and less even than he ever remembered them being before. Arriving at Number Four, he barely said a civil good morning to Mrs Kesselman, and once at his bench, sliced and cut his way to the first tea-break of the day in determined silence. Mr F always took the opportunity the tea-break presented to be alone for ten minutes, and would usually smoke his cigarette and drink his tea standing out on the front steps – they were reasonably sheltered, even on a cold or wet day – so as he made his way downstairs at ten o'clock with his tea, feeling in his pocket for his papers and tobacco, he was not best pleased on this morning of all mornings to be prevented from reaching his usual smoking post (on the fourth of the stone steps leading to the front door) by Mr Scheiner, asking would he mind stepping into the office for just a moment.

The time had come, Mr Scheiner explained, for his nephew to move upstairs. The boy had done well in the machine-room, he said, but it was no proper place for a young man down there with all those girls, and he might as well start learning the tricks of the trade now as anytime, what with his sixteenth birthday just passed. So would Mr F please take him upstairs and get him started at the cutting bench.

"I have told the young man," he said, "I am putting you to learn with the best. The best: so any trouble, and he is straight back downstairs in this office, Mr F. Straight back down."

★

Mr F, of course, had no choice but to accept his new apprentice. He had overheard one of his fellow cutters saying a young man with that attitude was lucky he was family, because they'd never've given him the job – but apart from that, he couldn't remember having seen or heard too much of the boy. Being downstairs, of course, he had really been Mrs Kesselman's department. He could remember the dark blue suit he'd been wearing when they were introduced, and thinking it far too flash for a work-day, but after that, hadn't paid his presence in the building any particular attention.

I was right about that suit, he thought, as he watched the boy hang up his jacket on a peg by the cutting-room door. And he was; it was a copy of the kind of fashionable outfit Mr F had only otherwise seen in pictures of television actors or singers in his newspaper. The dark blue jacket was high-buttoned, and cut as close as possible across the shoulders and under the arms – *Tight in all the wrong places,* thought Mr F, looking the boy up and down. *Just the sort of thing that makes you look as if you're trying to find the nearest mirror. Not to mention that hair.*

"Good morning," he said, as the boy crossed the room towards him.

"Good morning, Mr F," said the boy, rather ostentatiously cheerfully, holding the white cutter's coat he'd helped himself to.

And forward with it, thought Mr F.

"Get that on properly, and we'll start," he said.

The boy did as he was told, and buttoned himself up into the long white coat with its cutaway front. He left the top button undone, showing a little more of his smart, narrow tie than was strictly necessary; Mr F noticed this, but decided he wouldn't say anything unless the boy did the same thing again tomorrow morning. Without explaining anything, he walked straight over to his place at the cutting bench, and pushed aside the bundle of smoke-grey mink he'd been in the middle of sorting. He was clearly not best pleased at having to stop what he was doing and start showing a junior around the place instead, but equally clearly thought they might as well get straight on with it. Without a word, he collected the instruments of his trade from where they were scattered around the bench, and began to lay them out in an exactly spaced row for the boy's inspection.

"Right," he said.

★

The tools of the furrier's trade are strange ones, and seem at odds with the delicacy of the material they are used to handle. The blunt, black, wide-jawed metal pinchers used to nip and stretch the skins as they are nailed to the boards; the knife-like steel combs; the wooden bats which are slid like letter openers into the stomachs of the uncut pelts when they are first razored open; the pins and nails; the whetstone with its anointing oil and the heavy leather strop – even the strange fish-shaped brass handles of the tiny cutting-knives themselves – they all look as if they are designed to pierce, or wound; to damage, or, indeed, to hurt. Laid out together in a row, they couldn't help but look like the preparations for some scene of torture, or like the emblems held aloft by

the stony-faced angels attendant on some cruel martyrdom
or passion. Last in the row, incongruous amongst all this
metal, was a small and innocuous-looking cardboard box.
This, Mr F picked up and opened; then he tipped its
contents out across the bench. Razor blades, each one
wrapped in its own protective paper. He selected a blade,
unfolded the paper, extracted it, broke it diagonally in half
using a strange sort of hinged wooden box which snapped
shut like a mousetrap, and then fitted one of the two fine-
pointed slivers of steel into a brass handle. He did it all in
four quick moves, as if he wanted to prove to the boy how
expert his large white fingers were in handling something
that could so easily slice them to the bone. Then he picked
up one of the pelts he'd pushed aside. He slid a wooden bat
into its stomach, and picked up the knife again – but before
making the incision, he paused, and pointed the blade at the
boy; the strong sunlight from the long window caught the
edge of it.

People sometimes say that knives look wicked, and
these blades do. They look eager.

"Now," he said, "look, but don't touch."

Look, but don't touch unless I say so: isn't that the
sentence with which the education of a new boy always
begins?

*

Although he has ingratiating good manners when he needs
them, this sixteen-year-old (whose name, by the way, is
Ralph Scheiner) has little or no time for older men, starting
with his own father. Being the youngest child, and an only
son, he has grown up secure in the knowledge that all will
always be forgiven him – and this has not made him
especially kind, or wise; although he gives the impression of

always doing what he is told, the world, as far as he is concerned, is his oyster. This is 1967, after all, and like his two older sisters, who are eighteen and nineteen respectively, he can surely scent the new-found freedoms of the coming decade. They, of course, have already to face the prospect of imminent marriage – both their mother and their father have already told them as much; but the boy is still all smiles. He is quite sure that he has all the time in the world. Much as he hates having to turn up for work every day on time, and being constantly told what to do, he has decided that he may as well give his new profession a run for its money – that he may as well behave himself so long as he's on his Uncle Maurice's premises. He knows how to handle *him*. His sisters have been teasing him, and asking spiteful questions at Friday night dinner about how he's taking to the family business now that he knows how much sweeping is involved; but he has shrugged all that aside. After all, hasn't he been moved upstairs already? He knows that this so-called apprenticeship is just a preliminary; knows that once he's worked his way around the different bits of the building they're going to take him to one side and talk to him seriously about whether he'd like to join the firm. His father has already boastfully hinted as much. Six months, he's decided he'll give it, before deciding whether the place suits him. Who knows; he might just decide to branch out in another direction entirely.

He doesn't know what that direction might be, as yet, but he wouldn't be at all surprised if he thinks of something.

Yes, he tells his mother as she passes him his supper-plate; he does much prefer it upstairs, with the men.

With a trace of fine dark hair just becoming a regular feature on his perfect top lip, and his broken voice already well settled, this smartly dressed young man is as dangerous a creature as he looks. In theory, his position as a junior on the Lane ought to mean that he is at the bottom of the building's pecking order, but in practice everyone in the workrooms at Number Four knows that this so-called "apprenticeship" of his is meant to equip him for one day being their boss. This privileged position is further compounded by his sixteen-year-old good looks; not only is the boy the youngest male in the building, he is also by some stretch the best-looking. Quick, dark and bright-eyed, with striking collar-length nearly-black hair, he is one of those neatly built young men who not only knows exactly what they look like (Mr F was right to assume his fondness for mirrors), but is already well-versed in the uses such looks can be put to. Those dark eyes may give very little away, but they are expert at quickly sizing up everyone and everything that surrounds them; while they do it, their proud owner smiles at almost everyone, almost all of the time. He believes in first impressions, you see. As a result, in the six weeks since he first made the Monday morning journey from Hendon to Skin Lane, even those who might naturally be inclined to treat their employer's nephew with suspicion or even hostility have been systematically charmed. In particular – as much as his father and uncle's joint decision that the best way for him to learn his way round the family business would be from the bottom up had initially rankled – the boy has made a great success of playing fox amongst the chickens of the downstairs workroom. Just as they usually did, his hair, his dark eyes and his suit had all won him immediate approval amongst Mrs Kesselman's girls (if not from the lady herself.) The more whispering he heard at tea-break, the more jokes were made at the expense of him and his tightly cut trousers as he bent over to get at the fur-scraps caught under the treadles of the machines with his broom – the more he liked it. He was used to women making a fuss of him – it was all they ever did, at home – but this kind of attention was new. It had distinct possibilities.

He especially liked the nickname the girls had chosen for him. One of them in particular had been trying to knock him back a peg or two – to wipe the grin off his face for once – but her irony had backfired, and the name had stuck. Mrs Kesselman, who'd seen far too many young boys like him come through the building to fall for this one's charms, always referred to him rather disapprovingly as Our Young Mr Scheiner – reminding him every time she did it that he was only there pushing a broom round her machine-room because of who his uncle was – but everyone else downstairs called him just *Mr Schein.*

The nickname doesn't translate, exactly. There was an Andrews Sisters' song that some of the older girls still used to sing at their machines, just to make fun of him, which had a line in its sing-along chorus that ran *Bei Mir Bist Du Schein, Bei Mir Hast Du Chein* – and that's where the pun had first started. I suppose it more or less meant he was Mr Handsome, "Mr Beautiful"; The Beauty. Or just *Beauty*, really. That's what I'm going to call him, anyway. The name fitted the boy like a glove, and oh, did he know it. Everything about him – the way he looked, the way he carried himself – well, the way he got treated in that downstairs workroom, he may have been pushing a broom, but you'd have said he was less of a dogsbody, more of a mascot. Even Mrs Kesselman, when she overheard her girls chattering about him, didn't blame them. *With those looks*, she thought to herself as she watched him bend over his broom, *I should be surprised?* She knew he was a danger, and that she'd have to watch him, but was sure she was up to the task. She also of course knew something that the younger women in the room didn't yet know; that the bloom on the boy's looks would soon go, as it does in all fine-skinned, dark-haired young men of his type. *Still*, she thought to herself, watching the way the younger of her girls especially darted glances at him from out of the corners of their eyes, *from now until his fifth wedding anniversary... good luck to them.*

The first afternoon after he'd been moved upstairs, the girls found themselves free to discuss the boss's nephew with even more than their usual candour. Radio London was playing at top volume, as always – and as always, the afternoon sing-along to the chorus of Miss Vikki Carr's impassioned rendition of "It Must Be Him" had quickly descended into a mayhem of more or less single *entendres*. Joining in the laughter, Mrs Kesselman gave that indefinably suggestive-yet-dismissive shrug of the older woman who knows exactly what she's talking about. Raising one painted eyebrow into an even higher arch than normal, she turned to the girl who'd just shrieked out the most obscene suggestion of the afternoon, and said

"Listen; with a mouth like that, who wouldn't?"

★

"Listen," said Mr F, who wasn't used to talking to young men, but certainly knew how to address a cutting-room junior: "They used to call this business a mystery back in the old days, apparently; a mystery. But I can tell you now there's nothing mysterious about it. Years of application, and concentration, that's what it takes. Concentration, especially; that's the trick. Eventually, I'm going to show you how to use this – "

He showed Beauty the knife again, hafting it lightly in his hand so that the steel point danced in the light.

"But now, to start with... touch."

With one light sweep of the blade, he opened the pelt. Discarding the bat and the knife, he offered it to the boy.

"So go on; touch it."

Beauty took it, and was surprised by how light and supple it was. Dry as a piece of paper between his thumb and forefinger.

"Now the other side. Use your hand like a blade, up and down, up and down; like this."

He showed the boy how to lay the pelt on the bench and brush the fur using the side of his hand, once up and once down in two swift strokes, with and against the grain, leaving all the guard-hairs standing.

The boy did as he was shown.

"Now leave your hand resting on it – no; palm down."

To Beauty's great surprise, the furred side of the pelt was immediately warm to his touch. He didn't understand how this could be, from a dead thing; in fact what he could feel was the heat of his own body, returning to its source.

"Tell me what you feel then."

"I couldn't say, Mr F. Warm. I can't really describe it."

"Thirty-three years, and maybe you'll be able to. Right; basics; the most important thing in this business is choice of skin, and that – " he took the pelt off Beauty and blew on the fur to part it, then used his two thumbs to keep it spread and show the boy the tiny hidden split in the pelt his fingers had somehow detected with that one quick and apparently perfunctory stroking action, " – that is exactly the sort of weakness that if it gets past you at this stage can spoil a whole garment. Never waste time working on a spoilt skin – " He emphasised his point by pointing the blade of the knife at the boy's chest, then, placing the pelt fur down on the bench, he sliced it carelessly across with the knife and threw the two pieces to the floor.

"Oh and never try and conceal a spoilt skin, either," he added "Even if it means more work matching a new one. There's not much gets past me."

Beauty nodded. He was surprised to see a skin thrown to the floor like that – he wasn't going to say anything, but it seemed like a waste. He suspected that Mr F just wanted to make an impression – and he was right, actually, on both counts. The skin could have been salvaged; and yes, Mr F did want to make a proper impression on the boy straight off. As he saw it, his first job was let him know who was the Head Cutter, and who the apprentice. Who knew what was what, and who needed showing.

And so the first lesson, with its reluctant teacher and its devious, dark-eyed pupil, proceeded.

★

The first task the boy was set to master, after he'd been shown each of the tools in turn, was to memorise the names of all the different skins.

High on the rear wall of the upstairs workroom, away from the windows, hung a silent menagerie of samples of all the beasts that Skin Lane handled. Mr F collected a long hooked pole, climbed up onto a bench, and started to throw the pelts down for the boy to catch. As he tossed each one down, he called out its name.

He started slowly, and with the obvious ones – but he didn't bother to check if the boy had caught one fur before unhooking the next. He'd obviously been along this rail many times before.

"Squirrel," he called out, sending the creature flying through the air.

"Mink – "

(This one was named almost dismissively, as if no one could not know the title of that particular sharp-clawed and unnervingly luxurious rag as it flew towards Beauty's face.)

"Persian lamb…"

Now it began to be clear that the slow start had been just to make the job look easy. As Mr F worked his way along the rail, he began to pick up his pace, and Beauty was soon struggling to catch pelts whose outlandish names gave him no idea at all of what sort of creature had once worn them – half the time, he'd never even heard the word before, never mind seen the beast –

"Mouton; Miniver; Coney – "

(Mr F was deliberately giving him no time to think; the skins came flying.)

"Ermine, Fisher, Marmot – come on, catch them, don't drop them on the bloody floor – Marten, Musquash – "

(The cascading pelts threatened to overwhelm the boy; his arms were full, and as fast as he tried to pile them on the bench, they threatened to slip onto the floor. Still, Mr F barked out the names.)

"Kolinsky, Civet, Beaver – unsheared – "

Christ, thought the boy as he just managed to catch the heavy, greasy-looking skin, *Beaver – he's got the whole of bloody Noah's Ark up there –*

"Caracul... Colobus... Fitch – come on, don't stand and stare at them, just get them on the bench – Blue Fox; Red Russian; pair of Whites – "

The boy was doing his best, but even when there was a name he thought he recognised, the clawed and bushy-tailed animals that came flying through the air at him (and they really were animals, these ones, complete with tail, head, feet, the lot) still bewildered him. The colours were all wrong, for a start. What Mr F called a "blue" fox was really mostly black – and the one he christened "Red Russian" was a strange sort of gold colour – and this could never have been just a *fox*, surely; Beauty held up the pelt to check, and its sagging spine stretched all the way between his out-stretched hands, looking as if it had come from something that could tear a pack of dogs apart just for fun. And then there were the two white ones, "White Fox" – that was what he was sure Mr F had shouted, and that was what the paper label definitely said, but still, this was a creature which he hadn't even known existed. Were they real? (Beauty had time to think all of this only because there was a pause in the proceedings; Mr F had to get down off the bench and move to the other end of the rail to reach the last few samples.) He inspected them, discovering that this pair of glamorous vermin came complete with dry, hard ears; with cross-looking little yellow glass eyes and black-nosed snouts that made them look as if they wanted to yelp or bite; twined together, nose to tail, they looked like a vicious version of his mother's powder-puff. Checking that he wasn't being watched, Beauty ran his fingers through the luxurious ivory fur, and wondered how much these glamorous little beasts were worth. He remembered that he'd seen something like this once before, draped around the naked shoulders of a film star in a poster for a film – a film which he'd immediately wanted to see. It felt strange to be fingering something that was so clearly meant to be wrapped around a woman. A woman *like that*. His hands seemed very bare all of sudden – gloveless; he stroked the fur again, and wondered how easily it could get dirty. It could certainly get warm, he thought – but then suddenly there was another shout; Mr F was back up at the rail, and Beauty had to quickly throw the white foxes down on the bench so as to catch the next beast in mid-air.

He didn't think Mr F had seen him, stroking them like that. And anyway, it seemed that handling things meant to be worn next to a woman's skin was considered a normal part of the business. One he'd obviously better get used to. Handling them like it was the most ordinary thing in the world.

He'd never really thought about it like that.

*

Only once during this whole exercise did Mr F's voice relent. When the rail was finally empty, he left Beauty at the bench, busily trying to remember which beast he'd been told was which, and when he came back, he was carrying a large flat cardboard box, which he put down on the bench, shoving aside the heap of furs to make space for it. Inside the box were just three dark, gleaming pelts, lying side by side under a layer of white tissue paper. The way he peeled it back, you could tell how precious they were.

"Sable," he said. "And not just any old sable. These are what they used to call 'Imperial' – the wild ones, Russian; male winter skins. The darkest you can get – and the hardest skin in the world to match. If ever Mr Scheiner lets you cut one of those, then you'll know your apprenticeship's over. Go on: feel it."

The boy touched the skins; the electric points of light on the almost-human, almost-black guard-hairs sparked silently as his fingers disturbed them.

Softer than anything, he thought. *Soft as a girl.*

"Well, what d'you reckon?"

The boy paused, as if considering. Then he also shoved the heap of furs aside to make some space (the white foxes spilt unobserved onto the floor), lifted one of the sables out onto the bench, and ran the side of his hand roughly up and down it, like a blade, back and forth, with the grain and then against it – just as he'd been told. Then he looked up, paused again, and tried on a grin.

"I reckon," said Beauty, very seriously, but still grinning, "I reckon the most important thing, in this business, is choice of skin."

Maybe it was because he was tired, but Mr F had to laugh – and this was such an unusual sound in the workroom that a couple of his colleagues looked up from their work to see what had happened.

"You – " said Mr F, not able to stop himself from

smiling at the boy's nerve, but stabbing with his finger at his chest, making it clear he still had a long way to go before any liberties could be taken, "You had better get on with learning your way round that lot. You'll find the labels on the feet."

Wherever that odd bark of laughter had come from, the moment soon passed; Mr F's voice was already its normal blunt self again. You could see he wasn't angry though; as he put the sable back in the box with its companions and carefully laid them back to rest in their bed of tissue paper, he was still half-smiling himself. Leaving the boy to his study, he closed the box, and took the precious pelts back to their place of honour on whatever high shelf he had got them down from.

Watching him do it, Beauty decided there and then that this old trout was going to be even easier to handle than his Uncle Morrie – easier, even, than his father. Having decided that, he turned his attention back to the pile of jumbled skins on the bench and began looking for labels. Feet, paws, tails, snouts, stomach – you could hardly tell which was which, never mind what was called what… Gingerly, he picked up the first beast by what he guessed was the scruff of its neck, and began to learn his way around his new and adult world.

ten

Although he hadn't exactly welcomed the task when he was first given it, Mr F was nothing if not thorough in the way he showed that boy round the workroom over the next three weeks. Whenever Mr Scheiner asked him how his nephew was getting on, he would always reply "Steadily, Mr Scheiner; nice and steadily."

Before he was allowed to touch anything himself, Beauty was expected to stand and watch every single step of the process. Day by day, Mr F went through it all; the matching, the trimming, the cutting, the damping (the boy hated that bit; hated having to wring out the clammy sponges, and hated the smell), the nailing, the stitching, the draping and finishing. At every stage, the exactitude and patience required were relentlessly stressed – in the seaming and shaping of a fur, as Mr F was always sternly pointing out, there is absolutely no room for error. Beauty was well used to appearing to defer to his elders and betters, and would smile and nod and take it all in, making (he was sure) a highly convincing job of appearing studious. Of course, when it came to attempting things for himself – especially in these early weeks – he was never as good as he thought he was. The nails slipped; the sponges dripped – but he persevered. As so often with young men of his age, he made all sorts of private bargains with himself to justify his submission to all this adult instruction. It wasn't so much, he reasoned, that he found the work difficult, but rather that he found it an insufficient challenge. Or as he would have put it, if asked: *Messing about with bits of skin, it's not exactly what you'd call hard work, is it?*

It was, however. And Mr F kept him at it until, step by patient step, the boy began to get the hang of the basic procedures. Actually, although he'd never have admitted it, the position of apprentice suited him very well. He liked the attention. He liked working at the top of the building, two floors above the women amongst whom he had served his time. Most of all, he liked the common understanding that he was taking his rightful place in the scheme of things.

Master and pupil weren't always together, of course. Mr F had his own work to get on with, and would often send the boy off to watch one of the other cutters working on one of the simpler procedures. But he never quite took his eye off him; the first sign of confusion or haste, and he would be there. Mr F did not believe in teaching by allowing people to make their own mistakes. When he was explaining or demonstrating something for the first time, he would reel off his instructions as if he was quoting from some manual, one he knew whole pages of off by heart; but then he would also keep up a running commentary of these instructions under his breath even while he was keeping his eye on his pupil from right across the room. It was as if he thought that somehow their recital could guarantee the task being correctly executed. The boy would be stretching a dampened skin across the nailing-board for instance, tugging it across the lines of the pattern with his mouth full of pins and trying hard not to tear or bruise anything, and Mr F would be watching him all the time, all the time repeating the words of the lesson – not really to the boy at all I suppose, but more to himself – very quietly, through half-clenched teeth;

A mistake made now cannot be corrected later... That's it...

Swiftly and firmly, and at the correct angle. Good boy. Any hesitation, and you'll end up with bruising.

Touch! Come on, boy, touch it!
– standing there and watching him; ready to cross the room at a moment's notice and show him all over again how to do it, but somehow not wanting to, holding back, *willing* the boy to stick to his instructions. It wasn't that he assumed the boy would get it wrong, exactly; it was just very important to Mr F that everything was done by the book. Line by line; step by step; nail by nail.

Thirty-three years, remember, he'd been doing this.

The voice Mr F used to mutter to himself like this wasn't particularly soft; it was quiet, but not soft. It was *firm.*

Go on then. Touch it…

Eventually, of course, something would clearly be just about to go badly wrong, and before it could he'd be straight across the room, leant over the board and taking the pinchers out of the boy's hands without a word. And then he'd start showing him all over again how to handle them, repeating his instructions word for word, right from the very beginning. *Right,* he'd say. *Back to basics. The most important thing, in this business…*

*

To produce the impression of a seamless fabric, which is of course what the discerning customer requires (nothing about the finished garment should suggest too crudely that it was once a collection of pieces of skin, much less bloody ones), every pelt in the pattern has to blend invisibly with its neighbour. To an untrained eye, like yours, or mine, or

Beauty's, all of the ninety mink pelts required for a full length coat, for instance, would look more or less the same; Mr F's, however, could detect a myriad variations in tone, weight and lustre. Not only has every skin to be exactly matched and placed in relation to its neighbours; an experienced cutter will ensure that the richest and fullest pelts are reserved for those parts of the pattern that will attract Madam's most careful scrutiny – the collar and cuffs which will frame her precious face and wrists – while relegating any weaker or less impressive skins to the underarm or lower back, areas which no mirror ever displays to even the most demanding of customers.

This matching of the skins is perhaps the strangest ritual of the cutting bench. Laid out in a long row, the pelts are thrown and caught and sorted and shuffled like the tokens of some mad game of patience – a game the rules of which no uninformed observer could possibly discern. If the exact shade of a pelt eludes the sorter, he will suddenly pause, snatch up the skin and beat up its hairs with the back of his hand or even with a cane, eye it carefully in the strong working light from the window, then suddenly throw it down into its newly allotted place. Anyone watching might well think the dead beast was being punished. The ritual is made all the odder by being performed in uncanny silence – even Mr F rarely talked to himself while he did it.

But when he was demonstrating the job to Beauty, he couldn't help himself. Half-way through matching another pile of smoke-grey mink – all the new ranch pastels were in fashion that season – he suddenly stopped, handed the boy a dangling skin, and told him to find a partner for it amongst those already laid out on the bench. The boy hesitated, unsure – and quite without meaning to, Mr F started muttering at him *Touch; come on, touch it;* but the boy still didn't move. So he took the skin impatiently out of Beauty's hands and showed him once again how to beat up the guard-hairs: *Up and down, up and down; with the grain, and then against. Touch. Remember?* Mr F stroked the skin twice more, held it up to the light, judged it, then threw it down, satisfied with its placing at last, and continued. As he worked, deftly sending the skins flying left and right, he kept his eyes glued to the bench, only occasionally standing suddenly bolt upright as another culprit was held up to the searching light and scrutinised – and no matter how fast he worked, he handled each of the recalcitrant skins with the same firm, fastidious care. It was a way of moving that looked odd in a man, Beauty thought. At least in such a big one... those big white hands of his, it was amazing how they could fly around. They weren't gentle, exactly, because it was all done so quickly, but you could tell it was skin he was touching – and all the time, Mr F would be muttering to himself. Almost as if no one else was there except the two of them, or even as if he was quite on his own – as if he was about to find the solution to whatever strange game it was that he was playing.

Come on...

The words were hardly even there, they were so quiet.

Come on...

The boy pretended to be absorbed by the strange dance of the furs over the wooden bench, but actually, he was watching Mr F most of the time. Watching his face, in particular. Watching the way his eyes narrowed as his big soft hands quickly and firmly stroked each pelt and laid it down – as if he could feel the colour as much as see it. As if touch alone could guide him in his choice. And all the time, as he worked, Beauty could hear the strange, intent sound that came creeping into the man's voice, so serious, and yet so soft and caressing. Very quiet, as if this was something for their ears only. Right down to a whisper.

Come on, touch it.

Bloody hell, Beauty thought, *anyone would think he was teaching me the facts of life, the way he goes on sometimes.*

*

The one thing in the workroom that Beauty had not yet been allowed to handle was a knife. It had been made clear to him from the start that when he was ready for that, Mr F would let him know. However, by the third week of April, the lessons were going pretty well, and the day was not far distant. The top button of Beauty's white coat was now done up every morning, and though he was only ever as attentive and as punctual as he needed to be – he was invariably the last one up the stairs at eight o'clock, and by the time Mr F got his jacket back on at the end of the day, seemed always to have already melted out of the building – Mr F felt able to report to Mr Scheiner that although he'd probably never make a first-class cutter, in another couple of months his nephew was going to know everything a young man considering management might need to know about the manufacturing side of things. In fact, he was going to think about starting him cutting on Monday.

A few reprimands had of course been required along the way. The second time Beauty had been late back at the end of a tea-break, for instance (dawdling on the off-chance of catching one of the new girls from downstairs in conversation, Mr F supposed), he'd had to say something. But a curt reminder that he didn't expect to be always the first one to finish his cigarette had seemed to do the trick straightaway. All in all, he was rather proud of the way he'd handled the boy. He'd never lost his temper with him – in fact, he hadn't had to, which was a surprise, given his initial misgivings. He was even starting in an odd way to approve of the young man. Certainly, Mr Scheiner's decision that anyone who was going to end up in management should start from the bottom up, he approved of that. It was the right and proper way of doing things – and Mr F was, as you know, a man who believed there was a right and proper way of doing everything. After all, look at how he himself had started; in the downstairs workroom, with a broom, keeping his head down. Mr F could see that in some ways the boy's situation was very similar to what his own had once been – and when he looked at him in that light, he had to admit that the boy was making really rather good progress. *He's rather like me, in some ways,* he said to himself, as he took his decision to announce that they would be starting work with the knives next Monday morning. *Rather like me at that age.*

Yes. Oh yes; he really did think that.

In his defence, I should say that the project of having an apprentice doubtless gave Mr F some kind of much-needed fixed point to concentrate on amidst all his private turmoil. He was probably unconsciously grateful to the boy in some sort of way – grateful to have something else to think about for a change. It must have been that. That, or the boy's looks.

*

Certainly it was true that since he'd started working with this boy – since he'd had Beauty to take his mind off things, if you like – Mr F's dream had been bothering him less. In fact, as he stirred the teapot, replaced the lid and lit the first cigarette of that Monday morning, he was able to congratulate himself on the fact that his dream had not woken him for twenty-three nights in a row. True, the fact that he knew exactly how many nights it had stayed away tells you that it must have been still preying on his mind – and, true, his sleep on many of those twenty-three nights, though unbroken, had not been particularly deep. He still often felt more tired than he ought – which was annoying, now that he was responsible for the boy's work as well as his own. Sometimes, when he got off the seven-twenty at London Bridge, he found himself flinching slightly at the rush-hour musket-volley of slamming train doors – and as he told himself, that really was a sound he should have been used to after all these years.

And of course he did still find himself occasionally staring at someone instead of reading his paper on the train like he'd meant to.

Though perhaps less often, recently.

And certainly not in the mornings.

That's right, he told himself, as he stubbed out his cigarette and poured the tea. After over three weeks, surely he was going to be left in peace now. He looked up at the kitchen clock to check the time, knocked back his tea, collected his hat, locked his door and set out for Peckham Rye station with a clear mind. Quite looking forward to the day, in fact – looking forward to showing the boy how to handle a blade. And then, barely half an hour later, Mr F found himself doing something he had never done before in his life. He followed a man in the street.

eleven

It was a bright, brisk morning. He had nearly made it into work, and at the moment when it happened, he hadn't been thinking about his dream or any of his questions at all. In fact, he'd been thinking about Beauty. About how he felt the boy was coming along, and about whether he was right after all to have promised him on Friday afternoon that come Monday morning they would take a look at the knives together. *It wouldn't do to rush him,* he thought. Preoccupied with these thoughts, he turned left up out of All Hallows Lane and onto Upper Thames Street, bowing his head to protect his face from the gritty wind which was whipping through the tunnel under Cannon Street Station. Nothing unusual in that. He can't have been properly looking where he was going, however, which was unusual, because just as he reached the mid-point of the underpass, the point where it is darkest, the point furthest away from the bright rectangle of daylight at either end of it, he let someone coming the other way – someone walking against the flow of the crowd – run almost straight into him.

Now, as you know, Mr F hated to be bumped into or touched like that – and he didn't always have the best of tempers, our Mr F, and especially not first thing on a Monday morning when he was trying to think something through. He recovered his balance, and turned, fully intending to shout something at the culprit's retreating back. But by the time he had collected himself, the man – who hadn't stopped or said sorry, but had just kept on walking, fast, as if he had some urgent appointment to keep

– had reached the eastern end of the underpass; Mr F opened his mouth to shout at him, but at that exact moment the man walked out of the darkness of the tunnel and in one stride emerged into the sudden April sunlight of Upper Thames Street. Something about the sight of this made Mr F stop; stop dead, and stare. What was it? There was nothing obvious to distinguish this man from all the other men in dark suits in that crowd – except of course that he was the only person who was walking the other way, the *wrong* way, you might say, against the westward tide of early morning faces. He was striding out into the light, while they were all trudging down into darkness. In fact, to be particular, at that moment, he was the only man in all that crowd whose face Mr F *couldn't* see. Perhaps that was what did it – that, or the fact that his hair, when the light suddenly caught it like that, at the moment when he moved from the dark of the tunnel into the sunlight, it was –

Was what, exactly? Mr F couldn't say. His voice died in his throat.

He didn't set off in pursuit at once. He stood there, staring at the man's retreating back, and the rush-hour crowd parted around him as if he was a pile or bulwark in the river. As I said, he'd never done anything like this before – he'd stared at men, yes, I've told you about that, but he'd never actually turned around on his way to work and followed one. All he could think of was that he had to make his mind up quickly, that he had to move *now*, or lose the man in the crowd.

In which case, he would never see his face.

So he decided not to think; he stepped forward, and breasted the oncoming tide.

★

His quarry was now at least a hundred yards ahead of him, and was turning left up Arthur Street. This is the street that curves up and away from Upper Thames Street, back up to where the north end of London Bridge becomes King William Street, and at ten to eight on a Monday morning, people literally pour down it. It's quite a steep hill, and Mr F was walking against the crowd; but our Mr F has a surprisingly strong stride when he needs it. All the time, he keeps his eyes firmly fixed on the man's back and on the back of his neck, hoping for him to look left or right, so that he can at least catch a glimpse of his profile. As he emerges at the top of the hill he loses sight of him for just a moment, and has to stop and scan the pavements of King William Street left and right... *There he is*; on the traffic island in front of the Monument, waiting to cross onto the opposite pavement. The rush-hour traffic coming south onto the bridge is heavy, and this gives Mr F time. He doesn't want to get too close, not yet – but by the time they have both crossed the road, turned left, crossed Eastcheap and started heading north up the eastern pavement of Gracechurch Street, he is only twenty paces away from the man's back. Now Mr F can see more of him; he's young, and neatly built – but there's still no sign of his face. He's moving just how a young man should move at the start of the day – swift, neat and determined. Cutting easily through the crowd in his dark suit. Dark blue, it looks like. Mr F wonders if he should try and pass him – pass him, and then look back, and – and while he's thinking this, suddenly, without warning, the young man turns right, into a hidden alleyway, and disappears. Mr F didn't see that coming; he didn't even know there was an alleyway there. Undaunted, he picks up his pace and turns down it. It's dark, and narrow, and apparently empty of people, and for a moment he thinks he's lost his quarry. *No; there he is* – and there he is, at the far end, emerging from the dark into bright sunlight again, walking straight round the corner to the left, giving away just a swift glimpse of his face as he turns the corner, and as that happens, his dark hair catches the light again. Mr F almost breaks into a run.

If he stopped for a moment to think, he would realise that this route is taking him further and further away from Skin Lane, into the labyrinth-like lanes of the northern City. Even if he can retrace his steps accurately, this wild goose chase is going to make him badly late for work – but he doesn't stop, and he doesn't think. He doesn't think at all. He doesn't remind himself that he has promised himself to stop doing all this. No; what he tells himself as he tries to control his urge to break into a run is that it's alright, he'll find him again as soon as he gets out of this alley. He tells himself that he's sure he knows where the young man must be heading; he's going to cross Fenchurch Street, and then head up Lime Street to Leadenhall and the City. Where else, at this time of the morning? He can afford to hang back a bit. After all, he doesn't want the young man to know he's being followed. He doesn't want him to spin round suddenly and confront him right there on the street. He doesn't want to talk to him; all he needs from him is to see his face – but not just quite yet. He has to manage this properly, you see. Do it the right way. Get his breath back, for a start.

Get somewhere where it's safe to look at him, but not be caught doing it.

There he is, up ahead again. *Good. That's better.*

Mr F lets the young man walk well ahead of him round the slow, crowded right-hand curve of Lime Street. Well ahead; at least fifty or sixty feet.

Which was a mistake.

★

When he reaches the entrance of Leadenhall Market, Mr F realises he has hung back too far; suddenly, he can't see his quarry anywhere. He stops dead, and looks around – and now he does actually break into a run; a panic-stricken run, ploughing through the morning crowd right into the middle of the market, not caring what people might think, right to where its four covered arcades meet in a crossing like that of some great high-roofed church. North, south, east and west. He stops, and stares wildly about him.

Where is he?

The central crossing of Leadenhall Market is held up by eight silvered, snarling dragons; the mythical wyverns of the City of London. Four pairs of the beasts support the glass and girders of its high-arched roof on their outspread wings, writhing under its weight. As all the guidebooks tell you, they are one of the sights of London – but Mr F has no time to look up at the Victorian wonders of a market roof. He's searching – south, north, east, west – searching for some glimpse of that tell-tale dark hair and white neck and retreating back. West, north, east, west again – but it's hopeless, it's as if some great human anthill has been ripped open and its inhabitants sent weaving and scurrying in every conceivable direction. There are faces everywhere. There are at least twenty dark-haired young men in every direction he looks.

It's hopeless. Hopeless.

He's gone.

Mr F stands there under the wyverns' outspread wings, and he is forced to admit defeat. He can hear a strange sound, which he eventually recognises as himself. He hadn't realised he'd got quite so out of breath. A slight film of sweat begins to turn cold on his skin, and as he stands there, he gradually becomes aware of everything that is happening around him. Shutters are rattling up, orders are being shouted; a whole cacophony of activity is being trapped and amplified under that high glass roof. And then he sees the rows and rows of black iron hooks, and he remembers what it is that Leadenhall Market actually sells.

Although there are a few office workers taking their morning shortcut through the market, most of the young men he can see are wearing white aprons; and all of those aprons are stained with blood. That thick sweet smell which is just beginning to make itself apparent is the smell of meat: cut meat. Something about this smell feels very wrong; there is too much of it. One or two of the butchers' boys look at him and wonder what this old man thinks he's doing, standing there in everybody's way like that. One of them brushes past him with a wicker skip of dead hares, spiking the smells of pork and beef with the richer stink of furred game, and Mr F becomes very aware of the movement of his heaving chest, and of the trickle of sweat which is beginning to make its way down the small of his back, and of the thumping noise in his head. This unsettling awareness of the clammy fact of his own body, combined with the sight of the rows and rows of carcasses hanging by their feet from the metal hooks, makes him realise what the problem is. This is exactly how he feels in his bathroom, in the middle of the night, when he discovers that the door has slammed itself shut behind his back; except that now, he's feeling it by daylight. Despite himself, he closes his eyes, but it's no good. It might as well be four o'clock in the morning. He can't help it – and with a sudden rush of blood to his face and neck, Mr F realises his big mistake.

His dream hadn't left him in peace at all; it was just biding its time. And now that it's brought him out here, it's going to teach him a lesson.

Standing stuck out there in the middle of the market, Mr F suddenly desperately wishes that there was somewhere he could wash his hands – he even tries shoving them in his pockets to hide them. He can feel the skin on the back of his neck and all over his face beginning to redden, and he looks down at his feet to try and hide it from the people around him – he's sure he can feel them staring. There's blood mixed in with the sawdust between the cobbles, and a roaring sound in his ears. *If you had actually caught up with that young man,* thinks Mr F, clenching his teeth and trying to make himself heard over the din inside his head, *what would you have actually done? Grabbed him – grabbed him by the shoulder and spun him round? Looked him in the eye? Well, then you'd have had to have said something to him, wouldn't you. Yes you would. Well, what, exactly?* **What?**

Worried that he is about to start shouting, Mr F takes hold of his left wrist with his right hand – he does that sometimes these days, when he is trying to get a grip on himself. And of course as he does that, his right hand closes over his wristwatch. Without thinking, he looks at it, and sees the time.

It's just gone three minutes past eight.

Without stopping to think, he turns on his heel and walks straight out of the market. He turns left into

Gracechurch Street, then right on Cannon Street, heading for Dowgate, College Hill and the Lane – he reckons he can make it in less than ten minutes if he keeps this pace up. He doesn't run; there's no need to make even more of a fool of himself than he has already. The crowds on Cannon Street are murder, and he nearly steps in front of a bus. Dowgate Hill; sharp left, and down. Another four minutes to go at most. Of course, if he had been walking up this hill and not hurtling down it, say if he had been out at dinnertime, getting one of his leisurely dinnertime breaths of fresh air, he might have stopped to admire the strange wrought iron snakes which twist themselves head down through the acanthus leaves on the gates of Dyers Hall, or that little gilded, dancing fox that crests the coat of arms above the doorway to the Skinners Hall so gleefully – but not this morning, thank you. This isn't a guided tour. He's not looking at anything unnecessary this morning, thank you very much, he hasn't got the time. He has to get to work. Has to get this bloody jacket off as quickly as possible. He has to get inside, wash his hands, get his white coat on, and get down to some bloody work for Christ's sake.

His face is like thunder.

Arriving at Skin Lane at just gone a quarter past eight, he takes the stone steps at the front door of Number Four two at a time, and goes straight upstairs; no one sees him on the way up, of course, because everyone else is already hard at work. He pauses just outside the workroom door, with his hand on the door handle, very aware that the other cutters are all going to have smiles on their faces the moment he walks in. They're all going to really enjoy how late he is – and now he is *really* angry with himself, angrier than he's ever been before. He takes a deep breath, and unclenches his fists. And then of course when he does open the door, and walks in, the first thing he sees is that blasted boy standing there waiting for him at his bench with his white coat all ready and buttoned right up like he's been told it should be, all smiling and eager and ready for him.

twelve

Mr F didn't even wish him good morning. Ignoring the more or less obvious stares from his colleagues, he hung up his jacket with only slightly more briskness than usual (he hoped the patches of sweat under his arms were not dark enough to show; he could feel their sudden coolness), and then collected his own white coat from its peg. The first thing he said to the boy, using a noticeably more cheerful voice than was customary at this time on a Monday, was an offhand

"Good weekend?"

This, of course, was highly unusual. And Mr F's voice sounded – well, as if it was making a point. The boy hesitated for a moment, and his face showed a flicker of dismay; just for a moment, he wondered if something of what he'd been up to that weekend showed in his face. No, it couldn't possibly. Whatever was up with the old boy this morning, it was best to humour him.

"Yes thank you, Mr F," he said. "Very nice indeed."

Mr F still wouldn't leave it, however.

"Sleep well?" he asked, turning away to look for something – which was just as well, because otherwise he would have seen Beauty half-raising an eyebrow for the benefit of his fellow workers. All of them, of course, were discreetly enjoying the sight of their notoriously punctual Head Cutter trying to pretend that nothing was wrong – and making such a clumsy job of it. Egged on by a couple of expectant glances, Beauty found he just couldn't resist extending the scene. Looking round to make sure everyone was watching him, and using his best butter-wouldn't-melt voice, he replied

"Yes thank you, Mr F," and then added, as if it was the most ordinary question in the world, "And you?"

Mr F, looking down to check his last button, was determined to prove that conversation was a game he could play too. Given the question, it was perhaps not surprising that his answer came out with a slightly strangled sound to it, but he was sure no one noticed.

"As always. Now," he said, looking back up and rather triumphantly handing the boy a small brass knife-handle, "let's see you fit a blade into that. Time to get cutting."

As he smoothed down his coat for the last time and checked that the rest of the tools were all in order, Mr F felt that at any minute now normality would be restored. Quite soon now, everyone would be hard at work. Every head would be lowered over a bench. Just as it should be.

That's better.

*

Even though the blade was of course a new one, fresh from its paper packet and freshly split in two, he told the boy that for this particular lesson he wanted to see him sharpen it. Beauty found the grindstone, oiled it, and then, having dutifully checked that the steel sliver was securely fitted into the brass handle (he intuited correctly that this morning, it was important to do everything by the book), began to flick the blade carefully across the stone, left right, left right, like a thrush with a snail. Just like he'd been shown.

Even though Mr F could see he was doing everything right, he insisted on reprimanding him.

"Now slow down. And watch what you're doing, please."

*

The boy stoops to his task. He is actually rather pleased that this day has finally come; if he passes the test (which, of course, he will), it should mean he won't be quite so closely watched in future. His shoulder curves slightly under the white linen of his coat, and he presses conscientiously down on the blade. He can just feel the sunlight coming in through the long window and touching him; it's the first real warmth of the year. The patient, repeated whisper of the blade across the stone seems oddly satisfying.

Mr F, meanwhile, turns away and takes a look round the rest of the workroom, ostensibly to make sure that everything else is in order. It has the desired effect; everyone looks back down at their work and concentrates very hard on what they're doing. Mr F checks the buttons on his coat again, starting with the bottom one, and with each button he feels more calm; he feels *safe*. The panic of the last fifteen minutes recedes, and begins to seem like something from another world entirely. The sunlight coming in through the window overlooking the church roof is strong and calm and steady; his breathing is now perfectly back under his control. He can concentrate. When he turns back to the boy, he notices that his hair, just where the shirt collar is lifting away as he bends forward over the blade, where the sun is catching it, is getting so long that it is starting is curl on the back of his neck, and *I really must talk to him about that,* thinks Mr F. Indeed, he is just about to say something to him, something sharp – but not too sharp, because he bears the boy no ill-will, and he really has got rid of the last lingering trace of this morning's foul temper now, really everything is as it should be, but then

Ah.

Here it comes.

but then, as he stares at the hair curling over the nape of the boy's neck, and at the exact way the individual vertebrae show through the skin just above his collar, and the way that the corded muscles on the side of his neck are just beginning to show as he cranes it forward and slightly to one side – just then, and for no good or particular reason that he can identify, Mr F begins to have the odd sensation (it is hard to say where, exactly – perhaps in the pit of his stomach) that everything in the workroom is coming to a gentle but conclusive stop. It ceases to matter. The sounds – for instance, the sound of a pincher methodically tapping on a nailing board somewhere behind him – are beginning to fade, and after all the noise and the crowds and the stairs and the rush of his morning so far, this is a great relief. They are replaced, inexplicably, by the reassuring and familiar sound of his kitchen clock. He feels oddly still. He finds that instead of worrying about how the boy is managing with the blade on the stone, about the angle of the blade and whether there is any danger of the stone slipping as he steadies it with his other hand, he is suddenly able, exactly as if he was working on matching a pair of particularly tricky pelts, to concentrate exclusively on the exact colour and texture, the density and lustre, of the dark hair curling on the back of the boy's neck.

Remember, it all comes down to choice of skin.

He wants to touch it.

The important thing is, touch.

But he knows that that wouldn't be a good idea.

If he was matching pelts, of course, he would reach out and run the his hand firmly over the skin and then drag it back against the grain, to feel the exact quality of the guard-hairs' warm, soft resilience – but he knows he can't do that to the back of a young man's neck. But then he also knows – quite suddenly, and to his great surprise and almost, I should say, to his relief – that he doesn't actually need to. After seventeen previous attempts, you see, he knows that he's just found the exact match he's been looking for – and right here, would you believe: right here on his own cutting bench. Right where he least expected to find it. Yes; Mr F has just found the answer to his question – the question that he has been carrying to and from Skin Lane for weeks now, chafing away at him, nagging at him like a memory or a back-ache does – the question that now joins the clock ticking in his mind with all the clarity of a chiming hour;

Where have you come from:

Where the hell have you come from?

As always with Mr F, the answer to his question also comes in the form of a sentence. He can actually *hear* it – whispered, right in his ear. Because, you see, suddenly, everything fits. This young man is exactly the right size, the right build and the right shape. The hands sharpening the blade are just delicate enough, and his hair – well, you always need a good working light when you're matching pelts, and fortunately the light from the long window is strong this late April morning, and as it catches his hair just where it curls slightly above the collar, it makes it clear that it is an *exact* match; an exact match for the hair Mr F sees spread across the harsh white enamel of his bathtub at four o'clock every other morning of his strange and tortured life.

Even under the glare of that naked bathroom bulb, and here again in the sunlight pouring through the cutting-bench windows, it has those same elusive shadows. Look: *Sable.* And no ordinary sable. *Imperial. The darkness that is never quite black; the lustre that no dyer can ever convincingly counterfeit. How odd,* thinks Mr F – and he knows that he has plenty of time to think all of this, even in the short moment it will take the boy to finish the last sweep of the blade across the stone, because not only has that small staccato whisper faded away with the rest of the sound in the room, but the ticking of the clock has died away now too, and he feels sure that if he was to look down at his watch, that too would have stopped – *How odd,* he thinks; *when this boy next looks at me – when he turns to me and looks up and asks* **"D'you think we're ready now, Mr F?"** *– I will finally know what the face of the man in my dreams looks like.*

What will I say to him, I wonder? What?

Actually, when the boy turns and says that, Mr F controls his voice perfectly. Oddly enough, he knows exactly what to say. He replies

"Well, let's find out, shall we?"

*

Mr F takes the knife, tests the edge of the blade against his thumb, and prepares to show the boy how to make the first cut. He worries that his right hand might start to shake if he doesn't do it straightaway – ever so slightly, just as it does sometimes in the dream when he has just walked through the blood from the window and is slipping his front door key into the lock – and he knows he is being watched, and he doesn't want the boy to see his teacher hesitate. So he doesn't; he picks up the first of the pelts they are going to be working on today, a bundle of plain ranch mink being cut for the collars and cuffs of a big retail order, and lifts the point of the blade above the waiting skin. He takes a deep breath, and calmly reiterates the lesson for the day:

"The first cut on any skin is the most important," he says. "A mistake made now cannot be corrected later. The blade needs to move swiftly and firmly, and at the correct angle. If it swerves in the wrong direction, the exact alignment of the seams required by the pattern will be spoilt; any hesitating or snagging, and the fur will be bruised by the knife."

Mr F knows all this, of course; he knows it better than anyone. After all, he has been doing this for years. And the boy has heard this passage from the manual several times before – but it needed to be said. Just as he always does, Mr F stretches the skin of the pelt ever so gently with the thumb and forefinger of his left hand, so that it will part readily as soon as the blade touches it. All he has to do now is move the blade. He has done it a thousand times before. He looks down.

*

People say that the sound of a pelt parting under the knife is like paper or parchment tearing, or like the whisper of a turning page, but actually it is like the sound of nothing else; it is the sound of skin. Perhaps it is in anticipation of this sound that, as he prepares to lower the blade, Mr F looks down for a moment, and sees, or thinks he sees, not the delicate leather of an animal pelt stretched there between his thumb and forefinger, but something human. Specifically, he sees the taut white skin of the young man in his dream; he sees the blade about to open up the thick, meaty muscle covering the ribs directly above his heart. Of course, seeing this, he flinches. The blade jumps – just a quarter of an inch – and for the very first time in all his years at the cutting bench, Mr F feels the icy bite of the knife on his own flesh.

As if to punish him for the stupidity of his error, the blade catches him on one of the tenderest parts of the body, the taut web of skin where the thumb branches away from the hand. The cut is a nasty one, down to the meat, and like all wounds to the hand, it immediately begins to bleed profusely. Without hesitating, the blood – real blood – wells up as clear and bright as the very best quality rubies. But Mr F is quick too; he drops the knife as quick as you'd drop a red hot saucepan handle, then digs into his right-hand trouser pocket and whips out a clean handkerchief and clamps it on the wound straight away, just like you're supposed to. However, his blood won't be denied its new-found freedom; it soaks through the handkerchief in less than a minute, turning the clean white linen into a scarlet mess. To make matters worse, Mr F knows that to staunch bleeding from a wound to the hand, you have to hold it up above your head; he is forced to show the bloody rag to everyone in the room. Though he doesn't curse or shout, everyone stops what they're doing and watches him, so that when the blood begins to run down his forearm, everyone can see it. Small nicks to the thumb or forefinger are nothing unusual in the workroom, but a deep cut like this one, with a real flow of blood – that never happens. No wonder everyone is staring. Seeing their faces, Mr F now does begin to shout; at the boy, of all people, first, but then at everyone. He wants him out of the way, he wants him downstairs *now*, he wants Mrs Kesselman up here with the iodine straight away, he wants everyone back to work: *What the bloody hell do you think you're all staring at,* he shouts. They've all seen him deal with accidents before – when it happens to someone else, he is quick and quiet and method-ical – but they've never, so far as they can remember, ever heard this man raise his voice as high as this. One or two of them, as they reluctantly lower their heads back to their work, do wonder what exactly is going on with Mr F these days.

In all this, the precious fur on the bench is forgotten. Unwatched, the first three drops of Mr F's blood soak slowly into the pelt. As it happens, the fact that the first cut is slightly awry won't render this particular skin useless – once Beauty has finished trimming it, one minor adjustment in the fitting of the underside of the finished collar, and the fault will be invisible. In a way, this means that this anonymous fur collar – one of nearly a hundred in the order – will be the very first work from their two shared hands. Hidden away inside it, unbeknownst to the customer, these three drops of Mr F's blood will always be there – like a pledge signed in blood in some old story, or like a signature on a painting, hidden from sight under layers of darkening varnish.

I saw a painting once where the artist had actually done that – signed his work in blood. It wasn't in a gallery, but in a church. Unnoticed down in a corner, there was a strange streak of scarlet running across the filthy floor of the prison yard where the scene in the picture was supposed to be taking place. If you followed it back to its source, you realised that this was a ribbon of blood, running from a butchered saint's neck. And then, when you looked closer, you realised that the blood was resolving itself into the scrawled letters of the artist's name. When I saw that, I thought it was as if the man who had painted the picture wanted to say to me, *Well, you did ask what this actually cost.*

*

Surprised by the blood, and even more by the stony sound

of Mr F shouting at him, the boy did as he was told and ran downstairs for Mrs Kesselman immediately. She, seeing the look on Mr F's face as he stood there in the middle of the room with a bloody handkerchief clamped to his hand, knew as soon as she walked in through the workroom door that he'd lost his temper with someone, and suggested diplomatically that since Mr Scheiner was out this morning, why didn't they inspect the damage in the downstairs office. She'd never seen him quite like this – positively white-faced. Sitting him down while she got the iodine and lint and needle and thread ready, she did her best to calm him down; when Mr F told her that the accident had all been *that bloody boy's fault,* she clucked her tongue and said she was sure there was no need to be quite so hard on our young Mr Scheiner, we all had to start out in this business somewhere. Mr F felt himself about to hiss at her, *Actually there's every fucking need, Mrs Kesselman, since you mention it,* but fortunately at that point she had got the handkerchief off and was starting to dab at his wound with the iodine, so he had a legitimate reason to clench his teeth and hold his breath. The rest of the stitching, dressing and bandaging was done in silence.

The thought of going back upstairs and being asked by the boy if he was alright was intolerable, so when Mrs Kesselman told him she'd just get one of the girls to make him a good strong cup of tea before he went back up, he said no, he'd rather she just went up and told the boy to take the rest of the day off, and that they'd carry on tomorrow, if she wouldn't mind. He'd just sit here for a bit. Not quite sure what to make of the news that Mr F of all people was sending someone home early when there was a big order to be completed by the end of the week, Mrs Kesselman nevertheless thought better of enquiring exactly was upsetting him like this, and did as he asked.

★

Mr F sat in that office for a full ten minutes before deciding that the coast was clear. However, once he got back upstairs, he soon discovered that there's not much a cutter can do with only one un-maimed hand. By two o'clock, the silence in the workroom (nobody was saying anything), coupled with the steady tapping of pins into nailing boards, was driving him mad. By half past, he'd had enough, and when it got to the afternoon tea-break, without telling anyone he was going, he hung up his white coat and left.

At first he told himself not to pay any attention to his wound and just get on with things. But now that he was on his own, sitting on an almost-empty 3.02 train and feeling completely out of place, he couldn't help it; the ache from the cut was beginning to deepen and spread. He closed his eyes, and let the sensation work its way across the back of his hand and into his wrist. That way, at least he had something to concentrate on. Something to keep at bay the sound of the sentence that he'd heard whispered in his ear back there in the Skin Lane workroom, and which had now wormed its way into the front of his mind and was beginning to run insistently round and round and round his aching head. The train rocked its way along the long slow bend from London Bridge Station to Bermondsey, from Bermondsey to the Queen's Road, and from Queen's Road Station to Peckham Rye. As the train pulled into his stop, Mr F screwed his eyes up tight. He didn't want to hear it. *Didn't want to hear it.*

Wasn't ready to think about that at all.

By the time he got home, at the peculiar hour of half past three on a Monday afternoon, the cut was hurting badly. Because he always kept his front door key in the right hand breast pocket of his jacket, and his left hand was now pinned into a tightly wound crêpe bandage, it took him some time to get the key out and into the lock. Getting his jacket off and hanging up his suit and rolling up his shirt-sleeves also proved awkward. Scrubbing his one good hand properly proved practically impossible – and the wound was beginning to really throb now. A pot of strong tea and three cigarettes (rolling them wasn't easy, either) did nothing to calm it. By half past eight that evening, he gave up; he cleared his supper away uneaten, left the dishes unwashed and decided to turn in early. Before getting into bed, he went to the bathroom and took two aspirins. Then he lay stiff-backed in the dark and hoped that the pain would begin to wear off soon, and that he might get some sleep, and that the sentence hammering round his head would go away.

After half an hour, he was sure he could feel the blood beginning to seep out into the bandage again. He wouldn't be at all surprised if the sheets were spotted in the morning.

★

You might think that Mr F's dream would have left him in peace now, now that it had been broken (isn't it odd, by the way, that people say that, *Oh, you've just broken my dream,* as if a dream could be a piece of china, or a knife-blade). But in fact, that Monday night, his dream returned.

It returned, you might say, with a vengeance.

thirteen

It started the same way as always. As he turned the corner of the stairs, the red light from the window stained his sleeve; but only for a moment. The key slid into the lock and turned without hindrance, despite the fact that the hand that held it was bandaged – that's right; in his dream, it was now his right hand, the hand he made his living with, that had been cut and stitched. The front door clicked shut behind him, exactly as it always did. But then, once he had hung up the key on its hook by the door and hung up his jacket in the wardrobe, instead of continuing with his nightly ritual – the rolling up of his sleeves, the scrubbing of the hands – he somehow found himself already completely undressed for bed and standing stock still in the middle of his hallway. Just standing there, naked, and staring at the handle on the closed bathroom door. He knew what was in there, and he knew that he had to go in there and sort it out as soon as possible, but

That word again...

But what was he supposed to do, now that it has a name? What was he supposed to do with it, now that it belongs to someone he recognises?

Now that it has a face.

Now that he knows who to blame.

Standing there outside the bathroom door, Mr F looks down at his bandaged hand, his work hand, and he can hear his thoughts very clearly turning themselves into sentences again. He could even swear that in the stone cold silence of his flat he is standing there outside the closed bathroom door and talking to it, for all the world as if the dead body on the other side of it could hear him. *Now look what you've made me do,* he can hear himself saying. *People will say to me, how did you do that to your hand then, Mr F? The man who sells me my paper in the morning, the man who sells me my ticket, the man who sells me my milk – they'll all be at it.* "How did you do that then?" *they'll say. And what am I supposed to tell them – that I made a mistake? That I* **slipped**? *That I wasn't thinking – or I tell you what, how about this;* "I was thinking about the back of somebody's neck." *That'll do the trick I'm sure.* "I was thinking about the way the back of his neck – "

Well, the way it what?

What?

Mr F wasn't just talking now. He was shouting; shouting with his face pressed right up against the bathroom door. Staring at it, as if the wood wasn't there and he could already see what was on the other side of it. *The bloody cheek of it. Hanging there with a smile on its face...* He pressed his forehead against the gloss magnolia paint and closed his eyes and groaned. He knew the body was in there – no changing that. He just needed time to think. Time to decide what he ought to do about it. He needed a moment's peace... *Hanging up there by its feet like a fox ready for flaying. Like some piece of meat on a hook in bloody Leadenhall Market* – it made him wish he had his box of blades with him. That was it; that's what he ought to do. He remembered the moment in the workroom when he'd been steadying himself to make the first cut, and he'd seen all that meat. He put his right hand up on his chest, feeling with the tips of his bandaged fingers for the exact spot just below the sternum where he thought the first incision would have to be made. *Let's get to the heart of the matter, shall we?* he thought. What would be the best way – cut through the ribcage with a pair of trimming shears? Perhaps not; *be hard work getting through all those bones,* he thought, *getting through all those bars. You could do the whole thing with just the knife, of course. That's it; no need to go and get the shears at all, you can just use the knife, and cut upwards instead of down. Press firmly in with the blade to establish the entry at the navel – then rip up towards the sternum...* He talked himself through the entire operation... *feel your way in through the guts; reach up under the ribs...* His right hand clenched and flexed – which hurt – as he imagined all that grabbing and twisting and pulling – all the grabbing and dragging required to pull that ugly little beast out of its cage by the scruff of its neck. That was it; drag it out and cull it just like all the others. There it was, still beating, right there in the palm of his hand. He could just see it.

Mr F decided what he was going to do. What he *wanted* to do.

Needed to do, but

Need. Want. He wasn't quite sure. Couldn't quite hear which was the right word to use in the sentence. But he wasn't going to let that bother him. He went back into his bedroom. Avoiding catching sight of himself in the mirror, he pulled open the door of his wardrobe. It was empty, apart from a row of three suits hanging from the rail, each on a wooden coat-hanger. All three of them seemed to be cut from the same brown worsted cloth; he recognised them. Ignoring the question of how both of his old suits came to be hanging there in his wardrobe alongside his current one – which was impossible, obviously, because he'd thrown them away – he checked for which was the one he had worn to work that morning, the one least worn at the turn-ups and elbows. Finding it, he took it out and laid it, still on its hanger, on the bed. Then he stood and stared at it. He hated it – wished he had his knife again and could set to work on it right there and then. Hated it, because that brown suit lying there was really just about everything anyone might need to know about his life, *wasn't it, really* – he said, out loud, to no one at all. *Every single one of those thirty-three years. All the pay-slips, all the evenings, all of the weekends. Every single journey in to work on the twenty past seven. Says it all.*

Still, it had its uses. He reached down onto the bed, and one by one undid the buttons of the jacket – not easy, with your right hand in bandages, but he managed – and then with one neat gesture slid the trousers from their hanger. Holding them up by the waistband in his right hand, he took hold of the buckle of the belt with his left, and tore the belt from its loops. Then he threw the trousers on the bedroom floor – he didn't just drop them; he threw them, threw them against the bedroom wall so that they slid down onto the floor in a crumpled heap. They'd never be fit to wear in the morning now.

Then Mr F said, out loud again, in a voice thick with anger but oddly calm, and quite loudly – as if he wanted that young man to be able to hear him out there in the bathroom – *Right, young man. Now you're for it.* He transferred the belt buckle to his right hand, and then with his left hand wound the leather of the belt tightly around his fist, like a boxer bandaging himself before the fight, ignoring the pain, and leaving just the last foot and a half of the leather belt hanging free. He did it quickly and easily, as if this was a familiar action.

Where had Mr F learnt to do that? Had he seen someone else do it?

Who, I wonder. His father? I don't think so.

Now he did look at himself in the mirror. He raised his right hand for a moment, and stared at the picture that made; the wound was starting to hurt again now, to throb – but that didn't worry him. In fact, it made him all the more determined to finish the job. For a moment it looked as though it was himself he was going to beat, as if he was going to slash at the image of himself standing naked in the glass with the belt. But if that had been his intention, he clearly thought better of it. He walked out of the bedroom, back across the hall, into the bathroom (the light was already on, so he didn't have to stop for the light-switch) and without stopping to look at the face to check that it really was the boy, because he knew it was, who else could it be with that white skin – *If I told you once, I told you a thousand times; the most important thing in this business is choice of skin,* he muttered to himself as he drew back his arm – without taking any particular aim, he began to methodically slash with the belt across the legs, stomach and chest of the hanging body, once from the right, once from the left, then again from the right and again from the left, using the edge of the leather to cut at the flesh so hard he seemed determined to make it bleed. He worked very calmly, putting the full force of his body behind each blow; each time the leather fell, he would stop and look, to see if it had split the skin. It hadn't, so he would slash again, more furious still, pulling his arm right back in preparation before he landed the blow.

Mr F kept going until the pain in his hand became unbearable.

★

Although there seemed to be no blood in the hanging body that he could find, he himself had plenty. The pursed lips of the wound on his hand parted, and his blood began to seep through the bandage, staining it scarlet. Exhausted, he unwound the belt, and let it drop onto the bathroom lino. He stood there, breathing heavily, too tired to raise his arm even one more time. He stood, and watched, and waited. Waited to see the results of his patient handiwork. Waited for the moment when the first roses of bruising would begin to bloom beneath the boy's skin.

★

And that's where it ends, tonight's dream. With him standing there and staring at the body, waiting for whatever happens next. This means that there is no screaming; not tonight. Nonetheless, Mr F is still breathing prettily heavily when he wakes up at ten past four that morning. He reaches out and puts the bedside light on and sees that the bandage has come unwound and that there is, as he feared, blood spotting his sheets. His left hand is throbbing savagely, and his right arm – as he lies there, he is not sure if he is imagining this or not – his right arm and wrist ache. They ache just as if he'd been

Suddenly, he can't stand it. He can't stand the night-time smell of himself, and he can't stand lying there and hearing the disgusting sound of himself panting like some foul-breathed animal. He makes himself sit up, and swings his legs out from under the covers. He sits there in his pyjamas for a bit, the sweat cooling in the small of his back, and gets his breath back. He checks (he can't help it) to make sure that his suit trousers aren't lying crumpled anywhere on the bedroom floor, but they aren't; they're still safely in the wardrobe, where he hung them last night. Of course they are. He steels himself to get up off the bed and go to the bathroom and turn on the light and get himself a drink of water.

When he gets there he just has time to stare briefly straight at his face in the bathroom mirror, and to notice that his blue eyes are more fiercely pale than they've ever been, before he leans over the basin and is violently sick.

If Mr F shocks or disgusts you at this point in the story, then all I would say is: forgive him. In fact, in all that we are going to be seeing this man go through, forgive him. He had to fight this battle on his own. This was, after all, in another time, almost in another country – and besides, don't we all have to fight this battle on our own? When the knife strikes, none of us knows anything.

And don't accuse him; no one can help what they see when their eyes are closed. No one can be blamed for that – not Leda with her swan, not Pasiphaë with her bull, not the Lapith bride, grappling slowly on the bed with her very own centaur. Every bestial wedding is preceded by its dream. Isn't that why, at the circus, when the lion crouches and soaks the sawdust with its gushing piss, the children scream – because they long to see it leap? Long to see the man with the whip sent sprawling on his back; long to see the beast dine at leisure in the guts of its vanquished master. To see it lick his face, and take its pleasure.

So, as I say, don't blame or accuse him. In fact, wish him well.

fourteen

The next morning, the first cigarette of the day sickened Mr F, and he stubbed it out after one drag. Then, suddenly, standing there at the kitchen table, steadying himself (and again, this sensation was one that he felt first in the pit of his stomach; it nearly made him vomit again), he was struck by a mad hope. Maybe he'd simply got this all wrong. *Maybe it wasn't him.* Maybe it wasn't Beauty in the dream at all. The idea made him shiver.

He got dressed so fast that he tore the top button from his shirt (his fingers just wouldn't work properly; they felt cold), and he had to jam the knot of his tie right up tight to hold his collar closed. He couldn't find his hat, but for once that didn't matter; slamming the door shut behind him, Mr F went down his stairs two and three at a time (he should have been more careful on that worn stair-carpet; he could have come to grief) and then ran, all the way, to Peckham Rye Station. There was no queue at the ticket office, thank God, and he just made the early train. Arriving breathless at Skin Lane at twenty-five to eight, he found the front door still locked, but fortunately, as Chief Cutter, he had his own key. Once inside and upstairs, he checked his watch, and tried to think sensibly about what he ought to do to get himself ready for the boy's arrival. He went to the cupboard, and laid all his tools out in a row on his bench – but that only took a few minutes. He paced up and down the length of the window in his white coat, endlessly checking the buttons. Then he stood very still, and just concentrated on not letting his right hand shake. When he heard the first of his other colleagues coming up the stairs, he busied himself pretending to lay out his tools all over again; that way, no one had any reason to speak to him beyond a brief *Good morning.* He tried not to look at the empty doorway more than was strictly necessary. Then, at two minutes to eight, the boy arrived.

Somehow, Mr F managed to behave as if this was the start of a perfectly normal day. He even managed to say *Much better, thank you,* when the boy asked him how he was feeling this morning. They resumed their work on the pile of collars and cuffs.

Just occasionally, while he was working, Mr F had to pause and bite his lips, to force what felt like bile back down into his stomach.

That's what hope feels like, sometimes.

*

Not for nothing had this man spent thirty-three years concentrating; he not only managed to get all of his own skins cut by dinnertime, he also managed to take every chance he got to stare at the boy while he worked on his pile. Luckily, he knew that no one else in the workroom would think that there was anything particularly odd about him doing this, not even the boy himself; after all, Mr F was surely meant to be watching him like a hawk, making sure there were no slip-ups like yesterday's. This was the boy's first full day with a knife, remember.

Mr F was nothing if not methodical in his scrutiny. He checked the hair first, obviously. Its colour hadn't changed. The mysterious dark shadows were all still there, and when he saw this, his heart turned over in his chest. But then he told himself that he didn't believe any of that old nonsense about things like this happening at first sight; you always had to check for flaws. *Always check a skin thoroughly before proceeding,* that's what the book said. And so he did; glance by glance, he went on to inspect not just Beauty's hair and neck, but his whole body. The way the sleeves of his white coat covered his arms, and what that told him about the arms underneath. Everything the cut of his trousers gave away when he hung his coat up at dinnertime. The backs of his hands, which still hadn't got a single hair on them; the way he cupped his fingers when he smoked his cigarette at the tea-break.

Nothing.

★

Mr F was stubborn. He wouldn't admit defeat. Not on the Tuesday, not on Wednesday and not even on the Thursday or late on Friday afternoon, when the boy wished him goodnight. Even on the train home, he was still checking, going through everything again, piece by piece: the hair, the skin, the arms, the hands. The curve of each one of the boy's fingers. As he ran his Friday night bath, watching the steam from the hot water gradually obscure his staring face in the washbasin mirror, it occurred to him that the boy was probably running himself a bath at that very same moment – after all, cleaning up and putting on a fresh white shirt before going out on a Friday night, that was exactly what a young man of his age ought to be doing – and so he took this opportunity to check through everything again; he closed his eyes, and imagined being there to watch him get undressed. Imagined seeing everything. The flattened triangles of dark hair under his arms, left and right; the thin sheets of muscle across his upper ribs stretching like opening fans as he pulled his week-day shirt over his head.

His stomach. His fine-boned shins and ankles as he stepped into the bath. The hairs on the inside of his thighs, each one waving gently under the hot water.

But there was still nothing.

What about after he's got out and dried himself, then – Mr F got round behind him, and checked the colour of the damp hair curling on the back of his neck before he combed it; checked the colour of the skin on the back of his neck as he turned down his tight white collar; watched his fingers as they did it.

Still, nothing.

It wasn't working. No matter how hard he looked, no matter how hard he searched for the flaw – for that small, overlooked detail of skin or muscle or hair that was wrong, or was damaged, or that just didn't fit, just didn't *match –* he couldn't find it. He turned off the gushing taps, and for just a moment the surface of the scalding water in the bath became still; another mirror. He stepped into it, his mind a blank.

★

Twenty minutes later, Mr F gets out of the bath, puts on his dressing-gown and walks dripping into the living-room.

He sits down in his chair.

He doesn't bother with the tea or his tobacco and papers; he just needs to do this one last time. He has to be sure. He doesn't even put the fire on.

He closes his eyes. In his dream, he sees himself come calmly up the stairs, open the door, and proceed into the bedroom. He undresses, then walks into the hallway and pauses for a moment with his hand on the bathroom door

door-handle. Then, he takes a deep breath – and pauses again. He stands there, with his hand just resting on the door-handle, and is suddenly aware of a new feeling inside himself. There is an ache in his chest, and in his throat; it is the ache of unshed tears. Just before he opens the door and goes in, he promises himself that tonight, he is going to try very hard to change things. He wants to forget about the last time, the time with the belt – in fact he doesn't want to ever go back there again, not ever – no; what he wants to do tonight is to cut the boy down. He wants to get him down and lay him out on the bed. It doesn't seem right, leaving him hanging there right beside the open window like that.

He'll get cold.

He's going to go into the kitchen and get his knife from the drawer (why his knife from Scheiner's should be here in the flat he doesn't know – and he doesn't care; this is just something he needs to do). It shouldn't be hard – even the thickest of ropes will part like butter if you use a fresh blade, and take it strand by strand. He supposes that the only really tricky part will be making sure he doesn't catch the skin on his ankles – and then making sure the boy doesn't slip through his arms when the rope finally gives way of course. He thinks he knows how he'll do it – he's never taken the whole weight of somebody else's body before, but he's sure he'll manage. He'll have to stand on the toilet seat with one foot either side of him, and then hook his free left arm firmly around the back of his knees while he's working on the rope; that's it. Then, when he sees the final strands of the rope starting to give way, he'll wrap both arms tight around his legs – it'll be fine, he knows it will – and then, slowly, taking his time (bending his knees, bracing himself, using his back properly) he'll lower the boy down until he's got him safely laid out in the bath. Just like he usually does, he'll talk to himself all the way through it – just quietly, under his breath, nothing too loud. That'll help. It'll reassure the boy, too. Let him know that everything's all going to be alright. *I've got you. Daddy's got you. That's it. I've got you – there we go…* that sort of thing. Lowering him down, safe and sound, and then laying him gently down in the bathtub.

When he thinks about staring down at him like that, gazing at him lying there stretched out on the cold white enamel of the bathtub, Mr F forgets all about taking him into his bedroom. He thinks of something that he once heard as a child, in church, the phrase *to have and to hold*, and he finds himself wishing that his back wasn't aching like it is now, because then he could get down on his knees and find a way of picking him up somehow, of reaching down into the bath and lifting him up and cradling him in his arms – warming him up a bit. He knows that the boy is dead (that's another phrase that comes to mind, *dead weight*; he thinks he understands it now) but nonetheless he wants to hold him tight; to hold him tight and rock him back and forth and whisper gently in his ear *I've got you. I've got you. That's it; I've got you; sssh.*

Mr F sits there in his chair, thinking all of this, until it is dark. Eventually, of course, he nods off.

★

It's gone seven when he starts awake. He's cold – shivering, still naked under his wet dressing-gown. He knows he ought to get dried off and get himself off to bed before he makes himself ill. Oddly enough, as he gets up and starts doing all the things he has to do before he can turn the lights out and go to bed, Mr F is quite sure that the dream won't visit him again tonight. Why should it? Whatever message it had to give him has surely been delivered. Half-heartedly, he begins to lay the kitchen table for his supper – plate, knife, fork – and even gets as far as putting some water on for the potatoes, but then he turns the gas out again. It is still only eight o'clock, but he knows he is going to need all the sleep he can get. He also knows that he can't deny it any longer; he had been right first time. It was him. It was Beauty in the dream.

At the moment that he admits this, Mr F is standing at his kitchen table. He sits down. He places his hands, palm down, either side of his empty dinner plate, and then balls them into fists. He takes a deep breath. Then, with his fists balled and his eyes closed, he finally says out loud the sentence that has been running silently round his head for six days and nights now, the sentence he first heard whispered in his ear back there in the upstairs workroom. If the question he needed to ask the stranger in his bathroom was *Where have you come from,* then he now has his answer. He hears it sent back to him by the close walls of his kitchen.

You were here all the time.

In this strange manner, and with no one there to hear him, Mr F spoke of his love for the very first time.

2

"Those who suffer this disability carry a great weight of loneliness, guilt, shame and other difficulties."

Evening Standard, *July 4th, 1967*

Come the first week of May, something extraordinary happens to the streets of South London – even to the shabby ones like those through which Mr F made his way to work. Anyone would think some royal princess or beauty was about to arrive, the way those front gardens behave. Roses which have spent the winter as a tangle of dead thorns suddenly remember themselves, and bud; the honeysuckles wriggle free from their twists of rusty wire, and hurry up the trellis to secure a good vantage point. Red and yellow tulips form up in clumsy ranks beside the front paths, splashing their colour around quickly before the grass chokes them; purple and white lilacs ruthlessly elbow the privet hedges out of the way. As the air gets warmer, and big white clouds begin to pile up in the bright blue sky, neighbourhood after neighbourhood gives itself over to a frenzy of expectation. Mothers scrub their children in preparation for their very first outings to fragrant parks and blooming beauty spots; special trains are laid on to see the bluebells at Kew. Swifts and swallows begin to scream and twitter as they circle the domestic eaves, and in the windows of the haberdashers, rolls of floral prints presage the joys of imminent summer. Even the humble dandelions take their chance, and crowd the pavements. No space is wasted. Where the soil is too starved for a cherry or magnolia, there is at least a dog rose; where no rose, at least an elder or a white-flowered bramble. Buddleias claw their way out of the brickwork lining the railway tracks; by London Bridge Station, the bark on the plane trees splits open like sclerotic skin, as if the ancient wooden limbs were stretching in anticipation. One monster has grown so old that it has finally overcome the black iron railing encircling its trunk, enveloping it; as the bark strains to cover the metal, it flakes away in great sooty plates, revealing the pale pink flesh of the new life underneath. Everywhere, the blood quickens.

Some people, however, seem to notice nothing of all this. As they walk to work, their eyes stay down. They don't even appear to smell the lilacs. Clearly, something is wrong with them – but what, exactly?

I have a suggestion.

In the middle pages of the story, which were the ones which Mr F always more or less ignored when his father read it to him as a child, there is an elaborate description of the gardens which the Beast has built around his magic castle. These are stocked with every rarity his army of gardeners can obtain – arbours of roses foaming and tumbling in every known colour, tulips gleaming like jewels between hedges of clipped box – and so on. But the Beast himself takes pleasure in none of this. As the gravel of the long esplanades is raked by the setting sun, and he begins his evening round of inspection, he hears no birdsong – not even the scarlet macaws shrieking from their great gilded aviaries. For him, the evening is punctuated only by the lonely padding of his solitary paws. When he pauses to survey his domain, all he can ever see amongst all those fountains and marble statues is the absence of the one living figure he looks for; Beast that he is, when he lifts his muzzle to the air, it is never to catch the perfume of the jasmine, or a rose. Every night, he hopes the wind may bring him fresh news of the one whom all of this has been so cunningly constructed to lure. The sights and sounds of the spring are wasted on him; he lives only in his mind.

My point is that the little boy should have been encouraged to pay more attention to this passage. At least then when he grew up he would have had something to help him recognise his symptoms.

one

It may seem strange to us now, but at the time in which this story is set, people thought it was very important to be neatly dressed if you had to go and visit a doctor. It was the done thing; a mark of respect; a measure of the gravity of the occasion. There was also doubtless the lurking feeling that neatness – cleanliness – might in itself somehow ward off any possible bad news; news, for instance, that the infection had taken hold; that no, the tumour was not benign.

Perhaps that was why, on the morning of the second Monday in May, 1967 (which was a warm and sunny one), Mr F took such care with how he dressed for work. Such great care, in fact, that he almost made himself late; anyone would think that something in him would have preferred not to go. He shaved himself as close as he could, twice, with a new blade, chafing the skin on his neck quite badly in the process; then he scrubbed under his fingernails with carbolic until the quicks were nearly raw. Moving into the bedroom, he faced himself squarely in the wardrobe mirror, chin up, and knotted his tie as tightly as it would go – too tight, in fact, even for him; he had to relent and loosen it slightly. Then he sat on the end of the bed, and did the same with his shoelaces. Standing again, he worried that his brown suit was beginning to show some signs of wear, so took the jacket off and brushed it down. Then, having checked his appearance several last times, he collected his hat from the hallstand, locked his front door behind him and walked to the station with his most military stride. A casual passer-by, seeing him all dressed up and striding out like that in the warm spring sunshine, might have guessed he was a nervous lover, eager to create the right impression when that all-important pair of eyes caught their first glimpse of the day – they might even have wondered why he wasn't carrying a bunch of daffodils. But we who know him better will notice that the set of his jaw is too defensive for that, and that he is carrying both his hands ever so slightly clenched. Especially the left one, the one disfigured by a small but fresh scar. No, it's definitely not good news that this man is expecting.

Still, credit where credit is due; a brave face is always best, don't you think?

★

All the way to work that morning, Mr F really had only one thought in his mind: *Is it going to show?* Standing on the platform at Peckham Rye Station, he could feel the sunlight striking his face, showing him up. Every time he imagined or even tried to imagine what might happen the first time he found himself face to face with Beauty, his stomach turned, and his nerve almost failed him – indeed, if his feet hadn't been so used to the journey, he would have surely turned tail. There was a particularly bad moment on the train when he thought he heard the woman sitting next to him muttering *Just go home* under her breath at him, twice, and for a split second he even found himself considering pulling the emergency cord. But then he took some discreet deep breaths, and told himself not to be ridiculous – that was something people only did in films. He knew he was in danger of starting to talk out loud again, so he concentrated on keeping the sound turned down in his head. Fortunately, he was good at that. The fusillade of slamming doors at London Bridge Station sounded as if it was coming from a battle several miles away; once he was safely across the bridge, he managed the whole of the walk from there to Skin Lane in more or less complete silence. All he had to do, he decided, as he turned left out of All Hallows Lane, was concentrate. Concentrate on the big consignment of collars and cuffs which Mr Scheiner had insisted they needed to have ready for collection by the first tea-break. Gradually, a plan began to crystallise. If he left the job of parcelling up the order to one of his colleagues, he could surely legitimately spend the first part of the day downstairs in the office, checking the paperwork. That way, he probably wouldn't even have to wish the boy good morning.

*

It was stupid of him, in a way, to have headed down the stairs when he did. Having successfully got through the first half of the morning without seeing him, he had then debated with himself whether to stay put in the office or to risk smoking his mid-morning cigarette out on the front steps as normal for far too long. If he'd had the sense to just dispense with his usual timetable and go for his smoke ten minutes early, he'd have been safe; as it was, by the time he'd made up his mind the tea-break was nearly over, and the boy was just coming back up.

As I told you, the staircases at Number Four were narrow; so narrow that two people couldn't really pass in comfort. As soon as he saw the boy, Mr F stopped where he was; Beauty, of course, didn't. He had no reason to. This meant that in just a few moments their bodies were going to be only inches apart, and that the boy was going to have to brush right past him. Mr F couldn't quite believe that this was going to happen; but it was.

The sun, ridiculously, was streaming in through a landing window, and shining straight into his face. It really was a beautiful morning.

He pressed his back against the wall, and instinctively looked down at his feet (anything to avoid the boy's eyes). As he did it, he felt his stomach muscles contract under his shirt – he never liked to be touched, as you know, but this was different. Whatever he'd imagined, it certainly hadn't been this.

You or I might have experienced his sensations as exhilaration – or even pleasure. But for Mr F, they could only be panic. Terror. The stairs were just too narrow; there wasn't room to breathe – and where in God's name was he supposed to look?

Anywhere; just not at his face.

Especially not at his mouth.

Here he comes.

*

The extraordinary thing about these situations (I have no option but to assume you know what I'm talking about) is how very calm one manages to be. As the boy squeezed past, Mr F found himself saying, with that peculiar kind of mock-camaraderie that often infects a workplace on a Monday morning,

"Alright there?"

– to which the boy replied, in a cheerful grumble, and without pausing in his journey up towards the bright window,

"That tea-break never gets any longer, does it, Mr F? Still, nice to see the sun."

And that was it; the boy was already safely past and continuing up the stairs. There had been no contact; Mr F should have been able to unclench his stomach and start breathing normally again – but instead of concentrating on that, he found himself helplessly continuing the conversation. It was as if his idiot of a mouth just couldn't bear to let the boy go; as if it wouldn't do what it was told. It even shaped itself into a peculiar sort of half-smile as he called out – still not daring to look up at Beauty's retreating back –

"Yes it is – and no, it certainly doesn't. No peace for the wicked, as they say."

(Was that the sound of a laugh?)

"Too right, Mr F," the boy called back, after stopping for half a stair. He reached the landing, walked past the landing window (the sunlight flashed once from his hair – Mr F hadn't been able to resist looking up) and disappeared. If he had noticed the rather forced – indeed, half-strangled – sound of Mr F's voice, he didn't show it; if he thought there was anything odd about Mr F instigating such an uncharacteristically relaxed conversation – and on a busy Monday morning, too – he didn't show that either. As far as he was concerned, this was just another Monday morning. Rather a fine one – but apart from that, nothing special.

Mr F, however, had to wait fully two minutes before he got his breath back. He leant against the wall, closed his eyes (the sunlight was so strong he could see the blood in his eyelids) and took the time to realise the truth of his situation. For the boy, nothing at all had changed. But for him, everything had.

Bloody everything.

Jesus.

★

Given this change in his circumstances, it was perhaps unfortunate that on this particular Monday (*on the first day,* I almost said, *of our hero's new life*) Mr F should have had to spend so much of his time in a small room crowded with people. Just when he badly needed time to think, he was given none. This is how it happened.

On the Friday, Mr Scheiner had been seen hovering in the upstairs workroom, rubbing his hands together while he inspected the progress of the work. His visit was ostensibly to see how the big order was coming on, but also, he said, he wanted to have a quick word with Mr F. He was pleased to see that he'd got young Ralph hard at work, he said – and after he'd jokingly asked Mr F if the boy was behaving himself, he took him to one side and explained there was a job he wanted to discuss – a slightly delicate one. He was sorry to have to burden him with this at such a busy time, he said, but he was sure Mr F was understanding; a cousin of his wanted to bring a young lady in to choose her furs for a new coat, and she was, as Mr Scheiner put it, in a wincing half whisper, *not his daughter, Mr F.* No great favours were being requested, or done, in the matter of a discount – *costs are still costs, even for family, Mr F, as you well know* – but the cousin wanted to show off his connections in the trade a little ... bring the girl in, show her some styles and some samples, let her think she can choose whatever she fancies – *make her feel special, Mr F, that's the idea.* Obviously it wouldn't be suitable to bring this young lady up to the cutting-room, so what Mr Scheiner proposed was that Mr F should bring a selection of skin samples down to the office for lunchtime on Monday. The boy could help – it would do him good to watch his uncle working a customer – and Mrs Kesselman could be there to chaperone and take measurements when required. Fox, plenty of top-range mink and a couple of the fancier skins just to impress her, that was what was required.

Standing there on the stairs, Mr F remembered his instructions, which until that moment had gone completely out of his mind. So after he'd got his breath back, calmed himself down, had his cigarette and told himself for the twentieth time that morning that he had no option but to go back upstairs and pretend that this particular Monday of his life was just like any other, that's what Mr F found himself doing; getting things ready for somebody else to stage a seduction. He went upstairs, and started hooking a selection of pelts down from their rails in the ceiling and throwing them down to Beauty to catch – all the while still trying not to look too directly into his face.

*

The mechanics (I almost said, *the economics*) of the scene which took place in Mr Scheiner's office that Monday lunchtime were brutally simple. Everyone knew their place, and their allotted role; everyone knew the rules, and nobody was saying anything.

The office was a small room at the best of times, and by the time all the principal players were gathered, it began to be a warm one. When the girl arrived, she was already excited; however, she knew better than to let it show. As she was handed out from his car by Mr Scheiner's cousin (a well-preserved forty-five-year-old; his money's in handbags and belts), she swung her heels onto the cobbles of Skin Lane in conscious imitation of her film-actress idols. As she removed a stray hair from her mouth and looked up and down the Lane, her studied air of glamorous condescension was almost convincing, but not quite; although she behaved as if she just had been driven straight from Pinewood, Mr Scheiner was not all that surprised to be told that no, they hadn't had to drive far really, just from her parents' house. Once the introductions had been made, and Mr Scheiner had offered the girl his chair (she made a very good show of squeezing round behind the desk; that dress was tight) and

Mr F had laid out his first few samples, the bluffing continued. Leaning over her (he knew his cousin wouldn't mind), Mr Scheiner talked a blue streak at the girl, spreading his expertise before her like a peacock would its well-practised tail. He rattled on about the varying attractions of the different species he had selected for her to consider from the point of view of value for money, wearability and, of course, (a brief glance here over her head at his cousin) suitability as an investment. Mr Scheiner's act was skilfully pitched; he would never have talked in quite this way to a middle-class woman – to a woman with a husband in the City and two good-quality coats in her wardrobe already, for instance. In that case, he wouldn't have presumed to stand quite so close, and his manner would have respectfully implied that madam already knew all about value for money – madam's mother, after all, would have been sure to advise her daughter on the importance of quality when it came to choosing one's furs. But he knows that Maureen (that's the girl's name; she's a strikingly green-eyed red-head, and twenty-four) doesn't know about any of all that. To state the obvious, as you can see from her slightly overdone make-up and the would-be elegance of the way she's perched on the edge of that chair, she's making up this whole thing of being a lady as she goes along.

She does it, it must be said, pretty well. She lets herself be flattered, rather than patronised, by Mr Scheiner's attentions, and then she graciously takes off her gloves and gets down to the business of making her choice. Like a lady should, she flinches rather at some of the more outlandish pelts she is shown, and won't even touch them. The small shriek of dismay she produces at the sight of anything too obviously animal – the stiff black hairs of a colobus pelt, the dangling feet and claws on a bundle of untrimmed martens– has its desired effect, which is to make her boyfriend smile approvingly. He lights a cigar. The white foxes, which Mr

Scheiner had thought she might well fall for when he had seen how she was dressed, are toyed with for a moment, but then rejected as being too old-fashioned – *a bit too common*, is how she puts it. She is momentarily intrigued by the names of the different shades of ranch mink as they are recited for her benefit – *"Argenta"; "Royal Pastel", very nice – and this is "Autumn Haze" madam, our newest line*, purrs Mr Scheiner at her elbow – but none of their coffee, butterscotch or chocolate ice-cream colours seem to quite satisfy her. She picks up a long-haired red fox-skin – *Kamchatka fox we call that, madam; Russian, very nice* – strokes it, and giggles, and holds it close to her face and asks her boyfriend what he thinks. He of course would never dream of saying what he is actually thinking (he has half an erection – and besides, he has already agreed his discount with Mr Scheiner, and knows he can afford anything on the table); he merely shrugs, and indicates that he will consent to whatever makes her happy. There is a pause. Mr Scheiner and his cousin watch the girl with two distinct kinds of more or less well-disguised greed on their faces as she giggles and strokes her furs, but they are saying nothing. They let the girl have her moment; it's only fair. As she dallies, smoothing her pale hands first across one fur and then another – fox, mink, chinchilla: fire, smoke, velvet – the belt and handbag manufacturer glances across at Mr Scheiner, and can't resist blowing the thought *Women, what are they like?* out into the room with a mouthful of cigar-smoke. He's enjoying himself, too. He especially likes the way Scheiner's nephew or whoever he is can't help but stare; the kid can't be more than sixteen, but obviously already has a taste for the ladies. His eyes are like saucers. Generously, the older man takes these stares as a compliment on his own good taste in female merchandise, and at one point in the proceedings even gives the boy what he imagines to be an avuncular wink. Mr Scheiner, on his part, remembers the small explosions of dirty laughter the two men shared when this visit was first discussed on the telephone, and watches the way his cousin handles his cigar. He secretly enjoys the knowledge that the man isn't going to get quite such a good deal as he thinks he is. When the red foxes are rejected, he optimistically raises one eyebrow – the girl seems to be hovering on the edge of choosing a pastel mink after all, the most expensive of her options. Will she? Won't she? *Women*, Mr Scheiner thinks too.

Mrs Kesselman, meanwhile, waits patiently in her corner, and lets the men get on with it. Although she appears to be paying very little attention – she's only there, after all, to give some spurious respectability to the room before doing the measuring in private later – she sees everything. Personally, she rather admires the way the girl is letting the men think she is stupid. She does wish the boy wouldn't gawp at the customer quite so obviously.

Beauty, who wasn't sure if he'd even be allowed to stay in the room, since his only official role was to help Mr F bring the armfuls of samples down from the workroom – Beauty, meanwhile, can't quite believe his luck. He keeps himself quietly in the background – but makes sure that he has a clear view of everything. He is supposed to be learning the business, isn't he? When the girl twists one of the red fox-skins round her neck and poses with it as if she was on a magazine cover, he watches the way Mr Scheiner and his cousin briefly swap glances over her head, and takes note. When the cousin then winks at him, he is caught off-guard for a moment – but going on instinct, risks returning an appropriately discreet grin of his own. He wasn't sure if that was allowed, so is pleased to see that the older man apparently approves of his contribution. He thinks he's starting to get the hang of this now; this is how men behave, when they're all thinking about the same thing. In fact, as the scene draws towards its conclusion, he begins to feel that it is only right and proper that Maureen should include him in her appeals for judgement around the room. After all, it's not just the one man she's got to please with her choice, it's all of them – so long as she realises that, then he's happy to lend his approval. She certainly seems to; from where he's standing, he'd have to say that the young lady has looked up at him and offered him her smile a good few times more often than she strictly needed to.

Well, he is more her own age than any of the other men in the room. And let's face it, that cousin of Mr Scheiner's is no oil-painting, is he?

No wonder the boy's eyes are even brighter than usual.

Finally, Maureen asks to see the red foxes one last time. Mr F retrieves them from Beauty, and spreads them across the desk. One last little pantomime of hesitation, and Maureen announces her choice. It's going to be the foxes after all. She thinks that red colour will do wonders for her eyes.

Very good; the men approve. Mr Scheiner will send out a few telegrams and find out which of the brokers he knows has got the best Kamchatkas in stock this very afternoon – not always the easiest fur to find at this time of year, and not one so often requested these days (he commends madam on her distinctive taste) – but he's sure he'll manage. Meanwhile, once Mrs Kesselman has taken the measurements, perhaps a little lunch at that place on Queen Street where the fish is so good would be in order? Mr Scheiner's cousin couldn't agree more.

*

And Mr F?

If he had made any further plan for the day, it was only

to keep the boy at a reasonable distance; he didn't want any repetition of that unpleasant incident on the stairs. Trouble is, here in the office, there is nowhere else that Beauty can be except a couple of feet away – and to make matters worse, he has somehow ended up standing right behind Mr F. This means that he has to constantly worry that he might accidentally stumble back into him for some reason. Brush against him. He is also, because he is back in the room where Mrs Kesselman stitched it, unusually aware of the healing wound on his left hand. He remembers the slipping of the knife. The way the room went very quiet just before it happened. The incessant ticking of that distant clock. Whatever else happens, he has to make sure that nothing like that happens again.

Mostly, he manages the scene by not looking at anything or anyone too directly. He waits, with his eyes lowered, and does as he is told, clearing and re-stocking the desk with samples as Mr Scheiner instructs him; a lot of the time, he simply looks down at the floor. Because of this, he is more or less oblivious to the cat's-cradle of glances, signals and unspoken assumptions that is being woven above the girl's head through the cigar-smoke-laden air. It's not that he's prudish, just that this particular game is not one that has ever had anything to do with him; as always, he absents himself – and on this particular morning, of course, even more purposefully than usual. It isn't easy for a big man to efface himself, but he really works at it, and thinks he has almost succeeded, but then, just at the last minute, the girl asks him if she might just look at those three red Russian foxes one final time, and he has to turn to the boy to retrieve the armful of heavy, flaming pelts. At this point in the proceedings, Mr F suddenly finds that he can't keep himself or his eyes to himself any longer. Beauty, evidently not expecting him to turn round quite that suddenly, must have been slowly inching himself closer and closer in, so as to be in the best possible position for getting a good look at everything, because when Mr F turns, he discovers that the boy's face – the boy's bright eyes, and the boy's half-open *mouth* – is right there, only inches away from his.

To make matters worse – much worse – instead of immediately recomposing his features into those of a dutiful junior, the boy flicks on a quick conspiratorial grin, and shares it. He clearly expects Mr F to grin right back, as if they were in possession of the same secret.

As if that slight twisting of the lips was an agreed signal. As if they were thinking about the same thing.

Mr F –

Mr F can't think.

All of this happens very quickly – so quickly that only Mrs Kesselman sees it. She sees Mr F flinch, hesitate, blink, and then, clumsily, grab the armful of pelts from the boy and turn to lay them out on the desk with a dark cloud of disapproval spreading across his face. She thinks, of course, that Mr F is annoyed with the boy for staring at the customer like that, and *Quite right too*, she thinks – she didn't quite see why Mr Scheiner had seen fit to have him in the room in the first place.

But Mrs Kesselman misunderstood the moment entirely.

Remember, the young man's face was the one part of the body in his dream that Mr F had never really seen; in a way, it was the one part of it that he didn't yet know off by heart. And there it now was, suddenly right up close – closer to him than that of a fellow passenger on a crowded, standing-room-only, five-forty-nine train. Bright-eyed, slightly flushed, and freshly shaved. Lips coming together in an almost-invisible but unmistakably knowledgeable smile. Very sure of itself. Very *entitled*.

It was the face of a complete stranger.

No wonder Mr F flinched.

As he recovered himself, and as he laid the three beautiful fox pelts one after another down on the table like a fairy-tale promise in three parts (Beauty, Luxury, Wealth), Mr F was almost overwhelmed by a sudden feeling of *not knowing anything*. Of being the only person in the room who didn't know how he was supposed to behave. Almost, of being underwater. Was this how he was going to have to live now?
Was it?

*

Once Maureen had made her choice, and the attention of the room had been diverted to the subject of measurements, and lunch, Mr F busied himself with gathering up the furs, wanting to get out of the room as quickly as he reasonably could. But while he was doing it (avoiding so much as even glancing at Beauty, never mind asking him to help) he realised that even after being that close – being *face to face* – he still couldn't for the life of him remember what colour the boy's eyes were. Dark, certainly. And a bit *fiery* – except that that was probably just the effect of how hot the room had become, what with all these people in it. Black. Was that possible? Do men really ever have *black* eyes?

He needs to take another look.

(Plenty of time for that later. Just take the furs upstairs.)

He's sweating now. He *hates* that.

★

When she gave her detailed report on Maureen's hair-colour, make-up, dress-sense and demeanour to her colleagues downstairs in the machine-room, Mrs Kesselman couldn't help but express some reservations. Part of her wanted to applaud the girl for her nerve – *Well listen, at least a decent coat she gets,* was how she put it – but eventually, she had to concur with the generally uncharitable mood. Despite her attempts to play the lady, this Maureen customer was clearly no better than she ought to be – and as Mrs Kesselman always said, *No woman ever gets given a fur coat for good reasons; if it's not to keep her on her back, it's to get her off his.* One of the two new girls, who'd stood on a chair to watch her get out of the car through one of the downstairs windows, summed up the final verdict of the room with a quick, derisive laugh:

"Russian foxes, is it? I think someone's been to see that Doctor fucking Zhivago a few too many times."

Of course, there was nothing particularly personal about this animosity; it was a point of principle with the machinists that no woman who ever put on a Scheiner's coat was as special as she thought she was. They could all tell you exactly what the expression on Maureen's face would be once her coat was ready; when her once-in-a-lifetime bribe was finally lifted onto her shoulders by her gentleman friend. These women knew all about the reasons why, and the special occasions when, a man buys his woman a fur. Oh yes; every time they nipped two skins together, ready for the needle, they knew.

two

It never occurred to Mr F at any point in that first week that he ought to do anything about his feelings for the boy. Even that string of words – *my feelings for him* – wouldn't have been one he would have known how to use at this point. As far as he was concerned, that was the sort of thing that belonged in other people's mouths. No; what he did instead was to think. He thought about him all the time.

Ever since that moment when he'd been so close to him in the downstairs office, Mr F hadn't been able to get the expression on Beauty's face out of his mind. It worried at him every time he came to rest. Try as he might, he just couldn't get used to the idea that Beauty knew nothing at all about what he inevitably saw as being *their* situation. You might've thought that he would have worked out by now how to distribute the weight of the boy's presence efficiently across his daily routine, but no; the extra physical effort required now that the body of his dreams was actually in the same room as him for eight and a half hours every working day took him completely by surprise. Two completely contradictory waves of sensation would regularly pick him up and tumble him in their surf. On the one hand, he felt the boy's presence in the room as something so intimate that he was in constant danger of blushing and sweating; on the other, he felt completely estranged from him, as if he was watching him from across some great distance – the width of the Thames, at least. Sometimes, he would *hear* these two sensations; his head would pound with the agitated thumping of his blood and breath and half-formed thoughts

– but the whole dismal cacophony would be echoing inside an absolute and resounding silence. These feelings bewildered him; they crashed over him, leaving him bruised and floundering. Sometimes, he thought the battering would wear him out.

Nothing of this showed; for a man who was drowning, he kept remarkably calm. As he bent his big strong back over the cutting bench, he would match the movement of his hands to the rhythm of his breathing; one breath, one sweep of the blade. Instinctively, he became even more of a stickler than ever for the angle of the knife, the precision of a ruled line; when he nailed a cut skin, each pin would be *exactly* half an inch from the next. He concentrated until his hands ached. Sometimes, he would set himself the task of not looking up at the boy for an entire two hours, by the clock. The phrase *keeping your head down* could have been invented for Mr F, that week.

★

Talking to him, that was his main problem. On the Tuesday, for instance, come half past ten, he'd still uttered barely a word to the boy. If he kept this up, he knew that someone was bound to ask him the one question which he really didn't want to hear, which was of course *Are you alright this morning, Mr F?* – so, just before the dinner-break, he forced himself to go and have a brief but proper conversation. Nothing that involved looking Beauty in the eye, you understand, just a couple of brief practical suggestions on trimming a musquash he'd seen him hesitating over. Even this simple task proved fraught, however. The phrases which had come so easily in the early days seemed to lodge themselves clumsily in his throat; he'd hear the sentences forming in his head *(Go on then; touch it!)* – but wasn't at all sure that they'd come out right. Not now that everything had changed. It wasn't the actual words so much that were the problem, he thought, as what *voice* he ought to use. If he was sterner than usual, the boy might ask if something was wrong; and if he was kind, too kind – well then he was sure to think there was.

Even if he didn't say so...

All the time, he had the obscure sensation that he ought to be protecting himself – but he had no idea from what, or how.

When that Tuesday evening came, and the workroom finally emptied, its silence came as a sweet relief; not having to think about what he ought to say next was an almost physical pleasure. Glad to be the only person left in the building, he happily cut and sorted and stacked and tidied with no sound to accompany him except the occasional whisper of parting skin until well gone eight o'clock. But this brief respite from his confusing thoughts didn't last, of course. After he'd swept up – he always enjoyed giving an empty room a good sweep, Mr F – he found himself standing by his bench, holding the knife the boy had been working with on the musquash – and they all came flooding back. He tried to think of ways he could have handled the afternoon differently – specifically, to think of what else he could or should have said, but whatever sentence he tried – and this is Mr F, remember, the man whose head was usually so full of voices – he just couldn't hear himself get to the end of it. He'd set up the scene in his mind, the boy would turn to look at him, he'd open his mouth to speak – and all the sound would disappear, leaving only the boy's face and eyes.

In the silence, he became very aware of the knife again, still lying there in his hand. He found himself wondering just how long after he'd put it down the metal of the brass handle would have retained the heat from the boy's fingers.

There was certainly none there now.

He put the knife away and turned the lights out one by one; this wasn't getting him anywhere, he thought. Really he ought to go home, and just try again tomorrow.

★

He did – but (as he was finding) nothing in his new life was going to be that easy. Finding seventeen matching Russian foxes of an appropriate quality and price for Maureen's coat, for instance, was proving harder than Mr Scheiner had first anticipated. Despite several phone-calls to close personal acquaintances, the first half a dozen strings of pelts, being all unused stock from the previous year, had failed to yield anything suitable at all. The abortive task of sorting them had taken two entire afternoons, and at the end of the second of them, the Thursday, Mr F, exasperated, had given Beauty the relatively simple task of clearing the bench and restoring some order to the workroom while he went downstairs to report on their failure to Mr Scheiner. However, the boy, somewhat over-zealous in his clearing away, had then proceeded to re-string skins belonging to two different dealers in the same bundle, and when Mr F got back upstairs, this error of the boy's seemed suddenly to be some kind of last straw. Despite himself, he forgot to be speechless.

"Oh, for Christ's sake!" he groaned, noticing the mistake at once, his voice thickening with frustration. "Have I been entirely wasting my time with you?"

The boy of course had no idea what Mr F was talking about, but he could see that it must have something to do with the fox-skins lying heaped on the table between them. He knew he'd rushed the job, but decided it was better to play genuinely taken aback than to admit to any possible mistake.

"I'm sorry, Mr F," he said, "I thought I'd – "

"Well you're not here to bloody *think*, are you?"

Anger, it seemed, was lubricating Mr F's throat; he was shaking. "You're here to be *told*. If you're not sure how to bloody do something, then bloody well ask. D'you know what – " (here Mr F, as if surprised by his own sudden eloquence, looked right away from the boy, picked up his knife, and sliced through the string holding the offending bundles together with one short stroke) " – it's young men like you make my life a bloody misery. Think you know it all, don't you?"

Beauty knew better than to say anything at this point; he'd learnt from dealing with his father that it was always better to keep *shtum* when they got like this.

"Go on then," barked Mr F, with his back demonstratively still turned. "Clear off out of it and leave me to sort this mess, why don't you."

OK, thought Beauty, flicking his eyes to Mr F's wristwatch. It was nearly half past five. Hanging up his white coat and collecting his jacket, he did as he was told – and it was only when the boy was gone and the room was suddenly quiet again that Mr F realised where the voice he'd just used had come from. Yes, he was sure of it; *If you're not sure how to bloody do something...* He could remember his father shouting that at him, years ago. In the kitchen, probably. Or up the stairs. This discovery made him feel uneasy; after all, that hadn't been – well, that wasn't what he'd meant. He hadn't meant to blame the boy, exactly – after all, he should really have supervised the sorting, not left him to it... He was could hear himself apologising to the boy the next morning already; hear himself stumbling through some half-baked explanation in his own, ill-fitting voice. Making a mess of every sentence he tried.

He was dreading it already.

Jesus.

In fact, thought Mr F, there was only one thing about his new situation that was definitely an improvement, and that was the fact that his dream hadn't bothered him for seven whole nights now.

★

When he got home that Friday night, Mr F decided it was time to take stock. He rolled up his sleeves, ran the hot water, and as he scrubbed his hands made a mental list of all the things he had seen Beauty do or say in the course of the last five days. The one he kept on coming back to was the moment in the office on the Monday with that red-head, when the boy's eyes had been so black and close. What was it about the expression on his face which made him feel as if he'd never seen the boy before? That they weren't colleagues, but... what? What was the word? *Strangers.* He still couldn't put a name to it. And there was another moment, on the Wednesday, when he'd seen him laughing on the steps with one of the girls from downstairs during the afternoon tea-break. He wondered what had they been laughing about – about that young lady-friend of Mr Scheiner's cousin's, probably. If so, what was it about her that they found so funny – that they so obviously *shared*? He'd noticed that when the boy laughed, throwing his head back like that, he still managed to keep one eye on his audience, as if making sure that the effect was the right one *(he must remember to get some more carbolic – this block was nearly finished)*. Then, when the girls had all gone back inside, just before he'd followed them up the steps, Beauty had stepped back out onto the street – he hadn't known Mr F was watching him, obviously – and quickly squatted down on his haunches in front of one of the barred basement windows to see his reflection. He was obviously pleased with what he saw, because no major adjustments were required; he just ran his hands quickly through his hair. Then he stood up, tightened the knot of his tie, threw back his shoulders and took the steps up to the front door two at a time.

There; that's better. All clean.

Mr F put down the nail-brush, and ran his wet hands though his own hair – and then carried on staring at himself, less than three feet away in the washbasin mirror. At the two lines under his eyes, cut with a blunt knife. He wondered if Beauty had been checking himself for the girl's benefit, or just for his own pleasure. And he thought about the way his brothers used to do that, last thing; run the palms of their hands over their shining, slicked-back hair, and then grin at themselves.

White shirts. Black hair. Eye to eye in the mirror.

He wiped away the steam with the palm of his hand, and looked again. His own hair was greying; he smoothed it back again anyway.

What did they know that he didn't, these young men?

And why was he thinking about his brothers again – why, when he'd seen the boy crouching in his suit like that to see himself in the glass, hadn't he been reminded of himself – of himself at sixteen? He supposed it was his skin – and the hair of course – very different. But most of all it was the expression in the eyes. He'd never looked at anyone like that. Not that he could remember, anyway.

Why was that?

*

Later that evening, after he's drawn the curtains, turning his whole bedroom rosy, Mr F catches sight of himself in a mirror again. Full-length, this time. He wonders whether the boy is standing naked in his bedroom too, right at this very minute, thinking about Maureen. He can just imagine it. He tries to mimic the boy's stance, to capture that moment when he pushed up the knot of his tie like that and threw his shoulders back. Behind him, he can see his single bed, with its carefully smoothed counterpane, and really for the very first time in his life Mr F thinks about the difference that thirty-three years can make to a body. He looks in his wardrobe mirror, and he measures out those years. He thinks, as he looks at himself, that he is old, and ugly, and confused.

three

If only he'd known it, Mr F had had good reason to shout at the boy like that. He wasn't the only one whose mind wasn't entirely on his work these days.

Late that Thursday afternoon, all Beauty had actually been thinking about was getting the job done as quickly as possible and getting himself downstairs. He needed to be sure of catching somebody down in the machine-room for a few minutes before she went home, you see, and it was twenty past five already – and that was why he mixed up the skins.

This *somebody* was the girl with whom Mr F had seen Beauty sharing a joke on the front steps the day before. She was just about the youngest of Mrs Kesselman's machinists, seventeen if she was a day, and although she looked small and sweet (that was very much the fashion, that summer), she was the one who had first used Beauty's nickname to his face – and he'd had his eye on her ever since. He couldn't say exactly, but there was just something about her that he liked more than the others; there was always an edge to her laughter – and to the way he'd catch her looking at him. Because he was the boss's nephew, and because Scheiner's was such a noisy, cramped building, full of gossip and watching eyes (not to mention the fact that the girl was a *shikse*), he'd known from the start that he'd have to manage the whole thing without getting caught. But he was clever. Hearing her mention to one of the other girls which number bus she caught home to Poplar, he'd waited for a rainy night, and then gone and joined the crowds queuing at the bus-stops under Cannon Street. In the confusion and wet, it hadn't been hard to squeeze into the seat next to her. She'd been surprised, but had soon caught on. Ever since then, he couldn't quite believe how easy it had all been. They had to be careful about being seen together too much at work of course, but it was amazing what you could get away with if you tried. If ever they found themselves going up the front door steps together first thing in the morning, for instance, he could greet her with a broadly grinned *Good morning*, and she could reply with a tart *And to you* – and no one would think anything of it. Even the other machinists – who prided themselves on having the sharpest eyes in London when it came to men and their tricks – didn't pick up anything untoward as they giggled their way past him on the steps; that was exactly the sort of half-familiar, half-rude jokiness that everyone seemed to expect to see being traded between the two youngest members of their respective workrooms. He was supposed to be a flirt, and she was supposed to give as good as she got; as all the newspapers agreed (not to mention Mrs Kesselman) that was how all young people behaved, *these days*. It was now seven weeks since that first conversation on the bus, and nearly four weeks since the first time he'd pushed her up against a wall two streets away from where she lived and kissed her (she'd liked it), and still no one in the building had the slightest idea.

So now you know why the boy had hesitated when Mr F had asked him if he had had a good weekend, and why he paused on the stairs when he heard the phrase *No peace for the wicked*. Both times, he couldn't help but think about his girl – and couldn't help but smile, either.

Talk about getting away with murder.

★

That Thursday evening, however, he was genuinely worried

about being seen with her. Mrs Kesselman was the one person in the building he knew they had to be wary of, and loitering downstairs at any other time than his allotted breaks was always risky; however, he thought that if he could get downstairs on the dot, he'd be able to catch Christine while Mrs Kesselman was still finishing her end-of-day reckoning with Mr Scheiner in the office. He just needed a couple of minutes; he had to tell her he was sorry, but it wasn't going to be able to make their usual five forty-five rendezvous in Aldgate tomorrow night – his mother was insisting he come home early. He'd already worked out exactly what he was going to say; how sorry he was, but it was a family thing – she knew what his mother was like on Friday nights. And so on. Maybe, he was going to say, he could make it up to her later in the weekend. When he'd thought of that phrase, the boy had grinned to himself.

He was in luck; Christine (that's her name: Christine White) was the last girl out. The radio had been turned off, and the cloakroom next to the machine-room was empty. Soon as he spotted her, he was glad he'd made his approach so cautiously; it meant he could stand in the doorway and watch her tidying her hair and pulling on her coat without her knowing he was there. He liked that. Watching her. When he eventually coughed to let her know he was there, she jumped; he liked that, too. She only looked cross for a moment, however.

"What d'you want then?" she said, buttoning her coat up, briskly.

She knew from the look on his face what he was thinking – and she liked the fact that she'd been able to do that to him even with her back turned. Beauty said what he had to say – keeping his voice down, because they both knew that Mrs Kesselman was all ears – and tried out his line about hoping to make things up to her later. It seemed to go down fine. So, since they were alone, and the moment seemed propitious, he decided to push his luck. Speaking of later, he said, lowering his voice even further (and his eyes; he knew that was one of his best looks, looking down as if he was bit unsure of himself) and moving close to her, speaking of later, was she still on for Sunday? He hoped so (flicking the eyes back up again now, up through his locks of black hair, hooking her gaze with his), because he'd been thinking that maybe this weekend might be a good time for him to finally get round to –

At this point, when he actually said it, finally came out with it and actually said *that word*, the girl couldn't help herself, and let out a thin, gasped shriek of laughter – and then immediately clapped her hand over her mouth to stop herself.

Mrs Kesselman, one floor up in the office, heard it – Number Four quickly fell quiet once five-thirty had struck, and the boy had been reckless, and had forgotten to close the cloakroom door. She didn't go down to investigate, however. She recognised the sound of girls larking about together over a cloakroom cigarette after all these years – and besides, she had better things to do, like her accounts. Another ten minutes and she'd go and turn the culprits out – and tell them not to be late in tomorrow morning, thank you very much.

Downstairs, Beauty peeled Christine's hand away from her mouth, moved in a bit closer still (kissing distance), and asked her well, what about it? He hadn't planned any of this. But he's always liked the sound of that word, and now that on the spur of the moment he's come out and said it, actually said it to her, he thinks it rather suits him. She may look shocked, but her eyes are bright as buttons; and she's left her mouth half open. So he carries on. He suggests that they move their Sunday afternoon rendezvous, reference to the possible purpose of which had made her shriek like that, to Victoria Park. He knows it's only half an hour from her estate. Does she know it? Yes, she does. Great. And does she know about the shrubberies near the bandstand ?

Although they are both almost whispering now, the two of them have completely forgotten about the danger of Mrs Kesselman. The whispers are because neither of them can quite believe their own daring.

Of course she's heard about the shrubberies (and indeed, *of course* she has. The reputation of places like that are what both boys and girls talk about when they are alone in their separate packs. Or did you think it was only the boys?). The look on his face when he asks her that question (he runs his tongue involuntarily across his lower lip) makes her want to laugh or shriek again, as if she thought he was joking. But she knows he isn't. Something nips her between the legs when she see the particular way he smiles back at her, so she pauses and looks down at the cloakroom floor for a moment – just a moment – before she looks back up and says, not smiling at all,

"What time on Sunday?"

*

Lest you should be thinking she is some foolish innocent, this girl, I should tell you that she has campaign tactics of her own. This is the boss's nephew, after all. And she's ready. She's seventeen, she's a junior machinist, she has two younger sisters and a brother and she still lives at home – what else is she supposed to do? On Saturday mornings, when she walks past the stall selling bridal fabrics on Crisp St Market, Christine smiles a small, tight smile to herself. She's the quiet one of the family, Christine is – but she's pretty. She knows she is one of thousands, and she has her escape route planned. I don't know if you remember the words of that song, the one that seemed to be on the radio all spring and summer that year, the Supremes I think it was – *"You can't hurry love; You'll just have to wait"*?; well, when Christine walks past the fabric stall on Saturday morning, and that song comes on the stall-holder's transistor radio, and she smiles to herself like that, it's because Christine doesn't agree at all. In Christine's mind, the future takes a very definite form; in fact, she can already see it. She can see a silver-framed, five-by-four-inch black and white photograph, and in this photograph, she is wearing a long white dress. She can see exactly what style of dress it is; she can even see how lovely the bouquet of white spray carnations and maidenhair will look against the duchess satin and *broderie anglaise* she's chosen for her fabrics. She can see the shining silver of the photograph's frame, and the polished veneer of the sideboard it's standing on, and the whole brand spanking new living-room of the two-bedroomed flat where she's installed it in pride of place. In the photograph, she's holding on to the arm of her man respectfully, but firmly. He is slightly taller than she is, and strong-looking, and beautifully well-dressed – and she loves Beauty's hair when it's done like that.

Christine had thought she might refuse the boy when he finally asked her, at least the first time, might drive him crazy for a bit; but then, when it came to it – well, she couldn't. In that moment when she looks down at the floor, she tells herself that she does love him, really – him and his suit and his lovely dark hair. So she ought to let him, if he wants to. After all, it's nearly a month since she first let him open her mouth with his tongue; it's not as if they're just starting.

And fuck what her mother would say.

Just like Maureen, riding to Skin Lane to choose the furs for her coat in an older man's black Daimler, Christine knows that she is breaking the rules. They know they are gambling, these young women, and this probably explains why they laugh so much – and why their laughter never quite sounds easy. They are never quite sure if they are safe.

★

The rendezvous agreed, Christine ran to catch her bus. The boy stayed on, however – partly so that they wouldn't be seen walking down the Lane together, partly because he rather liked sitting on the bench in this empty cloakroom. He knew he was trespassing. He imagined the scene when the girls were all getting their coats on, chattering to each other and reaching behind their backs to untie their overalls. Saying things about him, he shouldn't wonder. He imagined the secret look on his girl's face when she heard them. *Bet she wants to tell them they don't know the half of it,* he thought.

He gave it three minutes, then decided the coast was clear. He stood up, ran his hands through his hair, and then, just as he got to the front door, walked straight into Mrs Kesselman.

★

Quickly reorganising his face, Beauty told Mrs Kesselman he'd just been in the machine-room, checking to see if anyone was ready for the next lot of trimmed musquash from upstairs. She didn't believe a word of it.

"Is that right, Mr Scheiner?" she said, "Well you can tell Mr Freeman we should be ready for it dinnertime."

He knew he'd been caught, but was sure she hadn't seen Christine leaving, otherwise she would have said so. Mrs Kesselman eyed the boy implacably, and then appeared to relent. She was never one to not speak her mind, Mrs Kesselman, but she had her ways of doing it.

"Still getting on alright up there with our Mr F, are

you? A bit fierce with the juniors he can be, until you get to
know him. Not an easy man always."

"We're getting on fine, thank you, Mrs Kesselman."

"Like him, do you?"

The boy appeared to think carefully before answering,
as if he didn't quite know how to put it.

"Well, he's always kindness itself to me, Mrs Kesselman
– but then I suppose he's got to be, being as how I'm his
boss's nephew. If I wasn't, I should think he'd be as much of
an old misery-guts in a suit to me as he is to the rest of the
world." He was beginning to overplay it a bit now, he knew
that, but he just couldn't resist it. "How come Mr F never
married, Mrs Kesselman? I mean, Head Cutter, been with
the firm almost as long as even you have, I should have
thought he'd've made someone a lovely – "

Before he could finish his sentence, the pretence of
affability slid from Mrs Kesselman's face like a cloud-
shadow passing over rocky ground, and left her features
their usual painted granite selves.

"On this subject I shouldn't presume to think anything,
Mr Scheiner, not if I was you. Time for me to shut up shop –
and for you, I should think, to be home."

She walked briskly across the hallway to where the
light-switch was, and paused with her finger on the switch.

"And now your uncle has you upstairs, I shouldn't
think you'd want to be down here quite so often. I should
hate one of my girls to get into any kind of confusion, Mr
Scheiner. *Farshtaist?*"

The Yiddish was like a slap; it meant he'd better make
sure he was never caught again, *Alright?* The boy wanted to
smile when he heard her say that, because he thought that if
this old woman reckoned part of her job was protecting her
girls from the likes of him, then she wasn't really very good
at it. But he didn't. He bid her a pointedly polite goodnight,
and left her to lock the door behind him.

Always polite, young Mr Scheiner.

Mrs Kesselman turned the lights out.

And clever with it, she thought.

★

But then young people have to be, don't they? The next Monday morning, Mrs Kesselman, just on the off-chance that Christine might be the guilty party whose laughter she'd heard coming up from downstairs that night, casually asked her if that was her she'd seen walking to Cannon Street station last Friday evening with young Mr Scheiner. The girl vehemently denied even the possibility of such a thing – catch her dead first, Mrs Kesselman, honestly. She didn't fancy him at all. *Not bloody likely,* you might say.

People think they can tell from your face what you've been thinking, that it shows in your face; but it doesn't, and they can't – remember?

So you see, Mr F isn't the only one in this story who's trying to work out a way to love.

four

Imagine two very different Sunday afternoons taking place that weekend.

Here is Christine, in her best coat – powder blue, white buttons, three-quarter length. She tells her mother what time she will be home from the cinema, and then catches a bus which goes in the opposite direction, making sure that none of her neighbours see her do it. And here's Beauty, standing sentinel by the park gates, waiting for her – for all his swagger, you can see by the way he combs his hair just once too often that he's a bit nervous. Here she comes. Now the two of them are walking hand in hand across the park, across its wastes of tired, hard grass, absurdly smartly dressed and formal in their demeanour considering what they're here for, taking the long way round to the rusting ironwork of the bandstand, to its dark trees and thickets. Once they're there – well I'm sure you'll have your own memories with which to complete the scene. The haste, the clumsy demands and negotiations, the clothing being hitched up or pulled down – the stinging dust of privet leaves in your eyes. All those things you have to endure when you're young, and there is nowhere else you can go.

Meanwhile Mr F, who has more privacy than he knows what to do with, and no one to ask him what time he will be home or where he's thinking of going this afternoon – here is Mr F, in his usual chair, in the living-room of his empty flat. He doesn't want to go anywhere. He wants to stay in, thank you very much. Now that it's the weekend, he wants to sit and roll one cigarette after another and let the cup of tea perched on the arm of the chair grow cold. He has things he wants to think about – that he *needs* to think about. He needs to think, for instance, about what it would be like to ask the boy to join him one weekend. To invite him along on one of his Sunday afternoon expeditions. For a walk. He isn't ever going to actually do this, obviously, but he still needs to think it through. Or for a meal, perhaps – a meal like one of those he's seen written up on the blackboard outside that Italian place half-way up Villiers Street. Except that they're not open on a Sunday. Perhaps he could cook something for him here then. What, exactly? (He's never even been inside that Italian café, though he always thinks it looks quite nice when he passes.) He's not sure what sort of meal would be appropriate. Tea, or dinner? Never mind; he keeps going. He thinks about what it would be like coming back here to the flat with him on the train. Passing through South Bermondsey Station with the boy sitting next to him. Coming up the stairs with him. Walking past the window. Putting the key in the door with the boy standing just behind him.

He wouldn't like that.

Never mind.

Once the front door is shut, he supposes it would be polite to show him round. But not the bathroom. And not the bedroom .He tries to imagine that – he even gets up and goes and stands in the hall and looks in through the open doorway at his bed – but it's no use, he can't. The counter-pane is too smooth and tidy. Too ready to show the slightest disturbance. He goes back into the living-room, to carry on the tour, but then he thinks of something else. He picks up the spare dining-chair, the one he never uses, and carries it into the kitchen and sets it at the kitchen table, opposite the chair where he always sits when he's eating. It looks nice there, and it fits quite well really – except that now he realises there isn't space for him to get to the cooker, so he takes the chair back into the living-room and tries it in the vacant space on the other side of the gas fire to his chair, the armchair. He looks from one to the other; they sort of make a pair. He turns the radio on, but it's an orchestra, and an orchestra doesn't feel quite the right kind of music for the occasion, so he turns if off again. However, silence isn't appropriate either – there's too much of it (he can even hear the clock in the kitchen) – so he puts the radio back on, and tries changing the station for once. It doesn't work; even with the sound turned down, the noise that starts coming out is too bright and too fast – too young, really, he thinks – so he turns it off again. He stands with his back to the gas fire (he can hear that sound too, the slight hiss of the gas) and looks at the two chairs again. They are angled slightly towards each other, as if the two people supposed to be sitting in them were going to have a conversation, or a smoke. Mr F looks first at the armchair, his chair, then at the other one. Then back at his chair. Then at his.

It's getting dark now.

The lovers have left the park; the gates are being locked.

Mr F realises that he's forgotten to make his dinner.

Much later, after he's eaten, he tries the radio again. The paper says there's going to be a programme on called *Music Through Midnight* – he would never listen to it normally, because it's on much too late for a Sunday evening, but whenever he's seen it, the title has always appealed to him for some reason. He's always liked the idea of the music being there in the dark even if no one is listening. When he turns the radio on, however, and the man comes on and announces the title of the programme in that deliberately soothing, scotch-and-soda voice they always use, it brings him no comfort. It's that word, *Midnight*; it reminds him that he has become one of those people for whom the dark brings no peace. He never sleeps properly now. Not like he used to. Even with his dream no longer coming to disturb him every other night, he's often awake until gone twelve, or one, or sometimes even two – and even when he does finally get off, he often wakes up again later. He listens to the voice telling him to stay calm and drift off if he can, but he knows it's no use.

Later, when he's lying open-eyed in bed, he thinks he can hear screaming. He starts, but then relaxes; it isn't a person screaming out there in the dark, but a fox, one of those city foxes that get into people's back gardens along the railway tracks. He's seen them from the train. She obviously doesn't care who hears her, this one, because four times in succession he hears her call. She's evidently not taking no for an answer – four times, she calls, with that unnervingly high-pitched yelp that is half-way to being human. The sound creeps into his bedroom though the gap under the curtains, and he can just see her, stretching her throat to the moon and screaming for her mate to come quickly. To come before the night ends. Screaming.

People think that it is in the tangle of bodies, in the actual congress, that one person invades another and takes possession of them; that it is on the bed that we give ourselves up. Well it is true that there is a surrender there that is unlike any other, but the real time they get under your skin is when you spend these hours alone preparing for them; imagining them. The hours when you find yourself wondering if these sheets would be too hot with two people under them. Or when you lie there on your back with both eyes open, as Mr F lies now, in the desperate early hours of that Monday morning, wishing that your nightmare would come back and plague you, just so that you can see your beloved one last time.

five

Mr F's ability to be two people – one when he was on his own, one on Skin Lane – was remarkable. That Monday morning, he blinked hard in his mirror (no more bad dreams for *him*, thank you very much), splashed the previous night off his face with two handfuls of hot water, and then proceeded to scrub and shave and cuff-link himself back into his week-day self as if nothing could please him more than the chance to get promptly back to work. All the way from Peckham Rye to Bermondsey, he gave himself a proper Monday morning talking-to, telling himself all over again that all he had to do was concentrate on this bloody coat and he'd be fine. Never mind all these things he doesn't know about; there's one thing he knows more about than anybody else in London, and that's cutting skin. *These foxes*, he told himself, *are going to have to be perfect.* This was his chance to turn out a really beautiful piece of work, something that he – no, something that *they*, he and the boy *together* – could be proud of. That was it. Thought the price-tag was everything, did he? (This was in reference to Mr Scheiner's cigar-smoking cousin; not the sort of man Mr F had ever liked.) Well, he'd show him. There were other things besides money that made something worthwhile. It was all so easy for him, wasn't it, bringing his girlfriend to Skin Lane like that, parading her in front of all and sundry, having it all approved of in public – whereas he, Mr F, he had to just stand there and – well, these were things which Mr F felt, but which he didn't like to put into words, not even in the privacy of his own head. *No, that's definitely it –*

he thought to himself, as he felt the train slowing down for London Bridge – *This coat* (he stood up) *is going to have to be* (collecting his hat off the rack) *bloody* (smiling quietly to himself as he stepped down onto the platform) *perfect*. Since he was last out of the carriage, he slammed the door behind him. Like a full stop.

★

Five new strings of reputedly prime-quality Russian red foxes were lying all ready for inspection on the bench that morning; Mr F called Beauty to his side, and they set to work. Every single skin had to be checked twice – there were twenty-four in every bundle – and it soon became clear that not one of them was going to have an easy time getting past Mr F and the scrutiny of his expert eyes. Either the red of the under-fur on the flanks was too brassy, or the white of the stomach too yellow; if the under-fur was right, then Mr F would spot that the guard-hairs on the shoulders were too brittle-looking, or too sparse, or that their lustre wasn't really anything special. On the rare occasions when the colour was judged half-way decent, Mr F's fingers would be sure to detect some hidden split or flaw in the skin itself; unimpressed by any considerations of beauty, his ruthless fingers stroked and probed every inch of belly, flank, neck and spine until it was found. At once, its weakness detected, the skin would be peremptorily thrown to one side.

As the day wore on, it began to seem as if nothing would ever satisfy him; *if he uses the words "right and proper way of doing things" once more time,* Beauty thought, *this old man is in danger of making a fool of himself.* Late in the afternoon, however, the very last of the strings began to show at least some signs of possibility. These skins were prime quality indeed; white-bellied, and with the soft, brick-dust-red under-fur of the flanks brushed over with garnet and mahogany as the pelt thickened towards the spine. Even Beauty could see that they were special; the guard-hairs across the shoulders and on the spine itself shone as if they'd been dipped in cochineal and then tipped in glittering Chinese black. Four of the skins in particular caught Mr F's eye; laying them side by side on the bench, he wondered out loud if they might work as a set for the collar and revers. But he still wasn't sure; running the palms of his hands again and again over the four pelts, up and down, restlessly, as if he was working the light into them like an oil, or a final wash of colour – he still couldn't make up his mind. He needed help. Apparently completely absorbed in his task, he stepped back from the bench half a pace, and muttered, quietly, out of the side of his mouth,

"Do they belong together or not?"

"Sorry?" said Beauty, surprised to be consulted.

"What d'you reckon?"

As if he genuinely valued the boy's opinion.

As if asking for it was the most natural thing in the world.

For all that this endless process of swapping and comparing the skins seemed rather pointless to him – *Just settle on something, and get cracking*, would have been his approach – Beauty was actually rather enjoying playing The Good Apprentice this particular afternoon. Now that he'd apparently been promoted to his Master's shoulder for the purposes of working on this coat, he felt much easier about the whole thing– and besides, he knew the part suited him (the way he'd spent his Sunday afternoon probably had something to do with his good humour, too). So he decided to play along. Casting aside what he was actually thinking about – which was just how white and unbruised that red-head's neck was going to look, framed by this lot – he adopted a suitable serious expression, and joined Mr F in staring at the skins. There was nothing wrong with them that he could see; but just because he could, and because he knew the old boy would fall for it, he answered, very seriously, and with a well-studied frown, that he wasn't sure the colours were exactly right.

"I don't know, Mr F. Do you think we've really got two pairs there?"

"I know what you mean," said Mr F, straightaway. "Get the rump-to-head match wrong on the rever, and it'll never sit right. How about like that?"

He deftly rearranged the pelts into a different order, and they both stared at them again. The boy was bluffing, of course, but he was good at it. As if he was really considering the matter deeply, he reached towards the skins, hesitated, and then swapped two of them over.

"How about..." he said, brushing the pelts up with the back of his hand so that the white of their two adjacent bellies blended into one snowdrift, then stepping back as if to scrutinise his handiwork – "How about that way round, Mr F?"

Beauty had been right; oh, how Mr F loved the seriousness of the ensuing discussion! Having the boy talk to him like this – and being able to answer him with such sureness – made him feel that everything was worth it. It made him feel confident again; feel *proud*. They must have spent a full half-hour selecting and trying and discarding alternatives, matching skin against skin, swapping comments in the private language of their trade – after all, as they laughingly reminded each other, with Mr F starting the quotation and Beauty finishing it for him, *In this business, the most important thing is choice of skin.* Eventually, the four pelts were judged worthy of becoming a collar after all, and reinstated in pride of place on the bench. The boy (of course) was happy to defer to Mr F's superior judgement; Mr F, while he appreciated his junior's contribution, thought that all things considered, he'd been right first time. He hadn't lost his touch; the skins were a perfect match. As he ran an approving hand over the beautiful pale red fur once last time, he rehearsed his credo again, out loud – and with real conviction:

"This coat is going to be perfect."

I suppose Mr F had good reason to be pleased with himself. But as one of the other men in the workroom remarked to a colleague under his breath when he heard Mr F saying that, he could have done that job on his own in less than half the time.

★

Come five-thirty, after they'd hung up their white coats and got their jackets on (it was getting a bit warm for jackets in the cutting-room by now) Mr F politely insisted that the boy went first down the narrow stairs. Once outside the building, they turned left together, and walked up the Lane and then up College Street as far as Dowgate Hill. Here, Beauty made his apologies; he'd arranged to meet a friend at Aldgate at a quarter to six, he explained, and really ought to be getting a move on. They bade each other a cheerful goodnight, and although Mr F had to actively resist the temptation to stand and stare at the boy's retreating back as he walked away up the hill, he continued his homeward journey with a light heart. He congratulated himself. Almost despite himself – because he knew it was dangerous to be seen smiling at him too often or too warmly, because then people might ask (the boy himself might ask, for God's sake) the one question he most wanted to avoid, which was of course *Are you alright, Mr F?* – he really felt that today, for the very first time, he had started to be able to enjoy the boy's company. The only thing he wanted – and this was why the work on the coat was so important to him – was for them to be a team. A pair. He wanted people to look at them and say *They do work well together, those two.*

Concentration, that was the trick. There really had only been one moment in the day when he'd faltered – the sight of a stray pelt lying leather up on the bench had suddenly disturbed him for some reason. It was the way the pale skin looked so unexpectedly helpless, lying there, open, waiting for the knife – but he'd covered it well, he thought. Pushed the skin to one side and got back to the task in hand straightaway.

All in all, he told himself, they'd made a good start. They were definitely *underway.*

There. That's better.

As he turned right down All Hallows Lane, a warm breeze from the river came up to greet him, and stroked his face. The buddleias were just beginning to crest the corrugated iron sheeting; another few weeks, and their coarse summer scent would start to make itself felt. Once again, he told himself that all he had to do was stick to his plan, and he'd be fine. He checked his wristwatch, and picked up his pace. If he hurried, he'd just make the five forty-nine.

*

But look at him; look at him, striding out to catch his train, the sun catching his face as he turns up onto the bridge. This man doesn't have a plan at all, does he? Look at his face, at the way he carries himself through the crowd, the

tell-tale set of his chin and shoulders. He has the characteristic expression of a middle-aged man who is trying much
too hard to look and move as if there is nothing at all
tugging at his mind except the imminent departure of his
train. Why else would he be frowning, on a lovely evening
like this?

Beauty, meanwhile, cutting through the black crowds
on Cannon Street as easily as a knife though butter, doesn't
really need a plan. He's sixteen. He pulls his comb out of his
back pocket and runs it twice through his hair without
missing a step. He's on his way to meet Christine – and he's
sure this whole situation will take care of itself, even if she
has been a bit funny with him ever since the park. It's not as
if it's anything serious, after all. He's young – they're both
young. His uncle has mentioned that he'd like a private
word with him sometime this week, but there again, he's not
worried. He's sure it'll be something about how he's feeling
about his progress through the family firm. Well, a few
weeks ago – and certainly last Thursday, with Mr F ripping
his head off like that – he'd have said that he wanted out, but
now, when he thinks about it, he wonders whether he
shouldn't consider staying on in the business after all. Or at
least waiting and seeing how he feels at the end of the
summer. It would certainly get his parents off his back, with
their constant questions. And he could do a lot worse. After
all, what does that old window say, the one he uses as his
looking glass? *And Son*, isn't it? When you think about it,
Skin Lane, he's made for it.

six

Sadly, that promising start with the skins for the collar turned out to be a false one. Finding the rest of the foxes for Maureen's coat took for ever. Eight weeks, in fact.

Partly, as I said, this was because good quality Russian foxes at a reasonable price proved even harder to find than Mr Scheiner had anticipated; mostly, however, it was because even when he did manage to track some down, his Head Cutter proved almost impossible to please. Whatever came in, it seemed that Mr F always found some legitimate reason to reject it. If the colour was right, the weight wasn't; if eight matching skins were required for the sleeves, the string under consideration would be sure to contain only five. Of course, the job wasn't strictly a top priority, but nevertheless, the sixth time he came into the office to report on a bundle of skins he'd been sent on approval and said that on inspection he really wasn't sure if they were up to Scheiner's usual quality, Mr Scheiner did privately want to ask Mr F what the fuck he thought he was playing at. Why didn't he just mix the weaker skins in the back of the coat like every other cutter on the Lane and get on with it? Anyone would think he didn't *want* the bloody coat to get made – but Mr Scheiner didn't want to offend him, and held his tongue. Unbeknownst to Mr F, he'd already had a quiet word with his nephew on the side, and promised Beauty that as soon as this piece was done, he was going to take him off the cutting benches and move him down to the office, where it would be just the two of them. Start looking at the management side of things – less skin, more phone and telegram. So in a way this coat was going to be the boy's final apprentice piece, and if Mr F wanted to be a stickler about it, then let him. It'd get made eventually. The young lady would just have to wait. And besides, who'd want to wear fox in this weather anyway?

Mr Scheiner was right about the weather. It was starting to get warm.

*

The old streets of the City are narrow, and even the wide new thoroughfares, with their facades of Portland stone or concrete, trap the heat and store it. The high wall of St James's church kept the basement and first floor of Number Four in shadow for most of the day, but come June, up on the top floor, even with the windows kept wide open, the workroom could become an oven. Under these conditions, even Mr F was obliged to discard his waistcoat and consider loosening his tie.

At the afternoon tea-break, the whole workforce would take the chance to spill out onto the cobbles of the Lane and get some fresh air. The cutters and machinists would mingle for once, and as he rolled his cigarette on the steps, Mr F would often as not see the boy surrounded by a cluster of his old workmates from downstairs. He was always amazed that the girls had the energy left to chatter and carry on like that, at this time of the day. He'd walk away from the sound, preferring to be on his own for a bit, even if it meant standing in the small patch of waste ground in front of St James's (when *were* they going to shift all the bomb-site rubble that still hadn't been cleared away?). But try as he might to concentrate on just enjoying his cigarette, when he heard the snorts of laughter, he'd always find himself turning round and watching. What for, exactly, he would never quite know. The boy would be in just his shirt-sleeves, with his shirt unbuttoned at the neck – tie off, throat exposed – and like Mr F, it seemed, those girls just couldn't take their eyes off him. Standing round him like they were in the chorus and he was about to do a number. Not that you could blame them – sometimes he really did look like one of those young men out of the newspapers, with his trousers and his hair. The way it curled on his collar like that. The way his skin, now that it was nearly summer, looked

The way it looked so young.

Then Mrs Kesselman would come out onto the steps and clap her hands, meaning it was a quarter to four and there was work to be done *if nobody minded* – and the girls would start to go reluctantly back inside, complaining as always. It would always be the same one who was the last in, Mr F noticed. Always the same one who put herself somewhere where she could keep an eye on the boy – not standing right next to him, necessarily, but always where she could see him. Mr F watched her face closely. She was pretty, he thought. Small – but pretty.

Back to work, he'd mutter to himself, giving his cigarette one last drag.

*

Beauty, of course, was quite happy to let Mr F stand there in his patch of rubble and stare; he was absolutely sure he had no more idea about him and Christine than anyone else. *Staring at me like that while I chat up my girl, the dirty old sod. What's his game? Smell us, can he?* He even played up for his audience's benefit, doing that young man's trick of laughing and throwing back his head to blow the last mouthful of smoke out from between his teeth before he stamped out his fag, showing off his hair. Then he'd whisper something

under his breath to his girl as they went up the steps –
something which would make her squeal with laughter. He
liked it when she did that. This may have been pushing it,
what with Mrs Kesselman standing right there at the top of
the steps, but – well, you remember how it is when you're
sleeping with someone and no one else knows. The constant
anticipation; the flirting; the getting away with it right under
people's noses. Like most young men, Beauty hadn't really
thought about what difference having done it for the very
first time would make to everything, but whatever he'd
imagined, it really hadn't been this. Sauntering up the front
steps in the June sunshine, he felt as if there was just a drop
too much blood in his head all of the time. It was all so
bloody *easy* – he stuck his hands in his pockets and watched
her go in up ahead of him through the black front door. For
instance, that first time, in the park – he hadn't really had to
break into her after all. She'd more or less consented. And
now… now, it was all going like clockwork. He was *in*.
Everything was rearranged, and not one single person was
any the wiser.

Just before he went inside, he turned back to look at Mr
F, still standing there squinting into the afternoon sun
amongst his rubble and weeds, and gave him a cheerful grin.

What could the old boy do, but smile back?

*

Mr F kicked at a stone. There were beginning to be far too
many of these tea-breaks, tea-breaks at the end of which he
was never quite sure exactly what he was going back upstairs
for. Because they couldn't start cutting until all seventeen
skins had been matched, there was no set sequence of events
or tasks he could impose on their days – nothing they could
ever get really stuck into *together*. An endless succession of
more or less unimportant jobs inevitably left him with far

too many hours in which his mind was free to wander, and instead of staying under his control, the days were slipping through his fingers. Alright, he thought, he had in a way got used over the weeks to this new and altered life of his – he no longer seemed to spend them simply lurching from panic to panic – but now, all he ever seemed to do was *wait*.

★

Oh, they were long, those summer afternoons of 1967. Shrieks of female laughter would drift up to the cutting-room windows from the machine-room in the basement; as ever, the girls' transistor radio would be playing its inane heart out, nibbling at the edges of his concentration. In the *Standard*, there were stories about young people gathering in their thousands on the grass in Hyde Park – but in the lanes and alleys of the City, there was no relief. Come six o'clock, the early evening crowds outside the pubs got louder, and thicker, and drunker. It wasn't just that people were thirsty with the heat; instead of merely laughing, the knots of young men would clutch their pints and throw back their heads and *bray* – there was something in the sound that made Mr F look hurriedly away. Sometimes, not content with crossing over onto the other pavement, he would even make a detour on his walk home. All those bodies, clustering in their thick black suits – they bothered him.

He did his best, of course. The morning after taking one of these detours, he would invariably give himself one of his stern talking-to's on the way back in to work the next day, promising himself he was going to do better. He would set himself his old task of not looking at the boy until after the dinner-break, or force himself to delegate the task of supervising a routine job to one of his colleagues. But for all his efforts, as the day wore on, Mr F would find himself prey to the same boiling down of time to a slow, treacly crawl that the rest of the City felt on those stunned, sweltering afternoons. One Wednesday – it was July by now – when at last some skins had come in that looked hopeful, the boy stood much too close to him as he held a flaming fox pelt up against the light, and for one long moment, everything seemed to stop entirely. As the boy brushed against him, he could suddenly think about nothing but their shoulders, separated only by the stiff white linen of their coats and the thinner cotton of their respective shirts. About how it would feel if the layers of fabric were not there. He faltered, holding the fox pelt up to the light for much too long. Fortunately, the boy thought he was just making up his mind about the quality of the skin – he knew that – but still, he wished the bench was between them, not in front of them. Anything – anything to have a reason to put some distance between them, some *air*. The moment soon passed, and when it did, he congratulated himself for not flinching, telling himself, silently, *That's better* – but even as he threw the pelt down on the bench and snatched up the next one, he knew he was in trouble.

That tea-break, sick with himself – and determined not to stand there mooning about on the Lane again, watching the boy out of the corner of his eye – Mr F walked down to the river at Queenhithe to roll his cigarette in peace. A gang of stevedores was working on the gantries reaching over the wharf, silhouetted against the sunlit water like some flock of great muscular black birds; but apart from that, he was alone. The men were whistling and calling to each other, and as he rolled his cigarette, leaning on a low wall by the river, trying to catch whatever breeze there was on his face, he closed his ears to the sound and ignored them. *Jesus; no peace for the wicked all fucking right.* What was he going to do with himself? He tried to think.

He wanted the summer to end, and he wanted it to go on for ever.

He wanted this bloody coat out of the way – and he wanted to tear every single skin they'd found so far with his bare hands.

He knew he was waiting, but no bloody idea what he was waiting for.

Jesus

He stared out over the dazzling river, and pressed both his hands onto the stone coping of the low wall separating him from the water. The stones were warm – Christ, but it was hot today. Another chorus of calls came down from the gantry, and he found himself squinting up at the scaffolding where the men were perched to see what the fuss was, shielding his eyes from the glare bouncing off the broken water with his hand. The reflected light drew a hard, white line round each body, picking them out as they reached and stretched… Realising what he was doing, he threw down his half-smoked cigarette and stamped it out, aching with fury and frustration.

★

Did Mr F really know what he was doing, do you think, dragging out the business of choosing the skins like this? I'm sure he'd never read or even heard of the names *Penelope* or *Sheherezade*, but it was certainly their old trick that he was up to. Somewhere in the back of his mind he must have realised that once those seventeen fox skins were all present and correct, the day when he would have nothing left to teach Beauty would be irreversibly inked into the calendar, and that when that day came – well, I suppose that if Mr F had tried to imagine for a moment what a day without Beauty would have felt like, his mind would have refused. It would have been like looking up and seeing all that dazzling, dancing water blotted out by an in-rolling wall of fog; like stepping out onto London Bridge and being suddenly enveloped in a chilly, endless and featureless world of no return.

Sometimes, of course, I can't help but wonder what might have happened if there had been somebody else there down by the river that afternoon: I mean if there had been somebody there to see him stamp out his cigarette like that, and be moved, noticing the obvious vehemence of the gesture, to ask him what he was thinking of as he stared out over the water like that (to ask him, perhaps, *Are you alright, Mr F?*). Do you think that then he might have been able to put his fears into words? After all, that's what it takes, sometimes, isn't it; a conversation with a stranger. Personally, judging by the set expression on his face, the way he is screwing up his eyes against the light from the river, I think not. I think he would simply have replied – after, perhaps, just a moment's hesitation – that all he was thinking about was work, and how he really should be getting back to it now. At most, he might have said something predictable about the heat. If the stranger had persisted – or if for some reason Mr F *had* decided to talk, had felt, suddenly, like unburdening himself a little – then… well, then, I don't think Mr F would have talked about himself and his problems at all. I think he would have talked about the boy. Keeping his voice quiet, and low (staring out across the river, and lighting another cigarette), he would have starting talking about how well they worked together, all things considered, and of how he thought the boy really was coming on by leaps and bounds. He would have talked at length about his diligence, his aptitude, his potential, and his charm. He would have commended his style of dress, and even his hair; would have portrayed him, that is, as a perfectly suitable choice.

He might even have said *you know, I think it would be nice if he got together with one of the girls from work – he is that age, after all. He'd treat a girl well, I'm sure. Not like they usually get treated by their young men. Take her out somewhere nice. Wherever it is these young people go.*

And I think he would have meant every word.

But there was no stranger, that afternoon. As he turned his back on the river, and decided it really was time he got back, Mr F suddenly felt sure that that was what he was so sick of: the sound of his own voice. He was sick of the sound of it forever bouncing off the walls of his kitchen or living-room; sick of hearing it run round and round the inside of his skull. And he was sick of this weather, too – sick of the sunlight, and sick of this everlasting heat; sick of the dazzle, and the sweat, and the laughter leaking up from the basement. As he trudged back up towards Skin Lane, he realised how much he was missing his dream. He missed the cool of his bathroom, the calming pallor of the gloss paint and the tiles and the mirror and the cold white enamel; missed the way the boy always looked so peaceful and quiet, lying there asleep with his eyes closed tight. Pausing in the shadow of a warehouse (no one was going to notice if he was five minutes late, not in this weather) he leant against its brick wall for a moment and took out his tobacco and papers again and started to roll one last cigarette. He remembered the good old days, when he could at least look forward to being alone with Beauty in the cool of the night. When he could stare and stare and stare his fill. He remembered that daydream about lowering him slowly down, laying him gently down in the bathtub and then kneeling by his side and brushing that stray lock of dark hair away from his face so he could sleep properly. He remembered how cool the touch of his forehead had been. How white his skin was. How sweet the weight of him, in his arms.

He remembered everything.

There. That's better.

Mr F opened his eyes. He did feel better, but he thought it might be a good idea to stay just a few more minutes leaning against this conveniently shady wall – calm down a bit before he went back to the Lane. Smoke his fag in peace. He didn't want to spoil anything when he got back. Slip up over anything.

★

If only he had known, that particular July afternoon, as it happened, was a historic one. Just a mile upriver, while our Mr F was leaning against his baking warehouse wall with his eyes screwed shut and imagining in vivid detail what it would be like to hold a naked young man in his arms, the House of Commons was beginning a debate on just that very subject. The Strangers' Gallery, that particular afternoon, was unusually crowded; the journalists, as they reached for their pencils and began to scribble, found themselves having to struggle for elbow-room – and if only Mr F had been paying as much attention as some other people evidently were, that's my point. If only, for instance, he had read his *Evening Standard* with a little more care the next day (read the lead article on page twelve, for instance) then it might have given him something else to listen to besides the sound of his own voice. If nothing else, surely

realising that he ought to have been using the word *we*
instead of always just that same cross, worn-out *I* in his
angry mutterings would have helped; realising, that is, that
he couldn't have been the only man on the five forty-nine
train home from London Bridge that night who instinctively
checked to see if any of his fellow passengers had noticed
the slight change in his face when his evening paper fell
open at that particular page. I'm not saying that he would
(or should) have started looking round the carriage to see if
he could spot any fellow sufferers, eager to start up a
supportive conversation, or anything like that – but surely it
would have helped him to know that he wasn't alone.

To know that he wasn't just imagining all this.

As it was, Mr F took one look at the headline and
decided that the article couldn't possibly be about him.
After he'd spent barely a minute scanning it, he turned
sedately (no one *was* watching him; he'd checked) back to
page four, which was where they always told you what was
going to be on the radio that evening. The only thing that
had really caught his eye in the article was a small detail in
the last paragraph. For some reason, the young journalist
who had written it had seen fit to mention the fact that the
House hadn't risen from its debate until nearly half past six
in the morning – until 6.21 a.m., in fact. What a relief it
must have been for them all, Mr F thought, to step out into
the fresh morning air after having had to talk about all of
that nonsense all night long. He always loved the sensation
of stepping out onto an empty pavement first thing on a
summer morning, before it got too hot. Before London got
really going, and the streets were still cool and quiet. Before
all the voices started. Before you realised that nothing was
ever going to change.

seven

You wouldn't have thought it could have got any hotter – but it did. Later that week, the front page of the *Standard* announced (alongside short paragraphs announcing *Abortion debated* and then, later, *Abortion to be legalised*) that the temperature in the City had twice reached eighty-one degrees. Every afternoon, clouds towered up over St Paul's, threatening thunder, and down in the basement of Number Four, Mrs Kesselman was obliged to let her girls lapse into all sorts of undress; come five-thirty, the cherubs carved over the windows of St Michael Paternoster rolled their eyes in fat-lipped disapproval as they clattered home tired and sweaty over the cobbles. Even up on London Bridge, the air was as warm as blood. The stone pavements, punished by the baking sun all day, gave back their heat, tormenting the homeward-bound crowds.

However, that was the very week – a week when no one in London could either remember or imagine being cold enough to want to put on a coat – when one of Mr Scheiner's contacts finally came up trumps with a supply of red foxes. The skins were dazzling; luxurious, heavy and fiery. Even Mr F could find no fault with what he was being offered.

It was time for the cutting to begin.

★

Any potential customer or colleague being shown round the premises that week, and seeing Mr F and his junior hard at work on Maureen's coat, might well have been moved to comment to Mr Scheiner on what a good team they made. *That nephew of yours, you've certainly got him up to speed,* would probably have been the phrase. And it was true; now that Beauty knew that there was light at the end of this particular tunnel, he was a model of diligence. He did exactly as he was told, passing the blade or cane or bat or nail exactly as and when required, and in dutiful silence. Mr F, on his part, sliced and stretched and pinned as if it was February, not July; having finally found seventeen skins which met his demanding standards, it seemed as if he couldn't wait to get the coat made. Never, it seemed to his colleagues, had his knife moved with more determined skill – and everyone in the workroom could see that, just as Mr F had promised, this coat was indeed going to be perfect. The pelts themselves were spectacular, and their beauty was to be allowed to conceal no botch or compromise; despite the heat (despite the sweat that sometimes slicked his hands) the blades and nails that opened and punctured them were never once seen to stray or slip.

By the end of the second week of July, all seventeen of the skins were already cut and on the boards. Beauty was given the job of damping them down, checking when they were dry enough for lifting, and passing them over to Mrs Kesselman for seaming; Mr F, meanwhile, was glad to tell his boss that the assembled coat should be on the stand in just three or four days. Mr Scheiner (*Oy! At last!* he muttered, the moment Mr F closed the office door behind him) straightaway lifted the receiver and called his cousin to arrange the young lady's final fitting. When he heard the coat was nearly ready, the cousin wanted to discuss the price again, of course – but Mr Scheiner was having none of that. He always enjoyed giving as good as he got from the customer, family or no.

"And how is business by you that suddenly you go tight

on me, eh?" he shouted at his cousin down the phone. "No, listen... it's a great pleasure knowing you too."

He knew the game; they both did. The offended tone was as cheerfully insincere as it was dramatic.

"Well a price is a price, my friend – even for family."

When they'd both stopped laughing, he brought the phone closer to his mouth, and lowered his voice as if there was someone else in the room.

"No but listen to me, my friend – this coat, the girl is going to love it."

The customer was unconvinced.

"No really."

At that price, the customer said, he should fucking well hope so.

"Worth every penny. Trust me."

On the other end of the phone, Mr Scheiner's cousin told him exactly what return he was expecting to get on his investment.

"Hey," said Mr Scheiner. "Nice life!"

His cousin promised he'd give his girl a call and arrange to come by the Lane just as soon as was convenient – she was usually pretty free. There was more than just money in the chuckle Mr Scheiner gave as the heavy black receiver of the office phone clicked back into its cradle. *Nice life indeed.*

*

Upstairs in the workroom, Beauty was squeezing out a filthy-smelling sponge into a bucket of water. Although he had never said anything, the one part of the job he'd always really hated was this damping-down the work on the nailing-boards. It was something about the way the dead skins began to smell alive again once they were wet, he thought. And especially in this heat.

eight

The date for the final fitting of the coat was not agreed without some negotiation; Maureen's diary (and indeed Maureen) turned out to be not quite so entirely at his beck and call as Mr Scheiner's cousin had anticipated. Eventually the last Friday of the month was agreed upon, and Mr F told would he please have the coat ready on the stand by that lunchtime.

The day before that, the Thursday, was probably the hottest day of the entire summer. The City baked, and burnt, and, unable to face the crush of London Bridge that evening, Mr F stayed late in the workroom – up there by the open windows, there was at least the possibility of getting some air. There was no real *need* for him still to be there at seven o'clock, fussing with the coat on its stand, but I imagine that besides the air he simply wanted to have a chance to take one last quiet, private look at this coat of his before it was taken out of his hands. The customer might never know with what care, and cares, it had been created – but he certainly did.

He had carefully draped it on a stand in the middle of the workroom – not the usual canvas tailor's dummy, but a headless wooden shop-window figure kept especially for displaying garments to customers. He settled the coat across its shoulders with a quick shake. It had already been given its first comb-out; all that was needed now was the one last formal fitting before the customer chose the silk for her lining and the fur was passed over to Mrs Kesseleman for lining, finishing, packaging and dispatch.

He stood back, and looked at it. It was, though he said so himself, quite a piece of work.

★

By seven o'clock on a July evening, the top-floor workroom at Number Four was no longer tortured by the direct glare of the sun; at that hour, the only light that reached the room was that reflected off the worn white stones of St James's tower and steeple, still baking on the south side of the Lane. It seeped in through the long window over the cutting benches like a rich gold stain, or dye, and in this strange, heavy light, as the shadows in the corners of the room began to gather, the colours of the coat seemed to deepen, and grow richer; to smoulder, and blaze. For the last time, Mr F let his wandering fingers find each of them in turn; the brick-dust red of the under-fur; chestnut spiked with black towards the spine; the cochineal-tipped-with-jet of the glittering guard-hairs; the hidden flashes of soft white belly. Because the coat was still unlined, it couldn't help but seem animal; there was something about the helpless sight of all that bare, seamed skin resting directly on the senseless dummy that made it look as if the coat was eager for a wearer made of flesh and blood again. For something that would let it move. As if he was answering this need – placating it, almost – Mr F fetched a steel comb and cane from his bench and began his final preparations. Methodically beating up the guard-hairs on each of the skins in turn, then combing them out, he worked across the shoulders of the coat, then down each of the sleeves in turn, and then, slowly, down the softly flaring back. As always, he moved his powerful hands with both decision and care, bringing the fur alive with every long, sweeping stroke.

His face was calm as he did this; his mind, quiet. I don't know if it was Beauty he was thinking of as he worked like this – of all the times their hands had accidentally touched, perhaps; of all the long hours of co-operation and frustration – but I do know that no lady at her glass ever combed out her shining hair at the end of the day with strokes as firm, as steady and as gentle as those Mr F used on that coat. Even though he had no dressing-table mirror in which to contemplate himself while he did it, he did look as though, finally, his thoughts were settling themselves into some sort of order; as if, briefly, he was at peace.

As if he felt… as if he felt *himself*.

It was probably a full three or four minutes before he realised that there was someone else there with him in that upstairs room, watching him.

★

"That's looking lovely, Mr F," said Beauty, quietly. "Reckon she'll like it?"

Mr F had no idea how long the boy had been standing there. He didn't turn round; there was a brief pause, and then the steel comb, which had hesitated in mid-stroke, completed its movement. Each stroke was long, and full; down; down; down, the comb went. Still he didn't look round – Mr F was always one for concentrating on the job in hand. His eyes stayed on the gleaming fur. If he was startled, his voice didn't betray the fact. If anything, it sounded deliberately calm.

"I should think so."

The hand kept moving. The eyes stayed on their task.

"And what brings you back here at this time in the evening then – you should be home by now, shouldn't you?"

"I was just meeting my friend up at Aldgate again, but he had to go home, and it's too bloody warm for the tube tonight... so I thought I'd walk back this way a bit first."

Flicking his eyes to the workroom mirror, Mr F could see the boy as just a dark, elegant silhouette, framed in the workroom doorway.

"I'm surprised the front door was still open."

"Mrs Kesselman was just locking up. She said you were up here."

"Like you say, it's too hot for a train."

I suppose it was the warmth of the evening, or maybe the light, or perhaps just because it was gone seven and the building was so quiet, but they were both talking softly now, as if there was something in the room that shouldn't be disturbed. There was another pause, and then the boy left his place in the doorway, and came closer, to watch the work. Still, Mr F never once took his eyes off the fur. With that look of concentration on his face, and in his white coat, he really did look like a doctor.

"I just thought I'd give it one final comb-out. You never can tell with fox, not until you actually see it on the customer. See that?" He flicked the comb across the right shoulder, just where the fur crested a seam "You can never be sure it's going to lie right at the top of the sleeve. It's the way it falls – just here – "

Whatever had been going through his mind when he thought he was alone, Mr F now seemed completely absorbed in the fur itself. He ran his hand back and forth across the seam, trying to settle the guard-hairs to his satisfaction. The boy couldn't see what, if anything, was wrong, but obviously something was; Mr F had stepped back from the dummy and was now flicking his eyes from shoulder to shoulder. The boy did the same, but he still couldn't see it.

"Here – " said Mr F. "I'll show you."

He put his comb down on the corner of the bench, lifted the coat off the dummy by the shoulders, and held it open for the boy to try on. He did this as if it was the most obvious and natural thing in the world.

"What?"

"Slip your jacket off, and I'll show you. Come on."

Beauty did as he was told, crossing the workroom to hang his jacket on the coat-hooks by the door and then coming hesitantly back in just his shirt-sleeves. Mr F was still patiently holding out the coat.

"Let's be having you," he said.

★

Beauty turned round, and reached clumsily back with his hands to find the armholes. He'd never had someone hold a coat out for him before, and wasn't quite sure how it was done.

"Careful your cuffs don't catch on the canvas, she's still not been lined, remember – "

But Beauty needn't have worried; Mr F had done this a thousand times. Once his cuffs were through the armholes, Mr F slipped the unlined skins up his arms and dropped them across his shoulders in one elegant, well-practised move. A big old full-length mirror was propped against the far wall of the workroom, and he led the boy over to it. Standing behind him, and watching what he was doing all the time in the glass, he worked as firmly and quickly as a seamstress with her mouth full of pins. As a dresser in the wings, when her young man's just been given his three- minute call.

The light was just catching the gilt of the mirror-frame, turning the boy into a picture; but he ignored that.

He ran his hands along the top of each shoulder-blade

and then up and down the top of each arm in two deft, separate strokes, flicking his hand away at the end of each outward or downward stroke, persisting until the fur over each of the shoulder seams finally hung in one soft, rounded, unbroken fall.

"See?" he said.

⋆

All the boy could see was how extraordinary he looked. Seeing himself framed in scarlet and gold, he couldn't help but be impressed. He reached up with both hands and ran them slowly down through the luxurious fur of the lapels, pressing his palms to his chest, watching the hairs divide for his fingers. He let out a low whistle.

"Lucky bloody tart," he said, softly. And then grinned at Mr F in the mirror.

Mr F met his eyes, but only very briefly. He walked back to the bench to retrieve his comb.

"That front still needs some work," he said. "Come back over here, where the light's better."

The boy did as he was told – but the coat felt strange. It was both too heavy, and too light; he didn't know how he was supposed to walk.

"Stand straight for me, then."

Mr F moved round in front of the boy, and, keeping his eyes well away from Beauty's face, started working on the lapels and the front of the coat with his comb. Of course, he was gentle; but again, he worked systematically and quickly, lifting and smoothing the hairs of each pelt in the pattern in turn, imperceptibly encouraging the fur to respond to the body it was now draping. As he worked, the barest beginning of a breeze from off the river started to come in through the open windows – but no sound at all. The City goes quiet very quickly on a summer evening.

The light thickened.

*

When he was finally satisfied with the hang of the front of the coat, Mr F moved back behind Beauty again in order to give the shoulders one quick last comb. He was concentrating so hard on his work that he didn't notice quite how close behind the boy he was now standing; not, that is, until he saw the fur of the collar move. It was his breath, catching it just where it touched the nape of the boy's neck.

When he saw that, he stopped what he was doing.

Just for a moment.

And in that moment, he became aware of a very odd sensation – an ache, almost – in the down-turned palms of his hands, which were hovering just inches above the fur on the boy's shoulders. It was as if they ached, literally, to touch something. He knew what it was, of course. He'd worked so hard to shut down his mind – ever since the warm, sudden shock of hearing the boy's voice in the doorway like that – that it came as no real surprise that his body was now thinking for itself. It wasn't the fur his hands wanted to touch; they'd already done that. It was the boy's hair.

As he stood there, trying not to breathe too hard, and grateful that there was no mirror in front of them now to reveal his face to the boy, all of Mr F's inchoate desire suddenly came down to this one wish; to this one, simple, longed-for gesture. And of course, standing as close behind him as he was, he could so easily have made his wish come true. The back of the boy's neck was only inches away. He could simply have leant forward, blown the fur aside, kissed the waiting skin, and then run the spread fingers of his hand (his right hand) up the nape of the boy's neck and into his hair. Nothing was stopping him from doing just that. Nothing at all. Nothing.

★

The boy didn't notice the breath on the back of his neck; but he could feel the growing heat of the fur. He found himself thinking about how much it was going to cost the man who was buying it, this coat – his uncle had told him the price – and then thinking about what it must feel like, being able to do that for your girl.

He started imagining her, putting the coat on.

The way it would look on her.

The look on her face.

As the distant smell of the dark river came in through the windows, the boy's cock began to stir. He would have liked to have gone and had another look at himself in that mirror, if only Mr F would stop fussing with his shoulders.

★

Mr F knew he had to do something to save himself, so he gathered himself, and made his move. Stepping round to the front again, he then took two paces back, as if to assess his handiwork, putting some much needed distance between himself and the boy. Once safely there, however, he almost undid himself. As he looked across from one shoulder to the other, trying to judge if the fur was lying absolutely correctly, his eyes couldn't help but graze the boy's face; and the third time he did it, their eyes met.

★

Nothing happens. The two them stand quite still, eye to eye, and barely three feet apart. Both of them seem to be holding their breath, and this time, there is no mirror between them.

The pause seems to go on for ever; how long it actually was, I couldn't say.

It is the boy who breaks it first. Still looking Mr F straight in the eye, and just (Mr F is sure he sees him do this) just slightly raising one eyebrow, he says, quietly,

"Christ, you get bloody hot enough in this then. She won't be keeping this on for long, will she?"

Still, Mr F can't tear his eyes away. He knows this feeling. There is no sound in the room at all.

The boy's eyes have never been this black.

"But then," he says, grinning, "I suppose that's the idea."

The eyebrow rises.

"Eh, Mr F?"

The silence continues. Mr F's mouth is dry; but he has a sentence in his head, and eventually, he manages to start saying it;

"Well – "

But now there is a sound; of all things, Mr F thinks he can hear the ticking of his kitchen clock, getting louder. He holds out his hands, as if – well, ostensibly as if to take the coat, but that's not it, actually, not it at all – and as he does this, he completes his sentence, raising his voice slightly to cover the sound of the clock

" – then you'd better take it off, hadn't you."

As he holds out his hands towards the boy, one of them – the one with the scar – shakes. Just slightly. Just as it does when he slides the key into the door in his dream. And he is suddenly very aware of how much the back of his throat is starting to ache. He knows he can't say anything else now, not a single thing more; and anyway, the boy must be able to see the expression on his face in this fiery evening light. And he must know what it means. He must.

Why else would he slowly, gently grin at him like that, as he begins to slip the coat off, looking him right in the eye, saying –

"You're right, Mr F. I better had. Don't want to wear it out, do we?"

★

Beauty slipped the coat off in two distinct movements. The left shoulder was peeled back slowly, carefully (pulling open the collar of his shirt just ever so slightly) – you might say, deliberately. The right, however, was slipped off so easily and apparently carelessly that anyone watching the scene would have thought the boy was trying to prove something – trying to prove, for instance, that nothing at all had just happened, or almost happened, there in the strange golden twilight of that silent room. Or at the very least to prove that whatever it was that might have happened or have been allowed to happen, its moment had definitely just passed. Handing the coat to Mr F as if it was some discarded rag, he collected his jacket off its peg by the door, shrugged it on, hunted briefly through the pockets of his hanging white work-coat till he found his cigarettes, tucked them away in his jacket, and turned to go. At the very last minute, he seemed to suddenly remember something he thought he'd better say before he went; he turned, and framed himself in the doorway exactly as he had done when he'd first appeared.

"And I'd better get off bloody home anyway – " he said, cheerfully, "My mother, she's dreadful if I stop out late."

He flashed Mr F one last shadowy grin, and nodded towards the coat.

"So goodnight, Mr F, and like you said – that's bloody perfect, that is."

And with that, the boy turned on his heel, and went.

★

As he clicked the front door of Number Four shut behind him, and jumped down the front steps, Beauty couldn't help but laugh. It was remembering that look on Mr F's face when he'd said that line about the coat coming off in a hurry that did it – he knew it was wicked, teasing the old boy like that, but honestly, he just couldn't help himself. Talk about helpless!

Beauty has just learnt something, you see; he's often wondered about Mr F and his funny looks, and now he knows. Oh yes – he knows that feeling, that feeling when your two faces are just a few inches apart, and there's too much blood in your head, and the next thing that happens has to be a kiss. He's not stupid. *Well, well, well; the randy old goat*, he thinks, as he pauses on the bottom step, smiling; *I wonder how long that's been going on.* The smile splits into a grin – he couldn't believe the way the old boy had swallowed that old story about meeting his "friend" up at Aldgate again. She'd been there alright, just as arranged. She couldn't stop long, because her sister was waiting at home, or something like that – he hadn't really paid much attention. Not that he'd minded – he was seeing her Sunday anyway. After she'd gone (it must have been that last kiss at the bus-stop that did it) he'd just felt like a cigarette – and reaching into his pocket, had discovered that he'd left the packet at work. Which is why he'd come back.

He stops, and as he reaches into his pocket for his cigarettes, unconsciously gives a swift tug at his still-half-stiff cock on the way. Pulling out a fag, he starts to whistle – and the sound is echoed down Skin Lane by the high walls of the church. He turns the corner, and starts his walk up the Hill to Mansion House tube station; if there was a tin can lying in the gutter, he's feeling so bloody good, he'd kick it.

★

Up in the workroom, Mr F hears the whistling drift in through the open window.

Standing there in the middle of the room, he too knows that he's just learnt something. He knows that he has just had his chance, and that he didn't take it. Still holding the empty skin of the coat, he strokes it, one last time, and then presses it to his body. Fur absorbs scent easily – it will hold a woman's perfume, for instance, for days. But now, even when he buries his face deep in the collar, and breathes as deeply as he can, there is no smell of the young man's hair there at all.

Mr F looks across the workroom at the naked wooden dummy. At its unfeeling wooden breasts.

nine

The black front door clicked shut behind him. He locked it, pocketed the key, and walked down the steps. The palms of his hands had stopped aching – and they'd stopped shaking, thank God – but when he got out on the Lane he noticed that they still felt

Felt what? What was it, this sensation? *Emptiness. The palms of my hands feel empty.* Was that it? He tried clenching them into fists, marking his palms with his nails, but it was no relief.

It was all he could do to keep on walking. He hated these cobbles, sometimes.

On his way home that night, Mr F tried, but he could think of nothing to help him make sense of what was happening to him. As he turned down All Hallows Lane, past the dying thickets of buddleia (when *had* it last rained?), the thumping of the blood in his head was amplified by the dull thump of a pile-driver working on the foundations of the wharf, preparing them for the long-threatened demolition work on London Bridge. The sound was as slow and heavy as his heart. How were they ever going to break all that up, he thought, looking up at the bridge? It was impossible – granite, wasn't it? Not to mention all those hundreds of great slabs he trudged over twice a day. The ones that never wore away, not in a hundred years, not even under all those thousands of feet – thousands of them, every Monday morning... If they were going to do it, he wished they would stop talking about it and just get on with it – tear it down, smash it – but the thumping, as it faded away behind him, sounded interminable. Hopeless.

The blackened maw of London Bridge Station, looming up to greet him with its stopped clock and screech of train brakes and gunfire of slamming doors, seemed infernal. Like he always did, he snatched a late copy of the *Standard*, but as he squeezed into his seat on the train, he knew he was going to keep it folded shut. What would be the point? The last thing he needed was all those grubby words chattering and droning away at him again. Who did they think he was – one of those dreadful *people* they were always writing about, one of those *unfortunate girls*, one of those *men*? He felt sorry for them, frankly. The front page of the paper had a big picture of some city going up in flames, (this was the night of July 27th, and the city was Detroit) but that had nothing to do with him either – the last thing he wanted was ink all over the palms of his hands, thank you very much. He sat and stared out of the train window at all the baking roofs of all the houses of all the people he didn't know.

When he got home, he let the light from the bloody window wash right over him on the stairs; he didn't care. Inside, the flat was stifling, even though he'd left the windows open in the bedroom as well as the bathroom; getting ready for bed, he knew that with the air as warm as this, he would have to sleep with just the one sheet to cover him, which he hated. He pulled the coverlet off, and threw it against the wall.

The sight of the empty bed made him think about the boy.

He imagined him framed on the blank rectangle of his sheets with some girl – not Maureen this time, but that little girl from Scheiner's who was always hanging around. He imagined them entangled, tied up in each other – touching each other all over. Sweating. Touching each other like he could never touch him – no, he could never touch him like that. Never touch him in any sort of way at all. Not even his hair. Didn't he know that if he touched him, he'd hurt him?

He wished there was something else he could throw against the wall.

There was a thin film of sweat on his back now, and he couldn't face getting under the sheet. He knew exactly how it would twist and knot round his legs, so he decided to sit out the heat of the night at his kitchen table.

*

Sat there with his hands pressed flat on the table to take away the ache in his palms (did someone once tell him to do that when he was a child, keep his hands on the table? Haven't we seen him make that gesture before?), Mr F decided that he might as well do something useful as just stare at the kitchen wall. He'd smoked enough for one day, so instead of rolling another cigarette, he decided to try and get some of the sentences hammering round his mind out of his head for once and write them down. It was almost the middle of the night by now, and his mind was so tired with the heat and the newspapers and the boy that at first he couldn't for the life of him remember where he kept his pen or the notepaper and envelopes, but then, after some searching, he found them right where he realised they were supposed to have been all along, which was in the middle drawer of the living-room sideboard. He brought them back into the kichen, put them down on the table, picked up the pen, sat down, put it down again, thought for a moment, then picked it up again and leant over the paper and started.

*

Mr F writes like children write; with that same look of fierce concentration. He screws up his face and breathes heavily through an open mouth, holding the pen so tight that his hand begins to sweat, and cramp. This is a big thing, you see, for Mr F to write his sentences down – to get them out of his head and onto a piece of paper. His wrist aches.

He finishes, and then thinks of something else. Finding that he has run out space, he turns the piece of notepaper over, and scrawls something across the back of it. He puts down the pen, and rubs at the smudge of ink on the first joint of his index finger. Now that he has done it – said what he wanted to say – he doesn't want to read it through, not even once; he folds the paper, licks the envelope and seals it down with a thump of his fist. Now what? He doesn't have an address to send it to – but of course that doesn't really matter, because this letter was never meant for sending anyway. He leaves the envelope lying on the kitchen table – he'll think about what to do with it in the morning. Now that his mind is cleared of some of its angry rubbish, he thinks he deserves to sleep. So he goes into the bedroom, and climbs under the sheet; he thinks he might as well try. As he lies there, he doesn't think about his dream, or any of its pictures, because it's too hot for any of that nonsense. And anyway, it's been so long since it last bothered him, he can hardly remember what happens any more.

ten

Some nights, the air itself seems to thicken. All across London, people leave their bedroom windows open; their sheets grow damp, and their dreams play themselves out with heavy, sweat-stained slowness. Mr F's was no exception.

As if conserving their energy, the sickeningly familiar images prowled around him in the dark, taunting him with their power over him by making him wait – it had been a long time, after all. Helpless in the heat, he had to lie there on his back and wait; wait for the key; wait for the light-switch: wait for the slow swinging open of the bathroom door. And then, when the dream had finally had enough of toying with him, and took him – when the proceedings reached their climactic moment, and his neck arched back and his throat opened to emit its terrible, helpless, howling scream – it left him hanging. The sound in his throat died away in a series of obscene gasps and pleas for mercy, and, horribly, he didn't wake up. There was no release; no return to the relative safety of his darkened bedroom. He opened his eyes, and discovered that he was still in the bathroom, slumped on the floor with his back to the door, bathed in sweat, his mouth hanging open and tears pricking his eyes. And the body was still there, too.

He didn't dare move. This had never happened before. What was it waiting for?

Was the next move up to him?

Using the door to support himself, he slowly got to his feet. Nothing in the bathroom appeared to have changed. The light from the bare bulb still picked out every detail. Holding his breath as much as he could – he could hear too much of himself, and he wanted there to be silence – he checked. He looked again from the defenceless hands to the perfect, hairless chest; from the spread, tangled locks to the limp meat of the upside-down genitals. Nothing had been disturbed; everything was as it should be. *At least he looks peaceful*, thought Mr F. He moved one pace closer to the bath, steeled himself, and looked down at his face – at Beauty, lying there looking more asleep than dead, his pale features resting on the hard pillow of that cool white enamel. *Best place to be, on a night like this*, thought Mr F.

Then he saw it.

The pulse, beating in the side of the boy's neck.

His first thought was that this was not possible; that it was just his fear, making him imagine things. And it was true, he could feel something very cold taking hold of the pit of his stomach. Without taking his eyes off the boy's neck or off the vein he thought he could see ticking there, he slowly reached out towards the hand-towel on the rail at the side of the washbasin, ready to whip it to his mouth if he started to vomit. But his reaching hand stopped in mid-air, because

He knew it was coming, and it did.

Beauty stirred; gently, as if the enamel of the bathtub was indeed the linen of a pillow, and he wanted to nestle his cheek deeper into its softness. His right eyelid trembled, and then, without warning, both his eyes flew wide open. Both pupils staring straight at Mr F.

Of course.

*

The boy's eyes had never been this black – jet-black – and in this bright light, they blazed. They held Mr F firmly; he could look at nothing else. He tried doing the usual – tried to find the familiar shape of the door-handle behind him, to turn it, to get out – but as his fingers scrabbled at the smooth gloss paint, he knew it was going to get him nowhere. Helplessly, he watched, as the impossible began to happen.

Beauty rolled his head back, and looked straight up at the bathroom ceiling for a moment. Then he took a deep breath, as if he was about to execute a dive. Ribs inflated, he lifted the back of his head slightly off the enamel of the bathtub, looked at his feet, braced himself and then, in one single, astonishing movement, and in one breath, jack-knifed the entire upper half of his body upwards, reaching up until he was grasping the metal brackets of the cistern with both hands. Then, bending his knees slightly, and taking all his weight on his arms, he pointed his feet like a dancer and deftly released them from the rope – which for some reason wasn't lashed and knotted tightly around them tonight, but instead was simply tied into a sturdy single loop, the kind the trapeze artistes at the circus use when they finish their act by descending, spinning, head down, from the very crown of the big top, hanging by just the one amazing heel. At the sight of this, Mr F involuntarily looked to see if the young man's hands and wrists were whitened with French chalk; suddenly, he thought he knew how Beauty had managed to clamber into his dreams like this, knew (at last!) exactly how and why this boy had been able to climb undetected up the fire escape and in through his bathroom window night after night – even the statue-like perfection of the boy's physique was explained. Suddenly, it all made sense; his memory had come to his aid. This boy hadn't been telling the whole truth when he'd told them he'd come straight to Skin Lane from school – let's face it, he'd never have got a body like that just from playing in a school gym. No; he'd run away to join the circus. That was it. Beauty was one of the very same team of three young men (the youngest brother, perhaps, the one who climbed last and highest on the wires) who Mr F could remember being taken to see at the Battersea Park Circus by his father. Now that it came to him, he could remember it all (why had he forgotten this for so long?); the music, the gusts of hot air, the wild smell of the turf even though you were inside – and best of all, the feeling of your nine-year-old hand being held so tightly as you were led firmly through the crowd to your seat. Then the music changed, the trumpets blared, and there they were, the three black-haired brothers, all in their spangled white leotards – there they go, climbing and swinging and swinging higher and higher! And then, when they let go of their trapezes, they seemed to the astonished child to hang in mid-air – impossibly; to just hang there, for ever, suspended in mid-air above his upturned face as the music played and the beams of the search-lights caught the rhinestones on their costumes and turned them into stars, bright against the blue midnight of the canvas – to hang there for oh the longest time – hang there, and then fall again, falling so that the child wanted to cry out, cry out in delight or anguish, and then of course applaud in wonder as the youngest one was caught – caught, always, just at the last minute, by that pair of strong, outstretched, reliable, brotherly hands –

But no; Beauty's skin was white – dead white – and his forearms were corded with muscle as he strained to keep his grip on the cast iron supports of the cistern, just like the acrobats' had been each time they swung themselves back up onto their trapezes – but they weren't powdered. He was still himself. He took his full weight on his arms (they trembled slightly with the effort), and then slipped his feet out from the loop of rope. Then, elegantly reversing his movement, the muscles of his stomach unclenching one by one like the fingers of a magician's white-gloved hand as they slowly spread a pack of cards, Beauty carefully lowered his feet to the bathroom floor. Releasing his grip, he brought his arms down from over his head; then he stood there for a moment and recovered himself, ribs flaring in and out and chest lifted, his arms held straight down by his sides. His fingers were extended, and both palms flattened a quarter of an inch from his thighs. He was standing exactly as a gymnast stands in the moment before he leans forward, breaks into a sprint across the mat, launches himself onto his hands and then springs back up, up, twisting and tucking as he goes – but of course there was no space for acrobatics of that kind in the bathroom of Mr F's flat. The young man was preparing himself for quite a different sequence of actions. What he did next, simply, was to take two small, measured steps towards Mr F, looking him all the time in the eye (Mr F, in his dream, thinks *I must look him in the eye the next time I see him*). Then, standing by the washbasin, and without raising his shoulder at all – only trained dancers and gymnasts can do this – Beauty elegantly let his superb right arm rise- not locked straight, but gently bent at the wrist and elbow, just like a dancer's when he accepts the crowd's applause after an especially elegant leap, or like the prince at the ballet when he greets his guests in the royal ballroom, his hand held elegantly open as his arm extends in welcome. As he did this, he came one short pace closer, and then, without waiting to be asked, he reached up and placed his right hand on the back of Mr F's neck, just where the spine enters the skull. He looked at him, exactly as he had once looked at him in the mirror in their workroom, framed and illuminated by that golden evening light. Their two pairs of eyes met, and then – just as he had on that previous occasion – he raised one eyebrow. He held Mr F in his gaze for just a moment more, and then, without breaking it, he gently – but firmly – (and at this moment he was not a prince, or an acrobat, or a dancer, Mr F knew that; he was himself, Beauty, the very same boy who he stood next to and worked with every day; he recognised him absolutely) – he gently guided Mr F's face towards his own, and, with a strange, sweet solemnity, did what Mr F had so longed for him to do back there in the workroom; he kissed him.

★

I'm sure you are familiar with the phrase *He took my breath away*. Well, that is exactly what he did. Because now Mr F did finally wake up, and when he woke, gasping, in the dark and drenched with sweat, his mouth was tearing at the air exactly as if he was a diver who'd wrenched himself free from some submarine obstruction at the very last minute and only just made it back to the surface in time, his lungs screaming with pain. The amount of noise he was making, you'd have said he could hardly stand it. His eyes were still screwed tightly shut; tightly shut, against all that bitterly salt water.

In great, hungry, noisy gulps, he filled his lungs. The heaving of his chest gradually subsided, and he recovered; it took a couple of minutes, but eventually he found he could breathe almost normally. He even stopped crying. He pulled the sheet up round his chest – his pyjama jacket was wet, and even on this hot night, he could feel it turning clammy. He turned the bedside light on, and then turned it out again. At last, he laid his head back down on the pillow.

Try as he might, he couldn't get the look in Beauty's eyes when he kissed him out of his mind.

As he lay there, he was sure that he could still feel the

memory of that strange hand cupping the back of his neck; and he couldn't believe how empty his mouth felt, now that it only had his own tongue in it.

Look at him, lying there. Why should he need me to give him strength – to watch over him, and always be worrying how he's feeling? Surely he'll find it himself. Isn't that what we believe, that we do always somehow find the strength? That the path will lead out of the forest; that the riddle will be solved; that the child never dies.

eleven

He was haggard, the next morning. As he was shaving, he couldn't help but stare, and at his mouth especially: the mouth that had been kissed in the night. The two lines under his eyes seemed to be cut a bit deeper this morning, and his expression, he thought, had changed. It wasn't just a question of pale skin or dark circles; he was sure, from the look in his eyes (those oddly pale blue eyes of his), that you could tell they had been gazing at something terrible.

And it was true; there was something different about them this morning. Just as in some old masterpiece (one of those big dark paintings that Mr F, like most people, would always walk right past in the National Gallery), some gloomy landscape dotted with gesturing figures whose pigment has begun to fade and wear thin, so that a road or path in the Roman *campagna* can now be seen winding its way through the forehead (that is to say, through the mind) of some young man sitting down and wearily re-tying his sandal-strap, a path winding away between the rocks into some unknown future, bright or dark... so, now, for the first time, Mr F's dream was beginning to make itself subtly visible in his face. It was starting to *show through*. His eyes had taken on an odd glitter – no one else might have been able to spot it straightaway, but he knew. He knew.

And it wasn't just his face; his body was changing too. Buttoning himself into his shirt, he inspected himself in the wardrobe mirror. His ribs, the concave stomach, the tautening skin; he looked leaner. Hungrier. He was surprised not to see a mass of scars.

Some mornings, as he stood in his suit by the kitchen table and waited for the tea to brew, Mr F would have liked to throw back his head and howl.

He noticed that the letter he'd written to Beauty the night before was still lying where he'd left it, its envelope still unaddressed. He picked it up, screwed it into a ball, and tossed it into the enamel pail under the sink with all the other rubbish.

twelve

As I think I mentioned, arranging an actual date for the final fitting of this coat had not been exactly easy. What had happened was that Maureen, offended that she'd been made to wait so long for these bloody foxes she'd been promised, had decided to punish her boyfriend a little. No, she'd said, when he'd called her to say Cousin Morrie was finally ready for her to come and try them on, she couldn't just pop down into town at his earliest convenience. He'd have to tell his cousin she wasn't free until the next Friday, as it happened. No, she couldn't just get the train in. She didn't feel like it. Yes please, she would like him to pick her up in the car.

All of this meant that the atmosphere in the Daimler wasn't exactly friendly even before they started their drive into town that Friday; then, to make matters worse, at the very first set of lights that stopped them (the traffic was unusually heavy, and moving like treacle), he had to go and say something unnecessary about her outfit. To be specific, he said he thought that that skirt was a little on the short side, considering it was only a fucking coat they were trying on. She countered, frostily, with the observation that in this weather she thought her new ensemble (a sleeveless Princess-line two-piece in French Navy viscose linen) was entirely appropriate. If the last time she'd been to Skin Lane was on a warm day, this one was making the leather upholstery decidedly sticky. And anyway, since he didn't like it, it was just as well he didn't have to wear it.

After that, they'd hardly exchanged a word the whole of the rest of the way – but then, as Maureen thought, but didn't say, *He wouldn't, would he?* He could be a real bore when he got like this – but she was determined to win. This coat was going to be her treat, not his. And anyway, she was right about this heat; sticky wasn't the word.

She was; all the way from Northwood to Harrow and across into town, you could tell that the terrible thunderstorms which were to make all the papers ten days later were already on their way. As they laboured down the Archway Road in thick traffic, she could see the clouds piling up right across London.

★

It was nearly one o'clock by the time they got to Number Four. The coat had been brought down from the cutting-room, and was draped on the wooden stand in the downstairs office, ready to meet its new owner. One glimpse of the finished article was enough to dispel Maureen's bad temper entirely; her squeal of delight mixed with lust when Mr Scheiner opened the office door for her and she saw the coat standing there, all ready and waiting, was entirely genuine – as was the girlishly breathless question she immediately turned and addressed to his cousin, eyes shining and lips parted, all thoughts of any hostility between them immediately forgotten:

"No! Is that really for me?"

His reply, though not quite so immediate, was just as sincere. *That's more like it*, he thought; and now that he'd brought his woman to her senses, he couldn't resist tipping his cousin the wink as he ushered her into the office to claim her prize.

"Go on then," he said, brusquely. "Get it on – and now try telling me I don't treat you like a lady."

Of course, Maureen couldn't wait. There was a slight

tempering of her enthusiasm when she discovered that the coat was still unlined – she wasn't sure how she felt about having all that naked skin straight on top of her, so to speak – but once it was on, her eyes got even brighter. *So this is what it feels like*, she thought, hugging the coat to her, turning up the collar just like Julie Christie did in the film. She'd always known red was her colour. The only problem was, there wasn't a mirror anywhere, which was a shame. She could tell from the expression on the men's faces what she looked like, but she would have liked to verify their evaluations for herself. Fortunately, Mr Scheiner suggested that perhaps – if she didn't mind – they could use the old mirror in the upstairs workroom for the actual fitting, since the men wouldn't be back from their dinner-break for nearly another half-hour. He was sorry, he said, but the mirror was too big to get down the stairs – Number Four wasn't really set up for ladies. *Not a problem*, said Maureen.

★

Going up the narrow stairs, with Mr Scheiner leading the way and the rest of the party right behind her – her boyfriend next, obviously, then that dreadful grim-looking Head Cutter person in the white coat, then Mrs whatever-her-name-was – oh, and that boy who couldn't keep his eyes off her legs (not that she really minded) – it occurred to Maureen (the thought made her giggle out loud) that they were so bloody steep, these steps, it was just as well she'd got her new coat on, otherwise, in this outfit, somebody might have got themselves a free eyeful! Once they were up in the workroom, Mr Scheiner apologised again for the rather makeshift mirror – which he asked Mr F and Beauty to move over by the window if they wouldn't mind, so they could all see what they were doing – and for the disarray of the room – but, as he said, Scheiner's was really a manufacturer's, and private fittings not their usual line. Being as how this was a family job, however (a quick glance here to his cousin again)... he was sure she appreciated. And now if madam wouldn't mind standing in front of the mirror for a moment, Mr F would just check the fit for her.

Maureen didn't mind at all.

Family, she thought, framing herself in the mirror, *that'll be the fucking day*. She wondered whether to try a quick smile at her boyfriend – something suggestive but demure, just to see if he'd get the point – but decided against it. Besides, looking at him would mean stopping looking at her lovely new coat. At the way the flaming red skins looked next to her own pale one. At the way it made her look as if she knew exactly who she was, and where she was going.

Mr F meanwhile, had moved in behind her and started work on the fitting. First, he quickly combed out the back. Then, in exactly the same way as he had done with Beauty the night before, he lifted and dropped and stroked the shoulders, settling the fur across the seams. As he did this, his hands hesitated, several times – something was clearly bothering him .Was it the fit, or embarrassment at being so close to this woman – or something else? The heat, perhaps? Whatever it was, he kept working, his eyes flicking expertly from seam to seam, from mirror to coat, front to back. Finally, when everything seemed to be hanging to his satisfaction, he asked if madam wouldn't mind walking a few steps, just so he could see how it moved.

If there was one thing that Maureen really knew about, it was how to be stared at. She shook out her hair, turned her back on the mirror and walked away from it with the kind of controlled flounce that suggested that it had just said something rather unfortunate to her; six kitten-heeled paces later, she stopped and looked back over her shoulder as if she was considering forgiving it; then turned front to face it again (all in one well-practised swivel), turned up the collar again and ran her hands down over the lapels of the coat a couple of times, stroking the luxurious fur where it lay across her breasts. As she did that, now she did make a point of catching her gentleman friend's eye in the mirror. Just to make sure he was looking at her exactly how she wanted him to. He was. Then she looked back at herself. She had been right about the colours. Her eyes had never been this green.

"Well I don't know about anyone else," said Maureen, "But I think it fits like a dream."

★

This was the point in the proceedings when Mrs Kesselman, who had not really been over-concerned about this particular customer's reaction in the first place, and was now very definitely wishing they could just get on to the question of linings and have done with it, began to notice how rather unwell Mr F was looking this morning. Positively grey-faced, in fact; she really thought he looked like he might be about to faint. She waited until the coat had been gently peeled away from Maureen's bare shoulders, and was back on the stand (she knew Mr F wouldn't have wanted her to say anything right in front of other people), and then, when he was helping her to lay out her samples of lining silk on the workbench, discreetly asked him, in her best *sotto voce*,

"Are you alright, Mr F?"

She was not to know that this was his least favourite of all questions: he looked at her as if someone had just slapped him.

★

What had happened was this; try as he might to concentrate

on the task in hand, every time he looked up to check the hang of the coat in the mirror, it had been Beauty that Mr F could see standing there, framed by its dusty gilt. Each time it happened, he had glanced away, of course – but then he had had to look back, in order to carry on with the fitting. He couldn't help it; the picture in the mirror kept on changing. It was Beauty, not Maureen, that he saw press the furs against his chest like that; Beauty, slightly raising one eyebrow. His memories of the scene that had been played out between the two of them the night before even came complete with the sight of himself fussing anxiously around the customer's shoulders like some busy old attendant or nurse, and now, when he saw that, for the first time he realised that that was exactly what he must have looked like last night; like an old woman, fussing. And then, when Maureen had looked up at her boyfriend like that, looked him right in the eye, he could have sworn that that blasted kitchen clock had started ticking again somewhere in the room – and he'd suddenly become aware of just how warm the workroom was getting again, warmer, even, than it had been last night. Stifling, in fact. He'd managed to finish the fitting alright, but only just – he found himself swallowing, and becoming acutely conscious of how his mouth was both dry, and empty; he had no idea of where to look (in the mirror? At the floor? Down at his trembling hands?) – and all the time, the ticking was definitely getting louder, and his hands were starting to ache as well as tremble, and his fingers to disobey. And then, when the girl had said that thing about the dream, about it all being like something out of somebody's dream, then – well, when Mrs Kesselman had seen fit to whisper that question of all questions right in his bloody ear, that really had been the last straw. He just couldn't stand to be in that room a moment longer.

★

"Yes. Yes of course I'm alright," he hissed at her – perhaps louder and more furiously than he meant to – "Why shouldn't I be?" Seeing Mr Scheiner shoot him a quizzical look, he remembered to keep his voice down. "But if you wouldn't mind managing without me, I think perhaps I ought to go and get myself a glass of water from downstairs – really, it must be this heat."

With that, dropping the silks on the bench, he fled. Maureen, still hard at work in the mirror, appeared not to notice this whispered dispute going on behind her back; Mrs Kesselman, puzzled, made the best job she could of covering her colleague's hasty exit by suggesting that Madam might like to join her at the bench now, if she wouldn't mind. Of course, Mr F's departure did mean that Mrs Kesselman then had to display her lining samples to the customer with only Beauty as an assistant – which didn't best please her, since (as she had to point out to him) he apparently didn't know his moire from his pongee, and barely seemed to have his mind on the job at all. However, after only a couple of minutes of picking up first one square of silk, then the next, Maureen did manage to finally choose a suitable lining with only a minimum of fuss – *cinnamon*, she fancied, would go best with the red, didn't everyone think? – at which point Mrs Kesselman was able to gratefully relieve her of the coat and march it downstairs to start her girls working on the lining at once. Beauty, meanwhile, she told to get on with clearing away the samples as quick as he liked.

Next Thursday afternoon at the latest, Mr Scheiner promised his cousin, by way of delivery, and they shook hands. Maureen's hand, of course, he kissed. Like a lady's.

"And may I wish you well to wear it," he said.

★

So; everyone was happy – even Beauty, dutifully clearing away the samples. He thought Maureen had looked smashing in her new coat, and was actually quite proud of having helped make it. She was a bit old for him, obviously – but still, smashing. He hadn't enjoyed Mrs Kessleman reprimanding him for getting the samples mixed up in front of everybody like that – but there was no point in getting worked up about that. Funny to think that one day quite soon he wouldn't be coming up here every morning – he was quite going to miss it in a way.

He did briefly wonder what was making Mr F look so poorly this morning – but only briefly.

★

Mrs Kesselman, making her way downstairs, hoped that she might catch Mr F later in the morning, to see if he was feeling better – but what with checking her stock of cinnamon silk, and getting two of her girls started on cutting the lining for the coat straightaway, she never did.

Which was probably just as well.

★

What, he muttered to himself, beads of sweat breaking out on his forehead, *is wrong with me this morning?* (Locked in a cubicle in the Gents toilet, Mr F was having trouble rolling his cigarette; his hands were all over the shop.) *Eh, what?* **What?** Mrs Kesselman's question had just been the wrong thing at the wrong time – that was it. Although he was surprised she hadn't asked him earlier, actually, the way he was looking this morning – when he'd had this fag (*damn* his hands, shaking like this), he was going to have to splash his face before he went back upstairs. And then when that bloody girl had started flirting with Scheiner's cousin like that in the mirror, and he could have sworn he'd heard his kitchen clock ticking again, same as last night – well it was enough to give anybody the bloody shakes. Which was not good, for a cutter. And on the subject of last night (he still hadn't managed to roll his cigarette – his papers seemed to have got damp, somehow. Or perhaps it was the sweat; sweaty fingers, that was it), on the subject of last night, how come it was alright for everyone else in the world to look each other in the eye, put their hands over their breasts and make eyes in the mirror and let everyone in the room know exactly what they were thinking about, when he couldn't manage it without starting to practically choke to death? And when they did it, there were no signs of shame at all so far as he could see; no blushing or blinking or shaking hands for them, thank you very much, oh no; *nothing*, actually, unless you counted the bloody giggling. The whole schemozzle was all as clear as bloody daylight, apparently – not that they had any reason to act ashamed, those two, because when you thought about it there wasn't anything actually strictly speaking *shameful* about them carrying on at all, actually, was there? Was there? Alright, they weren't married, and he was at least twenty years older than her, but who minded about that in this day and age? And how could anyone – mind – with Mr Scheiner standing there grinning like the Chesire cat the whole bloody time and using the word *family* every chance he got, not to mention a boy, a sixteen-year-old boy if you don't mind, being invited to stand and stare at the whole bloody business. It was *vulgar*, yes, coming into his workroom and parading themselves in front of everyone like that was *vulgar*, but you couldn't say it was *shameful*. Only secret things can be shameful, everyone knows that (Christ, he wishes his hands would stop shaking now, there's going to be tobacco all over the fucking linoleum). But why is that? Eh? Why was the way he looked at the boy any different to –

"Jesus Christ – " Mr F shouted, spraying Golden Virginia across the cubicle floor, forgetting entirely where he was. "What is *wrong* with me?"

– but then the sound of his own voice made him remember that there might be other people nearby on the stairs. Pulling himself together, he gave up on his cigarette, and threw the mess of tobacco threads and limp papers into the toilet bowl. He pulled the chain, unlocked the cubicle, walked out, splashed his face in the washbasin, washed his hands (of course) and took a deep breath before he opened the Gents door and headed back upstairs. He could hardly hide in the toilet for the rest of the day.

He came out through the door with his chin up. He started up the stairs, fully determined to put his bravest face on when he got back to his bench, but

But.

★

No peace for the wicked – wasn't that what Mr F had once blurted out to Beauty as he squeezed past him on the stairs? Well, there was certainly none to be had this particular Friday. No sooner had he started climbing quietly back up to the workroom, carefully drying his hands on his handkerchief, than he became aware of something blocking the light from the window on the landing above him. He looked up, and saw Beauty turning the corner of the stairs, coming down two treads at a time, evidently in something of a hurry. There was no time to go back, so Mr F just stopped where he was and pressed his back against the wall.

"Sorry," the boy said, meaninglessly, as he bundled past him.

Safe, Mr F breathed out again. But then – then, it all happened so fast. He just couldn't help himself; without even thinking about it, he turned, and watched Beauty's retreating back as the boy carried on down the stairs. Which was a mistake, because two steps before he reached the bottom of the flight of stairs, Beauty first slowed down, then seemed to hover for a moment, and then came to a halt.

Mr F's stomach turned over.

Why is it that young men can always tell when they are being stared at, even from behind?

*

As it happened, up until this point, Beauty had been having rather a good morning. As I said, he'd enjoyed seeing his handiwork finally on the customer (especially that particular customer) – and unlike Mr F's, his enjoyment of the sight of Maureen framed in the mirror hadn't been in any way complicated by memories of himself trying on her coat the night before. That had been a joke; she was very definitely the real thing. In fact, apart from a brief flicker of distaste as he'd run up the front steps at five to eight that morning – a distaste which had expressed itself in the quickly dismissed thought *Here we go again* – he hadn't really thought about last night's encounter much at all. True, the old man had seemed to be in a bit of a state this morning, right from the kick-off – but he'd be surprised if that was anything to do with him. Probably something about his precious coat – or just the heat. (Beauty, you see, was used to flirting with people to make his life easier, or indeed just to amuse himself; it wasn't as if he had gone out of his way with Mr F in particular. And now that last night had happened – well, it was true that he'd never had another man look at him in *quite* such an obvious way before – not so far as he knew, anyway – but he was sure it was nothing he couldn't turn to his advantage.) So he had had every intention of carrying on down the stairs without thinking twice about Mr F, or of stopping to talk to him – because his uncle had ended the brief chat they'd just been having by asking him to check with Mrs Kesselman downstairs and see whether she needed him to get on the phone for another piece of that cinnamon lining, quick as he liked – but then, as he squeezed past him on the stairs, Beauty somehow just knew – knew, by instinct or sixth sense or whatever – that those beady, ever-critical, prying, washed-out-looking pale blue goat's-eyes of Mr F's were going to follow him down the stairs, and when they did – he could feel the man's eyes on his arse, swear he could, feel them burning a hole right between his shoulder blades – well, suddenly, he'd had just about enough of all this. First there was Mrs Kesselman ticking him off over the silk samples in front of a customer (and a very gorgeous customer she was too) making him look like some sort of an idiot, and now here was old goat-face giving him the eye again. No, really, he could get sick of this – he is the boss's nephew, for Christ's sake. And hadn't his uncle just confirmed that one week from now he was moving him down into his office to start work in management? This was definitely something that needed putting a stop to. So he stopped, turned round, and said, in his best pointedly casual manner,

"You alright, Mr F?"

*

Cornered, every animal has to decide whether to fight or flee; Mr F chose the former. Bracing himself against the staircase wall, and staring straight ahead of him, he stood his ground – it was probably being asked that particular question for the second time that day that finally did it.

He knew he had to say something, but of all the things he could have said, he managed to get it down to just the one, hoarse, stubborn word:

"What?"

"I just thought you were staring at me a bit funny this morning, and I wondered if I'd done something wrong again?"

"Staring? Was I?"

"Yes you were, Mr F."

Feeling that some kind of roaring wave was about to close over his head, and fighting the impulse to close his eyes until it had passed, Mr F took a deep breath, and turned to look at the boy – who was standing six feet below him at the bottom of the flight of stairs – full in the face. He had to keep his jaw clenched, but he still managed to speak his mind; Beauty wasn't the only one who'd had enough, you see. Mr F's voice was level, and quiet, but clear. If it shook, it was as much with anger as with fear.

"My name is not Mr F. To you, sonny, it is Freeman: Mr Freeman. If you wouldn't mind. Or you can call me sir, if you like. Is that alright?"

The boy said nothing, so Mr F continued.

"Staring, was I? – I'll give you staring – "

Beauty came back up those stairs so quickly that Mr F had no time to do anything except instinctively jerk his head back against the wall as if to avoid some blow – and now he had to close his eyes. After quickly checking up and down the stairs that no one was coming, the boy had pinned Mr F back against the wall by placing one hand either side of his face; now he leant in right up close against him, so that their mouths were only inches apart. His face was twisted into a sneer, and his voice into a vicious whisper.

"Don't you talk to me like that, you miserable old – I've

seen you. Ever since I bloody started – looking me up and down like I was something nice on toast. Well let me tell you this, mate: you're too fucking ugly and you're too fucking old."

Beauty knew exactly what effect his being this close to the old man was having; he could see the sweat starting to break out on his forehead above his tightly screwed-up eyes. He loved how scared the man was. Unseen by the boy, the palms of Mr F's hands were starting to press themselves against the wall behind his back, as if beginning their search for that elusive bathroom door–handle. The spite-filled whisper filled his head, and he could feel Beauty's breath all over his face.

"You'd like to kiss me, wouldn't you," the boy exulted in a whisper, deliberately manoeuvring his lips within reach of Mr F's. "Wouldn't you?"

Then he moved his mouth round to Mr F's left ear, and lowered his voice to a soft, salacious drawl, the one he specialised in using with his girl.

"Well I've got news for you. I'm all fixed up in that department. So you, Mr F, can go and fuck – " Beauty put a full stop between every word; "Right. Off. Alright?"

*

Mr F couldn't open his eyes, and he couldn't breathe – but he tried; he tried. He knew what it was he had to say – could even hear the sentence in his head. Only three of the words would come out, however, and even they were too quiet; he sounded exhausted.

" … leave me alone"

"What did you say?"

With a great effort of concentration, he tried again.

"Why – "

"Yes?"

"Why can't. You. Leave me alone."

The boy couldn't resist enjoying himself for just one moment more. He smiled, and made his victim wait. Then, finally, still smiling, he whispered, right in his ear,

"Leave you? Oh, alright Mr F – if you say so. I'm sure Uncle won't mind – and I quite fancied going home early anyway. It being a Friday. My mother will be pleased."

He wondered for a moment about whether he ought to add insult to injury by telling Mr F about his uncle's plans for him next week, but no – he'd let the old boy get the bad news later. Let him stew. Beauty pulled his hands away from the wall, settled his jacket and ran a hand through his hair. For his parting shot, as he sauntered back down the stairs, all he called out over his shoulder was:

"I'll see you on Monday morning, Mr F."

★

Mr F listened to the sound of the footsteps going away down the stairs, and waited for the moment when he couldn't hear anything else except his own breathing. He knew he had to pull himself together, because he didn't want Mrs Kesselman coming and finding him like this and asking him that dreadful question again. With his eyes still closed, and his head leant weakly back against the wall, he gradually got his breath back. Then he started quietly whispering that dreadful word to himself over and over again;

Why? Why can't you? Why can't you? Why?

The word hammered round his head for the rest of the day, thumping at him like the beat of his blood – or like a pile-driver. As he crossed the concourse at London Bridge Station that evening, Mr F found himself wishing that someone *would* stop and ask him Mrs Kesselman's dreadful question again, or at least stare at him – anything, anything just so long as he could justify turning on some rush-hour stranger and releasing all the dreadful pent-up feelings of the day by screaming or shouting at them *Yes, what is it? Tell something is wrong with me, can you? Read it written all over my fucking face? Well do tell me, Doctor, please – it would be such a relief to know.* But no one did stare at him, of course. People are used to their fellow passengers looking half dead on a Friday night. Like the cherubs of St Michael's, they avert their eyes.

thirteen

It was a warm night again.

The man with the worn-out face climbed his stairs slowly; he was in no hurry. The treads, as always, creaked and sighed beneath his feet. As always, when he crossed the threadbare carpet on the second floor landing, the scarlet light from the window momentarily stained the white skin on the back of his hand as he fished for his front door key in the breast-pocket of his jacket. He seemed not to notice; he slid the key in the lock, and it turned. The front door swung silently open, just as it always did; just as it always had done. Everything was the same.

But the man who heard the front door click shut behind him so loudly, and who then stood aimlessly in the hallway of his flat with the key still in his hand for several silent minutes, was not. The suit was identical – but this is surely not the same man who we met at the beginning of our story. Tonight, as he goes into his bedroom and stares at himself in his wardrobe mirror, he barely even recognises himself. He cannot account for himself; he cannot describe what he sees. If what he is feeling is a disease, then why is it that he no longer wants to be cured? If it is grief he feels (grief, that distorts his staring face), then it must be grief at losing something he's never even had – he thinks (maybe it's just the light in here) that he can see his face is burning with shame – but for what? For what, exactly? Looking at the unmade bed behind him, he remembers waking up, twisted in those very same sheets, his mouth distorted by a kiss.

He knows that if he could be sure of that particular

dream returning, he would lie down and close his eyes this very minute.

Not knowing what else to do, he crawls onto his bed – unwashed, unfed and still fully clothed. The room is hot, and dark, and red; the curtains are drawn, but all the heat of the day has collected in that small, stuffy bedroom. The evening light is making the curtain-linings glow like embers. Despite what he said back there on that narrow staircase, he doesn't want to be left alone at all; that sentence was a question, not a demand. Like a dog to his vomit, he goes back to that moment. Back to the obscene whisper in his ear. Back to the boy's hot breath on his face.

Back to knowing how close his lips were.

The pictures won't come of their own accord, he knows that. He'll just have to make them.

Some people use drink; some people use magazines. Mr F lies down on his bed, unbuttons his trousers a bit, screws his eyes up tight and uses anything he can lay his hands on.

*

First, for want of anything better, he goes back to that strange dark room in the National Gallery, the one where that mysterious stranger accosted him in front of the painting. If only he could meet him again; he'd love to pick *his* brains. He looked like he knew a thing or two. He'd ask him if he had any good advice to give, or if he knew anyone, or could tell him of anywhere he could go. But it's closing time; the room's completely empty. Just like the last time he was here, there is a drumming sound (it must be the rain on the ceiling), and it is too dark to really see what's on the walls. He concentrates. Ah! – that's more like it. Somebody's flicked the invisible switch; all the lights come on together, and there they are, the paintings, framed in gold, and glowing. He prowls slowly round them, counting. After all, he's got all night. There are seventeen of them, just like before. But saints and soldiers and statues and Jesus won't do, not tonight, and so he makes the pictures change. What he wants to see is all those men he used to stare at in the street back in the early days – especially that one in the dark suit who he lost sight of in Leadenhall Market. There he is. Naked, now, of course. Naked, framed, lit and labelled. Open to inspection. Laid out across the canvas as if he was stretched across a bed. All the pictures are like that; white limbs, dark sheets. In some of them, the varnish is so heavy that he can't really see all the things he wants to see – almost the whole picture is darkness, swallowing up the arms and legs and straining, thrown-open mouths in deep, peaty shadows. He gets up close to one, to see if he can make out any more of the details, but they've put a sheet of glass over the picture to protect it, and of course the more he stares, the more all he can see is the reflection of his own anxious face getting in the way. That's no bloody use; he doesn't want to be looking at himself. He's sick of the sight of himself. He wants to try something else.

So he goes to visit one of his other favourites, another gloomy gallery – except that this one isn't full of paintings, but stacked with rows and rows of glass cases. Maybe the mysterious stranger with the glasses will be in here – it always makes him feel like that, being in these big empty galleries just as it starts to get dark, that maybe he's going to meet somebody. Just before closing time is always best. Best for catching somebody's eye. All the animals are certainly watching him – he knows that. He stares back at them – at all those rows and rows of labels; all those bright, glass eyes. They're all here, just as he remembers them: the dusty peacock; the shambling rhino with the straw stuffing spilling from the splits in its hide; the snarling black panther crouched forever on its forest branch, baring its discoloured teeth and painted red tongue; all watching. As he moves slowly through the gallery, the silence thickens; all he can hear is the sound of his own feet. And now this dead menagerie is not enough; he decides he wants to see them come to life. He remembers how it used to be at the zoo, with his father holding his hand – that hot excitement of the lion house, the coughing of the wolves, the lunatic chattering of the monkeys. He remembers the sight of hairy fingers plucking and pulling at the wire; remembers paws, determinedly pacing the gravel at the bottom of a cage. When he was little, he always wanted to know what would happen if the animals ever got out – what would happen if the bars of their cages were discovered prised apart one night. Would he hear them coming up the stairs in the dark? And if somebody had left the bathroom window just wide enough open for something or someone to crawl in through – what then? Would they come to him? Now he is grown up, and knows that he can do anything he wants; so he begins to fill the gallery with muffled, echoing screams, with the noise of wings thrashing in a desperate attempt to escape, and with the sound of frantic, scrabbling claws. Soon, his wish is granted; the howls and bellows begin to be punctuated by staccato notes of shivering glass, and one by one the rows of cases begin to smash and splinter, birthing their captives into freedom. He watches wide-eyed as all around him the beasts twist, dig and tear at the pins and wires they've been threaded and maimed with; he smiles. There's blood everywhere; the animals are so desperate to escape, they slice themselves open on the broken glass. Some writhe and die in spitting, thrashing fury – but some get free. Quickly pulling on his white coat, he calls out their names, and the survivors assemble. They're all here. The solitary panther shakes the dust from his petrol-black fur; the colobus perch in screeching pairs high on a window-frame; the foxes prance and bite and pirouette, mixing their colours (steel, ivory, flame), filling the room with their hot, generous stench. As the menagerie swells in number, he continues to bark out the names: Civet; Chinchilla; Fitch; Coney; Miniver; Marten. He calls, and they come; as the ranks swell, his feet are lost in a living carpet of bickering, swarming mink. Fur flies, guard-hairs sparkle, teeth are bared; the rich, animal stink rises around him. Then something in him senses another presence in the room. The animals can evidently feel it too, because they all begin to stir. Hackles rise. Muzzles and snouts are lifted to the air, scenting for clues. Then the cacophony of cries and calls begins to intensify; as if in welcome, the wolves throw back their heads, and sing. The colobus leap to a higher vantage point, peering and craning their necks, hissing and chattering as they bare their gums, tearing the curtains as they swing and climb. The panther digs in its talons, curls its tongue and lets out its unearthly, eldritch scream.

There he is, at the head of the stairs. Coming down step by steady step; accompanied at every elegant pace by a glorious chorus of howls, shrieks and snickers. The animals fawn at his naked feet, and dance, eager to touch his hands – but he never looks down, never once stumbles. The heaving rout of bristle, hair and fur obediently parts, and he continues his descent uninterrupted. The smell and the heat are overpowering, but he doesn't care; down he comes, with his arms outstretched and a strange, gentle smile beginning to flicker across his face. Oh yes, here he comes, with his superb arms, his dark hair and his never-so-black eyes; with his lips, parting in welcome; with his outstretched hands, offering to gently lead his guest of honour forth into the magic kingdom of everything he has never had.

★

Well, you know what it can be like, those hot summer nights. By the end of that weekend, Mr F's sheets were stained, and knotted, and heavy with sweat.

As I said; like a dog to his vomit. Like a beast.

fourteen

That Monday morning, his eyes didn't open until ten minutes to seven. Even without shaving, by the time he had scrubbed away the stink of the night, it was too late to run for the seven twenty train. The seven thirty-nine was then delayed at South Bermondsey, and so it was gone ten past eight when Mr F found himself stooped in an ungainly run down the cobbles of Skin Lane, trying to make up for the lost time.

Because it runs more or less directly east to west, most of the Lane is in clear sunlight by that time in the morning; not the black-painted front door of Number Four, however. Set back from the street at the top of its iron-railed flight of eight stone steps, that remains in shadow. This means that the steps, if the front door is closed, are probably the nearest thing the Lane has to a private place at that time of day. Of course, the front door isn't ever closed, not during working hours; but if two people from Number Four should want a moment's privacy, they could do a lot worse than slip out onto the steps and pull the door almost closed behind them. At ten past eight, after all, everyone in the building would already be hard at work; so long as they slipped out unnoticed, and then kept their voices down, they should be fine.

But on this particular morning, they weren't.

They should have heard him coming, half-running on the cobbles like that – but I suppose they were too intent on their conversation.

★

Mr F had already got his foot on the second step before he saw them; he stopped in mid-stride, catching his breath, his hand resting on the iron rail. When he saw them standing there like that, his first thought was to wonder how he could ever have missed it – they were so obviously a couple. There could be no other reason why the girl was looking up into the boy's face like that, and holding on so tightly to his sleeve. Then he realised that something must be wrong; the girl looked terrified, and the boy's face was dark with anger. They were both in their work clothes (Beauty in his coat, Christine in her overall), and they clearly shouldn't have been out on the steps at that time, but Mr F knew at once that it was more than being discovered that they were scared of. When Christine saw him, her face went white, and her voice died half-way through her sentence – Mr F only caught the first half of it;

"But you've got to," she was saying, "You've to got to help me, otherwise – "

The words trailed away to nothing, and she stared helplessly at Mr F. She almost looked as if she might be going to cry. Then she looked back at the boy, as if she was expecting him to tell her what she ought to do next. But he didn't; he stared straight past her, at the wall, tight-lipped with fury. The girl half-turned back to Mr F, as if she was going to come down the steps to him and ask him not to tell anyone what he'd seen, please – but the boy grabbed her arm so hard that she winced. She stopped, tore herself free of the restraining hand, wheeled round to face the boy (Mr F thought for one moment that she was actually going to hit him) – and then turned and fled back into the dark interior of Number Four in a clatter of heels.

Mr F waited; he expected the boy to say something now that she'd gone, to explain what was happening – but he didn't. He scowled, and stubbed at a stone step with the toe of his shoe, biting his lip. Then he turned and followed the girl, pushing the front door in so violently it swung half back on its hinges behind him.

After a decent pause, Mr F followed him in, taking care to go slowly up the stairs – partly so as to give himself time to think what this strange scene could have been all about, partly so as to give the boy time to calm himself down. But when he got up to the workroom, the boy wasn't there. He assumed he must have stopped off at the office to see his uncle about something, and carried on without him. Just before lunchtime, when the boy still hadn't appeared, he went downstairs and asked Mrs Kesselman if she'd seen or heard anything of him; but she hadn't. Christine was there at her machine, and when she saw Mr F come in, she got up and pretended to go and look for something in the opposite corner of the room, keeping her back well turned – he thought about it, but decided that he couldn't ask her if she knew anything, not with Mrs Kesselman there. He spent the rest of the day not being able to concentrate; under the circumstances, he didn't know if he should be grateful for the boy's absence or not – but then, when one of his colleagues enquired where Beauty was, immediately offered up a complicated story about Mr Scheiner having sent him up to a warehouse on Golden Lane to enquire after some delayed stock. He wondered why he'd concocted such an unnecessarily elaborate lie. By five o'clock, he'd got so little done that he felt he ought to stay late and make up for it, but for once, even the quiet of the empty workroom couldn't calm him. At just gone six, he put down his knife and hung up his white coat and made his way downstairs.

Beauty was waiting for him at the bottom of the steps. He must have been waiting for some time, because he looked anxiously up the moment he heard the front door open. Maybe it was because Mr F was looking down at him, but he immediately thought the boy looked different. He looked younger, and smaller – and though he was working hard at not showing it, the strain in his face made him look scared. Clearly he was worried someone might see them, because he stepped back out into the Lane and looked left and right to check who else might be around. He was smoking, nervously, the cigarette cupped in the fingers of his right hand. Mr F stopped when he saw him, of course, but then, seeing that whatever had been troubling him that morning was still making him frown, he came down the steps – slowly – fully intending to ask what was wrong, and if he could help – but then Beauty suddenly flung his fag-end down on the cobbles and stared aggressively straight up at him, making him stop half-way. Squinting up at him, and trying to make it sound as if he wanted to talk shop – but with a very odd and belligerent crack in his voice – the boy said

"Can I talk to you for a minute, Mr F?"

Yes, said Mr F, hovering on the third step down, yes he supposed he could.

Beauty glanced anxiously up and down Skin Lane again. Mr F was about to suggest heading left and then right onto Queen Street, down towards the alleys and wharves by the river, where they were almost sure to find a corner where they could be alone at this time of day – but the boy was in a hurry. Without even saying *Follow me*, he turned on his heel and set off sharply to the right; then, after less than a dozen hurried paces, he dodged immediately left again, up through a wrought-iron gate, up four worn Portland stone steps, and straight in through the front door and into the cool air and silence of St James's church.

Which was a strange place to take a secret.

fifteen

As any architectural historian will tell you, the chief glory of St James Garlickhythe is its light – not for nothing is the building known as "Wren's Lantern".

The exterior of the building, however, does little to prepare the visitor for its luminous interior. Like almost all of the City churches, it is – or was, until the widening of Upper Thames Street in 1973 exposed its secrets to four lanes of thundering traffic – a hidden building, one that had to be squeezed into dark, cramped site. If you stand on Skin Lane immediately outside the steps of Number Four and look up, for instance, only the golden cross at the tip of the beautiful urn-crowned tower will be visible above the blank rendering of the high wall that faces you. The height of this wall also conceals the building's chief architectural sleight of hand – the eight majestic semi-circular clerestory windows which are set into the hipped, slate-tiled roof – the same roof that Mr F could see whenever he looked up from his bench and out of the cutting-room window. For a hundred years, these windows were choked with gloomy Victorian stained glass, but the fires of January 1941 (which mercifully left the building structurally intact) not only shattered them, but also melted the surviving fragments beyond repair. Post-war economy dictated plain glass for the restoration, and so on a sunny high summer's evening – at ten minutes past six on an evening in late July, for instance – the forty foot high ceiling, which is the highest in the City excepting that of St Paul's itself, is once again flooded with the clear, all-pervasive sunlight that the architect intended.

Reflected back down from the ceiling into the body of the building, this light makes everything about the structure of the church seem as lucid, as cleanly phrased, as a well-preached sermon. Nothing is concealed.

Beauty, however, was not looking for light; he led Mr F to the one windowless corner of the building. Immediately inside the front door is a gloomy, wood-panelled ante-chamber, from which a second set of doors leads into the body of the church itself. To the left and right, the rising curves of a handsomely balustraded double staircase lead up to the organ gallery, and underneath the turnings of these stairs are dark corners just big enough for two people to stand in; Beauty chose the darker, left hand one. The double doors leading into the church proper were closed; before Beauty started talking, he checked that he could still see the patch of bright western sunlight that came slanting in through the open front door and across the flagstones of the vestibule floor; if anyone else came up the steps, he wanted to make sure he would see their warning shadow in plenty of time. The corner was cramped, and this meant that the two men were uncomfortably close together. Beauty avoided Mr F's face, looking instead at the floor. Again, there was no explanation.

"That bitch has tricked me," he muttered.

It was said with real vehemence, and with the wounded assumption that no one could help but sympathise. Angry as he was, he instinctively kept his voice down – as did Mr F.

"What are you talking about?"

"That bitch Christine downstairs, she's tricked me. Only tells me this bloody morning she's bloody pregnant, doesn't she?"

The boy spat out the words through half clenched teeth, and with his mouth twisted into something approaching a smile – as if they were both supposed to know that this situation was so stupid it was almost funny. From

the way he said it, you might have thought the two of them
were in a pub, and that he was keeping his voice down so
that the words wouldn't carry over the sound of the juke-
box. Mr F expressed no surprise at what he was being told,
or at how he was being talked to; he had no idea at all what
the boy wanted from him. He waited for a moment, and
then used the only instinct which came to hand, which was
to be practical. He continued to speak quietly, and gravely;
the boy's replies were quick, and bitter, as if Mr F's
questions were challenges.

"How long has she known?"

"Two weeks, she reckons. Said she was waiting to see if
she came back on this weekend, but no fucking luck."

"Is she sure?"

Only now did the boy's eyes flash up from the floor –
straight into Mr F's.

"D'you think I'd be bloody talking to you about it if she
wasn't?"

Mr F had never seen him like this before; the eyes were
hard as glass, and his mouth thin-lipped. Vicious.

"Is this what were you talking about this morning?"

"Then she tells me it's me who's got to sort it out.
Reckons her mother'll kill her otherwise." The boy sucked at
his teeth, and then turned his eyes full on Mr F again;
"Haven't got a fucking cigarette, have you?"

Mr F had, but he didn't offer one; he knew the boy
didn't really mean it. He watched his face; the way he was
biting his lower lip. The way his eyes keep darting away,
down to the floor again, as if there might be an answer to his
problem down there. Then Beauty took a deep breath, and
his face brightened into a strained smile again – as if he felt
better now that he'd got all that nonsense off his chest, and
felt free to get on and say what he'd really got to say. Before
he got to his point, he did his trick of looking Mr F straight
in the face, half-raising one eyebrow – like men do.

"Anyway, I've decided what to do. *You're* going to sort it out. I can't ask my uncle, he'll go mad, so you're going to do it."

The next pause, of course, was longer.

"And how do you think I'm going to do that?"

"You go to someone and you tell them it's you got her pregnant. And then you pay for the operation."

Why isn't he asking his father for help – Mr F knew the answer, even as he thought of asking the question. Still, he kept his voice low, and patient; he was concentrating, I suppose.

"What makes – " he faltered, and cleared his throat with a small cough. "I'm sorry. What makes you think I might want to help you?"

"You have to."

Mr F couldn't tell if his next line came straightaway, or after a whole minute of silence; all he could think about was how quiet it was in here.

"Do I?"

"Yes, you do." The boy stopped for a moment, and swallowed.

★

He's sure he knows how to do this; he's seen it done in a couple of films. He just has to keep looking the old boy in the face, and he won't be able to help himself. *Act like you've got a big stiff blade in your pocket*, he thinks.

"Otherwise, I tell my uncle about you. About the way you look at me. And you lose your job."

Now there is a very long pause. Mr F looks as though he is weighing up his options; he frowns. The boy tries not to show it, but he is starting to think that Mr F is going to refuse to co-operate, and if that happens, he has no idea what he will do. But as it turns out, he shouldn't have worried; Mr F already knows that refusing to help this frightened, bullying boy is something he can't even think of. He isn't considering his options at all – Mr F hasn't seen as many films as Beauty has, and certainly none with a scene like this one, and so he has no way of knowing what his options are (one; staggering away from the camera with a heart attack; two, taking a blade or fist across the face; three, being foolishly brave in tremulous close-up). No: the only reason Mr F is taking so long to speak is that he is wondering quite how all of this can be happening to him. Wondering quite how the air can be so still and so *thick* this evening; quite how this can be him, standing here in this church, hearing and thinking these things. How did he get here?

Beauty misunderstands Mr F's silence entirely, and is forced to improvise a trump card. A more experienced player might have been better able to disguise how far out of his depth he was when he played it; as it was, Beauty rather overdid the casual swagger, and almost stumbled on his line. His chest-out, chin-up stance barely concealed the fact that he was sixteen, and badly afraid. His sneering mouth told one story, but his urgent, too-bright eyes, another.

"If you do it, you can have me."

"What?"

"You heard. You can have me. Can't kill me, can it?"

★

The longest silence follows. Mr F says nothing. If this *was* a film, and Mr F's big helpless face was to be trapped in a close-up at this moment, his expression would reveal nothing. The audience in their darkened seats would only see what a big, strong man he is; what a big man, to be stricken so dumb. If he looks like anything, it is like an ox, chained in the slaughterman's stall; an ox, the moment before the bolt breaks its skull and its knees buckle. Of course, he knows what the boy means. But his mind is a calm blank.

The boy has to push him. *Stupid old goat*, he thinks.

"You do want me?" he asks, fiercely

After what once again feels like a very long time – after all, he already knows the answer to the question, and surely might as well just say it – Mr F hears a voice (but not his own, surely?) saying – whispering, almost – hoarsely, but quite clearly, *Yes, I do*. But the boy doesn't seem to have heard him. He's losing his patience; he needs his answer now, so that they can get on to the details of where and when and how much – so he hisses at the old man *Go on, say it*, and this time, in reply, it is quite definitely his own voice that Mr F hears – absolutely his own voice, speaking up clearly and openly in that cramped, dark space of stone and wood-panelling: no question. He hears himself say it, out loud. Just the two words;

"I do."

If someone had been there, and had heard him say that to the boy, what unholy ceremony might they have thought they were witnessing? If they had been eavesdropping outside the front door, say, or if they had been sitting crouched and unseen up on the curving staircase above the couple's heads – well, they would doubtless have had to strain to catch the conversation as it drifted up through the balustrade, but nonetheless, there would have been no mistaking those final words. Mr F said them with as much quiet sincerity as any bridegroom who ever stood before an altar.

sixteen

Mr F had no idea at all what he was supposed to do next. His mind paced around the problem all that afternoon and evening, but could find no point of purchase or entry. He knew such things happened; he even knew they were in the news. He'd read something about it once somewhere – he was sure he had. In the *Standard*, that was it. He wished he'd read that paragraph properly now, because he couldn't remember if it had said they were making the law on getting the operation harder, or easier. Easier, probably, he thought. Which was good, he thought. Good for the women – but how did that help him? He didn't know anyone who would know where to go – and he couldn't think of anyone to ask, not for the life of him.

Was this something that men were just supposed to *know about*?

Was that it ?

When, standing in his kitchen the next morning, he finally hit on the solution, it seemed obvious: after all, this girl of Beauty's couldn't be the first one at Number Four to have ever got herself into trouble. So at the end of the morning he went down to the machine-room under the pretext of needing to discuss some stock and then, when the last of the girls had left for their dinner-break (Christine didn't look up from her machine the whole time he was in the room, and he was careful not to stare at her), he simply closed the door and informed Mrs Kesselman that he was afraid he needed her help with something. He didn't use

Beauty's story that it was him who had got the girl pregnant – that didn't seem necessary – but just told her that the boy had come to him in genuine distress, and confided in him as the only adult he felt he could turn to in this very personal matter. He said that he felt obliged to do what he could for the boy. He spoke plainly and soberly, as if she could be expected to understand that this was the right way for an older man to speak on behalf of his protégé. It was strange, knowing that she would believe him.

Mrs Kesselman went very quiet for a moment, and held on very tightly to a corner of one of the workbenches – so tightly, the knuckles of her hand went white under her rings. Keeping her face turned away from Mr F, she muttered something vehement in Yiddish under her breath. Even when she spoke up again, she still didn't turn and look at him.

"Well I can't say I'm surprised at your story, Mr F. Our young Mr Scheiner, that is one young man I have never liked. Shall you be going to say anything to his uncle, I wonder?"

Mr F said he would leave that to her in due course, but first they had to take care of the girl.

"Yes indeed," said Mrs Kesselman. Now she did turn round. She looked older; but her eyes were very bright. Her voice was oddly matter of fact, considering how very angry she was.

"I shall arrange the necessary. And perhaps, Mr F, perhaps meanwhile... perhaps you would please to make sure that Christine and I don't have to be seeing that little boychik of yours anywhere near our machine-room."

That was it; no further discussion necessary. She would talk to him again as soon as the arrangements had been made.

People sometimes wondered how it was that Mrs Kesselman, with her piled-up hair and black-pencilled eyebrows and small, ferocious body, always managed to think of everything – how she managed to look so tired and so proud at the same time. I think it was because she knew who was really running that building. They say nothing, these women, but they look after their girls. They have to; it's a full-time job.

★

Beauty ought to have been terrified, of course – terrified that the girl might corner him on the way home one night and start screaming at him in the street; terrified that his uncle would suddenly appear with a face of stone and ask him to please step down to the office for a quick word. But if he was, he did a good job of concealing it for the rest of that week. Of course, it helped that he thought he was the aggrieved party; in fact, under the circumstances, he thought, he was holding up rather well. When Mr F gave him his brief report on his conversation downstairs, there was a tricky moment, because that did raise the question of Beauty eventually having to keep his promise – to pay up, as it were – but they both knew that there was nothing further to say until Mrs Kessleman had arranged delivery of Mr F's side of their bargain. Nobody needed to make a scene. Not yet, anyway. He just had to keep out of everyone's way. Speak when he was spoken to. And meanwhile, of course, he could rely on the fact that no one in the workroom would really even notice that Mr F was being slightly more stern-faced than usual, and that they barely spoke to or looked at each other – why should they? They had their work to get on with, too.

It may sound far-fetched that the two of them simply continued working, in silence, and in the same room, for the whole of the rest of that week; but have you ever stopped to wonder about how many white-faced secrets there are in the buildings around, for instance, where you work?

When, that Tuesday evening, Mrs Kesselman had confronted Christine in the cloakroom after work, she didn't let her waste too much time on crying, but instead simply advised her (sharply) not to confide her little secret in any of her colleagues. Two days later, she interrupted Mr F at his cutting bench half-way through the morning to ask if he might step downstairs with her for just a moment. On the stairs outside the workroom, having closed the door behind them, she told him that she would be needing thirty-five pounds, in cash, and first thing tomorrow morning. She also took the opportunity to say she'd be grateful if he'd arrange to have that Russian fox coat passed and dispatched now that the lining was finished, as she didn't want it littering up her machine-room any longer than necessary. She hoped *that* young lady wasn't going to let herself be made a fool of; first Mr Scheiner's cousin, and now Mr Scheiner's nephew –

"You see, Mr F, this is where the young people learn it," she said.

Thirty-five pounds, and first thing tomorrow, she reminded him.

*

That Friday, the fourth of August, Mr F was late for work again; instead of going straight to Peckham Rye Station, he walked across to Camberwell Green, and withdrew thirty-five pounds from his Post Office account. When he got to Skin Lane, he called into the office and apologised for his lateness, blaming a delay on the trains – that's one of the things that has changed about Mr F, as I'm sure you've noticed; these days, he can lie calmly, without preparation or thought. I expect he wishes he had learnt how to do that earlier in his life. While he was in there, Mr Scheiner finally got round to telling him his bad news, explaining that as from next Monday he was bringing the boy downstairs to be under him in the office for a bit. He was very grateful to Mr F for giving him such a good grounding in the raw skin knowledge – essential in this business as they both well knew – but now the lad needed to start getting the money side of things under his belt.

"After all, the cost," he said, "The real cost of things – that's what it all comes down to, Mr F, as I don't need to tell you."

Mr Scheiner was surprised by how well the man took it; Mr F hardly seemed to mind at all, but merely said (with his usual curtness) that he was sure the boy would be a great success, whichever part of the trade he ended up in.

Truth was, this news really didn't seem that important. Mr F could hardly bring himself to imagine – never mind worry about – anything that was going to happen as far away as next Monday; at the moment, it was all he could do to think about the things which were strictly necessary.

When he gave the small roll of pound notes to Mrs Kesselman, he noticed how her face snapped as tightly shut as her handbag.

★

It was the Friday lunchtime when Mrs Kesselman actually took the girl away. As luck would have it, Mr F saw it happen. Christine was wearing her powder-blue coat, as if it were a special occasion, and had done her hair and face; Mrs Kesselman was walking her down the cobbles of the Lane as quickly as she could, jerking at her hand as if she was a child or doll. As he watched the two of them go, Mr F realised he'd never really noticed before quite how tiny the girl was; as he saw her being hustled out of sight, with whatever small part of himself that was left to have any feelings for anyone else, he felt sorry for her.

Mostly, however, he was already thinking about what was going to happen tomorrow in the upstairs workroom, which is where he had just arranged to meet the boy at eleven o'clock that Saturday evening.

seventeen

Of course, Mr F had already had quite a bit of time that week to consider the practical problem of where and when he was going to take collection of his payment. The flat was out of the question – the thought of catching sight of himself at work on the boy in the mirror at the foot of his bed was obviously intolerable – and the workroom seemed a much better bet all round. He had a key, and Skin Lane at eleven o'clock on a Saturday night would be as dead as the proverbial. He even thought he might get some sort of satisfaction from welcoming the boy back to the very spot where he'd first made his heart stop beating.

When it came to it, the actual conversation regarding the completion of their bargain had been brief – and he'd organised the moment well. He cornered Beauty on the landing outside the workroom right at the very end of the Friday morning tea-break, immediately after he'd been down and handed over the thirty-five pounds to Mrs Kesselman; that way, since their other colleagues were already coming back up the stairs, the boy had no time to argue. In fact, all he had time to say in response to the naming of the time and place was a slightly startled *Alright, Mr F*, which was good, because – as Mr F quietly pointed out to him as the footsteps got closer on the stairs – any trouble, and he was going straight back downstairs to get his thirty-five pounds back off Mrs Kesselman, and then what was Beauty going to do?

Desire, you see, can make you pretty blunt – and in fact ever since he'd heard himself pronouncing those two fateful words in St James's church, Mr F had been living in a new and much simpler world. The twelve weeks he'd spent stumbling through a sweaty labyrinth of doubt and supposition suddenly seemed a long way behind him. He even found, to his surprise, that he rather liked the fact that the only questions he now had to answer were the straightforward ones of where, and when, and how much.

Don't make the mistake of thinking, however, that just because his voice and manner are now so forthright, Mr F is at any kind of peace. If he appears calm, it is only the calm of the Thames as it slides past the granite piers of London Bridge at the height of the tide; beneath the surface, the full force of the river is clawing at the stone, seeking some crack or flaw. For instance, watch this man's face as he lowers himself into the bath he takes after travelling home that hot and sweaty Friday evening. As he slowly lowers his body into the too-hot water, he flinches; he can't help but think that the next person to see it like this will be the boy, and once again, he is ashamed of himself, ashamed of how old and tired his skin looks. He tries telling himself at least he's only got the one scar – and let's face it, after all he's been through, he should be covered. *Oh well*, he thinks, *they must all be on the inside.*

Watch the way his mouth twists to one side as he allows himself to let slip that odd little half-laugh of his.

And now, after his bath, watch him as he makes his tea and collects his Golden Virginia and prepares to sit out the night in his living-room chair. He doesn't towel himself, or get dressed – he sits there naked and dripping under his dressing-gown. What does he care? There is no question of him sleeping – and he doesn't want to. All he wants is for this night to be over and for the morning to have come. He lays out his tobacco and rolling papers next to the cup and saucer on the arm of the chair, but he doesn't touch any of them. He simply sits, and stares, clenching and unclenching his fists. Occasionally, his head rocks forward, and then lurches back up again as he forces himself to stay awake; he doesn't want to miss the moment when the first grey light begins to show through the crack in the living-room curtains. The flat is so quiet, he can hear the ticking of the kitchen clock. He looks down at his watch, and it stubbornly insists that the time is still only ten minutes to midnight; but then, ten minutes later, when he looks down at it a second time, he could swear that neither of the hands has moved. So he sits there and forces himself to stare straight at the wall, for what feels like at least an hour. Then he looks again, and sees that somewhere in his agony of waiting, in that thick, intolerable silence, with no bells sounding, midnight has indeed passed; it's five minutes past twelve. He thinks to himself *This is it then. It isn't tomorrow; it's today.* He remembers the sound of the pile-drivers working on the foundations for the new bridge, and he thinks *That's it, isn't it. You slug the stone again and again and eventually, the cracks start to appear. From then on, it's only a matter of time. Only a matter of time till down it all comes. Stone by stone by stone.*

Mr F, you see, is realising that he has never lived in the present tense before.

Imagine how the next few hours must feel for this man. Not able to stand sitting still in his chair a moment longer, he starts to walk up and down the hallway in his dressing-gown, swearing occasionally under his breath like a man with a fever. Have you ever seen a beast pace its cage – some desperate creature like the ones which so fascinated Mr F on his childhood visits to the zoo? That's exactly how he paced his hallway carpet in the early hours of that dreadful morning, tracing a figure of eight into its pattern as if it was the gravel flooring of some barred and wired pen. All the classic signs were there; the dour, slow shaking of the captive's head; the practised turn at the bars (or in this case, in front of the locked front door); the determined, ritual padding; the occasional pause to scent after something that the beast has never, in all its captive life, tasted, but which it can never stop pursuing in its mind. Except, of course, that Mr F is no beast; beasts can't tell the time, and he has been given the exact hour of his release. He can almost hear it already, the sound of that key turning in the lock...

At exactly twenty past six, even though it is a Saturday and there is no actual need for him to stick to his weekday routine, he goes into the bathroom and begins to shave, with great care, and a steady hand. After all, today is a big day. He splashes his face and washes his hands, and then stands there in front of the washbasin mirror and anoints his hands with the lanolin lotion, wringing and wringing them until every drop has been absorbed. That accomplished, he moves into the bedroom and lays out his shirt, his tie and his brown worsted suit on the bed – just as he always does when he's going to Skin Lane. He begins to get dressed.

Imagine being him, as he does up the buttons on his shirt, and then the ones on his trousers, and finds that half way through that latter job his fingers freeze, because he suddenly sees a picture of himself undoing them again in just a few hours' time. When the time comes, will he be clumsy? The mirror on the wardrobe door is inescapable; how could anyone ever want *him*? Want to kiss *him*? He turns his back on it and, fumbling with his flies, finally gets the buttons done up.

Imagine being him as he stands there, looking down at his bed now, at the smooth counterpane, and finds himself thinking about what it will be like to get Beauty's tongue in his mouth at last; to get the skin on the back of his neck between his teeth. To find out how easily he actually bruises – because he knows he will have to force him. There will be no giving. Imagine how, as he bends down to knot the laces of his shoes even more tightly, all the blood rushes to his face.

You see, he is filled with such rage.

Now it is seven o'clock. Normally, he is out of the house by five past; but today, he knows that he still has another fifteen hours to go. Even though they don't need it, he takes off his shoes again, and carries them into the kitchen, where he spreads a newspaper across the kitchen table and polishes and brushes and buffs them until they have never shone so bright. Not for nothing he did he watch his brothers getting ready to go out on all those distant Saturday nights, you see; at least he knows how to put on a proper show. Then, worrying that there will be a smell of boot-polish lingering on his hands, he removes his links and rolls up his sleeves and goes into the bathroom and scrubs them again. The water is almost scalding, and he works so hard on his hands that he almost takes the skin off. By eight o clock in the morning, he's ready.

★

People talk about killing time, but you can't.

Imagine what this man must have gone through, getting through the remaining fourteen or fifteen hours of that long August day, with his kitchen clock counting every unforgiving second of them out loud. God knows how he did it; but he did. Imagine *being* him, at nine o'clock that evening, sitting on the foot of his bed again, still fully dressed, his hair combed and his jacket on, staring at himself in his mirror, his reddened face framed against a bedroom wall stained with a strange, ruby light (he's kept the curtains closed all day). He is so angry, he has had to sit down; but he doesn't know with whom.

If you find that you can't quite imagine what this forty-seven-year-old is feeling as he sits there at the foot of his single bed, then that is probably exactly right: he cannot imagine what he is feeling either. He tries; as he stares at himself, and at the empty counterpane on the bed behind him, he tries to picture what is about to happen to him – to play spectator to something that he has never seen. As you watch him confront himself in that mirror, look over his shoulder, try and remember very exactly what you did with the last stranger you took into your bed. Then think what you would have done, and what you would have felt, if you had known nothing. Nothing. If you are old, imagine youth; if you are young, imagine age. Imagine your body becoming that of a stranger. Imagine the sensation of it being *not yours*, as you discover what it feels like to do this, or to have this happen to you, for the very first time. Imagine it happening with sickening slowness, or with shocking speed, that discovery.

And then imagine knowing it has come too late.

That's how he feels.

While you're at it, lift yourself up, and now imagine the hands of all the clocks of all the churches, banks and head offices of the City of London moving silently and steadily towards the allotted hour of this fateful rendezvous; eleven o'clock. Do you see? There is nothing you – or he – can do can stop them. In the empty upstairs workroom of Number Four Skin Lane, imagine the beasts of the silent menagerie hanging head- and claws-down from their rails in the ceiling, all waiting; all waiting impatiently for some passing prince or huntsman to come and cut them open and give them a second life. Imagine thunderclouds parting, so that a giant summer moon can stare down wall-eyed at the city, touching all of its statues and memorials into shadowy animation. On Dowgate Hill, imagine the wrought-iron serpents on the gates of Dyers Hall starting to slither head down through their iron acanthus leaves, out across the pavement, eager to entangle your unwary ankles; above the doorway of Skinners Hall, watch the little heraldic gilded fox get up on its hind-legs and start dancing with malevolent, lunatic glee. And now, watch as the great silver wyverns on the roof of Leadenhall Market themselves smell carrion and begin, finally, to stir. As they come clambering down, watch how their barbed metal tongues stretch, and flicker; that is how they detect the stench of their next meal, you see. It is a law of nature that a dream carried for too long inside you must, eventually, begin to rot.

eighteen

When Mr F got to Peckham Rye Station, the entrance hall and ticket office were both deserted. Eventually, he tapped on the thick greenish glass of the ticket-office window, and a small, neatly-dressed clerk appeared as if from nowhere, fresh-faced and apparently quite unconcerned to be working so late. Mr F thought that he knew all the staff at the station, but this young man was a stranger.

"Good evening sir," said the clerk, "And where are you travelling to?"

Of course, Mr F gave the simple answer ("London Bridge," he said, "Thank you.") but as he reached into his pocket to find the correct change he couldn't help but think that tonight, the thousand and first time he has made this journey, he actually had no idea at all where it was taking him. *Perhaps that's what I should have said,* he thought, rummaging in his pocket: *"At this time of night, young man, I have absolutely no idea."* He wondered what the clerk would have made of that. As it was, all the young man said, in an oddly kind voice, considering the enquiry was so routine, was

"Single?"

"Yes," said Mr F, looking at him more closely, "Yes, I suppose so."

" One and three then, thank you, sir. "

As he slid the correct money under the window, Mr F almost laughed; *Single? Too bloody right mate,* he thought.

"There we go, sir. Have a good night."

"Thank you. I will."

The young man behind the glass disappeared back to wherever he'd come from, and Mr F slipped his ticket into his trouser pocket.

All the way up the stairs to the platform, it was so quiet that all he could hear was the sound of his own footsteps. *A good night...* he thought; *And to you, sonny.* He wondered why he hadn't asked the young man for a return... It just seemed the right thing to do at the time. He supposed getting back home was something he'd have to worry about later. Worry about *after*.

It felt odd, to be wearing his suit by moonlight, and to be standing out there on the platform exactly where he always stood, but with no one else about – because the platform, like the rest of the station, was completely empty. The moon was almost full, and making everything that ought to have been familiar, strange. It was as if the edges of everything – the empty benches, the platform clock, the sign for the gentlemen's lavatory – were being picked out against a slightly more heavily inked background than usual. As if each one was more distinct – more *itself*. And it was the same with the sounds; London is never silent, but late on a summer's night it does sometimes get quiet enough for the odd shriek or scream of laughter rising from a nearby street to be distinct, and surprising. This was one of those nights, and Mr F, as he stood there on the empty, silvered platform, watching for the lights of the train to appear round the bend of Denmark Hill, was aware of everything.

Everything.

He'd calculated which train he needed exactly, of course. The twenty minutes past ten; fourteen minutes to get to London Bridge, then fifteen minutes to walk to Skin Lane (without hurrying; it was still warm, even at this time of night), leaving him a full ten minutes to get himself ready.

The clock-face at the end of the platform clicked its way round to eighteen minutes past, and the train came round the darkened hill.

Good.

No turning back now...

The carriage (the second carriage, same as always) was almost empty too. A young man and his girl were sitting right at the far end, and opposite the seat Mr F chose, one fat middle-aged man, with his tie at half mast. His face was unshaven and his chin dropped heavily down on his chest – he was deeply, fully asleep. Mr F watched the city slide past the windows. Queen's Road; South Bermondsey – the young man and his girl got off there. Where were they going? he wondered. Home? Their home? There was no one else left in the carriage but him and his soundly sleeping companion. *His* night was over, you could tell that. Look at the way he was letting himself go, slumping down in his seat like that. Mouth open. Too tired to care. Empty.

When he got off at London Bridge, the great polished expanse of floor between the barriers and the station entrance, normally so crowded and scribbled over, was as bare as a blank sheet of paper. All but two of the windows in the ticket office were dark, and only a very few tired, late travellers were making their way out of the station to cross the bridge. Some of the placards wired to the front of the kiosk for newspapers still held Friday night's headlines, and everything had that very particular feeling only the City has at night – that sense of the whole place having been mysteriously and completely evacuated. Outside, the streets were almost bare of traffic; a single figure up ahead of him crossed the road at will. Two traffic-lights winked from red to green, unheeded. As he left the station, the warm wind from the river touched his face, and without thinking he looked up, as he always did, at the stopped clock on the ruined façade.

When he looked at it each morning, Mr F had always just thought *Oh, still ten minutes to twelve*; but tonight, something about this familiar sight too seemed strange. The clock-face seemed bigger, and whiter, than it ever had before. Perhaps it was the moonlight making it look like that, he thought; making it shimmer slightly – making it almost too big, and too white. Then, for the first time in his life, it occurred to him that the stopped black hands (ink-black; jet-black) were actually telling him the time. *Ten minutes to midnight*, he thought; that's it. He smiled gently to himself. *How could you?* he thought, still staring up at the hands of the clock, at their shadows, etched in soot on the pale white clock-face; *How could you have walked past that every day for thirty-three years, and never seen the proper time?* He knew there was no point in looking down at his wristwatch to see which one of the two timepieces was right. It wasn't twenty-five to eleven on a Saturday night at all; it was ten minutes to midnight.

Ten minutes to midnight, on Saturday the fifth of August, 1967. Or, as the voice in his ear puts it,

About bloody time.

★

Despite himself (he knew he wasn't going to be late), Mr F picked up his pace slightly as he stepped out onto London Bridge, putting that tell-tale military swing he sometimes

used into his stride. The moon was picking out the muscula-
ture of the black river-water, and he could see the currents
heaving under its oily skin. High tide. One late bus passed
him, travelling north, its yellow light spilling briefly onto the
pavement, but even that was almost empty.

As he approached the City, looming up ahead of him,
he found himself wondering if he'd ever really seen it before.
Of course, in a way, he hadn't; not like this. All those closed
stone faces of all those sleeping buildings, stacked one
against the other, lit only by the moon. All those great
respectable facades of banks and head offices, with their
rows of blind windows; all forty-seven, locked-for-the-night
churches of the City of London. All that power. As he
walked towards it, *Money*, he thought; *it must need silence to
sleep in*.

As he reached the north end of the bridge, the
emptiness of the streets began to seem uncanny. Somewhere
under his feet, he knew, the tube must still be running
through its hot tunnels, and up on Cannon Street he could
see one of the late buses still making its dutiful way from the
West End to the East – but no one gets on or off in the City,
not from St Paul's to Aldgate, not at this time of night; the
pavements were all his. The illuminated clock-faces still
pronounced the time, and the gilded flames on top of the
Monument still preached their warning sermon – but to no
audience except Mr F, and he had other things on his mind.

Because the streets were so empty, there was no reason
for him to follow his morning route, avoiding the crowds;
but he did, of course. He turned left on Arthur Street, then
sharp left down the dark steps of Miles Lane; passed briefly
along the stinking waterside, up All Hallows Lane and then
left again under Cannon Street. At night, the underpass
here is lit with a thick, yellow light, and in high summer,
each of the lamps wears a slight halo of mist, softening the
shadow-less sodium glare. Half-way through the tunnel –

exactly half-way – Mr F stopped. He remembered (it was his right shoulder that remembered it first) the sensation of that stranger bumping into him – and the memory made him clench his hands. Stretching them out in front of him, he could see that they too were stained yellow, as if they belonged to somebody else.

It was the strangest feeling, to be walking alone in his workday suit along this particular pavement and to have no one in his way – almost a blasphemous one. If he were to make the tunnel ring with a sudden scream, he realised, no one would hear him; if he felt like it, he could step off the pavement and walk down the middle of the road. He had always felt solitary as he walked through this tunnel, even in the thickest rush-hour crowd, and now its very emptiness was making him remember all those mornings when he had fought his way through the crowd with gritted teeth, aching to be left alone, to be *untouched*.

Well, his wish has been granted. Despite the warmth of the night (it is clammy in that tunnel), he shivers.

He emerges from the tunnel, waits for a solitary taxi to pass, and crosses the road up to College Street. There are no streetlamps here, and the moonlight comes into its own. He passes St Michael's; the haughty stone cherubs are as sightless as ever. The trees of the church garden cast ink-black shadows.

Skin Lane.

The sound of his heels striking the cobbles. The sound of his breath.

The point of St James's tower, bone-white in the moonlight above the great black wall. The gold cross, silvered.

The black front door, almost hidden in the dark.

★

Going up the steps, he has the key all ready in his hand. He quietly unlocks the door and then, as he had agreed he would, leaves it unlatched behind him. Even though he knows the building is empty, he goes up the six flights of stairs in careful silence, and without turning on any of the lights; once he gets into his workroom, however, he does flick the switch. He hangs up his jacket, and even catches himself reaching for his white coat. No, he decides, that won't be necessary. Not for this.

Ten minutes to eleven.

Looking out of the window, he can see the lights of the workroom spilling onto the slates of St James's roof, and so he turns them off again. There's no need to advertise. And he's sure the moonlight will be bright enough. Not wanting to give himself too much time to think, he finds two last things that need doing to fill in the final few minutes. He lays all his tools out in a row on the cutting-bench, just as he did on their first morning together, and then he drags the big mirror out to where it was when they did the final fitting of the coat.

He checks.

Everything is ready. There is nowhere else to go.

As he stands there beside his bench with the windows behind him and the lights all off, his eyes and ears complete their adjustment to the darkness and silence all around him. He is sure he will hear the boy the moment he pushes the front door open; sure, because tonight, he can sense everything. He can even feel the night air touching the soft skin on the backs of his big white hands. He slowly flexes them, then curls them into fists.

nineteen

It had never crossed Mr F's mind that Beauty wouldn't come; but in fact, he almost didn't.

It hadn't been easy to get out of the house, for one thing; his mother had seemed to know (in that annoying way of hers) that something was wrong. All week, noticing that her one and only was somewhat more subdued than usual, she'd been asking him if he was *alright* (that question again) and then, on the Saturday afternoon, when he'd evasively answered her that he was feeling fine but just felt like "going out", she'd suddenly wanted to know exactly where he was going, who he was meeting, and exactly what time he thought he'd be back home. After the week he'd had, Beauty just couldn't help himself, and flew off the handle at her – which was never a good idea, not with his mother. She was never one to let a man have the last word – not even her pride and joy. Fortunately, his father had weighed into the scene with a shouted *No, but the boy should be out – he should be meeting people. When I was his age, never I was at home* – and under cover of this paternal approval, Beauty had coughed up a hastily improvised story about some school friends and the cinema and a coffee bar, and that had seemed to satisfy them both. The irony was that he'd then had to get himself done up to the nines before he went out – the suit, the shirt, the hair, the works – so that he really did look like he was going on a date. He got the tube in as far as Tottenham Court Road; since it was still ridiculously early for his appointment with Mr F (he wished he'd kicked up more of a fuss now, and made him arrange the rendezvous for a more reasonable time), he planned to sit out the couple of spare hours in the Astoria, and then get the number twenty-two across to the City. Outside the cinema, there were two girls who giggled and gave him the eye. His first instinct was to saunter over and talk to them, ask them if they were meeting someone or would they care to join him – but just as he was preparing to make his move, the blonde one of the pair leant over and whispered something in her companion's ear, eliciting a shriek of laughter. The look on their faces gave Beauty a sickening thought, which was that they were laughing at him because they thought he was *one of them* – one of those over-dressed boys who loiter, so conspicuously single, on West End street-corners late at night: dismayed (except, of course, they were so wrong it was *funny*) he was just about to stride right over and disabuse them of their mistake when two boys of his own age got off a bus outside the Dominion, and noisily hailed the pair from across the street. It was bloody odd, he thought, to be watching the four of them set off down Oxford Street for their Saturday night together, laughing and carrying on, while he was

Well, while he was what, exactly?

Telling himself to just get on with it, Beauty moved round the corner and had a smoke, and then (now that the coast was clear) went back and bought himself a one and six to watch something called *The Pleasure Girls*, which was all they had on at the Astoria that he fancied. If two stupid bitches got the wrong idea about him just because he was wearing a smarter cut of suit than either of their boyfriends could evidently afford, he told himself, that wasn't his problem. The picture was dull (it had been playing for over a year, and the sexy poster was really a con; so far as he could see, it was really all about some upper-class girl giggling a lot while various boys in cars tried to get her out on a date);

kicking himself for having wasted his money, he left before
the end. Having nearly a whole hour still left to kill, he
decided the only thing to do with the spare time was to
walk.

The walk, of course, gave him more time to think about
those two girls, and the way they'd stared at him, and
laughed. *Bloody hell*, he thought, *you'd've thought they could
tell I was hardly the type.* That was really the only reason why
he'd come out tonight, you see – he knew he could have just
not shown up if he'd felt like it – because he wanted to clear
the air. He knew about men like Mr F – obviously he did –
and quite honestly, it didn't bother him that much, so long
as they kept themselves to themselves; Mr F hadn't,
obviously (in Beauty's book, staring was as bad as touching
) – but you could hardly say that that was because he'd been
encouraged. Now that the situation with Christine was all
sorted out, no one owed anyone anything, and if anyone
thought they did, then they'd got another think coming,
frankly.

He was sorry, but that was all there was to it. Whatever
happened, nobody was touching anybody. Alright?

The streets were getting emptier now. There was still a
bit of traffic on the main roads, but cutting across Holborn
Circus and down Shoe Lane, for instance, he didn't pass a
soul.

As he headed up Ludgate, the illuminated clock-face on
the right-hand tower of St Pauls told him, disappointingly,
that it was still only just gone half past ten. He slowed
himself down. Obviously, he didn't want to be the first one
to get there – he couldn't think of anything worse than
having to hang around waiting for the sound of footsteps,
looking as if he was the one who'd asked for the date. No; he
wanted to walk in, say what he had to say, and then get
straight off to Mansion House tube and back home again –

there was going to be enough trouble explaining to his mother why he was out so late as it was.

When he came down Garlick Hill, the clock on St James's said ten to eleven, so he was still early. Even though it had been a good twenty minutes since he had passed a single pedestrian, he still stopped and looked up and down in both directions before turning the corner into the Lane; once round, he ducked straight up onto the front steps of Number Four, grateful to have their well of shadow to hide in while he got himself together before going inside. He pulled his comb out of his back pocket, and ran it through his hair a couple of times; he thought about having one last cigarette, but decided against it. Eventually, judging it was now time to go up, he cleared his throat, and tried the black front door. It gave silently under his hand; one firm push, and it would yawn open. Beauty wasn't quite ready for that, however. He shook his hair, took a deep breath and ran through his patter in his head one last time. *I'm sorry, Mr F, but I just needed someone to help me. I don't know why I said that about, you know, about you wanting me – and I know it wasn't fair, but really I didn't know what else to do, you see. That girl tricked me, and I just panicked –* all that. Keep playing the sympathy card, that was the trick with this one. After all, it wasn't as if he hadn't had plenty of practice getting round him over the last three months – and if push came to shove, and the old boy got shirty, he'd just have to tell him where to get off, and that was all there was to it. After all, what was the old goat going to do about it? Come bundling into the office on Monday morning and start shouting the odds and telling his Uncle Maurice all about it? He didn't think so. He just had to lay on the charm, and remember what his main problem was; keeping all of this from his parents. If they ever heard about any of this… *You just have to get yourself through the next quarter of an hour, and this problem really is all sorted out. No one got hurt, no one is any the wiser, and Monday morning is another day.*

Somewhere behind him, one of the city churches began to ring eleven o'clock.

Right. Deep breath, and –

Beauty pushed at the black front door again, more firmly this time, and it swung silently open. One last moment of hesitation, and he walked straight into the waiting rectangle of darkness. Then, trying to make as little noise as possible, he began to feel his way up the turning flights of stairs.

★

Beauty's caution was to no avail; Mr F knew exactly when he was coming. He counted the footsteps on the last flight of stairs.

Three. Four.

The boy was moving very slowly. Was it the dark, or was he scared?

Seven.

Eight.

He must have stopped. Mr F held his breath. He could already see it, the moment when he would appear, framed in the doorway.

Thirteen.

Fourteen.

With a kick to his stomach, Mr F realised that the slight, dark figure was dressed exactly the same way as he had been the first time he'd ever laid eyes on him. High-waisted four-button jacket, neatly tight-cut trousers; white shirt, dark tie. He'd even combed his hair (Mr F can see all of this, even though the doorway is in almost total shadow; he has a beast's eyes. He can even see how black the boy's eyes are tonight, and how his skin seems to collect the light, even in this near-complete darkness). Except that now, it is summer. Now, it is a dark, high-summer night, not a cold February morning, and there is nothing in the way. In fact, there are only twenty-odd feet and the cutting-room benches keeping them apart.

No wonder there is a slight tremor in Mr F's voice when, after a short silence, he says

"So you came then."

★

Beauty could see Mr F silhouetted against the window, but he couldn't see his face. Deciding that it was best to take the initiative, he set out across the room, starting straight into his spiel as he went.

"Look, I'm sorry, Mr F; I know you must think I'm – "

but Mr F cut him off in a voice that sounded like a dropping axe:

"Thank you."

Straightaway, there was something in the room that the boy hadn't prepared himself for: feeling. He stopped, and waited – warily, not knowing what was coming next.

"And is that supposed to make me feel better?"

Now the voice was almost a snarl. And it was thick with anger – that was it; anger, coming off Mr F in black, turgid waves, like a smell. The room was suddenly much too dark for Beauty's liking, and the door too far behind him. This wasn't the same man he was used to dealing with at all. With the light from the window behind him like that, he looked taller – heavier, even – than usual; bull-necked. The usual tricks weren't going to work with this one.

Neither of them moved.

Because whatever light there was in the room was behind him, Mr F's face was in darkness. It was only when he turned away to look for something on the bench behind him that it was briefly caught by the moonlight coming in through the window. For a moment, Beauty thought that Mr F must have decided to wear some sort of strange white carnival mask for the occasion; the man's face looked almost like one of those plaster ones you see up over the arch at the theatre. Dead. It was something like that time when he'd cut himself – except that now his mouth was gaping, a black hole, with the lips pulled right back, and his forehead looked as if it had been raked by someone's nails. In which case, why wasn't he making any noise? And what was he doing scrabbling around on the bench like that? Had he lost something?

As if he didn't want anyone to see him like this, Mr F stayed with his back half-turned to Beauty for what seemed like a full minute, hunched over, fighting to get his breath back. Still, the boy didn't dare make a move for the door.

Mr F had spread both his hands palm-down on the bench, and Beauty could see that they were half-clenching into fists. Then the right one moved, and found what it was looking for.

When he saw his fingers close around the brass handle, Beauty's first, ridiculous thought was that Mr F was going to suggest they started working on something together. But there was no piece of work laid out on the nailing-board that he could see, nor anything on any of the stands; everything was as neat and tidy as they'd left it on Friday night – and anyway, how could they possibly get any work done with the lights off like this? So the knife must be for something else, he thought.

Well, for what, exactly?

It was only when Mr F turned back to face him, and started to swing his arm back in preparation, that Beauty realised what was about to happen. Even though the man's face was in darkness again as he started to come slowly round the benches and towards him, he knew exactly what that movement of the arm meant – knew that he ought to start backing away towards the door, right now – but for some reason, his feet wouldn't move. It seemed that all he could do was stare, stare fascinated at the way the moonlight was catching just the point and edge of the blade – at the way the small brass handle of the knife sat so lightly and so neatly on the palm of Mr F's outstretched right hand as he worked his way towards him, holding it out now as if offering it for his inspection, coming round the benches towards him and saying *Well then; recognise our old friend here?* There was still one last cutting bench between them, and Mr F must have realised that the boy was about to make a dash for it, because he came over that bench so quickly and so lightly that Beauty didn't even have time to think about which way to run...

And then there was no point in him moving, not an inch, because Mr F was holding the blade of the cutting knife right close to the side of his neck. He'd come over that bench so fast, you'd've thought he'd practised the move a hundred times.

★

Beauty hardly dared breathe. The blade was lying on the right side of his neck, the tip of it just stinging the skin beside his Adam's apple. Mr F's pale blue eyes were right up close to his now, and staring straight into them. He'd never seen them this close before. Set in such a dark face, they looked as pale and fierce as a gas-jet, just where the flame is hottest. He could feel Mr F's slightly foul breath on his cheek. He'd never quite realised until now just how big and bulky the old man was. How powerfully built. For a while, the only sound was Mr F's fierce breathing. Then Beauty forced himself to find his voice.

"What are you doing?"

"I'm showing you how it's done. Remember?"

Whatever the answer was supposed to be, the boy couldn't think of it. The point of the blade shifted a fraction, pricking him.

"No? Then let me jog your memory. *'Always use the knife swiftly and clearly; any hesitation, and you will bruise the skin. The first cut is always the most important; a mistake made now cannot be corrected later. The blade needs to move swiftly and firmly, and at the correct angle. If it swerves in the wrong direction, the whole pattern will be spoilt.'"*

Now that he hears them, the boy remembers the words; he remembers them being recited in this very same room. But now Mr F's voice is completely different; it is harder, and wilder. It is somebody else's. As the hot, rank breath strikes Beauty's cheekbone with each phrase, the words sound as if they are meant to wound or sting; if they were a whip or belt, they'd be meant to cut the flesh open. He knows he is being punished, even if not what for, so he stands stock still, and waits for Mr F to make his next move.

The words stop.

Beauty is used to the workroom being silent, because everybody knows that Mr F won't stand for too much chatter at the benches – but tonight the silence is different. This is the sound of there being absolutely no one here who can help him. He can't think of any way out of this, and he closes his eyes.

When he sees him do that, Mr F, still holding the blade of the knife against his neck, reaches up with his left hand and takes hold firmly of Beauty's tie, just below the knot.

Beauty can't help himself; as he feels that slight change

in the pressure round his neck, he involuntarily jerks his head back, and gasps.

And waits.

The first cuts come so quickly and lightly that the boy hardly feels them, much less sees them coming. With a delicate adjustment of his wrist, Mr F lifts the knot of the tie, gets the tip of the blade in behind the button which holds Beauty's collar closed, and severs the threads of cotton holding it in place with one neat flick; then, in one firm outward stroke, he slices through the fabric of the boy's tie, just to the side of the knot. Beauty feels the air reach his throat as his collar falls open. Mr F slides the cut tie away from around his neck, and lets it drop to the floor.

"And what else did I tell you?"

Beauty is too frightened now to reply. He still daren't open his eyes, but can sense that the blade of the knife is hovering just above his left breast.

"Come on, come on."

The boy manages a whisper;

"I don't know, Mr F."

"I told you it would take years. *Years*. Thirty-three, in my case. Thirty-three fucking years… before you can really do a skin justice."

Beauty has more sense than to move; he knows the next cut is coming. And indeed it does; without ever once touching his skin, Mr F moves the blade button by button down the boy's shirt-front, severing each one in turn. Beauty hears them as they bounce on the floor. To get at the last two buttons, of course, Mr F has to pull the shirt out from the waistband of Beauty's trousers. He does it simply and efficiently, removes the buttons with his knife, and lets the cloth fall open. Then he steps back half a pace, to inspect the way the shirt now lies open from neck to navel and beyond. His eyes appraise the gleaming white skin of the boy's chest and the faint trail of dark hair on his stomach as expertly as if he was aligning the seams of a coat on the stand.

"Patience, you see. *Patience and concentration.* That's the trick."

He sounds calmer know, and Beauty thinks that he knows this sound. This is how he talks when he talks to himself; how he talks when he isn't thinking about anything except his work.

"I think we'll have that jacket off now," says Mr F.

*

Never having done it myself, I cannot imagine with what ceremony or trembling fingers a bride and groom begin to slowly un-hook or -button each other's clothes in the first dark hour that they are left alone together. But I do know how Mr F set about stripping his beloved, there in the cutting room of Number Four, Skin Lane; without hesitation. Of course, no one can handle a knife like that unless they have been doing it for years; neither could they dismantle a garment back to its constituent pieces of fabric so swiftly unless they knew all the tricks of seaming and pattern-cutting and lining – but still, it was wonderful, the way he did it. Not once, no matter how boldly he sliced down or across or up, did he ever even graze the boy's skin. Using his other hand to lift, pull and steady the fabric – sometimes running the tip of the blade delicately over the stitching of a shoulder-seam so that it would part – almost gratefully – of its own accord, sometimes running the full blade ruthlessly down through the more resistant cloth of a cuff or collar – he cut away first the tight-fitting jacket and then the white cotton of his shirt from Beauty's body with extraordinary skill, never once pausing in his task. As each piece came away, he tossed it to one side without even looking at it, so intent was he on the job in hand. Seam by seam, the boy's skin was freed from its covering; the workroom floor might as well have been that of a bedroom, the way Mr F littered it with pieces of discarded clothing – and all this time, remember, he was working in almost no light at all. It was almost as if he knew the contours of Beauty's body so intimately that there was never any need to consider exactly where the next deft flick or lunge or slice should land; no need to calculate just how close, beneath the intervening cloth, the flesh might be to that heartless, exposing blade.

Anyone would think he could already see the boy naked. In his mind's eye.

Only when the warm night air was free to reach every part of Beauty's torso did Mr F pause and step back again to admire his handiwork. The boy's back was framed in the mirror behind him, and it looked as pale and lovely in the moonlight as any of the picture-gallery beauties Mr F had once so hesitatingly admired; his spine was traced in one single daring downward brushstroke of shadow, dark against an ivory ground. Now, Mr F didn't hesitate; he inspected every inch.

"Very nice," he murmured, to himself. Then, very softly, so that the boy wouldn't have known what he was saying if he hadn't heard the words so many times before, he whispered the sentence

"Never waste your time working on a spoilt skin."

From the gentleness with which he said it, Beauty had hoped this might be the end of it. But Mr F wasn't finished.

"And the rest," he said, pointing with the blade of the knife at the waistband of Beauty's trousers.

★

This boy has never undressed for anyone before; that is, he has never considered the possibility of being the one who gets watched while he undresses. The unaccustomed feeling is hateful to him, and because all he wants now is for this to be over, he does it the only way he knows how, which is as quickly and clumsily as possible. As if he was at the doctor's, or being examined at school, he unbuckles, unbuttons and unzips himself, and then pushes his trousers and his underpants down around his ankles in one single, defiant move. Then, hobbled, he stands straight back up, and looks Mr F right in the eye. He can feel the air all over him, and that Mr F's eyes are all over him too. He knows the man can see the rest of him from behind in the mirror. He grits his teeth.

So there, at last, it is. The body Mr F had been dreaming of all these wretched nights. The body, he now thinks, he has been dreaming of *all his life*.

He steps a few feet back, so that he can take in the whole thing. He looks it up and down.

As he stares at it, wondering, just as he used to in his bathroom, at the inexplicable whiteness of its skin and the soft, shining darkness of its hair, he hears, but doesn't speak, the sentence which inevitably comes into his mind; *"It all comes down to choice of skin."* Now he has, truly, made his choice. This is the one. And this – *now* – is the time: the building is empty, the front door is closed, the city is silent – and surely it must be midnight by now. All he has to do is to walk forward, reach out his hand, and begin.

Why, then, does he not?

Why does he not put down the knife, and touch him?

Why is it the boy who, not able to stand it any longer,

has to be the first to speak – because speak he does, desperately trying to stand up straight with his trousers wrapped round his ankles, desperately trying to keep the tears out of his voice, the shame and the fear, spitting his words out:

"Come on then if you're going to."

★

Mr F's right hand, the one holding the knife, begins to shake, ever so slightly. Somewhere in the room, he begins to hear the mocking, insistent ticking of a kitchen clock. Still, he does not move.

The boy senses his hesitation, and his fear makes him sarcastic:

"Something stopping you?" he says.

Much as you or I might want Mr F to answer that question, he cannot; perhaps, like all beasts, he is after all dumb. At this point, you or I might have said – or cried out – the words we'd learnt from one of the stories; *If you had never woken me, I could have slept for ever* – or, *If you had not come to torment me, this would never have needed to happen…*; even, *If you had not been so beautiful, I would never have needed to punish you like this* – but Mr F said none of these things. He stood there, dumbfounded, until, at last, unable to stand his silence any longer, the boy almost shouted at him.

"What is it?"

Still nothing. Still, the trembling hand, and the clock.

"Afraid, are you?" said the boy.

★

In answer to that most terrible of questions, the beast,

goaded beyond endurance, did finally find his voice – but not the one that you might be expecting. Tradition dictates that at this point in the story he should speak with an animal roar, one that will echo down the corridors of the castle and shake its foot-thick walls with its fury; but in this telling of the tale, the only sound that Beauty hears is that of a single, broken-winded man, in a darkened room, saying, in a voice more truly like that of a child than his own, just the one, hollow word:

"Yes."

That one word, however, is enough. The silence is broken, and the fatal sentence has been begun. The clock is still ticking, but Mr F struggles to make himself heard against it. Step by step, he tries to complete his explanation.

"Yes, I am. I am afraid. Because – "

Tears threaten to waylay him, and he pushes them back. He knows that for this to work, he has to say every single word out loud.

"I am afraid, because I have never. Never. I have never – "

He shakes his head – just as if he really was an animal. Then throws it back, and gasps, as if for breath. There is silence again. The ticking grows louder.

Seeing him struggle like this, Beauty, remarkably, does not taunt him. He can see that Mr F is fighting for the words with which to speak about something dreadful, something that is lost deep inside himself, and of all the things he could be, he is gentle with him. I suppose it must be because he has never seen a man like this before; there is even an odd kind of astonished tenderness in his voice, when he asks,

"What, Mr F? Never been what?"

Even in the darkness, he can see the old man's eyes are starred with tears.

"Because no one has ever – "

Mr F knows what he is going to say – what he must say

– and he braces himself to get the word out; that one word which he knows never can be, or should be, and never has been said to him. There is no one to hold him now, no one to reassure or talk him through this; no one to hold him gently by the shoulders and whisper in his ear *That's it, I've got you; there we go; that's better.* He must do this on his own. He knows that.

"No one has ever – "
Here it comes…

But the missing word is never spoken.

He cannot do it; if he admits that, he may as well turn the knife on himself. Instead, he looks helplessly down at his still trembling hand, and with a sickening lurch of his stomach, he knows what is about to happen next. He wishes he could fight it, but, gasping for breath, he begins to drown. His tears overcome him in great agonised gulps, and as they begin to course down his contorted face, he cannot help himself. With an inhuman scream (he is a red-tongued panther; a stuck boar; a maddened, blinded bear) he again draws back his right hand in preparation and then, as if the caged beast had seen its freedom through a swinging-open door, he makes it across the few feet that separate him from the naked boy in one single uncanny leap or bound, swinging the blade back up and across in one dreadful slashing arc towards his throat as he goes.

Don't be frightened; don't flinch, or look away. I promise you, there will be no blood. What happens is this.

*

As the arc of his hand completes, the scream strangles in Mr F's throat, and his hand stops: just in time. The boy has jerked his head back, and again he feels the sting of the blade as it rests against the taut skin of his neck. Instinctively, he has closed his eyes; his mouth gapes open, but there has been no time for him to make a sound. Mr F, who has never been able, remember, to properly see this boy's face in his dreams, and could rarely if ever bring himself to look openly or frankly at it in real life – in the flesh, so to speak – now does see it; and right up close, in a shaft of moonlight.

He sees it, you might say, for the very first time, and for the very first time, the mask of its beauty cracks open. It has always been the face of a stranger; but not now. Now, he recognises it.

Thank God, the sight is enough to stay his hand.

He rests the knife against the boy's throat, and stares in astonishment: and now, the tears come in earnest. Mr F cries; he cries so hard and so much that the hot tears go splashing down his face and onto the boy's naked chest. Hardly daring to believe that the knife still has not opened his throat, Beauty slowly opens his screwed-shut eyes. Without thinking, as he sees them blink open, *Oh, you poor boy*, Mr F murmurs; then, letting the knife fall away, but still gazing at the boy's moonlit face, *Oh*, he begins to sob; *oh, you poor boy. You poor, beautiful thing* – and then, with his other hand (the words still tumbling out between his sobs) he reaches out and runs his fingers – gently; so gently, as if touching the breast of a frightened bird – first through the boy's dark hair, and then across his face.

It is himself, you see, that Mr F thinks he is seeing; his own face, at sixteen.

That is why he is crying.

It is himself at sixteen that his hands are aching to console; it is himself, at sixteen, whose cheek he now so gently strokes. His own dark hair that he so tenderly caresses.

As Mr F does this, Beauty shudders and screws his eyes closed again – not understanding at all that the danger is now past, he thinks that the fingers are going to clench into a fist, grab a handful of his hair and use it to pull his head roughly back, exposing his throat to one final sweep of the knife – and so Mr F gently withdraws his hand, and runs the back of one finger across the boy's cheek again, so that he will open his eyes again and look at him. As he does, and their eyes meet, Mr F simply, unceremoniously, drops the knife to the floor, as if to prove his change of heart; then he uses the back of his hand to wipe his own face, across and back, as if it was some workroom rag. He seems not to have realised that he has been crying, because when he finds that his hand, coming away from his face, is wet, he stares at it, and then touches his fingers to his lips as if to see what this unexpected liquid could possibly be. As I promised you, it is not blood. Quite involuntarily, and after all these years, Mr F tastes his own tears.

★

When he hears the clatter of the knife on the workroom floor, and sees the expression on Mr F's face, Beauty finally realises that the dreadful thing which he'd feared might be going to happen to him in this room now isn't. In fact, he can see that this man would rather die than hurt him, rather *die* – and perhaps it is because of this, as much as out of simple shock, that he starts to have to gulp back tears of his own. Inch by inch, his body is flooded with the sweet, utter relief of realising that he is safe.

Mr F still has his finger to his lips.

Beauty tries his best to stop his eyes welling up and making a fool of him – but it's not that easy. When they start to trickle, he has to knock his tears back where they came from with a manly swipe of his knuckles – and then, to make matters worse, as he starts to collect himself, he realises that he is still standing there stark bollock naked in front of another man – wet-chested and naked and snivelling like some little boy. He stoops, and struggles to get what's left of his clothes back on, quickly pulling up his underpants and then, clumsily, his trousers. But he wants to cover himself with more than just his clothes; when he's done up his belt, and sniffed back the last of his tears, he attempts an odd and entirely inappropriate attempt at a cheeky grin. He knows that the crisis has passed – and now that he's safe, is already prepared to propose that the two of them look back on the whole thing as some sort of a ridiculous aberration. After a decent interval (he can see that Mr F is still in a bit of a state, and although he is a man of the world, he is not without feelings), he says

"You know, Mr F, what you need to do is to find yourself someone who does want to do it. It's not as if you're that bloody ugly."

Mr F looks at the boy, but as if there was a great distance, not just a few feet, separating them. As if there was a gap, I suppose, of some thirty-three years. But he wants to be kind. So as if he already understood that what the boy had just said to him was true, and as if life could possibly be that easy, he gives him the best he can do by way of a smile in return, and says, exhaustedly,

"Yes. Yes. You're right – "

and then he says something he has said to Beauty once before –

" – I do."

(Of course, it is too soon for Mr F to mean what he has

just said. But later – perhaps years later – he will remember those words of Beauty's. Believe me, someone only has to speak them to you once.)

He smiles at the boy again, more fully this time, and then, as if to thank him for his generosity and wisdom, for his *kindness*, of all the gestures he could make at the end of this strange and violent scene – of all the ways that one man can touch another – Mr F reaches out his right hand and once again, and this time without hesitation, does the very thing that he had once bitterly sworn to himself he would never, should never and could never do. He runs the fingers of his right hand gently through the blue-black miracle of a young man's hair.

*

And as he did that, as if on cue, the first bells of the forty-seven deserted churches of the City of London began to chime their long, staggered midnight.

twenty

The unexpected does happen. A woman hurrying down the street in flat shoes turns her anxious gaze on you, and you realise that she is not a woman. Some twenty years before the events of this story, the tablecloth spread for a children's picnic in Victoria Park is torn by bullets from a fighter plane, dodging its pursuer through the towering clouds of a perfect July day; twenty-four hours later and seventy miles away, the waves of a popular holiday beach cough up the sodden body of its pilot onto the shingle. A tumour skips a generation and kills a child right in front of her adoring grandmother's eyes. A centuries-old glass vase in a case in a silent museum – silent because it is 3 a.m., and the building is empty – suddenly shatters. A man in the middle of his life finds himself overcome by tears; and as Mr F stands there, alone now in the middle of that darkened room, he is amazed to discover that he is not just crying again, but weeping; weeping helplessly, surprised by some sudden, nameless and uncontrollable grief.

3

"Here is my prediction for the rest of the weekend: this might be a good time to explore new ground, mentally and physically; for considering a change of course in business."

"Katina"; horoscope for Aries, Evening Standard,
Saturday, August 5th, 1967

In the version of the tale which Mr F knew as a child, the very moment that the magic tears of pity touch the lips of the dying Beast, rockets whoosh up, an invisible orchestra begins to play, and the transformation scene begins. In our story, however, things happen differently. Beauty scurries away from the scene half-naked, tear-stained and glad to be heading home (even if it is with only a white workroom coat to cover himself), already preparing some unlikely story about a jacket and shirt lost in a late-night dance-hall brawl – a story which in the morning will make his mother suspicious, his two sniggering sisters green with envy, and his anxious father swell with pride.

And the Beast... well, the Beast is left alone, and nothing about the way he looks changes at all. Claws do not retract into fingernails; no stained and bared incisors re-align themselves into a smile; no stinking, mite-infested, hump-backed hide splits open to reveal the handsome and well-proportioned muscles hidden beneath. Instead of his flesh, in our story it is the walls of his imprisoning castle that must now dissolve. Now that he has tasted tears, no longer will he be content to wander in stoic silence through the pointless, untenanted Versailles of his obsession. The nights when he would stagger though its enfilades of ever vaster apartments, sometimes catching sight – or so he thought – of an image of a hurriedly retreating stranger, only to find when he lurched love-sick towards it that it was once again merely his own reflection, multiplied in the unfeeling mercury of a hundred gilded mirrors, each one staring coldly across the empty spaces of an ever partner-less ballroom – those nights are over. The magic castle, together with the evil spell of loneliness that built it, must be cast down.

This is how it was done;

one

Realising that it was time for him to go home, Mr F wiped his face, and took one last look around the room in which he had spent the best part of his life. The benches, the nailing boards, the rows of laid-out tools – they were all there. Every empty place was swept and ready, dutifully expecting its Monday morning worker. He wondered how many times exactly he had stood here at his bench (he ran his hand across its scarred surface), patiently working away. Thousands, probably. *All those bribes,* he thought. *All those dirty secrets.* He gathered up all his tools, and put each one back in its proper place. Never untidy, our Mr F – not even now.

What he did next may surprise you – but to him, it was merely necessary. Stooping down to reach under his bench, his fingers searched amidst the hidden jumble of discarded fur-scraps and rolled-up paper patterns till they found the small can of oil which he sometimes used for the sharpening of his knife-blades. For that, only one or two drops on the stone were required; for this job, however, he was going to need the whole can. He unscrewed the cap, and laid the can down on its side at his feet, letting the oil glug slowly out and gently spread itself into a soft, shining stain across the wooden planking. There wasn't that much – those cans were tiny – but he was sure it would be enough to start things off. When the small dark puddle seemed to have completed itself, and before the oil could soak away into the wood, he reached into his pocket for his matches – how funny, he thought, that he should have bothered to bring his tobacco and papers on this rendezvous. What had he been thinking – that they might have shared a cigarette, once their transaction was complete? Whatever the reason, he was glad he had them now. He knelt, and interrupted the silence of the room with the rasping flare of a match. Then, gently – gently – he applied the flame to the pool of oil. The oil took it gratefully, and quickly; at once, pale blue fingers began to dance above the floor, sending new shadows dodging around the walls and into the corners of the room. He watched, fascinated, as they began to pluck and stroke at the debris under the bench. He could smell the first scraps of fur evaporating into acrid smoke, and if he really listened, he could even hear them. It sounded like... like the whisper of a turning page.

He did nothing to either stop or encourage the flames; for once, the Head Cutter was content to let his juniors get on with their work unsupervised. He stood and watched them for a moment, and then, deciding they could manage perfectly well without him, left them to get on with the job. Collecting his jacket from its coat-hook by the door, he made his way quietly back down the stairs. And then, as discreetly and quietly as he had arrived, closing the front door behind him as he went, he left Skin Lane.

*

At first, the flames were modest; they licked tentatively at the debris under Mr F's cutting bench, but seemed embarrassed to go any further. One or two of them hesitantly fingered the remains of Beauty's clothing where it lay scattered on the floor, but clearly were unsure of whether they were allowed to disturb it or not. Once they had whetted their appetite on the leavings under the bench, however, they felt emboldened: and once they had scrambled up onto the bench and got their first glimpse of the racks of furs hanging from the ceiling at the far end of the room, they became shameless. They leapt from bench to bench, scuttled across the floor, and when they reached their destination, grasped and grabbed at the hanging furs with cackles of real greed. Anyone would have thought it was a competition; as soon as they got their hands on something they liked, they stroked and clutched at it with obvious glee, pressing it to their bosoms and then tossing it aside, rifling their way through the rails like greedy old women, chuckling and hissing, hurling great flaming bundles of skins aside in their impatience to get to the next treasure. They raced through the cheaper racks of musquash and ranch mink at speed, clearly eager to get to the really valuable stuff. The foxes – red, white, silver – were greeted like long-lost sisters, embraced and then swiftly rejected, sent flying to the floor in stinking, blackened disgrace. Panther, ermine, colobus – they didn't care what the label said; nothing would satisfy them now. They ransacked the room, shattering the gilt-framed mirror, rifling through drawers, hurling open cupboards – sending a newly discovered cache of oil-cans up in flames with great explosive shouts of laughter. Even the box containing Mr F's precious sables was not safe from their vulgar, rapacious attentions. Heat rises; up on its high shelf, the cardboard of the box was peeled back by firm, invisible hands. The covering tissue paper was dispensed with in one hot breath, and then, after just a moment's delicious hesitation – as if the flames were enquiring of this newly unwrapped treasure, *Is that really for me?* – the dense, oil-laden pelts were kissed into extravagant, fiery life. There was no stopping them; the laughter turned into a full-throated roar.

However, their orgy of destruction couldn't go undetected for ever; such wanton antics always draw the attention of the neighbours eventually. The smoke given off by burning fur is of a peculiarly dark and noxious quality, and as the top floor windows on Number Four Skin Lane began to shatter, it poured out into the London night, and sank in heavy trails down the side of the building. Three streets away, the night-watchman in the lobby of an office block was alerted by the smell, and at once reached for his telephone. Barely ten minutes later, bells began to ring, and help was on its way. Of course, as far as the flames were concerned, the fun still wasn't over – and they were determined to enjoy themselves as long as they could. Crashing down the stairs like uninvited guests, they made short work of the papers in the office and then, clambering down into Mrs Kesselman's well-ordered domain, they systematically wrecked each and every one of her precious machines (anyone would have thought they bore a grudge); they even twisted the metal bars of the basement windows beyond repair (that'd teach her), making sure that the heat of the fire scorched the walls of the church opposite in the process. They seemed to take particular pleasure in destroying the window just to the right of the door; its painted legend *And Sons* was first rendered illegible beneath a sticky black coating of oil and ash, then punched into fragments by a fist of escaping heat. The paint on the black front door bubbled and seethed in useless protest at this outrage – so they kicked that out, too. Even when the building was more or less ransacked, and help did finally begin to arrive, these wicked women still found new ways to cause mischief. The smoke painted strange smears of oily smut on the flushed faces of the first firemen to arrive on the scene; even as it died, the fire found ways to smudge its stinking black secretions across their handsome young cheeks and upper lips. They pushed its bitter smell right down their hard-working throats; slipped ash under their tongues, forcing them to spit; worked it deep into the hidden folds of their clothes, into seams and linings and pockets. Invisible and filthy fingers helped themselves to the young men's tousled, sweat-stained hair.

★

Mr F was already half-way across London Bridge when he heard the first wailing of the sirens. He stopped, and looked back over his shoulder at the sparks showering up into the sky, briefly silhouetting the tower of St James's church in black against a blaze of gold as the roof of Number Four finally gave way and opened itself up to the night – but then he kept on walking. He'd never cared much for fireworks. The night was still hot, but the air was just beginning to stir in earnest over the river; he was grateful for the slight sea stink of it.

It isn't often that you see the whole of London Bridge with just one person on it; still all lit, but entirely empty, and with the whole of the sleeping City laid out in silence as its backdrop. This is the last time we shall ever watch him walk across it – and it is also, come to think of it, one of the very last times that anyone will walk across that particular pavement late on a summer's night. Barely ten weeks from now, the work of demolition will be in full swing, and the old stone bridge will soon be down and gone for ever. However, that's the last thing on Mr F's mind. He knows there is no point in hurrying for a train – not at this time of night – and so he loosens his tie, and slips his hands into his pockets as he walks. Although nothing about his face has dramatically changed – in fact its features have almost been restored to the same ordinary expression they had when we very first met him (and his face, of course, is neither flushed nor smoke-stained; he got out well before the flames took hold of the building) – it is nonetheless the face of a man whose life has just entirely changed. People always talk as if the great discoveries in life come suddenly, don't they – but it doesn't look as if that was how Mr F experienced it at all. His face, as he walks across the lamp- and moon-lit bridge, looks strangely composed. The words that Beauty had spoken to him there in that upper room seem not to have hit him yet; in fact, it does not look as if they are going to *hit* or *overcome* him at all. True, he had broken down and wept after the boy had left – but it looks to me as if there is to be no single moment this morning when our hero staggers and sinks exhausted to his knees or down into his kitchen chair; no revelatory moment when he gives way and weeps again, this time for joy.

I should say, rather, that those words unfolded; unfolded through that night, and through the rest of his life. That they changed *everything*.

But I get ahead of myself; first, let's get him safely into bed.

★

From London Bridge to Peckham Rye is a good walk. To a lesser man, or one whose stride wasn't sustained by that calm exhilaration peculiar to a journey home in the early hours of the morning, it could well have taken a couple of hours. Mr F made it in just over one.

It felt strange, picking his way though a tangle of streets he normally only ever saw looking down from the train. As he made his way through Bermondsey market, the shutters were all pulled down and the stalls all padlocked closed; he had the place entirely to himself. He walked down a street of silent warehouses, and then past an empty children's playground – behind its black chain-link fencing, there was an odd sort of peace in its vacant stretch of tarmac and row of still, deserted swings. This was 1967, remember, when one day in London really did stop before the next one began, and so it was only when he emerged out onto the Old Kent Road that he began to encounter the very first traffic making its way into the centre of town. He wondered where the one or two lorries that passed him were heading – Covent Garden, he supposed. He imagined all the vegetables heaped up in the back, the potatoes and cauliflowers and cabbages – all with the chill and smell of the earth still clinging to them, ready to be tipped out and sorted through and shouted over. It felt good, somehow, the thought of the next day beginning like that. That *simply*. Not entirely sure of his route, he followed his nose, heading south, and then let the iron railings of a park lead him into Peckham Hill. Now he was beginning to recognise the occasional building; as he crossed over Peckham High Street, the sky to the east was just beginning to shade from true darkness to whatever that colour is just before you can truly say *it lightens*, and he knew he must be nearly home. There were still no lights on in any of the sleeping shops or houses – the beacons on a zebra crossing still flashed silently on and off to an entirely empty road – but the air was definitely cooler on his face. It was that exact moment in the night when you can somehow sense the darkness *thinning*, preparing to give way before another morning. The City was well behind him now; on these last few streets, each of the terraced houses was just the right size for a family .The front gardens which had been riotous in May were almost over, straggling and thirsty, but they still looked oddly pretty with the shadows covering just how tired they truly were. As he looked at the privet hedges, and at the last few exhausted roses glimmering on the rose-bushes, at the neatly closed front gates and at the curtains drawn in the upstairs windows, he wondered if any of the people sleeping safely in those bedrooms had any idea at all of what his life was like. He wondered what they'd think about it, if they knew; and he wondered what it would be like to crawl into one of their tidy little houses and curl up in its kitchen like a stray dog, and never go home again.

As he turned into his own street, it was gone half past two, and the very first birds were just beginning to twitter.

He pushed open the front door of his building, and walked quietly across the tessellated tiles of the hallway. He didn't stop to turn on the light; after all these years, he knew his way. The mahogany banister felt cool and solid under his hand. Climbing, he noticed for the first time how very tired he was; he made his steps gentle, and for once the worn stair-carpet accepted his feet, and the treads made no sound. As he turned onto the second-floor landing, the grey and yellow lozenges of the stained-glass window were still all blank; the bevelled edges of its border caught what light there was, and reflected it back at him in a hard, knife-like gleam, but it was still too dark outside for there to be any colour in the light. Nothing stained the back of his hand as he paused, and reached into his breast-pocket for his key. He went gently up the final flight of stairs, and quietly slipped it into the lock.

Once inside, he didn't close the door behind him right away; he paused, and listened to the familiar silence of his hallway. Was it any different this morning? Yes, he decided; it was softer.

When he did close the door, he pushed it closed slowly, so that he had time to relish that quiet, particular *click* as the mouth of the mortise accepted the tongue of the lock. *Home*, he thought.

He went into the bedroom, and slid his jacket onto its waiting hanger. Then he went into the bathroom, took out his cuff-links, and rolled up his sleeves (the slight sound the links made as he dropped them onto the glass shelf by the washbasin reminded him of that *chink* of his father's wedding ring; how odd, he thought, that he should still remember that, after all these years). He didn't put the light on – not because he was scared of seeing anything untoward reflected in the mirror, but because now there was no need; the first faint glimmer of morning was just beginning to make itself felt outside the bathroom window. And besides, the half-darkness was kind. He didn't bother to run the hot tap, but instead, just filled the basin with cold. Scooping it up with his big, pale hands, he began to wash them with that same wringing motion that he always used – but this morning the movement was gentle, and patient. Careful. He couldn't help but recall the sensations he'd felt when he'd run his fingers through Beauty's hair, and he didn't want to wash all that away. Not just yet. While he worked, he watched himself, knowing that tonight, there would only be his face in the mirror. Goodness, he looked tired.

"Still, thirty-three years," he said quietly to himself. "Not bad."

He scooped up two palmfuls of the cool water, and splashed the last of the tears from his face. He even ran his two wet hands back through his hair to dry them, and looked himself straight in the pale blue eye.

"There," he said. "That's better."

★

As he climbed into his bed, Mr F knew he was exhausted. For the first time in a long time, he didn't even think about how he should arrange his limbs, or what he should think about once the light was off. He was content just to lie there with no pyjama jacket on, without even the sheet pulled up over his naked chest, and to watch the light slowly beginning to draw a definite line beneath his curtains. It wasn't very long before his eyes closed, his head rolled gently to one side on the pillow, and he slid gently into a long, deep and dreamless sleep.

4

"If this is to be permitted, the next questions is: To what extent?"

Hansard, vol.749, p. 1439 (Sexual Offences Bill, 1967)

Why do they read them to us night after night, those stories – it can't only be because we beg for them. Perhaps they hope their terrors will be tamed by repetition. Or is it because something in them wants to drum the lesson of that famous final sentence into our receptive heads: " – and so they lived happily ever after, for years and years and many years to come"? If that is the reason, then their efforts are wasted; Mr F wasn't the only child who was never really interested in or believed those words. To him, as to so many others, they were merely the necessary prelude to the smoothing of the eiderdown and the subdued click of the light-switch. He settled down to sleep each night secure in the knowledge that all the ordeals and tribulations and excitements would be repeated again tomorrow; as his eyes closed, he knew, despite those final words, that the story was not and never could be over.

He was right, of course. Those stories never do tell you what really happened ever after, do they – or even what happened next. That is not their place; what happens next, as far as they're concerned, is your affair. They will escort you out of the dark wood, but then you're on your own. Which I suppose means that now that we've reached this particular point in the story, that image of Mr F lying there on his bed as the dawn breaks, eyes closed and head thrown back, asleep in peace at last – that really should be the picture at the bottom of the last page. That ought to be where we leave him.

However, to soften the blow of his departure, I will tell you everything else I know.

The most important thing, I suppose, is that Mr F never saw Beauty again. Not even in his dreams.

Although none of the huddled knot of employees who gathered outside the ruins of Number Four that Monday morning knew it at the time, the preceding Friday afternon had been the very last time when Scheiner's of Skin Lane ever really existed as a family firm; certainly, that was the very last time when all our protagonists were ever assembled in the same building at the same time. As it turned out, the shattering of that pane of painted plate glass in the ground-floor window to the right of the front door – an inconse-quential detail, you might have thought, amidst so much destruction – was to be prophetic; there was quite literally going to be no "And Sons", no handing down of the business from one generation to the next. When a distraught Mr Scheiner had telephoned his older brother in Hendon in the early hours of the Sunday morning to tell him the dreadful news of the fire, he had assured him that the business would soon be back on its feet; that evening, however, Beauty's mother had pointed out to the boy that there was little or no point in him going in to work on the Monday, what with there now being no office for him to actually move down into – he should let his Uncle Morrie get things sorted out with the insurance before anyone made their next move. As the week passed, the boy not unnatu-rally found himself beginning to think that he actually might be better off out of it, all things considered, and at that Friday night's supper he announced to his parents that he

fancied a change of direction – into men's retail, for prefer-
ence. There was some heated discussion across the table,
but eventually both his parents conceded the wisdom of
their only son's wishes, and a suitable opening was soon
found for him in another relative's premises, this time at an
address in Newburgh Street, W1. He never went back to the
Lane; not once.

It also became clear, in the course of that difficult week,
once the chastening details of his inadequate insurance
policy had been explained to him by the bank, that Mr
Scheiner was going to be obliged to go into partnership with
an existing firm if he was going to stand any sort of a reasonable chance of resurrecting his business. 1967, in
consequence, was the last year in which he was listed in the
London Fur Trade Directory as trading under his own
name. Mrs Kesselman's stock of silk labels, each one
proudly embroidered with that single word in an elegant
copperplate, was never replaced – indeed, that red fox coat
commissioned by his cousin must have been one of the very
last garments to go off the Lane with a Scheiner's name-tag
stitched into its lining. So it wasn't just the story of Mr F's
obsession or of Beauty's apprenticeship that came to an end
in the flames of that fire; everything that had seemed so
tightly interlocked around those premises was, in the space
of just a few weeks, dispersed. Since the new partner's
premises were up at Elthorne Road in Archway, and most of
the machinists and cutters had already sought employment
elsewhere by the time the move was made, almost the entire
workforce had to be replaced; a lot of people never saw each
other again.

Mr F, for instance. After thirty-three years – no less – he
never went back to Number Four either. Not to work,
anyway. When Mr Scheiner asked if he'd be moving out with
him to the new premises, he informed him (to Mr
Scheiner's considerable astonishment, it must be said; they

didn't part on the best of terms) that he was sorry, but he'd recently been offered a post as a senior cutter with a rival firm round the corner on Great Trinity Lane, and since he very much wanted to stay in the neighbourhood, had decided to accept it. Actually, the second part of this answer at least was a lie. Although he did end up working on Great Trinity, which was only a short stone's throw up Garlick Hill from the Lane itself, the truth of the matter was that he didn't much mind where he worked now, just so long as it was somewhere new – and so long as he could keep himself to himself when he got there. He didn't want anyone thinking that they knew him, you see; not now. *Not now that I don't even know myself*, was how he put it. He wanted to be able to concentrate on this peculiar but not unwelcome feeling of not really knowing what was going to happen to him next for as long as possible, and he knew that staying with Scheiner's would stop him doing that. He wanted to *start over* – that was the phrase, he decided. *Start a clean slate*. For instance, he'd already decided that he was going to insist on everyone at the new premises calling him by his full name, from the very first day. Mr Freeman. It sounded right, somehow.

As it turned out, the new place suited him. It was smaller, and he liked the fact that he could still take more or less the same walk to work every morning; but he also enjoyed discovering, at ten to eight on the Monday of his second week, that he no longer felt quite so compelled to take his old circuitous route simply in order to avoid the rush-hour crowds. That morning, as he reached the northern end of the bridge, he decided on the spur of the moment to try turning left and walking straight down Cannon Street just like everybody else – and finding that he rather liked it, he stuck to this way of doing things from that moment on. It saved him a good five minutes on his journey – not to mention the fact that that way, he didn't have to walk past the corner of the Lane first thing every morning. It wasn't that he was avoiding it as such (the first day he took his new route, he stopped for a moment on the pavement just outside Mansion House tube, and talked this all through with himself); no, he just didn't want to be reminded of everything every single day, thank you very much. If he did go back, it was going to be deliberately – because he wanted to think about something, or to answer one of his questions. He would visit when he wanted to, and avoid the place without making any great fuss about it the rest of the time. *Sounds to me like a good way of doing things,* he told himself (standing there, deep in conversation with himself, with the commuters pouring up out of the tube around him – cursing him for getting in their way, some of them). *Proper.*

Every time he did go back – which was usually as part of one of his lunchtime walkabouts, and I should say at least once every week, at least for the first few months – the thing he couldn't help but remember was the way Number Four had looked that very first Monday morning after the fire.

★

Although he had prepared himself, the simple fact of turning the corner onto the Lane at ten to eight in the morning and seeing that what had always been there to greet him no longer was, was still a shock. He stopped, dead, and stared.

The walls of the building had almost entirely gone – and remember, when he had closed the black front door behind him that last time, they had still all been standing. To add to the devastation, the thunderstorms which had been looming over London for days had finally broken late that Sunday afternoon in torrents of rain, and in consequence, there was water lying everywhere. Despite the rain, the stink of burnt fur still hung in the air; because of it, the familiar cobbles of the Lane were coated in a sticky black paste of foul-smelling ashes. Picking his way slowly through the oily puddles, Mr F began to see how complete the destruction had been. Not a single roof-timber or window-frame remained.

Nobody in the small huddle of people down at the end of the Lane was saying anything. Mrs Kesselman's girls were standing helplessly around in disconsolate ones and twos, staring in disbelief at the hole where their workplace should have been. Mr F looked for the boy amongst them, but couldn't see him anywhere; he wasn't especially surprised, or worried. The feeling was odd – or rather, the absence of feeling; as he stood there, keeping his distance, he realised that in contrast to every other Monday morning of that summer, he didn't much mind not seeing Beauty one way or the other. Like a lot of other things, Mr F thought to himself, that madness was probably all over now. Seeing the shell of the gutted building, so incongruously filthy and empty in that strong August sunlight, with the City of London scrambling to rush-hour life around it (the eerie silence on the Lane made the traffic up on Cannon Street seem very loud that morning) only confirmed his sense that he had done the right thing, drawing a line under things like that. Making an end .

Nobody had seen him yet, and he was glad; he wanted to keep this sensation of standing up straighter than he usually did to himself for just a few minutes longer. He looked up at the empty space where the top floor of the building should have been, and thought about his white coat. It should have been hanging on its hook by that gaping doorframe, waiting for him to come and button himself up in it just as he had done every Monday morning for more years than he cared to remember – but he was glad it was now a sodden black rag, lying buried somewhere under all that filthy brick and timber. As he stood there, Mr F wasn't at all frightened of being discovered or of betraying himself. He knew that no one had the slightest reason to suspect him of any involvement in the fire – and that the only person who knew for certain he had been there that Saturday night had every reason to keep his secret.

When he finally stepped forward and made his way through the little crowd to the front, looking for Mrs Kesselman, one of the machinists spotted him, and asked him "Are you alright, Mr F?" – as if he should be feeling the loss more deeply than they were; almost as if this was a funeral, and he was immediate family while they were merely guests. This morning, his least favourite question in the world gave him no trouble at all; straightaway, he told her that *Yes, thank you,* he was fine.

And he was; underneath the stink, there was an undoubted freshness to the air.

He found Mrs Kesselman right at the foot of the shattered front steps, staring stony-faced into the sodden remains of her machine-room. Of the eight steps, only the bottom four were left, and even two of those had been split right across by the fierceness of the heat. The metal handrail reared up and away from its wall in a grotesque question mark. Above that, instead of the front door, was simply a gaping hole, giving onto a confusion of twisted metal and charred timbers; there was nothing left. Nothing. He went and stood beside her, thinking that she of all people might need comfort – but when he offered to put an arm round her shoulder she stopped him with a firm but gentle lifting of her hand. I suppose that when it came to twisted girders and scorched walls, Mrs Kesselman had seen a lot worse in 1941. She didn't turn round – but she did manage half a smile.

"God willing, all fires should be on shabbas, Mr F; that

way, nobody gets hurt but the bank," she said, quietly.

"That's right, Mrs K," replied Mr F, staring over her shoulder at what he had done. "Thank God nobody got hurt."

★

The euphoria of that morning wore off, of course; Mr F didn't suddenly forget about Beauty, or become a different person. Often, over the next year, he would catch himself wondering what the boy was doing, or wearing, or saying. But he never tried to find him .The new job suited him, as I said, and he worked at it patiently and silently for the rest of his working life, keeping himself to himself and staying on in the same small top-floor cutting-room until he retired. Everyone there respected him – and always called him by his full name; for some reason, his nickname never caught up with him again. Eventually, as the trade on the Hill began to fail and disperse, this Mr Freeman (as I suppose I should now call him) gained some notoriety at the very end of his career by becoming the very last fur-cutter left working in EC4; although some brokers and commissioners still survived through to the late 1970s, and a very few into the 1980s, his new employers had the distinction of being the last manufacturing furriers working in this part of the City. When he retired, you might say that that strange trade and all its secrets vanished from that dark, crowded nest of streets entirely.

What happened to everyone?

Mrs Kesselman – of course – went with her old employer up to Archway, and worked at the new premises until her retirement in 1985. She travelled on the Northern Line all the way up to N19 from her flat in Finsbury every single day; she got stouter, but she never once changed her make-up, her ferocious care for her girls or the colour of her raven's-wing hair.

Christine, not surprisingly, took the opportunity to move elsewhere. After three years as a junior machinist at Calman Links up on Golden Lane, she married, and moved into a third-floor flat in one of the council blocks that went up at the beginning of the seventies on the top end of the Commercial Road. The young man she shared it with may not have been quite what she'd once thought she was looking for – he worked as an assistant caretaker – but even after her second child was born, she still thought they looked good together. Every weekend, when she dusted her framed wedding photograph, she would still stop and look at it before she replaced it on the sideboard – him in his best dark suit, and her in white duchess satin – and she would still, usually, smile.

Mr Scheiner, although the fire was a terrible blow to his health, made a good stab at rebuilding his business. He was one of the first in the trade to take seriously the move towards synthetics and "fun" furs – coney, dyed mink, fake sheared beaver – that characterised the end of the decade. One of his first big earners on the new premises, only two seasons after the fire, was a mini-length coat in synthetic red fox. The garish colours, and the assembly-line work required, had almost nothing to do with the traditions of the firm; but the mark-up was fabulous. He finally ceased trading in 1977. (The original of that coat, by the way, was a great success during its short career; a couple of its nocturnal outings were even marked by the excited glare of flashbulbs. Eventually it was put into cold storage, having been replaced by something even more expensive – this one having been bought for its wearer by, it must be said, a man with *real* money – but even while it was locked away in darkness, its glamour and beauty continued to wreak their havoc. One photograph of Maureen wearing it to a first night made it onto page three of the *Evening Standard*, and was later widely reproduced as one of the defining images of the decade. You may be sure that over the years plenty of other young women noted the expression on her face as she stared so boldly straight into the camera out of that crowd, her flaming hair piled high on her head, and knew in their hearts that if she could do it, then so could they.)

And Beauty?

I think we can safely assume that whatever business he ended up in, that boy was a success. With his looks, and his confidence, he was made for the coming decades.

There. I think that's everything.

★

So – there he goes, our Mr F. Lost from sight. Absorbed back into the City, just like any one of countless other strangers whose body you can vaguely recall, but whose face or name you can't now quite remember. Still, that's what happens, isn't it; their strange and lurid stories flare up briefly as you hear them, but then, when they are gone, eventually, they are forgotten – and you realise you never really knew anything about them except the story you were told.

There's not much left by way of any physical traces, either; that whole world of which Mr F was part has pretty much gone now too. Garlick Hill is now a street of office-workers just like any other; no one loiters, and the brass name-plates announce credit brokers and shipping insurers. Even some of the streets themselves have gone; if you were to try and retrace Mr F's original morning journey now, for instance, you'd find that the Miles Lane steps have been swallowed under an eight-storey office-block. The maze of alleyways and bombsites flanking Cannon Street Station has been tidied away into a concrete riverside walk, complete with benches and informative signposts; the bottom end of Dowgate Hill has been carved open by a road-widening scheme, and Upper Thames Street itself is unrecognisable, choked with traffic night and day. And, of course, the old London Bridge itself has gone. The spacious new pavements on its replacement never bring their crowds to such a black, thick boil as the ones Mr F had to carry his secrets through; nowadays, there's room for everyone, even at ten to five. Of course, the water still heaves against the piers of the new bridge at the turn of the tide – but not quite so threateningly as people always say it used to. On the wide new concourse of London Bridge Station, the crowds still stream to and from their trains just as they always did – but that unnerving rush-hour fusillade of slamming doors is a thing of the past. The trains for Peckham Rye now arrive at platforms fourteen and fifteen, not eight and eleven – and of course, you could stand there at the ticket barrier in the morning rush hour and watch the 7.08, the 7.20 and even the 7.37 train come in, and you know – he wouldn't be on any of them.

Extraordinarily, considering how much else has gone, the clock on the ruined fragment of the old station's façade has survived. It still says ten minutes to midnight – not that anyone ever bothers to look up at it. No one ever thinks that's really the time.

Number Four Skin Lane is still there – but only just. The site is now occupied by the late 1960s building that was erected after the fire. It's more or less the same size and shape as the building that Mr Freeman knew, however – it gives you at least an idea of what it must have been like. You can still look up and see the long windows of a top-floor workroom, which was rebuilt almost exactly as it was. You can even see where they incorporated the four surviving stone steps in the flight leading up to the new front door; I suppose someone must have thought they made a good "feature". If you peer in through the barred ground-floor windows you'll see the new workrooms that replaced the old half-basement Mrs Kesselman and her girls had to put up with; spacious, better-lit, and well-equipped – but all under a heavy layer of dust. The new premises were built too late, you see; the trade was already faltering, and no one ever really succeeded in giving the reconstructed building a new life. It's been empty for years now.

Like I said; he's gone, and that whole world has gone with him. *Took all their secrets with them* – that's what people who worked in the trade say about old-timers like Mr F. *Ah yes*, they say, smiling to themselves, *those were the days – the bad old days!* (They always laugh when they use that phrase: why is that? Do they miss them?) *The bad old days.*

Those bad old days which are gone, and over, and forgotten, and finished – we all know that – except

Except that of course, like me, I'm sure you can't help but speculate about what happened to him. About how he *lived*.

Well, he must have kept on buying his copy of the *Standard* to read on the train home every night – don't you think? Most people do. And if he did, did he ever come to think that any of those stories might actually be about him? Did anyone ever tell him that? Do you think that if we went carefully back through the files for next ten years we might even find his name *in* one of those stories – or his face, perhaps, caught by the camera in the midst of a crowd on the Mall or in Trafalgar Square on one of those "historic" days when the *Standard* always tells you exactly how many

thousands of people the police think turned up to cheer –
still in his three-piece brown worsted suit, of course...

Perhaps not.

I agree; crowds are never going to be this man's
favourite thing. And those really aren't his parts of town.

No, I expect he will just sit quietly at home on those
days and watch the crowds on his television, cup of tea and
rolling papers laid out on the arm of his chair as always –
except, of course, that I doubt that even when he is old the
corner of this particular customer's living-room is ever
going to be filled with a television set. I think he'll always
prefer the radio – prefer having just the voices. And I think
any staring this man has left to do will still all be done out
on the street, or up on London Bridge. Yes, that's it; even
when he passes fifty – and sixty – even in November, when
all he can see are faces and backs of necks and hands, I still
think this man will be keeping an eye out for beauty – if not
for Beauty – on his daily walk to work across those newly-
widened pavements.

Well then, if we can imagine him in winter, what about
in June – in the dog days, when ties are loosened, and the
City begins to sweat; when the scaffolders appear high up
on their building sites like so many gods – what then? Will
anything be different, when he catches himself staring at
them? Will he *smile*?

And let me ask you this; can you imagine Mr F ever
standing in front of his bathroom mirror in a clean white
shirt, slicking back his hair with both hands, and wondering
how he looks? I mean, wondering how somebody else might
think he looks on this particular Saturday, or even Saturday
night? Can you see him smiling, as he steps onto an evening
train? Is that possible? Surely

Surely it's too late for that.

*

I don't know about you, but this would be my only wish: that some several weeks or months or even years after that night when he slept so deeply and peacefully through the dawn (for who knows how long these things can take), this man will once again be disturbed by dreams. Dreams in which he hears that sentence of his – the one he never completed back there in that upper room. Dreams which dare him to speak out loud that dreadful word he has never yet found occasion say – taunt him with it; whisper it, lasciviously, in his ear. In the dark hours, or the early hours of the morning, as the strip of light grows under the curtains – I don't really care. I just want them to come. I want him to wake up hearing himself say it.

I suppose I just don't like to think (or believe) that once a man has acquired the gift of dreaming, he should (or even can) ever lose it.

Perhaps, of course, he'll be fine. Perhaps I shouldn't worry too much about this one man amongst so many – a man who, even after all this, I still don't really know that well. Perhaps he doesn't need my good wishes, this Mr F; perhaps it won't be a dream that haunts him ten years from now, but a memory, the memory of some sordid or marvellous meeting which I am too timid to imagine on his behalf. Some marvellous lesson of the flesh that he'll sit there in his armchair with his cold tea and his Golden Virginia and replay in his mind until he remembers exactly what sound his voice made when he said that missing word.

As I say; I can't tell. It's not the place of stories to tell you if dreams come true.

Now that I think of it, I said I'd told you everything, but there is just one more thing.

When the flat in Peckham Rye was cleared out by the council after Mr Freeman's death in late November 1995, one of the things that was found amongst all the rubbish was a letter. This was the same one that we watched Mr F sit and scrawl at his kitchen table at the very height of his miserable infatuation with Beauty, the one he never sent. It was found in a blank, unopened envelope, tucked away at the back of a drawer. As I told you at the time, he had left it lying in the middle of the table that night, and then the next morning screwed it up and threw it away without even re-reading it. What I didn't tell you was that he never actually got rid of it.

When, two days later, he went to empty the kitchen pail into the dustbin out by the front garden gate (a job he hated, because of the smell he always worried it left on his hands), he noticed the envelope sticking out from amongst some potato peelings. He slipped it in his pocket, and then when he got back upstairs opened it up, extracted the letter and smoothed it out with the back of his hand on the kitchen table. The notepaper was damp and badly stained, but he could still make out almost all of the words. When he first read them, he could barely remember writing them; the sentences sounded like somebody else's (he didn't know this, of course, but he shouldn't have been surprised; it isn't often that the words another man wrings out of you at three o'clock in the morning still seem to belong in your mouth when you recall them by the light of the next day). He read it through twice. Then, instead of tossing the letter back in the garbage, Mr F did something strange. After he'd sat there thinking for several minutes, he folded the paper neatly in half, and then went into the living-room and rummaged in his sideboard drawer until he found another, clean envelope. He sealed up the letter with one decisive lick, went back into the kitchen, and tucked it away in the drawer of the kitchen table. That is where it was found, twenty-eight years later, amongst all those annoying things that everyone always keeps, but never seems to use – the stray pieces of string and the packets of unused paper serviettes; the blunt pencils, the scraps of fuse wire, and the spare key for the kitchen clock.

Why did he do that?

Why did he keep it, this letter full of things that could never be spoken out loud? Surely he knew that it could never be sent? And why did he seal it up so carefully again in an unmarked envelope before he put it away, when he could have just shoved it into the back of the drawer as it was? Was it to hide its shameful message, blurted out in the middle of the night? To protect it from prying eyes? Or perhaps he kept it out of some obscure instinct that the day was bound to come when he would need proof that everything that was now happening to him had actually happened: but if that was the case, surely he would have got it out and re-read it at some point. The envelope, however, was still unopened, twenty-eight years later. Had he learnt it off by heart? Is it possible that he simply forgot that he'd ever written it?

Of course, what was in the drawer of that kitchen table meant nothing to the council workmen who cleared the flat – it was just part of the rubbish of somebody's life. Even the table itself was hardly worth lugging down the stairs – a heavy, old-fashioned thing. It was the same with that stained-oak wardrobe in the bedroom – but lug it they did, giving the flaking paintwork on the frame of the stained-glass window another dent on the way down. They weren't being particularly disrespectful, or careless; the detritus of a life means nothing unless you know its stories. To you, for instance, because you know some of the things that were once reflected in the bevel-edged mirror on its door, the sight of that wardrobe standing with the rest of Mr F's furniture out on the tarmac of a station car-park, awaiting a buyer at a second-hand furniture sale, might have been a forlorn one – but not to anybody else. After all, it's not as if it was worth very much. If you'd looked inside, you would have seen no one had even bothered to clear it out. There was still a whole row of those clumsy old-fashioned wooden coat-hangers, the ones your grandmother probably used to use, hanging up on the rail inside – and stuffed onto one of the shelves where the socks and underwear should have been, the jacket of some tatty old brown worsted suit, so badly worn at the elbows it was no use to anyone. Under the jacket, there was what looked like some sort of old shoe box, wedged in the corner next to a pair of ruined but still impeccably polished brown leather oxfords, and with a thick rubber band round it. Inside, tucked away amongst a litter of all the usual personal papers (birth certificate, ration card, demob notice, rent-books), was even more rubbish – why do people keep these things?

A photograph of a group of workers standing outside a black-painted front door.

A child's ticket for Billy Smart's Circus, Battersea Park, dated March 27th, 1929.

A ticket-stub from the Odeon, Leicester Square, and a torn ticket for the Regent's Park Zoo – this last item still has the word *Daddy* written in clumsy pencil, faintly visible on the back.

A battered copy of an old children's book of fairy stories, half its dog-eared pages missing – and tucked inside it, presumably for use as a bookmark, a creased and folded black-and-white newsprint photograph, carefully cut from the *Evening Standard* for Friday the 14th of October, 1967. Under the caption "Triumph", this last shows part of a crowd of excited admirers surrounding the singer Marion Montgomery as she makes her exit from the stage door of the Talk of the Town. One of the women in the crowd is wearing far too much make-up, and what looks like a three-quarter-length red fox coat.

As I said, why do people keep these things?

Anway, here is that letter. The handwriting is clumsy – childish, even. In places (especially in the scribbled note on the back) it is almost illegible, and I have had to fill in the occasional word. From its contents, you might think that it was tears that had blotted the ink; in fact, it was drops of sweat that coursed down Mr F's face as he wrote it.

July 27, 1967

I don't think you're ever going to write to me, are you, so I'll just have to make the first move myself. Trouble is, I don't know how to say it. I was reading the paper this week on the train, and it said that people like me are bound to have problems, and I think this is the biggest one of all for me really, this not knowing how to say things. The general gist of the paper seemed to be that its stupid, what I am, but I don't know that, do I? I don't know anything.

Which I think is probably your fault.

Where are you I wonder. Are you in bed my darling, if you are then wont you let me lie down next to you when you are sleeping. I want to wake up in the middle of the night and to listen to the sound of your breathing. When I am sure you are asleep I will lean over and look at your face all over, at your eyelashes and your eyebrows and your hair. Then I am going to lean right over, because it looks as though you might be going to say something to me in the night, look your mouth is moving ever so slightly. I wonder do you talk in your sleep, probably I know I do. Then you frown a bit and I reach over and touch your face just between your lovely black eyebrows and that will make the frown go away. And then you'll go back to sleep properly and I'll go back to sleep too even though this bed is small for two people and too hot.

Goodnight then

PS I say I don't know anything but that's a lie. I know what you look like.

And here is what is scrawled on the back; his final words.

Still look on the bright side, not knowing anything doesn't that mean anything can happen

And right across the bottom of the page:

Goodnight darling

Goodnight

Fuck me

How strange – strange, I mean, that he should have used those particular phrases; strange that a man who had never yet shared his bed with another should have had dreams of such accuracy. It wasn't at all what I was expecting when I opened the envelope.

Some people of course may say that such dreams or convictions are hardly likely – but then, Mr F himself could hardly be said to be likely. In fact, a lot of people would say that a man like him should not, or could not, or most probably – and this I think is the worst thing of all – *did not* exist, but

But he did. And he did write that letter. How else are we to explain the fact that you are holding a copy of it in your hand?

Lights out now.

Goodnight.